D1600673

PERCEPTION
of POWER

BRUCE THOMASON

BATJAK™
PUBLISHING

DEDICATION

There are fewer than one million law enforcement officers charged with protecting the more than 325 million people in the United States. Perception of Power *is dedicated to all those brave men and women who serve on the thin blue line.*

ACKNOWLEDGEMENTS

Perception of Power would not be possible without the talented support of the following people:

To Jen Zdunkiewicz: You keep outdoing yourself in your insightful editing of my novels. You cheerfully skewered my use of slang terms more suitably rooted in the sixties and seventies, and your comments on communications officers' on-air terminology were helpful since I haven't sat in front of a dispatch console since 1967.

To Commander Gene Paul Smith: For sharing your knowledge of SWAT tactics and sniper rifle capabilities and techniques.

To Tom Taylor: For your technical advice on the operation of concrete trucks and what happens when they fail to stay upright.

To my daughter, Holli Honchen (RN): For educating me on degrees of traumatic brain injuries and the appropriate medical terminology.

And, as always, to my lovely bride, Jackie: *Perception of Power* is our third book to collaborate as author and editor, and the team effort has only gotten better. I value your judgments and insights even in those few instances when we have to agree to disagree on a plot point, character trait, or a particular piece of dialogue. Your goal is always to make the story better.

OFFICIAL DISCLAIMER

It's possible, maybe even likely, that I have made mistakes in areas unrelated to my field of expertise. Those include plot points utilizing the Uniform Code of Military Justice as well as certain military sniper rules and techniques, autopsy routines and processes, and hostage negotiator practices and procedures. In every case, I take responsibility for any errors and beg consideration of leniency from those experts in the various fields.

UNOFFICIAL DISCLAIMER

It's a novel. The characters are in charge. I blame them!

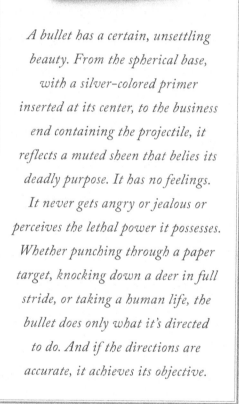

A bullet has a certain, unsettling beauty. From the spherical base, with a silver-colored primer inserted at its center, to the business end containing the projectile, it reflects a muted sheen that belies its deadly purpose. It has no feelings. It never gets angry or jealous or perceives the lethal power it possesses. Whether punching through a paper target, knocking down a deer in full stride, or taking a human life, the bullet does only what it's directed to do. And if the directions are accurate, it achieves its objective.

C lay Randall eased his bicycle into the parking lot of the convenience store, shivering from the cold rain that had pelted him for the past hour. Rolling to a stop under the store's awning, he dismounted with a groan. His back and legs ached from the fifty-mile ride. Most of it seemed to have been directly into the face of a stiff north wind, which was somewhat unusual for late March in Northeast Florida. Not for the first time, he wondered if his obsession with cycling was getting out of hand.

He pulled off his helmet, eyes reflexively scanning the interior of the store. Standing six feet and a solid one hundred, eighty pounds, Clay appeared younger than his forty-one years. He ran a hand through his sandy-blond hair, slight hints of gray just beginning to show at the temples.

A cop for almost twenty years in the Jacksonville Beach, Florida Police Department, it was second nature to watch everyone and everything around him. The store was empty of customers. The clerk sat behind the counter, a bored expression on her face as she flipped through the pages of a magazine.

He leaned his bike against the ice machine, briefly considering rolling it inside to ensure no one stole it. The sleek carbon-fiber bicycle had set him back four grand, an amount his wife argued could have been better spent on something more practical, like new dining room furniture.

Clay smiled as he thought of Dana. She was probably at her easel by now, creating another of her beautiful watercolor landscapes that generated an income several times greater than his salary as a public servant. Married seventeen years, he still felt like the geeky kid who somehow convinced the prettiest girl in school to fall in love with him.

Pushing through the door, he felt a welcome rush of warm air flow over his wet bike clothes. As the clerk looked up from her magazine, Clay said, "Morning. Got any fresh coffee?"

She smiled, "Just curious. Didn't you notice it's raining and fifty degrees outside?"

Gazing over his shoulder at the rain hitting the pavement, he said, "Really? Nope, didn't notice."

Laughing, she said, "The pot's fresh. Help yourself."

He poured a cup, savoring the aroma as the rising steam warmed his face. As he took his first tentative sip, a thump drew his attention to the entrance door. An old man in a wheelchair was trying unsuccessfully to push the door open. Clay quickly stepped over and held it open.

"I ain't helpless! Get the hell outta my way!" the man exclaimed. Hitting the power lever on the arm of the chair and motoring through the door, one of the wheels ran over Clay's foot as he passed.

"Hey, watch where you're going!" Clay exclaimed, dancing on one foot as he massaged his toes. He noted the man's filthy, disheveled clothing, wet, greasy hair plastered to his head, and a dirty, unshaved face. The wheels of the battery-powered chair were rusty, and the seat backing was cracked and torn in several places. Homeless, Clay suspected.

"Screw you," the man said, glaring over his shoulder as he rolled up to the counter.

The clerk studied the man with distaste. "What do you want?"

"Whataya want," the man mimicked, sarcastically. "I want food. What're you, stupid?"

"I've told you before. We don't give food away here. Go to a homeless shelter," the clerk replied.

"Naw, I don't think so. Shelter's too far away, and my battery's gettin' low. So I'll just get somethin' to eat and be on my way."

"Excuse me," Clay said, stepping up beside the man. "The lady made it clear she's not giving you food. So either buy something or pack it on out of here."

"Up yours. I ain't talkin' to you." Spinning his chair around, the homeless man rolled to a nearby rack and began grabbing bags of chips and peanuts and dropping them into his lap.

"Ma'am, I'm a police officer," he said, pulling his badge and identification from his pocket. "Do you want him to leave?"

"Please," she said. "I have to put up with this all the time. He thinks just because he's in a wheelchair he can do anything he wants."

"No problem," Clay said. Grabbing the chair handles and pulling the man away from the rack, he exclaimed, "Police officer! Stop what you're doing!"

The man touched the chair's joystick and spun around, his face contorted in fury. Pulling a large butcher knife from under his leg, he thrust it at Clay.

Leaping back, Clay stumbled. Before he could recover, the man charged forward, slamming the chair into his legs. Arms flailing, Clay staggered into a display rack that promptly collapsed, sending him to the floor amid dozens of candy bars, gum, and cookies.

The homeless man put his chair in high gear, banging into the door hard enough to knock it open. The clerk watched transfixed as Clay struggled to free himself from the rack. Scrambling to his feet, he bellowed, "CALL 9-1-1!"

He took two running steps, forgetting that his cleated shoes were designed for cycling and not running. Suddenly airborne, Clay landed flat on his back for the second time. Stunned, he sat up shaking his head, angry at letting a man in a wheelchair catch him off guard. Yanking his shoes off, he jumped to his feet and hit the exit door at full speed.

The rain came down hard as Clay raced across the parking lot. The wheelchair-bound man had already started across Beach Boulevard, one of the main arteries leading into downtown Jacksonville Beach. Clay reached the curb and started into the road after him. Suddenly, the shrill blast of an air horn brought him to an abrupt halt. His eyes widened in shock as a concrete truck roared past him only inches away, its huge tires splattering water over him in a cascade. *Damn, that was close!* he thought.

But he was lucky. The homeless man was not. As Clay stood at the curb watching helplessly, the truck driver locked down the brakes of the thirty-ton rig and yanked the steering wheel to the left. The homeless man stared in horror at sixty thousand pounds of metal and concrete hurtling toward him. Mouth open in a silent scream, he thrust out his arms in a futile attempt to stop the inevitable. The massive truck slammed into the man, the impact launching his body airborne as wheelchair parts scattered across the lanes of traffic.

The loaded truck slewed from side to side as the driver fought for control. For a second, Clay thought he would be successful. However, gravity finally won out, and the truck toppled onto its side with a deafening crash. The rig hit the pavement with such force that the concrete chute tore free from the drum, spilling wet concrete across the roadway. The truck, now fully on its side, spun around as it slid backward into the oncoming lanes.

Seconds before, a woman approaching Beach Boulevard from a side street answered her cell phone.

"Hey, Gina, it's Dad."

"Hi, Dad, what's up?"

"Listen, I wanted to talk to you about your decision to go through with—"

"Dad, just stop," she said with irritation. "I've heard your concerns already, and I'm not changing my mind. I'm divorcing Greg, and that's final. And if that creates a problem for you, then I'm sorry. But it's really not your decision, is it?"

"Listen here, young lady," he responded angrily. "You don't have any business talking to me like that."

"No, *you* listen, Dad. You haven't been on the receiving end of that man's verbal abuse toward me and my daughter. I'm getting out before he turns violent. And if you can't accept that, then maybe we need to stop talking!"

In her anger, Gina didn't notice the stop sign. Turning onto Beach Boulevard, she had just enough time to scream before the sliding concrete truck slammed into her small SUV. The force of the impact crushed the front of the vehicle all the way back to the passenger compartment.

Clay splashed through puddles of concrete and water as he ran toward the crash. In the rush of adrenaline, he was oblivious to the broken glass from the truck's windshield gouging his sock-clad feet. Running past the overturned truck, he saw the driver struggling to exit the cab, his face a mask of blood. The homeless man's broken and lifeless body lay sprawled in the street near the curb.

When Clay reached the SUV, he cringed. The windshield was gone, and the roof had bent upward in a V shape. The driver's window was shattered, leaving chips of tempered glass clinging to the warped window frame. Clay could see a woman pinned behind the steering wheel. The airbag had activated at the moment of impact, but it was clear the devastating force of the collision had rendered it useless.

A soft whimper drew his attention away from the woman to the back seat of the mangled car. Leaning down, he flinched at the sight of a little girl about five or six years old. Blood flowed down her face, the result of a four-inch shard of jagged metal protruding from her forehead. She was barely conscious, her head moving slowly side to side as her little hands fluttered in her lap.

He tried to reach the child, but the car's window frames had collapsed from the impact, jamming the doors shut. Hearing sirens in the distance, Clay said a silent prayer of thanks that help was on the way.

Turning his attention back to the woman, he reached into the car and pressed his fingers to her neck, hoping to find a pulse. After a minute of trying, he gave up. Although the woman's long dark hair partially covered her face, something about the angle of her jaw and chin seemed familiar to him. Gently brushing the hair aside, Clay suddenly got a clear view of her face.

He gasped in shock, "Oh, no!"

I t was Gina Starks, a close friend of his wife, Dana, since they were in high school. That meant the little girl had to be her daughter. Clay grimaced as he imagined his wife's reaction when she heard the news.

A faint voice from the front seat caught his attention. Leaning down, he saw a cell phone clutched loosely in the woman's hand. "Hello! Hello! Gina, what happened? Are you okay?" the voice asked, anxiety pouring from the tiny speaker.

Clay reached into the car and took the phone from the woman's lifeless hand. "Hello," he said.

"Who is this?" the voice demanded.

"Commander Clay Randall with the Jacksonville Beach Police Department. Who am I speaking to?"

"What's going on?!" the voice exclaimed. "I was talking to my daughter when she screamed, and then I heard a loud crash. Has she been in a wreck? Talk to me, officer!"

Clay thought about how he should respond. As a police officer, he had delivered death messages to parents, spouses, and children many times over the years. It was never easy. People reacted differently to the news that a loved one was never coming home again. Some were stoic, showing no emotion. Others became hysterical to the point that Clay had to call rescue personnel to treat them.

However, in all those death notifications, he had never encountered a situation quite like this. He knew not only the two victims but also the man on the phone. Referring to Gina Starks as his daughter was the giveaway. That meant the little girl was his granddaughter.

Clay said, "Mr. Barclay, your daughter and granddaughter have been in a traffic crash."

"OH, NO!" Barclay shouted. "How are they?! Are they hurt?!"

Speaking calmly, Clay said, "Mr. Barclay, I need you to come to Beach Boulevard and Sixth Street. Quickly. Can you do that?"

There was silence for what seemed to Clay like minutes but in reality was only a few seconds. "How do you know who I am?" the voice demanded harshly.

Ignoring the question, Clay said, "Mr. Barclay. I'll talk to you when you get here."

"I'm on my way," Barclay said, his voice cracking as he hung up.

Clay gently put the woman's phone on her lap, grabbed his cell, and dialed 9-1-1. "This is Randall. I'm at the crash scene on Beach," he said when the dispatcher answered. "Was the store clerk the one who called it in?"

"She was, Commander," the dispatcher replied. "Rescue is en route along with the fire department and all on-duty officers."

"Contact the fire department again. Make sure they've got their hydraulic can opener with them. An SUV was crushed by a loaded concrete truck, and there's a small child trapped inside. She's alive, but just barely. Also, contact Sergeant Crutchfield and have him call out the traffic homicide investigation team. This is a mess out here, so I need as many detectives as he can reach. Got all that?"

"Got it, Commander. Are you okay? We were told a homeless guy tried to stab you," the dispatcher said.

"I'm fine, but he's dead. He ran his wheelchair right into the path of the truck," he said. "Listen, a couple more things. Call the Chief and ask him to respond. And the police chaplain, too. I need them both out here ASAP."

"What do you want me to advise them?"

Clay paused, debating how much information to give at this point. "Just tell the chaplain there are two fatalities, and I need him at the scene. Nothing else. And ask the Chief to call me on my cell," he said, hanging up.

Police officers and emergency personnel arrived within seconds and went to work. Clay directed the officers to set up barricades to protect the scene while fire personnel began the delicate process of cutting away the mangled roof to get to the injured child.

Clay's cell phone rang. "Randall."

"What's going on?" Police Chief Mike Wilson asked in his usual, gruff voice.

"Mike, this is bad," he said.

"Don't keep me guessing. What is it?"

Clay recounted the confrontation at the convenience store and the death of the homeless man, pausing after explaining about the concrete truck overturning. "And that's the easy part."

"That was easy?"

"In comparison, anyway. After the truck overturned, it slid for a short distance on the wet road until it crashed into an SUV that had just turned onto Beach. It crushed the front of the car, killing the driver and seriously injuring a small child in the back seat."

When Clay paused again, Mike said, "What are you not telling me?"

"The driver is Gina Starks, Thomas Barclay's daughter, and the child is his granddaughter. Gina is dead, and I don't know if the little girl will make it. She has a chunk of metal embedded in her forehead. The fire department is cutting the roof off the car to get to her."

"Are you referring to *the* Thomas Barclay?"

"I am."

Mike didn't respond for so long that Clay said, "You still there, Chief?"

Wilson said, "I'm here. Has anyone contacted Barclay yet?"

"That's an additional complication," Clay said, relaying to Chief Wilson his phone conversation with Barclay on his daughter's cell.

"Is he already there?" Wilson asked.

"Not yet. And I didn't tell him his daughter was dead. I just said to get here as fast as he could, that there had been an accident."

"Okay," he replied. "I'll be there in five."

Clay clicked off as he watched the firemen continue their careful efforts to cut through the roof supports to reach the little girl. In the past few minutes, she had stopped moving, and rescue personnel were getting anxious.

Hearing his name called, Clay turned to see Detective Sergeant Joey Crutchfield approaching.

Crutchfield asked, "You okay?"

"No, definitely not okay."

Clay spent the next few minutes bringing him up to speed. As he explained, Mike Wilson arrived, standing by silently listening. Just as Clay finished, Thomas Barclay drove up, leaping from his car and running toward the chaos.

"Here we go," Wilson muttered, moving quickly to intercept Barclay before he could reach the car. "Wait," he called out, waving at Barclay. "Don't go there."

Barclay ignored Wilson, never wavering from his direct and determined path to reach his daughter's car. When he drew near, his eyes bulged at the sight. Falling to his knees, Barclay cried, "OH, MY GOD! SHE'S DEAD!"

The firemen had succeeded in peeling away a section of the roof to allow access to the little girl. Rescue personnel immediately began checking her vital signs. Clay raised his eyebrows questioningly at the EMT hovering over the child. The man held his thumb and forefinger a hair's breadth apart, saying, "An air unit's coming to transport her to the trauma center, but I'm not confident she'll make it. Her GCS is three."

Seeing Clay's confusion at the medical terminology, the EMT explained, "Vital signs are almost non-existent."

Gesturing toward Barclay, who was still swept up in an emotional storm, Clay said, "That's the dead woman's father, and this is his granddaughter. Do you know who he is?"

The EMT observed the sobbing man, shaking his head at first. Then recognition dawned, and his eyes widened. "Is that Thomas Barclay?"

Clay said, "The one and only."

"Aw, man, that sucks," he said, shaking his head. "Listen, considering who he is, I can get him on the flight if he wants to go. You know, just in case . . ." he said, his voice trailing off.

Clay said, "I'll get back to you."

Kneeling in front of Barclay, he spoke softly, "Mr. Barclay, I need you to listen to me for a second."

Barclay slowly raised his head, his face a mask of grief. "What?"

"Your granddaughter is being life-flighted to the trauma center downtown, and she needs you to go with her," Clay explained.

Confusion crossed Barclay's face, and then he wailed, "I forgot about her! Where is she?!" he demanded in a loud voice, lunging to his feet.

He gasped as he saw the paramedics gently strapping her small body onto a gurney in preparation for the helicopter flight. Rushing over to the closest EMT, he yelled, "IS SHE ALIVE? IS SHE GOING TO BE OKAY?"

Clay stepped in front of the distraught man, grabbing him by the shoulders. "Mr. Barclay, it's important that you stay focused. You can't do anything for Gina, but you can for your granddaughter."

Barclay glared at Clay, his fists doubled up. Suddenly, his shoulders slumped, his head dropped onto his chest, and tears flowed once again. Clay took his arm and led him without resistance to the area patrol officers had cordoned off for the helicopter to land.

The air unit arrived, and the EMTs hustled to get the little girl aboard and strapped down. As Clay shepherded Barclay to the helicopter, the police chaplain arrived and received approval to go along for support.

Clay watched as the helicopter lifted off for the twenty-minute flight to the hospital, profound sadness on his face. He had seen death many times in his career. It was an occupational hazard. Cops trained themselves to keep their emotions tightly under control to do the job effectively. However, the deaths of two police officers several years before, one of whom had been Clay's best friend, still weighed on him in times like this.

Mike Wilson watched the emotions playing out on Clay's face. He gripped his shoulder. "I'm sorry, Clay. This is tough, I know."

Clay shook his head, "If I hadn't decided to chase that guy, maybe none of this would have happened."

"Stop right there. Nobody forced him to steal food or to attack you. You were doing your job. You can't blame yourself for this." Glancing at

Clay's feet, the chief said, "You're bleeding. Go see the paramedics."

Clay looked down in surprise at his bloody socks. In all the turmoil, he hadn't realized he was injured. Head still down, he walked slowly over to the rescue unit.

Wilson turned to Crutchfield. "Joey, you're in charge."

"I'll take care of it, Chief."

Crutchfield watched Clay as he sat on the bumper of the rescue unit and removed his bloody socks so the EMTs could treat him. He had great respect for the man. As Clay's first field training officer, Joey had quickly recognized the young cop's drive and intelligence. The fact that Clay was now his boss was neither a surprise nor a problem for him. Joey liked to brag that Clay's rise through the ranks was because of the outstanding mentoring and training he had given him.

Joey had been a cop for more than thirty years. In his early fifties, he still had a full head of hair with little gray. Although standing an even five-eight, Joey always swore he was five-nine, a discrepancy he declined repeatedly to resolve by submitting to a tape measure.

After ten years as a patrol officer, he decided it was time to test for a supervisory rank. Scoring first in the process, he received a promotion to sergeant and moved into the detective division. There, he quickly established himself as a tenacious investigator who treated every crime as if it had been committed against a member of his family.

Shortly after his promotion, Joey had an encounter that earned him both a nickname and a reputation as a gutsy cop. One afternoon, a man armed with a handgun robbed a bank of several thousand dollars in cash. As he fled, the dispatcher notified officers of the suspect's physical description and the car he was driving.

Joey heard the call dispatched as he was coming back from a court hearing in downtown Jacksonville. Crossing the Intracoastal Waterway, known by locals as the ICW, into Jacksonville Beach, he saw a car fitting the general description of the suspect's vehicle approaching the bridge from the opposite direction.

As soon as the car passed, he made a quick U-turn and activated the lights and siren on his unmarked unit. The driver immediately pulled into the breakdown lane near the top of the bridge. Non-stop radio traffic by officers responding to the bank robbery prevented Joey from calling out on the possible suspect.

While he waited for airtime, he saw a clean-cut young man get out of the car, smiling and waving as he strolled slowly toward Joey's vehicle. His reaction was so unlike that of a man who had just robbed a bank that Joey made a dangerous assumption; he had stopped an innocent citizen. Taking his eyes off the man, he leaned over to switch to another radio channel.

Turning back just as the man arrived at his window, Joey saw a gun pointed directly at his head.

In a conversational tone, the bank robber said, "Sir, please put down that microphone right now."

Keeping his eyes on the gun, Joey dropped the mic onto the seat.

"Thanks. Very carefully now, turn your engine off and hand me the keys."

Not saying a word, Joey did as commanded.

"Good. I want you to take out the gun I know you're carrying, using your thumb and forefinger only. Don't try anything cute, or you'll force me to shoot you, which is something I don't want to do."

Still not speaking, Joey slowly pulled his weapon from its holster and handed it across.

"One more thing, and I'll be on my way," the robber said. "Every cop carries handcuffs, including you. Am I right?"

Joey pulled the cuffs from his belt and starting to hand them to the man.

"No, no. Those are for you. I want you to handcuff yourself to the steering wheel."

Joey complied, locking the other end of the cuff to his left wrist.

The robber examined Joey's keys, asking, "Is this your handcuff key?"

Joey shrugged and then nodded.

"Good, I think we're done here. Have a nice day, officer," he said turning and starting back toward his car as he slipped both pistols into his pants and pulled his shirt over it.

Joey swiftly reached into his coat pocket and then called out, "Hey, I need to show you something."

The young man stopped and peered at Joey, who smiled at him. He looked toward his car, then turned and came back.

He leaned down, the gun back in his hand, and said, "I'm in a hurry. What?"

Joey responded, "Meet Little Heat," as he pointed a small, five-shot, twenty-two caliber revolver at the man's chest and pulled the trigger.

Later, after EMTs transported the robber to the hospital, Joey had the embarrassing task of explaining to the chief how he had allowed himself to be handcuffed to his steering wheel. As he recounted the story, his chief was puzzled. "What's Little Heat?"

"That's my backup piece," he explained. "You know, it's little, but it packs a lot of heat."

From that day forward, Joey was enshrined in the folklore of the police department, affectionately and respectfully christened with the nickname, "Little Heat."

C hief, Thomas Barclay and his assistant, Louis Dunlop, are here and would like to meet with you for a few minutes," the chief's administrative assistant said over the intercom.

Frowning, Mike Wilson responded, "Okay, give me a minute."

He had dreaded this ever since the mayor called and insisted he meet with Barclay. It was politics, pure and simple. The Honorable Thomas Edward Barclay, III, United States Senator from Florida, was running for his third term and already touted by some in his party as a possible presidential candidate. Mike suspected Barclay was about to exercise his political muscle to try to force him into a decision he had no intention of making.

Anyone who knew Mike Wilson would say without question that he never succumbed to pressure. After a fifteen year Navy career, Wilson was one of the first African-American police officers hired into the Jacksonville Beach Police Department. His swift rise through the ranks to become the department's first black chief of police was not surprising to anyone who had the opportunity to work with and for him.

Chief Wilson grumbled, "The man shows up without an appointment dragging his hatchet man with him and expects me to drop everything to see him."

Lou Dunlop, Barclay's chief of staff, had called five times in the past month, always with the same questions. Why was Commander Clay Randall chasing a man who for all practical purposes had committed no crime? When he saw the poor homeless man heading toward the street, why didn't he recognize the danger and stop chasing him? Why did Commander Randall involve himself at all, considering he was not on duty? Dunlop's questions with their infinite variations had grown so contentious that the chief had told his assistant to decline further calls from the senator's office; hence, the political pressure.

Mike said to Clay, "You ready for this?"

"I've thought a lot over the past month about that day, and I've pretty much come to terms with what happened. Whether he believes it or not, I truly sympathize with Barclay. I can't imagine how painful it must be for him to lose his daughter and see his grandchild so severely injured. You know, it's a shame we couldn't measure the exact speed the truck driver was going because of the wet condition of the road. When he came past me, he had to be doing at least fifty in a thirty-five-mile speed zone. If we could prove that, it might make Barclay feel differently. Unfortunately, we can't, so he's not likely to change his mind."

Shrugging, Mike said, "I think you're right. But regardless, Thomas Barclay is a typical politician, so it's not in his nature to admit that he could be wrong about anything. Anyway, let's get this over with."

Pressing the intercom button, he said, "Ask the senator to come in, please."

"No need," a deep voice said. Mike and Clay turned as Barclay came striding into the office with Lou Dunlop following a step behind.

Barclay's perfectly coiffed, silvery mane of hair topped a face with a golden tan that Wilson guessed came from regular visits to a tanning salon in DC. Standing six-four, the man was impeccably dressed in a navy blazer, gray slacks, and a light blue shirt with a patterned red and blue tie. He looked and sounded every inch the Hollywood version of a politician.

In direct contrast, Lou Dunlop barely topped five-six in his shoes. Balding, he adopted a comb-over hairstyle that required substantial amounts of hairspray to hold in place. His cheeks and nose were a mass of spider veins caused by a combination of a skin condition called Rosacea and thirty years of hard drinking. His waist stretched the limits of his charcoal, custom-tailored suit. Dunlop was a man who loved good food and drink and never passed up an opportunity to partake of either.

"Good morning, Chief Wilson. I'm Thomas Barclay," the senator said, evidently forgetting Wilson had talked to him the day of the crash. "Your subordinate advised my chief of staff you were busy, but I'm on a very tight schedule. I have to fly back to Washington tomorrow, so I hope you can take a few minutes to meet with me."

As he talked, Barclay's eyes drifted around the office, noting the plaques and pictures on the walls. When Clay extended his hand, he saw a brief flash of anger cross the senator's face. Barclay stared at Clay's hand before reluctantly reaching out and gripping it powerfully. Keeping his face impassive, Clay gradually returned the pressure to the point that Barclay winced, jerking his hand away.

Clay said calmly, "Good morning, Senator. Please accept my sincere condolences to you and your family. My wife and I are . . . were good friends with your daughter."

The distaste on Barclay's face grew by the second as Clay talked. Ignoring his comment, Barclay sat down and crossed his legs, carefully preserving the sharp crease in his slacks. From his jacket pocket, Dunlop removed business cards for the senator and himself and placed them on the corner of the chief's desk as he took the chair to the right of his boss.

"Chief Wilson, I would like to speak privately with you, if I may," Barclay said, glancing pointedly at Clay.

Wilson responded evenly, "I'm afraid that won't be possible, Senator. Commander Randall's rank is second only to the chief of police in this department. Consequently, I have no intention of excluding him from this meeting."

Before Barclay could object, Dunlop put his hands on his knees, leaning forward, "Excuse me, Chief. The sole reason Senator Barclay and I are here today is to discuss serious acts of malfeasance by Mr. Randall. Do we think his presence will hamper our ability to speak freely? Yes, we do."

Ignoring Dunlop, Wilson continued. "Senator Barclay, surely your aide has briefed you on the numerous conversations I've had with him over the past month."

"I'm the senator's chief of staff, not his aide," Dunlop protested.

Wilson kept his eyes on Barclay as he continued, "It is my understanding from *Mr.* Dunlop that you blame Commander Randall for the death of your daughter and the injuries to your grandchild. I've explained to him each time we've discussed this that the commander acted responsibly when he tried to prevent a crime. He narrowly avoided serious injury himself when the man tried to stab him with a butcher knife. Mr. Dunlop has demanded, supposedly on your behalf, that I get rid of Commander Randall. That, I absolutely will not do."

Barclay glared at Wilson. "Chief, I understand your desire to protect one of your own. However, the fact remains that I have suffered the painful loss of my daughter and horrible injuries to my granddaughter as a direct result of that man's criminal negligence," he said, pointing at Clay.

"Senator, as Commander Randall said, we're terribly sorry for what happened to your family. However, I object to your comment that I'm protecting my own, as you characterized it. In this police department, if we're wrong, we're the first to admit it. But, in this instance, the commander doesn't need defending. The incident was thoroughly reviewed by the Florida Department of Law Enforcement as well as the state attorney, both of which completely cleared him."

Dunlop put a hand on Barclay's arm. "Senator, if I may?"

Barclay nodded curtly.

Dunlop spoke directly to Wilson. "Should the law-abiding citizens of this community be subjected to this menace to their safety? We say, emphatically, absolutely not! Randall had several questionable incidents in the past few years. It seems that whenever he gets involved in something, people wind up dead. The fact of the matter is that this man is a hothead who acts first and only thinks of the consequences when it's time to write up his reports. For example, consider the incident when those two officers were killed. If Randall had–"

Wilson said abruptly, "Stop right there, Mr. Dunlop. I'm not going to sit here and listen to you trash the reputation of this officer. He is a consummate professional and an honorable man."

Turning to Barclay, he said, "Senator, Commander Randall did his job that day and did it well, as he has done since the first day he pinned on a badge. I don't intend to take any action against him in this nor in any other incident unless someone presents *proof*, not baseless allegations, that he has done something wrong."

Frowning, Barclay said, "Chief, don't you work directly for the mayor?"

"I do. What's your point?"

"My point is that if I can't get your cooperation to rid our community of this . . . this person, perhaps I should discuss the matter directly with Mayor Adams. I have no doubt she will see things my way."

"Please feel free to meet with the mayor or anyone else you like, Senator. That changes nothing as far as I'm concerned. Commander Randall will continue to serve our citizens as long as I'm the chief of police."

In an icy tone, Barclay said, "Well, Chief, nothing lasts forever. It seems it may be time for a change in the leadership of this police department. Now, are you prepared to fight me on this issue? Because if you are, be warned that I can be quite persuasive, and I seldom fail to get what I want."

As Barclay spoke, Clay watched Dunlop leaning closer and closer to the edge of Mike Wilson's desk. Staring at the lapel of Dunlop's jacket, Clay stood abruptly, saying in a firm voice, "Hold on, Chief." Leaning toward Dunlop, he demanded, "Are you recording this conversation?"

Dunlop immediately sat back in his chair, his left hand brushing his lapel. "What is this crap?" he said sarcastically. "You're just trying to deflect attention away from your own screw-ups."

Clay grabbed the lapel of Dunlop's coat, turning it over to reveal a thin, black wire running from a microphone through a hole in the fabric into the inside pocket. Before Dunlop could do more than sputter, Clay snatched a miniature digital recorder out of the pocket, yanking the wire and mic free as he did.

He quickly examined the device before tossing it on the chief's desk. "The recorder is running, Chief. He must have turned it on when he pulled out the business cards."

Eyes blazing at Barclay, Wilson snapped, "I can't believe you would have the nerve to record a conversation without our knowledge! This is the most unprofessional and unethical behavior I've ever seen from an elected official, and particularly one who's talking about running for president!"

Barclay scowled, lunging to his feet. "This is outrageous! I've never been treated so disrespectfully in all my years of public service! I had no idea my chief of staff was recording this conversation."

"I find it hard to believe that he did this all on his own," Mike said, coldly, gesturing toward Dunlop. "He strikes me as a man who doesn't take a piss unless you tell him it's okay."

By this time, everyone was standing, and Dunlop was desperately trying to reach the recorder on Wilson's desk.

Clay snatched up the device before Dunlop could grab it. "I'm confiscating this recorder as evidence in a possible criminal prosecution for illegal wiretapping," Clay said. "This entire conversation is still being recorded, so I advise you both to shut up and walk out right now unless you want to hear your Miranda rights."

The expression on Barclay's face was raw and ugly. "You will regret this," he growled, shaking his finger at Clay and Mike. He spun on his heel and rushed out of the office, followed closely by Dunlop, his short legs churning to keep up with Barclay's long strides.

Wilson's eyes stayed on the open door as if expecting them to come charging back. Muttering a curse under his breath, he dropped into his chair.

Clay found the power switch and stopped the recording. "I can see a dirtbag like Dunlop pulling something like this. But do you think Barclay knew about it?"

Wilson shook his head. "Knowing Lou Dunlop, he probably didn't tell Barclay. That gives his boss total deniability if he's caught, which he was, thanks to your sharp eyes."

"You're right. We can't prove the senator knew about it. Even if he did, he covered himself well with that over-the-top denial on the recording. The only solid case is against Dunlop," Clay said.

When Wilson didn't respond, Clay continued, "What do you want to do about it?"

The chief paused before answering, his eyes on the desk blotter as he considered the ramifications of pursuing a criminal case against the chief of staff of a United States Senator.

Mike said, "You know where he's headed right now, don't you?"

"Sure. By now, he's halfway to the mayor's office."

"Yep," Mike answered. "And what do you think she'll do?"

My guess is the mayor will do whatever Barclay tells her to do. In my opinion, Denise Adams is just like Thomas Barclay."

Wilson agreed. "You also can't discount Dunlop's part in it. He's the one who gets things done for Barclay. He's a real prick, but you can't deny his skills. While Barclay parlayed his fast talk and charisma to make it to the Senate, Dunlop is the one responsible for positioning him to be a potential candidate for president. The man will say and do anything to accomplish his political goals. The crap he tried to pull today is vintage Lou Dunlop. And Denise Adams? We should expect nothing less from her than total compliance with Barclay's demands. That is, as long as it can be done behind the scenes where people can't see him pulling the strings."

Clay frowned. "What does this mean for you? And for me?"

Wilson smiled. "For you, it means nothing. You're not an appointed official like me, so no action can be taken against you in the absence of a serious violation of policy or law. Neither of which you've done. As the chief, I'm the only one who can take such an action. For me? I'd like to think Denise understands me well enough to know that I won't cave to political pressure. From her or Barclay. I retired once after I got a bellyful of our illustrious former chief, Gordy Cooper. Worst case, if they decide they want me out, I'll just retire again."

Clay shook his head. "But the mayor still needs a majority vote of the city council to remove you from office. And I can't imagine–"

Mike interrupted, "I know the law, Clay. And regardless of how the rest of the council members might feel about Barclay or the mayor, I doubt she could get a majority to vote to remove me."

"But–"

"But, nothing, Clay," Mike said, gently. "I'm not completely helpless here. I haven't lasted this long without learning a few tricks. If the mayor tries to pull that crap, I'll refuse. Then, if she threatens to take the matter before the full council for a vote, I'll encourage her to do that. I'd be happy to state my case in an open meeting with the media and citizens present."

"You're sure? I don't want you sticking your neck out for me and getting your head chopped off."

Shaking his head, Wilson said, "You just keep doing your usual good job and let me worry about that. This will all blow over. Trust me."

As the chief uttered those words, Senator Barclay charged into the mayor's office followed by Lou Dunlop. Mayor Denise Adams was talking to a constituent on the telephone.

Waving them to seats in front of her desk, she said, "Certainly, ma'am. I understand you don't want to see your taxes go up. However, the city needs additional revenue in order to continue to provide the outstanding services you've come to expect. We–", she stopped, interrupted by the caller.

Listening to the agitated woman, she saw Barclay gesture for her to get off the phone. With a small frown, she broke in on the caller. "Excuse me. I'm sorry to cut you off, but I have an important issue that has just come up and I have to take care of it. Please call the main number and make an appointment if you would like to discuss your issue further. Thank you, and have a good day," she said, hanging up without waiting for a response.

Turning to Barclay and Dunlop, she smiled, "Good afternoon, Senator. Lou. What can I do for you?"

Gritting his teeth, Barclay said, "I want that bastard Mike Wilson canned. Nobody talks to me the way he just did and gets away with it. And while you're at it, fire Randall, too!"

Her smile faded. "What do you mean? What did they do to you?"

"Wilson and Randall both talked to me like I was some, I don't know, like some homeless bum living in a dumpster. They threatened to arrest me over a tape recorder!"

"Who threatened to arrest you? And over a tape recorder? I don't understand."

"Senator, if I may?" Dunlop said in a soothing voice.

Barclay waved at Dunlop to go ahead, going over to a cabinet at the far end of the mayor's office that concealed a wet bar. Retrieving a bottle of scotch, he poured two fingers into a glass and downed it in one long swallow. Filling the glass a second time, he stood gazing out the window at kids tossing a football in the green space outside city hall called Latham Plaza.

"Mayor," Dunlop said, drawing her attention from Barclay, "what Senator Barclay is trying to say is that he went to the police department to discuss the incredibly botched investigation into the death of his daughter and the critical injuries to his granddaughter. Specifically, he wanted the chief to do something about Randall's culpability in this horrific incident. Was the senator shocked and dismayed to find Randall in the chief's office when we arrived? You bet he was. And when Senator Barclay asked to speak privately with the chief, the man refused to make Randall leave. Then he proceeded to lecture the senator about how Randall had done nothing wrong. He wouldn't listen to anything we had to say."

"Lou," she interrupted, "you still haven't explained the threat to arrest Senator Barclay over something about a recorder."

"I was just about to clarify that, Mayor. I wanted to put the incident into context for you first. You see, I strongly suspected Chief Wilson would take an adversarial position seeing as how he previously denied Randall had done anything wrong. So, what could we do to pressure the chief into doing the right thing? Well, I advised Senator Barclay that it would be to our, to *his* advantage to get Chief Wilson on record as denying any impropriety by Randall. Consequently, I brought along a digital recorder to preserve the conversation accurately in the event the chief later claimed something was said that wasn't."

"Okay, that seems reasonable to me," the mayor responded. "So why did he threaten to arrest you?"

"It was that guy, Randall," Barclay interjected, walking back over with his drink clutched tightly in his hand. "He claimed it's against the law to record someone without their knowledge. I don't remember ever hearing about any law like that."

Denise shook her head. "I'm sorry, Senator. I don't deal with criminal law. But if he said it, and Chief Wilson didn't dispute it, my guess is it's true."

"What? Are you taking his side?" Barclay demanded, leaning forward.

Holding up her hands, she replied, "No, no, please, Senator. Calm down. I'm not taking anybody's side right now. I'm just trying to understand what happened so I can help you."

Barclay said to Dunlop. "Lou, give us a minute."

Dunlop stood slowly and moved toward the door. "I'll be in the car."

Barclay turned back to Denise Adams as Dunlop left, quietly closing the door behind him. Neither said anything as Barclay took a sip of his scotch. The mayor went to the bar and poured herself a glass of white wine. Strictly speaking, policy prohibited alcohol on city property except during certain special events, but Denise Adams felt the rule was advisory rather than an outright prohibition.

Moving to the chair Dunlop had vacated, she leaned over and gently squeezed Barclay's arm. "Tommy," she said softly, using the nickname he allowed no one to use except her, "what can I do?"

Taking another swallow, Barclay eyed her over the rim of his glass, "You know what I want, Denise. I want Randall's head on a platter. Because of him, my daughter is dead, and my granddaughter is a vegetable."

Putting her wine glass on the edge of the desk, she took Barclay's drink and set it down beside hers. Leaning over, she wrapped her arms around his neck. "You poor darling. I'm so sorry."

In a grieving tone, he spoke. "You know, I can't get past the fact that my daughter would be alive today, and my grandchild would still be calling and asking me when are we going to the beach again. But because of *Randall* . . ." he spat.

Taking his face in her hands, Denise said, "Tommy, you have to let the hate and anger go. It's eating you up inside."

"I can't. I was talking to her on her cell phone at the very instant she died. Did you know that?"

"Yes, you told me," she answered softly.

Lost in the memory of that pain-filled day, he didn't hear her response.

"I was bitching at her about going through with the divorce from that jerk she married. Then she nailed me, saying I was only trying to get her to drop the divorce because I thought it might hurt me politically."

He rubbed his eyes with the heels of his hands as if trying to blot out the memory of his daughter lying dead in the car. "The last words we ever said to each other were hostile. She died angry with me," he said in an anguished voice. "Don't you understand? I can't let this go. I won't! I'm going to make him pay for what he did. I've crushed people far tougher than Randall and his boss. They're going to learn there's a price to pay for defying me."

Denise was stunned at the intensity of Barclay's emotion. "Tommy, I can't feel the depth of your terrible loss, but I do understand your anger and frustration. And I'll support you in whatever way you need."

Barclay sighed deeply. "I know you will. And thanks for sticking by me."

With a sad smile, she replied, "I'm happy to do it. I just wish I could be there for you every day."

She hesitated before continuing, thinking of the tragedies Thomas Barclay had endured. His wife of almost forty years had died of breast cancer less than a year before. Now, his only child was dead, and his grandchild lay comatose in a hospital.

Denise Adams had not had a storybook life, either. Pregnant at seventeen, she and her boyfriend both dropped out of school and got married. Three months later, she had a miscarriage. Six months after that, they were divorced.

Barely eighteen, in spite of future prospects that seemed dim, Denise Adams was determined to become successful. She passed her high school GED exam and then, with the help of student loans, went to the University of North Florida. In three years, she graduated with honors with a degree in political science, all while working two part-time jobs.

Intrigued by the political process, she completed a master's degree in the same discipline. After a painful breakup with the man she thought would be her life mate, she moved to Washington, DC to pursue her career. Over the next ten years, she worked on numerous campaigns, earning a reputation as a savvy political consultant. By her mid-thirties, she had become a vice president of a prestigious Washington political consulting firm and proved very successful in convincing top political candidates to hire her company to represent them.

However, Denise still felt unfulfilled. On a personal level, she had never married again, preferring relationships with no strings attached. Professionally, however, she wanted more. She wanted to run for elective office herself.

One evening while attending a political fundraiser, she had her first encounter with Senator Thomas Barclay, the event's keynote speaker. Although they were both dialed in to the DC political scene, their paths had never crossed until that night. As she sat listening to him, she thought to herself that he was the complete package. Senator Barclay was a dynamic, compelling speaker with a message that resonated strongly with her. She thought he was incredibly handsome, also. The talk around DC that he was eyeing a future bid for the White House made perfect sense to her.

As the event was winding down, she approached a group of supporters surrounding Barclay and introduced herself, suggesting her consulting firm might be able to assist him. Within a couple of weeks, he had hired her firm and begun working closely with Denise and her staff. Over the months, as the professional relationship proved beneficial to both Barclay and Denise's company, a friendship also began to develop between the two of them.

When she shared with Barclay her ambition to run for office, he was enthusiastic and promised to help her get elected, suggesting she start at the local level back home. Subsequently, after resigning her position with a generous separation agreement, Denise moved back to Jacksonville Beach. Within a year, Barclay had used his money and influence to ensure her election as the new mayor.

During a post-election celebration with Barclay at an expensive restaurant, he shared the news of his wife's cancer. Although visibly upset as he spoke of her losing battle, Denise could tell there was something he wasn't saying. On impulse, she reached across the table and squeezed his hand. The gesture seemed to comfort him, and he revealed that he and his wife had largely led separate lives for many years and that her illness made their already strained relationship even more difficult.

Although surprised, Denise immediately recognized the possibilities. She had grown very fond of the man sitting across the table from her. His handsome features and aura of raw sensuality were alluring, and the fact that he was a powerful man on the national stage made him all the more attractive. That night, they checked into a suite at the Ritz-Carlton on Amelia Island, beginning an affair that lasted through and beyond his wife's death late the following year.

———————

Taking Barclay's hand, Denise felt a slight twinge of guilt as she said, "Tommy, you've told me before that you're not ready to talk about it, but I need to know when we, you and me, are going to be able to be seen together publicly?"

Pulling his hand away, Barclay picked up his glass and drained it in one long swallow. "Come on, Denise. We've had this conversation many times. I know it's hard on you. It is for me, too. But it's been less than a year since Barbara died. And with what's happened . . ." he stopped, a troubled look on his face.

"I know. I understand how difficult this is for you."

"No, you *don't* understand. I've lost my entire family except for my granddaughter. The doctors still can't tell me whether she'll ever recover. My personal life is in chaos right now, but I have to set that aside and stay focused on my political future. Everything I do will be scrutinized, so I have to be careful not to come across as callous. The political fallout from that would be huge."

Taking a sip of wine, Denise said, "I understand the politics of the situation, Tommy. I really do. But we've been together professionally for quite a while, so I can't see it being an issue."

"You're right about the professional connection, but going public with a romantic relationship this soon after Barbara died and Gina and, and ..." he stopped again, swallowing hard.

Sighing, he continued. "Anyway, it could potentially be disastrous. In fact, Lou Dunlop bitches every time I bring up the idea. He's worried that when people find out about our personal relationship, they will start questioning when it started. He's also worried women voters will be turned off by me getting involved with someone so soon after Barbara's death."

Raising her eyebrows, she said, "It's been almost a year, as you said. No woman with an ounce of compassion or common sense is going to criticize you for wanting a companion after being married for so many years and then enduring your wife's long, brave battle against cancer. Tommy, I believe in you and what you can bring to this country, but this was supposed to be a package deal."

"I know," he said, reaching for her hand. "And it's going to happen. I just need some time."

Denise withdrew her hand, leaning back in her chair. "We've been dancing around this for a long time now. You've told me more times than I can count that you just need time, but then, when I bring it up, you say the timing is wrong. I'm beginning to think the timing is never going to be right."

"Don't say that. I just can't afford to do anything that could screw things up before the campaign even has a chance to get off the ground. A presidential campaign is a billion dollar venture today, and the big money people are starting to line up behind me. Without those people backing me, I have absolutely no chance of being elected. The guys with the fat checkbooks are not going to back a candidate who has some scandal in his background. You understand that, don't you?"

Denise shook her head, her expression flat. "Sure, Thomas. I understand. What you're saying is that being with me will screw up your chances of getting what you want."

"No, no, no, that's not what I'm saying," he said, shaking his head vigorously.

"Sure you are," she countered. "That's exactly what you're saying."

Barclay rubbed his face, frowning. *Women are all alike*, he thought. *They want what they want when they want it and the way they want it. And nothing else matters.*

"Look, Denise, Lou thinks we should wait at least until after the election before we go public with our relationship."

Seeing the consternation on her face, he hurriedly added, "That's Dunlop saying we need to wait until after the election. I've told him I don't think it's necessary to hold off that long."

"So how long is it going to be?" she insisted.

"Listen, what I've gone through over the past couple of years is almost more than I can endure. I just need you to support me. Not badger me. And what you're doing isn't helping."

The sharp lines in her face softened at his words. Touching his arm, she said, "Tommy, losing a child has to be the absolute worst thing a parent could ever endure, regardless of how old you are. On top of that, the horrible injuries to your grandchild make it so much more devastating. I can understand that. At least I can on an intellectual if not an emotional level. I guess what's making me unhappy is that I can't be there for you. Our stolen hours together are too little and too long between. I can help you deal with all this if you'll just give me a chance."

Barclay stood, leaning over and kissing her cheek. "Thank you for that. I appreciate your understanding. I'll figure out a way to make this, to make us, happen, and I'll be proud the day I'm sworn in as President to introduce you to the world as my wife, First Lady Denise Barclay."

With a small shrug, she stepped into his arms and held him tightly. "I guess that's as much as I can hope for right now. A chance for true happiness for us both," she said in a small voice.

Putting his hand under her chin, he gently tilted her head back, kissing her. Softly at first, then with increasing passion, they clung together. Barclay stroked her back, moving his hands lower and lower until Denise broke away, breathing hard. "Not here, Tommy. I can just imagine what people in City Hall would say if they saw me after one of our sessions."

Barclay grinned at her. "We get pretty wild, I'll admit. How about tonight? Same time and place?"

She smiled back at him. "Same time and place."

Barclay started for the door, then stopped and turned. "About Randall and Wilson. Can you take care of them for me?"

Denise hesitated before responding. "I have to think about the right way to do this. Mike Wilson has overwhelming support in the community.

For that matter, so does Randall. I'll need something that makes it clear that firing them was my only choice. I need public opinion on my side on this. And your side, too. With what you have at stake, you can understand that, can't you?"

Barclay said, "I guess I can. Just remember that I want both of them gone. So build your case. And make it happen soon, okay?"

"Okay," she smiled.

"See you tonight," he said, heading out the door.

One week later

A light rain pelted the windshield as Officer Summer Hayes headed back to Jacksonville Beach from the Duval County Jail. An eighteen-year-old kid in his daddy's new BMW had driven onto the median on State Route A1A, or Third Street, knocking down a light pole and earning himself a trip to jail for drunk driving. Summer had been tracking the car's erratic movements for a couple of blocks and had just made the decision to stop the car and check out the driver when it vaulted the curb.

Surprisingly, the kid wasn't hurt, a combination of the airbag deploying and his noticeably drunken state, she guessed. She had him undergo the standard field sobriety exercises, which he failed miserably, and then arrested him for DUI. The boy bawled all the way to the county jail, begging her to let him go so he could run away before his daddy found out about the car. Shaking her head, she wondered about the dynamics of a family in which a car held more value than the safety of a son.

Summer Hayes had been a police officer for five years, joining the Jacksonville Beach Police Department two months after completing a four-year hitch in the U. S. Army. At five-nine and a toned one hundred, forty pounds, she could hold her own with most men fifty pounds heavier, thanks to years of intense training in mixed martial arts. Twenty-nine years old, with dark hair and pale blue eyes, she had no shortage of guys interested in getting to know her better.

Summer had been involved in a deadly force incident during her first year in the department, exchanging shots with a killer after being wounded herself. The way she handled herself during that incident and afterward earned her the respect of her fellow officers, who gave her the ultimate compliment. They said Summer Hayes was a good cop.

Heading over the ICW, she keyed her radio, advising dispatch she was back in the city. The communications officer immediately cleared her for a meal break since there were no calls holding.

Glancing at her watch, she saw it was almost three in the morning. Nothing open but a couple of fast food joints and convenience stores, she realized. Visualizing hot dogs turning endlessly on an electric spit, growing darker and more wrinkled by the hour, she grimaced.

While she didn't consider herself a health nut, Summer tried to eat sensibly in spite of the typical cop's tendency to eat whatever was quick and inexpensive. She weighed the pros and cons of shriveled hot dogs versus the department's snack machines. Snack food, it is, she decided, hitting her blinker to backtrack to HQ.

As she approached the turn, a pickup came barreling up behind her, its bright lights blinding in intensity. The truck was only inches from her rear bumper as the driver laid on the horn.

Summer muttered, "What is this guy's problem?"

Continuing to slow, she watched in her mirror as the truck suddenly whipped around her and raced through the intersection toward First Street, running the red light. She could see a lone white male behind the wheel as the truck roared past.

Food would have to wait. The guy needed a reminder that cops carry citation books just for drivers like him. Hitting her overheads, she bumped her siren once to let the guy know she was pulling him over. The pickup, a rusted-out, white Isuzu, turned left onto First Street and kept moving at a low speed. Summer hit her siren again, and the truck slowed to a stop.

Advising her location and the vehicle description over the radio, Summer positioned the patrol car properly and stepped out, keeping her eyes on the silhouette of the driver as she approached. She inspected the bed of the pickup, noting a few items of trash and nothing else.

Reaching the cab, she stood a couple of steps back so the driver couldn't throw the door open and knock her down. "Sir," she said, "may I see your driver's license, registration, and proof of insurance?"

The man looked over his shoulder at Summer, a sneer on his face. "You always have to be in control, don't you?"

Startled, she said, "Len Westcott?"

"Surprised?"

Summer scowled. "No, I'm not. This is just the kind of stunt I would expect from you."

"A stunt, huh?" Westcott said, sarcastically. "I figured I'd try something a little more direct since you won't return my calls or text messages."

"Len," she said, shaking her head, "I told you months ago it was over. Why can't you get that through your head?"

"Because it's not over unless *I* say it's over," he said, his voice rising.

"You see? This is exactly why I stopped seeing you. You're a control freak. You were so jealous that I couldn't even talk to another man. Like I'm supposed to bow down to you and do whatever you say. Well, I don't think so."

Angry now, Summer moved closer to the driver's door. "Len, this isn't accomplishing anything. We're not getting back together. Get that through your head. Oh, and here's a tip. Don't ever pull crap like that again, or I'll put your ass in jail!" she exclaimed, shaking her finger at him.

Westcott's eyes widened in rage. Without warning, he threw the door open, slamming it into Summer. She fell, scraping her hands on the rough pavement.

Jamming the truck in gear, Westcott drove forward fifty feet before slamming on the brakes. Summer clambered to her feet, furious at being caught off guard. She could see him watching her in his side mirror, a smirk on his face.

Frustration boiled over, and she took off running, all thoughts of calling for backup forgotten in her desire to arrest him for the battery. Just as she reached the rear of the truck, Westcott hit the gas and drove another fifty feet before stopping again.

Breathing hard, Summer came to her senses. "Twelve-Thirteen, I need backup at the Seawalk Pavilion!" she yelled on her portable radio, her voice conveying urgency. Knowing officers would be racing toward her location from all over the city, she didn't wait for a response, starting toward the truck again.

Westcott suddenly spun the truck around in a U-turn and, with squealing tires and thundering engine, roared directly toward Summer. Shocked, knowing she couldn't get back to her car in time, she sprinted for the stage at the Seawalk Pavilion, drawing her weapon as she ran.

As she got closer, she fought back rising panic when she spotted the roll-down barrier abutting the front edge of the stage. The city had recently installed the barrier to stop people from climbing onto the stage after hours. That obstruction now prevented her from reaching safety. Spinning around, her back against the stage, she saw the truck was now only yards away, its headlights blinding her. She looked frantically to her left and then right. There was nowhere to go.

Time seemed to slow, and her vision narrowed to the point she could see only the truck as it barreled toward her. Summer raised her pistol and fired. The shots sounded muffled, as if they were coming from a great distance instead of inches from her ears. In slow motion, she saw the windshield star and then shatter. The thought flew through her head that, if she wanted, she could count the individual pieces of safety glass as the window blew apart.

Continuing to squeeze the trigger as fast as she could, she saw the extreme rage on Westcott's face. Suddenly, his head jerked backward, hands flying to his throat. Less than ten feet away by now, Summer dived to the side as the truck veered slightly to the right.

The front bumper clipped the heel of her boot, tearing it off as it barreled into the stage at more than forty miles per hour. The vehicle struck with such force that the rear end lifted off the ground, slamming back down as both doors flew open. Westcott's upper body slumped sideways out of the truck. His legs, crushed when the dashboard crumpled, held his body in the cab.

For several seconds, Summer lay on the ground, her eyes on the broken body of her ex-boyfriend. Shaking her head as she came out of the adrenaline-induced fog, she got slowly to her feet, drawing a sharp breath as she felt a shooting pain in her ankle.

Unable to tear her eyes away from the carnage only feet away, Summer holstered her weapon and pressed the emergency call button on her radio.

The dispatcher immediately responded, "Twelve-thirteen, are you seventy-seven?"

Feeling her racing heartbeat, Summer responded, "Negative. Shots fired. One suspect down. I need rescue and a supervisor at the Seawalk Pavilion."

"You advised shots fired?" the dispatcher asked.

In a rush, she blurted, "Ten-four! Shots fired. The suspect vehicle tried to run me down. He crashed his truck into the stage at the Seawalk Pavilion. He appears to be Signal Seven."

"Message received. Units are en route," the dispatcher advised.

For a couple of seconds, the radio was silent. Then the shift sergeant keyed up his radio, "Twelve-thirteen, are you injured?"

"The bumper hit my foot just before it crashed. I'm okay," she answered.

"Stand by. I'm on my way," he said.

6

Randall," Clay answered, squinting at the bedside clock. At three-thirty in the morning, the caller was almost certainly a dispatcher or one of his supervisors. Something unusual must have happened to necessitate the call, he reasoned. He wasn't wrong.

"Commander, this is dispatch. We have an officer-involved shooting at the Seawalk Pavilion. The suspect is reportedly Signal Seven."

Clay leaped out of bed, tucking the phone between his ear and shoulder as he struggled into a pair of jeans. "What officer, and is he hurt?"

"It's Officer Hayes. She's reporting an injury to her ankle, from what the sergeant is saying."

"Okay, call Sergeant Crutchfield and have him head that way along with the on-call detective. And contact the state attorney, also."

"Yes, sir. Uh, Commander? There's something you need to know. About the suspect."

Clay stopped dressing, focusing his attention on what the dispatcher said. "What is it?"

"The guy Officer Hayes shot is her boyfriend. I mean ex-boyfriend, actually."

Clay sat down on the bed, stunned at the news. "Is Hayes still at the scene?"

"She is. The sergeant has her in his car."

"Okay, tell him to freeze everything until I get there. And if you haven't already done it, notify Chief Wilson," he said, ending the conversation.

Dana stirred. "What happened? Are you going out?" she asked in a voice still heavy with sleep.

"Yeah, babe. Got an officer-involved shooting. One suspect dead."

Dana came wide awake at the news. Having experienced on a first hand basis previous traumatic events involving her husband, she was nervous whenever Clay went out in the middle of the night. "Is it still going on?"

"No, honey, don't worry," he said soothingly. "It's safe. I just have to take care of all the administrative stuff."

"Which officer was it?"

"Summer Hayes," he said, continuing to dress.

Dana shook her head. "She's really been through some rough times, hasn't she? Getting shot and losing her partner. I can't imagine what she's going through right now."

Not ready to share the information of the relationship between Hayes and the person she shot, he said, "It's all part of the job, Dana. Most cops go through their whole career without ever pulling the trigger except at the firing range. Then there are others who aren't so lucky," he said as he leaned over to kiss her. Brushing a strand of dark hair out of her face, he said, "I'll call you later after things settle down. Go back to sleep."

She laughed, "As if I could roll over and drift off to sleep now. I might as well get up. Just call me as soon as you know more."

With a wave, Clay was out the door, his mind already ticking off a long list of things he needed to ensure was done. In the time Summer Hayes had been with the department, she had distinguished herself as a mature, intelligent young cop who worked hard, wrote excellent reports, and seldom got flustered. Killing an ex-boyfriend sounded really bad, and Clay was hoping that the circumstances of the shooting were going to be in Summer's favor.

Five minutes later, he turned onto First Street from Beach Boulevard, finding it blocked with police cars with red and blue lights flashing. He left his car in the traffic lane with the flashers on and walked toward a large group of officers, firemen, and rescue personnel clustered around the crumpled pickup.

The driver's door was standing open, and Clay could see the body of a man hanging halfway out, a pool of blood directly below his head. He noted tire ruts in the grassy area in front of the pavilion leading away from the truck's final resting place. The erratic trail was clear evidence that the driver had abruptly changed direction several times in his pursuit of Officer Hayes.

The patrol sergeant exited his car and walked quickly toward Clay. As he approached, Clay saw Summer Hayes sitting on the passenger side of the sergeant's car, her head down.

"Commander, we've got a mess here," the sergeant said.

"So I gathered from dispatch," Clay responded, continuing toward the sergeant's car. "Hold that thought."

Walking around to the passenger side, he tapped on the window. Summer gave no indication she heard him. "Officer Hayes!" Clay said loudly.

Summer jerked erect, turning her head and seeing Clay. He opened the door and kneeled down beside her. "Summer, are you okay?"

"I guess so," she said in a soft voice. Seeming to gather strength, she said firmly, "Yes, Commander. I'm okay."

"Good. Alright, you know the drill. Give your weapon to the sergeant so it can be processed and–"

"Commander, he already took it. He gave me his backup," she said, indicating a pistol riding in her holster.

"That's fine. Critical incident team officers will be here shortly in case you want to talk privately with them about what happened. We'll need a formal statement from you, but it can wait until you've had a chance to rest and clear your head. Okay?"

Summer shook her head. "I don't need time to rest or anything. I know exactly what happened, and what I did wrong."

Clay's eyebrows went up at the mention of wrongdoing on her part, but she continued before he could respond.

"When I said wrong, I meant from an officer-safety standpoint, Commander. Not a policy violation." Shifting her eyes toward the pickup, she said, "His name is Len Westcott. I dated him briefly several months ago. It didn't take me long to discover he had a terrible jealous streak that came out every time he saw me talking to any man. When I told him it was over, he went ballistic, threatening to kill himself at first. Later on, when he saw that wasn't working, he started threatening me."

"Did you report this?" Clay asked.

"No, sir. I didn't say anything to anyone. I was embarrassed at my stupidity. For not seeing him for what he was. And I figured he was all mouth anyway, just like when he threatened to kill himself."

Mike Wilson joined Clay at the passenger side of the patrol car. "Officer Hayes, are you alright?" he asked.

"I'm fine, Chief. I'm sorry for all this," she said, gesturing toward the pickup.

Waving the comment away, Wilson said, "Go ahead. I didn't mean to interrupt."

She continued, "Len obviously had no intention of killing himself. He was just trying to play head games with me. A couple of months ago, I blocked his cell phone when he kept calling me at work and in the middle of the night on my days off. I thought he had gotten the message that we were done, but apparently not," she said, as her eyes shifted toward the pickup.

"Summer, if you want to wait and talk this over with someone, you can do that," Wilson said.

"Thank you, Chief. Commander Randall already told me I could wait, but I don't have a problem talking about it." Taking a deep breath, she continued. "I stopped the truck," she said, gesturing toward the pickup, "on First Street just north of Beach Boulevard. He blasted by me on Beach and ran the red light at A1A right in front of me. When I approached the pickup, I had no idea it was Westcott. He didn't have a truck when we were dating, and the registration came back to another name.

"That's where I screwed up. When I realized who it was, I stood directly in front of the driver's door instead of behind it the way I was taught. He slammed the door open, and it hit me and knocked me down," she said, showing them her scraped palms. "Then he drove forward a short distance and stopped. I was mad at myself for being caught off guard but also angry at him for what he did. I could see him watching me in his side mirror, and I let my emotions overcome my judgment. Instead of calling for assistance right then, I ran toward the truck. I was going to arrest him for the battery, but just as I got there, he took off again. That's when I called for backup.

"I realize now he was goading me into getting away from my patrol car. When I started toward him the second time, he whipped around and headed right at me. I knew I couldn't get back to my car in time, so I ran for the Seawalk Pavilion. I figured I could get onto the stage and be safe, but I forgot about the barrier the city put up there."

Clay and Mike were riveted, saying nothing to break her chain of thought.

"I turned around with my back against the stage. There was nowhere else to go at that point, and I was convinced I was about to die. So I shot at the truck. Five or six rounds, I think. I'm not sure. The windshield shattered, and I saw him jerk like he'd been hit. But the truck kept coming right at me. At the last second, it sort of swerved as I jumped to the side, and then it hit the stage."

"How were you injured?" Clay asked.

She regarded her bare foot, now tightly wrapped in an ace bandage.

"Apparently the front bumper hit my foot just before it crashed. The EMTs are saying they think I have an ankle sprain, but they want me to have it x-rayed to be certain, though."

"What happened after the crash, Officer Hayes?" the chief asked.

"I kept my gun pointed at him until I got closer. That's when I saw that one of the rounds caught him in the throat, and a second one hit him in the upper left chest. I checked for a pulse, but it was obvious he was dead. If only I had known what he was really like before we started dating."

"You're going to be fine, Summer," Clay said, squeezing her shoulder. "Just take it easy now. Here come the guys from the critical incident team. They'll stay with you while you go to the ER to have your ankle x-rayed."

She nodded her thanks as Clay and Mike headed over to Westcott's truck.

"What do you think, Mike?" he asked.

Wilson considered Clay's question before answering. "I think Officer Hayes is right in that she didn't practice the best officer safety. I also think she was put into a position in which she had no option but to use deadly force."

"My thoughts exactly," Clay agreed.

"Of course, this doesn't help when we have the mayor doing Thomas Barclay's bidding, just grasping for a reason to attack the two of us."

Clay glanced sharply at his boss. "You don't think she would use something like this to make political points with Barclay, do you?"

"Oh, I have no doubt that she intends to do whatever the senator wants. She's wrapped up so tight with him you couldn't shove a needle between them."

"Well, unless Joey and his team find something contrary to what we've been told, I don't have any worries about what Denise Adams might do. Or Thomas Barclay, for that matter."

"Keep in mind that he's a very powerful man," Mike cautioned. "You should never underestimate your enemies. And make no mistake about it. Senator Barclay has declared himself your enemy."

T he chief hunched over his computer as he debated what he wanted
to say to the press about the shooting. Under normal circumstances, the
public information officer wrote the department's press releases. But the
incident with Summer Hayes would generate a flood of media attention.
Not because a police officer killed someone, although that was still big
news. It was the fact that this particular cop had now been involved in her
second deadly force incident in her short career, and this second incident
involved an ex-boyfriend. Consequently, he felt compelled to write the
release himself.

Surprisingly, the media had not yet uncovered the previous relationship
between Summer Hayes and Len Westcott. They would, he knew. He
frowned as he imagined the potential political fallout.

"Hey, Mike, got a minute?" Clay asked as he walked into the office.

Wilson sat back in his chair, rubbing his eyes. "I'm getting too old for
this crap," he said.

"I heard you were doing the press release," Clay said as he sat down.

"I am," Mike said. "This is one that needs to be worded very carefully,
and it's better coming from me than from the mayor. I have a feeling
she'll put a negative spin on the situation if she thinks it will make the
department look bad."

"Are you going to say anything about Summer's previous relationship with Westcott?"

"If I don't disclose it up front, they'll scream cover up and then go into full-on attack mode. Of course, they could do that anyway. You know, female cop. Carries a gun. Stalks and kills her ex-boyfriend over a domestic quarrel or something equally ridiculous. That's why I've been through a dozen drafts trying to find the right words that will clearly explain what happened."

His assistant came to the door, saying, "Chief, I just received a call from the mayor. I told her you were in with Commander Randall and asked if she wanted me to put her through. She said no, that she wanted the commander in her office in fifteen minutes. And then . . ." she stopped.

"And then what?" Mike asked.

"She said to tell you that Commander Randall was to come alone. That you didn't need to be there."

"She said that?"

"Yes, sir."

"Don't worry about it, Chief," Clay said, getting to his feet as he saw Mike getting angry. "I'll find out what she wants and get back to you. You've got the press release to finish."

Wilson saw the words on the computer screen, but his mind was spinning, trying to decide whether to ignore the mayor's order and accompany Clay. If he did, and she ordered him out of her office, he wasn't certain he would be able to maintain his composure.

At last, with a brief nod, he said, "Okay, no doubt this is about the shooting, and she's probably going to blame you or me for it. Just listen to what she has to say. Keep your comments to a minimum, and make no commitments about anything."

"You got it, Mike," Clay said. "And who knows? Maybe we've got the mayor all wrong. Maybe she wants to say she's sorry for the way she's been acting," he said with a brief smile.

Wilson laughed. "Sure thing. You can count on that."

Five minutes later, Clay arrived at city hall, taking the stairs to the second floor. Reaching the hallway outside the mayor's office, he pulled his cell phone out and silenced the ringer. Seeing he was still early, he began scanning his emails.

"Commander, what are you doing?"

Clay turned and saw Denise Adams walking toward him, a folder in her hand. He said nothing, as he closed the email he was reading.

"Were you trying to eavesdrop on me?" she asked in an accusatory tone.

"No, of course not. Besides, it's obvious you weren't in your office, so how could I eavesdrop on you?"

"Then why were you just standing there?" she persisted, ignoring his question.

"Mayor, I'm working," he said, holding up his cell phone.

Adams studied Clay's face with skepticism. "Whatever," she said, sweeping past him into her office. "Come in. I need to talk to you."

Clay followed the mayor inside and sat down in a guest chair across from her.

Adams settled into her chair, placing the folder in a tray on the corner of her desk. She remained silent for so long it became obvious to Clay that she was trying to make him uncomfortable enough to speak first. Crossing his legs, he waited calmly.

The mayor broke the silence. "Commander, a half hour ago, I received a disturbing phone call," she said.

Clay remained quiet, his eyes locked on hers.

She frowned. "Do you have any idea who might have called me?"

Clay shook his head. "No, Mayor, I don't. I've been at the crime scene since four this morning supervising the investigation. I've also notified my officers about the shooting so that unfounded rumors don't get started."

Rocking back in her chair, she said, "Well, I can certainly understand about wanting to squelch rumors. About the telephone call I received. It was from Mr. Wayne Westcott. Does that name sound familiar to you?"

"I'm guessing that would be Len Westcott's father."

"That's correct. And as you can imagine, he's very upset that his son is dead. Shot to death by one of your officers. Wouldn't you agree this is a terrible shock to the Westcott family?"

"I agree. Although, had he been successful in running over Officer Hayes, there would have been a lot more people upset on the other side. Wouldn't you agree?"

Adams scowled. "Commander, your sarcasm is inappropriate, and I don't appreciate it."

"Mayor, I was merely pointing out that we almost lost an outstanding police officer this morning. She's the one I'm concerned about. Not the man she was forced to kill to save her life. I can feel sympathy for his family, but Len Westcott made a conscious decision to try to kill a police officer. As far as I'm concerned, he got what he deserved."

The mayor glared at Clay, her nostrils flaring. "Tell me, Commander. When did you or your chief intend to inform me that Officer Hayes was actually dating the man she killed?"

"She wasn't," he responded.

"Excuse me?" Adams said, her voice rising. "Are you telling me Wayne Westcott was *lying* when he told me not thirty minutes ago that his son was dating Officer Hayes?"

"I don't know if he's lying or simply misinformed. Here are the facts," he said, relaying the incident in detail, his voice growing more forceful as he struggled to control his anger.

"In conclusion, that's why Len Westcott is dead. And, no, they weren't dating and hadn't been for a long time," he finished, breathing hard.

"Well, that's quite a story. How do you know it's true?"

"Which part?"

"All of it."

"Physical evidence at the scene backs up Officer Hayes' account of what happened this morning. As for the relationship being over, Officer Hayes told me, and this was also confirmed by–"

"Let me guess. Her fellow officers covered for her, right?" she interrupted.

"Denise, I don't understand why you're going after this officer so hard. Summer Hayes is a good cop. We could use more just like her."

"Remember your place, Commander," she said sharply. "I worked hard to earn the title of mayor, and I expect to be referred to that way by a subordinate."

"Fine, *Mayor*," he emphasized. "My question still stands. Why are you going after Officer Hayes?"

"I'll tell you why. Because she's just one more example of a department that's out of control."

"With all due respect, I disagree. The Jacksonville Beach Police Department, *your* police department, by the way, is one of the most professional departments in Florida. Hell, in the country!"

"You know, Commander, your statement reveals one-sided thinking and incredibly poor judgment."

"Would you care to explain?" he asked.

Leaning forward again, she said with a smile, "I think you know what I'm talking about. You've developed a reputation for making, shall we say, rash decisions and taking actions that, quite frankly, have put this city in a precarious position, liability-wise."

"Mayor Adams," he said, "You're speaking in generalities. I have yet to hear anything specific that I've done wrong. In your opinion."

"Well, besides the screw-up that caused the death of Senator Barclay's daughter and–"

"Stop right there!" Clay exclaimed in a loud voice. "I did not cause the death of Gina Starks or the injury to her daughter, and I'm offended that you, as the chief elected official in this city, would make such a reckless and false statement."

Her eyes flashing, Denise snapped, "You're forgetting your place again. As mayor, I can have your job any time I get ready. All I have to do is say the word, and you're gone. No job! No pension! Nothing! So don't you ever talk to me that way again. Do you understand?" she demanded, trembling in fury.

Standing abruptly, he pointed his finger at her. "You can't fire me because I don't work for you. Of course, if you ever bothered to read the city charter, you would know that."

"You're . . . you're nothing but a small town cop in a crappy little police department!" she ranted.

With a smile, Clay shot back, "And being a small town mayor is somehow better, Denise?" Heading for the door, he continued, "I'm leaving. I have work to do."

"Come back here!" she shouted. "I'm not through with you!"

Stopping, Clay turned. "I've encountered some unethical politicians over the years. In fact, I ran across a couple of them just a little while ago. And you know what? You fit right in with them."

"You can't talk to me that way!" she sputtered.

"You gave up the right to be treated with professional respect a long time ago."

"If you walk out that door, you'll regret it!" she yelled, leaping to her feet.

Clay paused, his hand on the doorknob. Taking a breath to calm himself, he said, "What I regret is that I work for a city that has someone like you as an elected official. It might be interesting to know what the good people in this community would say if they found out that those, quote-unquote, fact-finding junkets you take at taxpayer expense always happen to coincide with Senator Barclay's trips. They would probably wonder how much fact finding is going on."

Her mouth dropped open. "You bastard!" she spit, her face a mask of hate and apprehension.

"Mayor, if you have evidence that either the chief or I have done something wrong, I suggest you take it to the state attorney. Meanwhile, I have a ton of paperwork to finish on this shooting. You have a nice day," he said, walking out the door.

Senator Barclay lay on his back, fingers laced behind his head as he watched the slowly turning blades of the hotel's ceiling fan. His eyes drifted around the spacious suite that an ardent supporter had comped for him. It was good to have friends, but better to have devotees. Friends weren't always willing to attend to your every need or whim. In contrast, true believers were, in Barclay's estimation, an indispensable asset to a politician.

He admired the woman beside him. Denise Adams had kicked off the covers in her sleep, revealing a naked body toned by many hours with a personal trainer.

Barclay reached over, tracing his fingers lightly along the side of her breast. Denise stirred, opening her eyes slowly. She smiled and turned toward him, throwing a leg over his midsection as she snuggled closer.

"What time is it?" she murmured.

"Almost nine," he said.

Her eyes flew open, and she leaped from the bed. "Oh, no! Why didn't you wake me up?"

"You were sleeping so peacefully I didn't have the heart. Besides, I enjoy staring at your fabulous body. Does that make me a pervert?" he asked with a leer.

Scurrying around the room searching for her bra and panties, she didn't respond.

"Hello, Denise. Are you listening?"

"Yes, yes, I heard you, Tommy," she said as she retrieved her underwear from behind a chair. "How did they get back here?" she muttered, sitting on the side of the bed as she slipped on her panties.

"You threw them across the room in a fit of passion," Barclay said with a grin.

"Yeah, right."

"Why the hurry, darlin'?" he asked, walking naked over to the built-in bar where he poured himself a glass of tomato juice and topped it with a generous shot of vodka.

"Tommy," she said, exasperation in her voice, "I have a ten o'clock appointment with the mayor of Jacksonville in his office. He's a guy you don't keep waiting."

Seeing a smirk on Barclay's face, she said, "I know, I know. *You* can keep him waiting all day, and he'll never say a word. But I'm the mayor of Jacksonville Beach, not a United States Senator. I don't have the option of being late."

"Okay, I give," Barclay said, stirring the drink with his finger before taking a swallow. "Do you want a little taste of this to calm your nerves?" he asked, raising his glass to her.

Denise eyed the drink with distaste. "A little early for that, don't you think?"

"It's going on five in the evening in Moscow, so, no," he smiled, taking another drink.

"Tommy, be serious for a second. I have a question."

Sitting on the edge of the bed, he said, "Okay, shoot."

"After my confrontation a few weeks ago with Randall, you told me I could get rid of him for insubordination."

"Right. I did. So?"

"Well, it turns out the city attorney told me I couldn't."

"That's bull," Barclay said. "You're the mayor. Everybody works for you."

"Not according to him. He said it takes a majority vote of the whole city council to do anything to the chief. And I don't have *any* authority over Randall."

Taking another swallow, Barclay smiled. "Then what's the problem? Tell Wilson to dump Randall if he wants to keep his job. After he does it, you use your influence with the other council members to get enough votes to send him out the door, too. Simple."

Brushing her hair, Denise shook her head. "No, Tommy, it's *not* simple. Not simple at all. Besides, Wilson has already made it clear that he won't do anything to Randall."

"Okay, so get your votes together now and fire Wilson. Then, you get somebody appointed chief who will agree beforehand to have Randall join Wilson in the unemployment line. This isn't hard, Denise. We do this kind of stuff every day in Washington."

"Tommy, this isn't DC. It's small town politics, remember? People would get very upset if high-ranking police officials were let go unless they did something illegal or unethical."

"They did! Well, Randall did, anyway. My daughter is dead, and my granddaughter will never be the same thanks to him. And the fact that Wilson refuses to get rid of the man is a clear dereliction of duty. A firing offense that your city attorney ought to be able to defend unless he has a mail order law diploma!" Barclay exclaimed.

"Calm down, Tommy. I didn't mean to get you upset. I'm just trying to help you understand that we need something more substantial than what we have now. If we had evidence that they committed a crime, like taking bribes or something like that, the city council and the citizens would back me a hundred percent, and we could get rid of them both."

His mind turning over what she had just said, Barclay responded, "That might not be a bad idea."

"What are you talking about?"

He shook his head. "Not now. Let me think about it. Talk to some people. You may have given me an idea that will solve our problem where Wilson and Randall are concerned."

Barclay drained his third Bloody Mary as he sat on the deck of the Mahi Grill & Bar overlooking the beach. Lou Dunlop sat across the table from his boss, a frown on his face.

"What's your problem?" Barclay asked, chewing ice from the glass.

Seeing the deck crowded with people enjoying the sunshine, Dunlop leaned forward, speaking in a low voice, "Thomas, do you think it's a good idea to be seen drinking so much? Some of these people are bound to know who you are, and you can bet they're not all supporters."

Barclay viewed the other diners, smiling and waving at those who caught his eye. He responded, "Lou, when I want your advice, I'll ask for it."

Dunlop leaned back, holding up his hands. "Okay, okay, don't get pissed. I'm just trying to help."

"Just doing your job. I hear you." Picking through the remains of his shrimp salad, he said, "Let's get back to Randall."

Dunlop shook his head, the frown back in place. "Thomas, do I still think this is a bad idea? Yes, in so many ways. Even if I can find sufficient dirt on Randall, it could still come back on you. You know, you haven't exactly hidden your feelings about the guy. There's a whole bunch of people around this town that have heard you say Randall should be gone."

"I don't care!" Barclay hissed angrily. "I want that man to feel just one-tenth of the pain I feel every day of my life since he killed my daughter!"

In a placating tone, Dunlop said, "I know you do. Believe me, I want the same thing, too. But we have to move carefully on this. One wrong move, and your run for president is history. The other side is already doing oppo research on you. Would they love to get wind of you trying to get a high-ranking police official terminated for personal reasons? You're damn right they would."

"Personal reasons?" Barclay growled. "Are you crazy? I'm not pushing this for personal reasons, and I'm not going to listen to you condemn me for trying to get justice for my daughter."

"Hold on, Thomas," Dunlop said, glancing at people at nearby tables to see if they were listening to the conversation. "I didn't mean anything disrespectful toward you. I'm just worried people may get the impression that maybe you're not emotionally strong enough to handle being president, what with the tragedy and all. No one who knows you will believe that for a second, but it's a given that the little people in flyover country will think whatever the media people tell them to think. And if the media start raising questions, you know how much power they wield."

"I'm well aware of all that. Trust me. I know the stakes involved, and I'm not going to do anything that will hinder in any way my opportunity, so get that ridiculous idea out of your head."

Barclay waved at the server and pointed at his empty glass. Shifting his eyes to Dunlop, he said pointedly, "Don't say a word. I know exactly how much alcohol I can drink and still function normally, and I'm nowhere near that threshold."

Dunlop shrugged his shoulders in resignation. "Okay, you're the boss."

"Nice of you to remember that. Now, back to Randall, are you on board with the plan?"

"I'll start digging," Dunlop said, his eyes on his drink.

"Good. How soon will you have something?"

"I can't tell you right now, Thomas. It's not like we're dealing with a hardened criminal with a rap sheet a mile long. The impression I've gotten so far is that Randall has never even had an immoral thought, much less actually done something illegal or unethical."

"Then you haven't dug deep enough. Everybody has secrets they hide from the world. It's your job to find them. If you can't do it, tell me now, and I'll find someone who can."

Dunlop shook his head, "Don't worry, Senator. I'll take care of it."

Barclay flashed a smile at the server as she placed his drink in front of him. As she turned to go, he lifted the glass, staring intensely at his chief of staff. "See that you do."

9

Jacksonville Beach Mayor Denise Adams called the meeting to order. She spotted Lou Dunlop sitting on the back row. As their eyes met, he gave a slight nod. Without acknowledging him, she continued scanning the council chambers, noting Clay Randall and Mike Wilson on the front row, their heads together in whispered conversation. She smiled inwardly at the thought that they had no idea what was about to happen.

With a quick look at the agenda, she raised her head and smiled at the audience. "On behalf of the city council, I want to thank you all for coming tonight. As your mayor, I encourage you to exercise your rights as citizens to express your opinions about an agenda item. Also, if you wish to speak to the council about any other topic of concern, please fill out a comment card and pass it to the city clerk."

Holding up one of the cards, she said, "I have one from a citizen who wishes to speak about an issue that is not on the agenda. Mr. Wayne Westcott. Please come forward to the microphone. You have five minutes to speak."

As Westcott struggled to his feet, a low murmur rippled throughout the chamber. The man leaned on a metal cane as he slowly made his way toward the podium. A portable oxygen machine hanging from a shoulder strap bounced against his hip with each step. When he reached the podium, Westcott paused to adjust the elastic strap holding the nasal cannula in place.

Taking several short breaths, he spoke softly, "Mayor, members of the City Council, thank you for allowing me to speak tonight on a matter of great importance."

The mayor responded, "We appreciate you coming here tonight considering your physical limitations." She continued, "For those of you who don't know Wayne Westcott, I want to take a few moments to share a little of his inspiring story. He is a fifth generation Floridian and a lifelong resident of Jacksonville Beach."

Glancing down at notes she had written before the meeting, she went on, "Mr. Westcott is a Vietnam veteran who won a Silver Star, a Bronze Star, and two Purple Hearts for injuries received during multiple deployments. As you can see, he has breathing difficulties caused by his exposure to Agent Orange during that terrible conflict. However, while those exploits are impressive, they are not the whole story. They do not define this man.

"As most of you know if you're over the age of thirty, or assuming you paid attention in American History class . . ." she paused, as laughter reverberated throughout the chamber. Waiting until the crowd grew quiet again, she continued in a solemn voice. "The Vietnam War was highly unpopular here at home. Soldiers were vilified. They were cursed, spat upon, and even called baby killers. Some were physically attacked by their fellow citizens. When Wayne Westcott returned from the war, his body broken, he would have had every right to be bitter at the way he and his fellow soldiers were treated."

Gratified by the fascinated expressions on people's faces, she said, "But that was not his way. No, Mr. Westcott was, and is, a different kind of man. He used the money he received from the G. I. bill to obtain a degree in business administration and then started a successful real estate firm. A company that today generates millions of dollars in sales and employs over one hundred people.

"He's not just a successful businessman, though. Far from it. Wayne Westcott is a philanthropist in the finest sense of the word. A man who donates generously from his own pocket to those less fortunate than himself."

Clay leaned over to Mike and whispered, "Isn't it amazing that the mayor just happened to have at her fingertips all this background information on Wayne Westcott? It's almost like she knew he was coming."

Without turning his head, Wilson responded, "You think?"

Winding up her praise, the mayor said, "And with that, I believe I've embarrassed the gentleman enough. Please continue, sir," she said, gesturing to Westcott.

"Thank you, Mayor Adams, for those kind words," he said, his voice weak but understandable. "I'll be brief. I come before you tonight on a matter that causes me great pain. My son, Len, was killed by a member of your police department. Shot down in the prime of his life. When I went to see your police chief, Mike Wilson, and his assistant, Clay Randall, to ask what happened," he said, turning slightly to point at the two sitting a few feet away, "they said my son tried to run over their police officer, and that's why she killed him. Now, I'll be the first to admit my knowledge of real estate is much greater than my understanding of police procedures. However, I'm at a complete loss to understand why, if, and I stress the word *if*, my son was trying to run over Officer Hayes, she didn't simply get into her car or get behind something to protect herself? Why did she feel compelled to expose herself in the wide expanse of lawn in front of the Seawalk Pavilion, if not to create an excuse to shoot my son? Your honors," he paused, nodding toward each councilmember in turn, "those are questions your police chief and commander have been unable, or unwilling, to explain to me. Nothing has been done to address this travesty of justice. This officer, Summer Hayes, has not been held accountable for her actions," he said, starting to wheeze and cough.

"Are you alright, Mr. Westcott?" the mayor asked in a concerned voice. "Can we get you a glass of water?"

Westcott continued to cough, nodding his head in response as he lowered himself into a chair beside the podium. The city clerk took a bottle of water from a cooler behind the dais and passed it to Westcott. Struggling to unscrew the cap, he managed to swallow several sips of water. When the coughing passed, he adjusted the oxygen level on the portable unit and took a few breaths, the color slowly returning to his face.

Standing again at the podium, he said, "I apologize for the interruption. When I get emotional, my breathing is sometimes affected. I'll hurry along because I know you have many issues to discuss."

"Don't worry about the agenda, Mr. Westcott," the mayor said with a warm smile. "Take as much time as you need."

"Thank you," he said. "For everyone in the audience, I recently shared with Mayor Adams my unhappiness with the way the police department responded to my concerns about Len's death. From that conversation, I sensed she had similar concerns about the appropriateness of the officer's actions. Therefore, I'm here tonight to ask her and her fellow council members for justice. Len was a loving son. A good friend to all those who knew him. A hard worker who always went the extra mile to get a job done. Now, I don't mean to imply that he was perfect. He had his faults, as we all do. But they did not justify the taking of his life. And particularly by a woman he loved and who he thought loved him."

The last statement instantly generated a buzz of conversation throughout the large room, leading the mayor to bang her gavel. "Please, folks, let's maintain order. Everyone who wishes to speak will be given the opportunity at the proper time."

Noticing a councilmember had activated his speaker light, she said, "Mr. Cooper, did you have a comment?"

Staring coldly at Mike Wilson, Gordy Cooper, the former police chief and current deputy mayor spoke, "Yes, Mayor. I would like to ask Mr. Westcott a question."

Adams said, "You have the floor, Mr. Cooper."

Leaning forward to speak directly into his microphone, he said, "Mr. Westcott, you made a startling statement when you spoke of your son and Officer Hayes having a personal relationship. Could you explain that?"

Westcott adjusted the oxygen flow on the machine before responding. "I can. Len and Summ–, Ms. Hayes, were together for quite a while. They even talked about marriage."

"Mayor Adams, may we have Chief Wilson speak to this allegation raised by Mr. Westcott?" Cooper asked.

She addressed Westcott, "Sir, do you have anything further before I ask Chief Wilson to answer some questions from the council?"

"I'm done, your honor. I just ask that you and the members of this City Council make the right decision regarding my son," he said as he turned and slowly made his way back to his seat.

"Chief Wilson, please come forward. The council has a question for you," the mayor said in a stern voice.

Mike rose without hesitation and walked to the podium. Folding his hands in front of him, his face expressionless, he gazed at his former chief. Years before, when Wilson was a division commander working under Gordy Cooper, he had walked away from the job when he could no longer endure Cooper's dictatorial management style. When a former mayor fired Cooper after an on-air meltdown during a press conference, Mike came out of retirement to become the new chief. Cooper had faded away to nurse his bruised ego before reinventing himself in a successful run for the city council.

As the silence stretched out, Cooper said, "Chief Wilson, did you hear the statement made by Mr. Westcott concerning a romantic relationship between your officer and his son?"

"I did," Mike said.

"And?" he prompted.

"Councilman Cooper, I'm not certain what you're asking."

"I'm asking you if the statement made by Mr. Westcott is true," his voice rising in irritation.

"That's an impossible question to answer with a simple yes or no."

"Well, why don't you take a shot at it, Chief?"

Ignoring Cooper's mocking tone, Mike continued, "First, let me say that I have great sympathy for Mr. Westcott's loss. At the same time, I cannot allow his statements to go unchallenged. Officer Summer Hayes and Len Westcott had, and I stress the past tense, *had*, a personal relationship that ended months ago. The confrontation that resulted in Westcott's death was instigated and escalated to its fatal conclusion solely by him, all because he couldn't accept that she had broken off the relationship with him. Now, I also want to address Mr. Westcott's allegation that Officer Hayes deliberately placed herself in harm's way so that she could use deadly force against Len Westcott. That is totally false. The evidence at the scene clearly showed that Westcott caught Officer Hayes in the open area in front of the Seawalk Pavilion with absolutely nothing to protect her from the speeding truck. The bottom line is that the young man would be alive today had he simply accepted that the relationship was over and not tried to kill Officer Hayes."

"That's a lie! She's a murderer!" Wayne Westcott yelled, clutching his cane as he struggled to his feet.

The room erupted in shouting. The mayor banged her gavel repeatedly, calling for order. All the while, Mike Wilson continued to stand motionless at the podium, his eyes shifting between Gordy Cooper and the mayor.

Clay stood and turned toward the crowd, watching in case anyone grew agitated enough to rush Mike Wilson or the dais where council members sat anxiously watching the uproar. As he scanned the room, Clay locked eyes with Lou Dunlop standing at the exit. With a sly smile and mock salute, he pushed open the door and went through.

Clay spun around, tapping Wilson on the arm. "Chief, Lou Dunlop just left. I've got a feeling he's the one who set this whole thing up. I'm going to have a talk with him."

10

Clay hurried out of the building, exiting in time to see Barclay's chief of staff about to back out of a parking space. "Dunlop! Hey, Dunlop!" he called, breaking into a jog.

The man smirked as he lowered the car window. "What's the hurry, officer?" he asked, then laughed. "Geez, I've always wanted to say that to a cop."

Clay ignored the comment. "Anything you want to tell me about what just happened in there?"

Dunlop shrugged, "Nope, can't say there is. Why do you ask?"

Clay leaned forward, resting his hands on the roof of the car. "You set the whole thing up, didn't you?"

"If you mean the remarks from the venerable Mr. Westcott, then my answer is no."

"I'm not buying it. The chief talked to Mr. Westcott right after the shooting. He was upset, but he understood his son was completely wrong. Now he's calling the officer a murderer. Somebody jacked him up, and I suspect it was you."

Dunlop shrugged again. "You're saying I'm the bad guy all of a sudden? I don't think so."

"Then why did you come? I've never seen you at a city council meeting before tonight."

"Hey, just doing my job. Am I trying to keep abreast of issues and concerns that Senator Barclay may need to address? Rest assured, I am."

Clay grimaced, "Does your habit of asking and answering your own questions irritate the hell out of people? Rest assured. It does."

"Cute, Randall," Dunlop snarled. Shifting into reverse, he said, "How about taking your hands off my car so I can leave. I have more important things on my plate than wasting my time with you."

"No problem," Clay said, stepping back from the car. "But remember one thing. We still have the recording that you illegally taped, and charges against you and possibly your boss are not off the table."

"You're bluffing, Randall. I talked to an attorney, and he said you have nothing. In fact, he offered to take the case pro bono if you and your boss were stupid enough to file criminal charges. And one more thing. I also talked to another lawyer who said he would love to take your asses to court on a civil rights lawsuit."

Clay shook his head, smiling at Dunlop. "You know, Lou, I thought you were pretty smart. Heading up a big-time senator's staff and all. But now? I'm not so sure."

"What are you talking about?"

"I tend to agree that your boss could probably skate the charges, but I'm confident the state attorney would take a case against you. So let me ask you this. Would arresting Senator Barclay's chief of staff for a felony, a crime committed in the great man's presence, by the way, possibly hurt his chances of being elected president? I think it would."

Dunlop opened his mouth to retort, paused, and then, without a word, put the car in gear and drove away.

"Did I just piss off the senator's chief of staff? I believe I did," Clay said with a grin as he headed back into the building.

Stepping into the council chambers, Clay saw the chief standing where he had left him, gripping both sides of the podium tightly as if to restrain himself from snatching it up and throwing it at the dais. Wayne Westcott was gone; however, judging from the glares he received from several people, some of the man's supporters were still there.

Councilman Peter Daniels was speaking as Clay slipped into his seat. "Mayor Adams, I have been a member of this city council for over ten years. And, with all due respect, I can say unequivocally that I have never before seen such an unwarranted attack on members of the city staff as I have witnessed here tonight."

Clay listened intently, thinking at first Daniels was talking about the comments by Wayne Westcott. He wasn't, as Clay quickly realized.

"Although I don't agree with the reason, I can at least understand the emotional turmoil Mr. Westcott is experiencing. However, the verbal attacks by Councilman Cooper on the integrity of Chief Wilson and Commander Randall are unacceptable. There are no facts to support such accusations. I have carefully read the entire police report, which is more than two hundred pages, including pictures and the autopsy report. There is nothing in those documents that in any way suggests Officer Hayes acted illegally or unprofessionally. In fact—"

"Mayor Adams," Gordy Cooper interrupted, "do we have to listen to this whitewash attempt by Councilman Daniels?"

Before Adams could respond, Daniels spoke angrily, "Excuse me, Mr. Cooper, but you're out of order. I have the floor, and I have not yielded it to you."

As the two councilmen glared at each other, the mayor scowled, saying, "Mr. Daniels has the floor."

Daniels continued, "What I was about to say before I was interrupted is that I have closely read the two most important documents in the file. That would be the independent investigations conducted by the Florida Department of Law Enforcement and the state attorney's office. Their reports unequivocally state that the actions of Officer Summer Hayes were in accordance with state laws governing the use of deadly force. In my opinion, this incident, while understandably tragic, should be considered closed by my fellow council members. We have important budgetary issues to tackle, and I suggest we get to them forthwith."

"Is there any other council member who wishes to comment on this topic?" the mayor asked drily.

When none of the other council members turned on their speaker light, she said, "Seeing none, I will go on record as saying that I disagree with the findings of FDLE and the state attorney. Furthermore, I believe we have a police department that is out of control and in desperate need of new leadership. This killing by a member of the police department is only the latest in a string of deadly shootings. If there is anything positive that can be said about this horrible incident, it is that, contrary to the others, Commander Clay Randall was not directly involved in this one.

"By terms of the city charter, the police chief serves at the pleasure of the mayor and city council. Conversely, individual members of the police department have a level of protection not afforded the chief. In other words, they can only be removed for cause, and only by the police chief. On several occasions, I have discussed Commander Randall's unacceptable performance with the chief. In every case, he has defended the man in spite of evidence to indicate he is unfit to serve our community. Therefore, I will entertain a motion that the city council conduct a shade meeting to discuss the ongoing employment of Chief Wilson. For those in the audience who don't know what that is, I'll explain. Under Florida's Sunshine Law, the public's business must be conducted in the open, in the sunshine, so to speak. There are a few exceptions to the law. When the city council wishes to discuss a personnel matter, for example, we can schedule what is called a shade meeting to convene behind closed doors to discuss the topic. The public as well as the media are excluded from such meetings. I hope that helps our audience members understand what we're talking about," she said with a smile.

"Now, in the event it is the decision of this council in a shade meeting to remove Chief Wilson, he will be removed from office in a public session. Perhaps his replacement will have a more favorable opinion about removing such other members of the department as he or she deems right and proper. Having explained the process, do I hear a motion?"

Peter Daniels and two other council members flipped their speaker lights on, but Adams ignored them. "Is there a motion?" she asked again.

Gordy Cooper said, "I move the city council conduct a shade meeting to discuss the continued employment of Police Chief Mike Wilson."

"There is a motion on the floor that the city council conduct a shade meeting to discuss the continued employment of Police Chief Mike Wilson. Do I hear a second?" the mayor asked. She watched in growing consternation as none of the other five council members spoke up.

After almost a minute of silence, she sighed loudly, a sound clearly heard over the PA system. "Motion dies for lack of a second. And with that, we will move forward with the agenda."

Seeing Mike Wilson still standing at the podium, she dismissed him with a wave of her hand. "You may sit down, Chief."

Without a word, the chief turned and walked out the door. Ignoring the mayor, Clay stood and followed him out.

F or the next month, an uneasy truce existed within the halls of
government in Jacksonville Beach. Thomas Barclay and Lou Dunlop were
back in Washington. As a member of the Senate Judiciary Committee,
Barclay was busy attending hearings on nominees for various federal
appeals courts. Meanwhile, Dunlop continued his behind-the-scenes
lobbying with rich donors, making promises of favored treatment when
Senator Thomas Barclay became President Thomas Barclay.

The mayor stayed closeted in her office, avoiding meeting with
constituents except those she could be certain agreed with her campaign
to rid the city of Mike Wilson and Clay Randall. Gordy Cooper was a
frequent visitor, taking every opportunity to stir up resentment against
the two men whom he believed were, if not actively complicit, at least
supportive of the decision to oust him when he was the police chief.

Of particular concern to Denise Adams was the fact that she had been
unable to speak to Barclay since the day before the disastrous council
meeting. Each call to his private cell number went immediately to
voicemail. Although she left several messages, he had not called her back.
Frustrated from nearly a month of continuing silence, she called Barclay's
office, hearing a voice that immediately set her on edge.

"Senator Thomas Barclay's office," his assistant answered. "How may I help you?"

Denise visualized the woman on the other end of the line; five-ten, gorgeous red hair that flowed in curly waves halfway down her back, a voluptuous body that business attire failed to hide. Denise's face reddened as feelings of jealousy flooded her emotions. She wondered not for the first time if Barclay might be having an affair with her.

Pushing those thoughts aside, she said in a crisp tone, "Yes, this is Jacksonville Beach Mayor Denise Adams. I need to speak to Senator Barclay."

"I'm sorry, Mayor Adams. Senator Barclay is in a meeting right now. Is there someone else who can help you?"

Struggling to remain calm, Denise said, "No. Wait, how about Lou Dunlop? Is he in his office?"

"Again, I'm sorry, ma'am, but he's in the same meeting with the senator. Would you like to leave a message for Senator Barclay or Mr. Dunlop?"

"For the senator, yes. Please tell him it's urgent that he contact me as soon as possible."

"And may I tell Senator Barclay the nature of this urgent matter?"

"No. It's confidential."

"Alright, I'll pass along your message, Mayor Adams. Does the senator have a number where you can be reached?"

"Senator Barclay has my numbers. Just ask him to call as soon as possible."

"Yes, ma'am," she said. "Is there anything else I can help you with?"

"No, thank you," Denise said, hanging up. She sat staring at the phone as she brooded over the silence from Barclay. Maybe he really was busy with his senatorial campaign in full swing. Barclay had told her how important it was to his long-range goal of running for president that he win re-election to his Senate seat by a large majority. A close win would potentially hurt him with the high-dollar supporters he needed for his White House run. And a loss? That wasn't a remote possibility, as Barclay had said to her on several occasions, describing his opponent as a clown with the intellectual acuity of a doorknob.

In spite of her irritation, she smiled at the mental picture of her last session with Barclay, her lover strolling naked around their hotel room with a drink in his hand. Thomas Barclay's ability to satisfy her sexually was incredible. He was handsome and intelligent and made her laugh, all qualities she valued in a man.

Those attributes, though important on a personal level, were not what drew her so strongly to Barclay. More than anything, she admired his driving ambition. He refused to allow anything to stand in the way of reaching the pinnacle, to hold the most powerful office in the world.

His single-minded pursuit of the presidency resonated with Denise Adams, for her political ambitions had grown every bit as strong. But she knew her chances were lessened without the backing of a powerful ally such as Thomas Barclay. Wending her way through local, state, and national offices was a long, expensive, and difficult process, maybe impossible, without the help of powerful friends. She was in a hurry, and her lover was the means to get her to her destination.

She could admit to herself with no sense of shame that she was using Barclay to get what she wanted. Just as she believed he used her to get what he wanted. A woman who could satisfy his prodigious sexual appetites. A woman who would one day soon be his wife, which shouted to the world his consummate virility. She was good with that if it got her what she wanted.

Marrying the future president was the first and most important step on her journey that, if everything went as planned, would result in her becoming what an extremely small number of others had so desperately desired but never accomplished. To be the first woman president.

As she imagined taking the presidential oath of office, her phone rang. Scowling at the interruption of her pleasant daydream, she snatched up the receiver. "Yes, what is it?" she asked brusquely.

"My, my, we're a little testy today."

A smile lit up her face. "Hello, Tommy. I was beginning to think you had forgotten me."

"No way, babe. It's been an absolute nuthouse here for weeks. In addition to my re-election campaign obligations, I'm up to my ass in hearings for a bunch of candidates for federal appeals courts. And as you can probably guess, the president's nominees don't share our political views, so we're having to dig hard and fast for any dirt we can use to bury them. But, hey, that's D-C-B-A-U."

"DC what?" Denise asked.

"DC Bullshit As Usual," Barclay laughed. "Anyway, my assistant said you called and wanted to talk about something confidential. What is it?"

Denise hesitated, unsure what to say now that she had him on the phone. Deciding to keep it light at first, she said, "I've missed you, Tommy. It's been quite a while since you've been home."

"I know, darlin'. I miss you, too. But like I said, it's been crazy here."

"Are you scheduled to be back here anytime in the next couple of weeks?"

"Hang on, let me check my calendar."

She could hear the click of computer keys as he accessed his calendar. In her mind, Denise could see him hunched over his desktop computer, his large fingers pounding the keys hard enough to break them. Barclay had not embraced technology willingly, still preferring a paper calendar to track his appointments.

"Tell me, Tommy. Have you moved into the twenty-first century now?" she asked in a teasing voice.

"Huh, what are you talking about?" Barclay asked, distracted as he scanned through his list of appointments.

"I'm impressed that, at long last, you've started using a computer to track your appointments instead of that archaic paper calendar you've used for years."

"Oh yeah, I'm a regular computer genius," he said. "Okay, I've got my calendar up. Hang on." Neither spoke as he read through the list of meetings. "Let's see. I'm tied up in hearings and meetings all this week and most of the next. My first open window is not until Friday the fifteenth. So, what does my calendar have to do with this urgent, confidential matter?"

Denise took a deep breath before replying. "We need to talk about Clay Randall," she said.

"What about him?" Barclay asked sharply, the easy banter gone from his voice.

"I would rather discuss it in person, Tommy. It's a little complicated."

"How so?" he persisted.

"Again, I really need to see you so we can talk about this at length without the distractions of your job. Is that possible?"

"Don't tell me you still haven't managed to find something you can use to get rid of that man."

"Like I said, it's complicated. And besides, we need time to talk about us. Where we're going. That sort of thing. The clock is ticking, and something needs to happen. That is if you still intend to keep your word."

"Come on, Denise," he said, irritation clear in his voice. "How many times do I have to keep telling you? I have to move carefully on this. If the timing is wrong, everything I've worked for will be for nothing."

"Well, we certainly can't have that, can we?" she said, derisively.

"You know, I don't have time for this today. So, if you don't have anything else, I have to go."

After a brief silence, she said, "I'm sorry, Tommy. It's just hard, you being up there in DC for so long. I miss you."

Barclay clicked the computer mouse to bring up his calendar again. Scanning it quickly, he said, "That's okay. We're both on edge, I guess. Tell you what. How about I fly in this Friday for the weekend? I'll reschedule a couple of things. It might piss off Lou since they're fundraisers, but he'll get over it. We'll slip down to St. Augustine and find a little out-of-the-way place to stay where we won't attract attention. Does that work?"

Denise smiled, "That sounds great, Tommy. Call me when you get in. I'll be home."

Having settled that, they spent the next few minutes talking about Washington politics. Barclay told her some of the dirt his staffers dug up on one of the candidates for the appeals court. By the end of the conversation, they were both laughing and once more at ease with each other.

12

Lou Dunlop stepped into the office as Barclay said goodbye to Denise. "Was that the honorable mayor of Jacksonville Beach?"

Barclay didn't answer right away, lost in thought as he continued to grip the telephone handset. Shrugging his shoulders, he said, sourly, "Yeah, that was her."

Lou sat down in one of two oversized leather chairs in front of Barclay's polished cherry wood desk, the chair's high back dwarfing his short frame. Leaning forward, he fished a hand-rolled Cuban cigar from the humidor on Barclay's desk. As his boss continued to brood, Lou snipped off the end of the cigar and lit up, then lounged back into the comfortable cushions while he got it going to his satisfaction.

"You know," he said with a deep sigh of contentment, "I just love the little perks that go along with this job. Like being able to smoke a fine Cuban cigar that's banned for the common folk."

Raising his eyes from the phone, Barclay said, "Lou, I'm kinda busy. What do you need?"

"You seem upset. Anything wrong back in the sticks?"

Barclay grimaced. "It would seem so."

"Something I can handle for you?" he asked, tapping ashes into a cut crystal ashtray on the desk.

"I don't know," Barclay sighed. "This thing with Denise is becoming a problem. Every time we're together lately, she brings up the topic of going public with our relationship. But the more I've thought about it, the more convinced I've become that it would be a political disaster. Besides, there's no comparison between what Alicia Comstock can do for me and what Denise has to offer. Politically and personally speaking."

As he spoke, Barclay pictured Alicia Stevens Comstock. In her late fifties, she was still an attractive woman. Tall and thin, her blond hair lightly streaked with silver. Thomas Barclay and Alicia Stevens had dated in college but eventually drifted apart, though they remained friendly. The following year, Barclay met and married Barbara, the daughter of a wealthy real estate developer.

Meanwhile, Alicia Stevens married Darren Comstock, the son of a rich and powerful oilman who spent millions of dollars to ensure his progeny would become governor of his beloved Texas. Throughout his eight years as governor, Darren Comstock kept his attractive, well-spoken wife, by then a successful corporate attorney, front and center, a political move that proved to be of great benefit to his career.

As her husband's second term neared an end, they talked about a run for Congress. Comstock wanted to step onto the national stage as a prelude to an eventual run for president, a rather ironic twist that Thomas Barclay thought about but never voiced to Alicia.

The good citizens of Texas voted for Darren Comstock in large numbers, ensuring his election to the Senate, and he and Alicia packed up and moved to Washington DC. Comstock quickly made a name for himself as a hard-working senator who wasn't afraid to reach across the aisle to ensure laws were enacted that helped the country and his home state.

Then tragedy struck. During a run for re-election, as he crisscrossed the state, a drunk driver ran head-on into the campaign bus, knocking it off the road into a ravine. It overturned, killing Comstock and three of his campaign workers.

Alicia was suddenly a widow, albeit a rich one, thanks to her law practice and her husband's estate. She briefly considered moving back to Texas before deciding to stay where the most powerful men and women in the country pulled the levers of power.

Though pursued by many suitors, she had no interest in another relationship. Other men paled in comparison to Darren Comstock. Having never had children, Alicia buried herself in her law practice and volunteer work.

Alicia had thought of Thomas Barclay occasionally over the years, wondering if he had ever pursued his dreams of running for office. One day, as she walked past the open door of a colleague's office, she noticed a man sitting across from the lawyer. She couldn't see his face from where she stood, but something about him seemed familiar. Seeing her standing at the door, the attorney invited her in to meet the senator-elect from Florida. As Barclay stood and turned toward her, the shock of recognition crossed both their faces.

That chance encounter led to Barclay taking her to lunch, where they spent the afternoon reminiscing about their long-ago relationship and catching up on major events in their lives since college.

As Barclay's political star began to rise, he and Alicia Stevens Comstock maintained regular contact, sharing legal and political gossip over occasional dinners. Though they had not resumed the intimate relationship they had in college, they became close friends.

"Thomas, where are you?" Dunlop asked.

Shaking his head as if to push the memories back into his mental closet, Barclay said, "Just thinking about something. No matter. Where were we?"

"You were comparing Denise Adams to Alicia Comstock."

"Oh, right. As you probably know, Alicia and I have grown very close since Barbara's death. We've even talked about the possibility of marriage. Since her husband was killed in that bus crash some years ago, she's never given any thought to remarrying. Until now, that is," he said with a smile.

"Really?" Lou said in surprise. "Well, boss, I believe Alicia Comstock would be a great asset to your campaign. There's no comparison between her and Denise Adams, as you said. Can we see as much as a ten point bump in the polls if you married her? You bet we can! And would she help you carry Texas? I think so. And the best part is that she's got no baggage like Adams."

"Exactly what I've been thinking," Barclay agreed. "In addition to the clear political benefit, she's my best friend, and I trust her completely.

Which is not something I would ever say about Denise. The sex with her is fantastic, but she has an agenda. One that doesn't fit with mine."

"So, what do we do about the good mayor?"

"I've told Denise more times than I can count that being seen in public as a couple is a bad idea, but she doesn't hear it."

"Oh, I think she hears it. She just doesn't like the message, so she ignores it."

"You're probably right," Barclay said. "Then there's Randall. She still hasn't done anything about him."

Lou took several puffs on his cigar before responding. "As I see it, there are two issues in play here, and both of them are problematic. One more so than the other."

"How so?" Barclay asked, pulling a cigar from the box and lighting up.

"Well, let's start with the easier of the two."

"Which is?"

"The deal with Randall."

"Why is that easier?"

"Because you can maintain plausible deniability with that situation. If the mayor succeeds in getting him out, and the talking heads ask you about it, you simply say you've been in Washington working hard for your constituents and that you're unaware of it. Then you follow that up by telling them you know Commander Randall personally and that you're deeply saddened to hear he has been fired, seeing as how he was so helpful to you on the day of the traffic accident."

At Dunlop's mention of the crash, Barclay's face clouded up. "You can't be serious. You're saying I should praise a man I absolutely despise?"

Dunlop's expression didn't change. "Yes, that is precisely what I'm saying. Besides, it's not like I'm suggesting you do something radical. You've been doing it for years. It's called politics."

"I'm not stupid, Lou. I understand the political process very well. I attack my opponents on the floor of the Senate. I write critical op-eds for the newspapers, and I go on the Sunday morning talk shows and rip them to shreds."

"Okay," Dunlop said, "So what's the problem?"

In a sarcastic tone, Barclay responded, "The problem is, with my colleagues on the other side of the aisle, I can verbally beat them up and then go have a drink with them. It's nothing personal. But with Randall, it's *very* personal. So much so that I can't stand to be in the same room with him, much less express sympathy for him."

Spreading his arms wide, Dunlop said, "Then I was wrong. This problem is as big as your second one."

Barclay exclaimed. "I hired you to make my job easier, Lou, not complicate it!"

"I'm sorry if I'm telling you things you don't want to hear, but that's my job. You know I'm always looking out for your best interests. And right now, if you want to know the truth, your interests would best be served by backing completely away from this campaign to get rid of Randall."

As Barclay opened his mouth to protest, Dunlop raised a hand. "Hang on a second, please. I know how important punishing Randall is to you. At first, I didn't understand why you were so hell bent on it, but now I do. And I accept that, which is why I suggested a scenario that gives you what you want without exposing yourself to a ton of political fallout."

Barclay was silent as he considered Dunlop's words. With a curt nod, he said, "Okay, let's say you've convinced me. For now." Seeing Dunlop grin, he continued, "But not to drop it completely, if that's what you're thinking."

Dunlop kept smiling. "I figured there was no chance of that. But this is a good compromise."

"Alright," Barclay said. "What's your take on the second issue?"

"As I said, I see it as the tougher of the two, and you've already identified it. It's your relationship with Denise Adams. And I don't mean your professional relationship, as one politician to another."

Barclay frowned, "I know, I know. This whole thing with Denise has gotten out of hand. It was just an exciting diversion when it started. She's a beautiful woman with a great body, and she knows how to use it, if you know what I mean."

Dunlop nodded as if he knew. "I can certainly understand your attraction to her. However, this would be a PR disaster if it came out."

"Then you have to ensure it doesn't."

"Whoa," Dunlop said, holding up his hands. "I can't guarantee that. Going out with Denise after your wife died might pass the smell test, although there are those who would claim you didn't wait long enough before you jumped back into the dating scene. But if it comes out that you had an affair with her while your wife was lying in a hospital wasting away from cancer, well . . ." he shrugged.

"So what do we do?"

Leaning forward as his eyes bored into Barclay, Dunlop said, "In politics, timing is everything. There are hundreds of operatives who will be checking every detail of your background trying to find even one speck of dirt that can be used against you. Consequently, we have to assume they'll find out about your earlier relationship with her. And if they do prior to the election, they'll hurt you with it. However, if you're married to a highly-respected woman like Alicia Comstock, that will give you some immunity. Even if they dig up the information after you're elected, it's old news then. It won't even be a blip on the scandal meter."

Barclay didn't immediately respond, deep in thought. "I guess I've been deluding myself," he said. "As much as I enjoy Denise's, shall we say, physical talents, the time has come that I have to end this. In addition to everything else, she's developed an irritating habit of telling me how to do my job. As if being mayor of a small town qualifies her to advise me on national and world affairs. At first, I tried to tell her gently that I'm not interested in her opinions, but she didn't get the message. Then, I told her straight up one day a couple of months ago to shut the hell up. You can imagine how well that went over."

"I definitely can. I've seen her temper on a few occasions, and it ain't pretty."

"I've been ignoring her calls for the past month, hoping she'd get the message."

"Thomas," Lou said gently, "I doubt seriously that ignoring her is going to work."

"You're probably right," he said. "I've got to make her see it's over. She insisted we have a face-to-face talk about Randall and our relationship, so I told her I'd fly down this weekend."

"With all due respect, I don't think that's a good idea."

"How did I know you would say that?"

"It's my job, Thomas. First, you have two fundraisers with some very rich and influential people wanting to back your run for the White House. If you cancel on such short notice, you can kiss that money goodbye."

"I told Denise you would object to it."

"Well, it's true. What do you expect? These guys are flying in from all over the country so they can give money to the man they hope will be the next president. If you don't show, will they slam their checkbooks closed so fast the wind will create a tornado? Trust me on this, they will."

Barclay scowled at his chief of staff. "Well, dammit, Lou, what am I supposed to do? I already told her I was coming."

Dunlop didn't answer right away, his mind formulating a convincing argument as he watched the smoke curling up from his cigar. "Okay," he said, "how about this? We know the money men aren't coming to see me. You're the attraction, the big show. So, I'll head down to Florida in your place and have a talk with the mayor. That way, you don't piss off your supporters, they drop their fat checks into your campaign coffers, and I gently but firmly deliver the message that the mayor needs to sacrifice for the greater good of the party and the country."

Barclay leaned back in his chair as he pondered Dunlop's suggestion. "It might work," he agreed.

Then he frowned, "But hang on. From her perspective, this isn't just some frivolous affair. She's in love with me, and she's not going to be happy being dumped by my chief of staff. Besides that, she's a very ambitious woman who has her heart set on being First Lady."

"I under–" Dunlop started to respond, as Barclay continued talking.

"And there's another problem. Once she's been dumped, regardless of who does it, she no longer has any incentive to get rid of Randall."

Dunlop groaned inwardly at Barclay's fixation with getting the Florida cop. He didn't like the man either. He was still angry over Randall catching him recording the conversation in the chief's office, and the confrontation outside the city council meeting had only solidified his loathing for him. It was clear, though, that Clay Randall was becoming a destructive obsession for his boss. An obsession that, if allowed to fester, could interfere with Barclay's ultimate political goal. Unfortunately, Dunlop knew, Thomas Barclay didn't see it that way.

At least he was coming to his senses with Denise Adams. He could understand Barclay's physical infatuation with her. What he couldn't comprehend was how the man had allowed his sex drive to overshadow his political ambition.

Dunlop thought back on his career. Working in the Clinton administration had given him a taste for the power and influence that fuels Washington DC, and he had chased after that feeling ever since. However, as the years passed him by, he began to feel like a minor league baseball player that gets called up to the majors at the end of the season, never to make it back again.

When Barclay hired him, Dunlop knew it would be his last and best chance to connect with a winner. He had worked tirelessly to help the man build a national following, and he had been successful. Now, if he could just maneuver him through the political minefields of Denise Adams and Clay Randall, Dunlop believed there was a very good chance he would be the chief of staff to the next president.

Dunlop noticed his cigar had gone out. He dropped it into the ashtray. He knew what he had to do.

"How does this sound? I'll go in your place and let her know you simply can't break away this weekend. You have to be back there early next month for a fundraiser in Jacksonville. I'll tell her you'll see her then. That will give you more time to prepare for whatever objections she raises and ensure you'll make your meetings this weekend. Now, about Randall. I agree with you that she'll probably refuse to help anymore with him once you drop her. So I'll take over and run with that problem."

"Your idea for handling Denise might work, but I'm not clear on how you can do something about Randall. You have no authority over him or Wilson."

Dunlop smiled. "You're right, I don't. I don't need to. I have an idea how I can create a situation in which Randall himself will choose to maximize his opportunities outside the organization. Either that or Wilson will have no choice but to fire him."

"What do you have in mind?"

Dunlop shook his head. "It's better you don't know. Plausible deniability, remember?"

Detective Donnie Pecora stood mute as Clay Randall glared at him. "I can't believe you could be so stupid," he said, angrily pointing his finger at the detective. "Sit, Donnie," Clay ordered.

Pecora fell heavily into a chair in front of Clay's desk as if his knees could no longer support his weight. He crossed his arms in a defensive posture.

"I've heard the condensed version from Sergeant Crutchfield," Clay said. "I want to hear the whole story directly from you."

Pecora cast a pleading look at Joey Crutchfield, who sat across the room, a thunderous expression on his face.

The young detective turned to Clay. "Boss, it's like this. I got a guy I jammed up on a cocaine deal. He's facing a minimum fifteen to twenty unless he gives up something good in trade. So he tells me he's got information on a pedophile here in Jax Beach."

"And how does he supposedly know this?" Clay asked.

"He saw a bunch of pictures on the guy's computer."

"How did he get access to the man's computer?"

"He claims he's the dude's accountant."

"What's the guy's name?"

"I don't know. He wouldn't give me that."

"Why?" Clay asked, frowning.

"Because he wants a guarantee that he won't get any prison time in return for the information."

"As I told you earlier, you have no authority to work a deal with this guy," Joey interjected. "That's done through the state attorney."

"I know, Sarge," Pecora said. "But I talked to the prosecutor handling the case, and he said he's interested in working a deal depending on how good the information turns out to be."

Clay said, "Set that aside for now. Before you continue, though, what's your guy's name?"

"Zach Petersen," Pecora said.

"Did you enter all his information into the CI log?" Clay asked, referring to the confidential informant logbook.

"Yes, sir, I did."

"Okay, go ahead."

Pecora slowly relaxed as he got into the story, uncrossing his arms and settling more comfortably into the chair. "My CI, uh, Petersen, said he was in the guy's house. Well, a house or condo, I'm not sure, just that it's somewhere on the south end of the beach. Anyway, Zach said he was there last week. They're going over the dude's taxes on the computer when the phone rings. The guy goes off in the bedroom to take the call and tells Zach to keep working. He said this was the first time the guy had left him alone with his computer. Zach said he was already suspicious of him because of some things he'd said."

"Like what?" Joey asked.

Glancing over at Joey, Pecora turned back to Clay. "Like, when Zach asked the dude about dependents for the tax filing stuff, he supposedly said he had none. Then he said something really weird. He said he wouldn't mind having a few dependents, as long as they were little girls. Zach thought that was kind of strange, so he asked him why. He said the guy played it off like it was a joke and changed the subject."

"Okay, so what happened with the computer?"

Pecora cleared his throat, then crossed and re-crossed his legs. "Well, Zach starts thinking the guy might be some kind of pervert, so he decided to check out his computer to see if there was *anything of interest*," Pecora said, using air quotes to emphasize the words Petersen used.

"Zach's a computer whiz, so he figured he could dig through the guy's files and then get out quick if he heard the dude coming back. He clicked on the Documents folder and started scanning various files. They were mostly memos and letters. You know, just the usual business stuff. Then he opened the My Pictures folder and found a bunch of files with multiple pictures inside. He opened one called, 'BabyGirls' and got a shock. He said there were by his estimate a couple of hundred pictures of little girls, all naked, posed in positions like in a skin magazine. Zach said he almost puked when he saw what they were. Of course, it didn't take him long to figure out this was something that could save his ass. I mean, literally save him from a trip to prison and becoming some inked-up dude's girlfriend, and–"

Clay interrupted, glaring at Pecora. "Donnie, your colorful description of prison life, although possibly entertaining to your fellow detectives, fails to amuse me. Get on with the story."

"Yes, sir. Sorry," Pecora said, his face turning bright red. "My CI grabs his flash drive and copies the picture folder. He got it saved and snatched the drive out of the computer just as the dude gets off the phone and comes back in the room. Zach tells him he's sick and hauls ass."

"Tell Commander Randall exactly when this took place," Joey directed.

Pecora glanced at his sergeant, immediately averting his eyes. "This was, uh, last Thursday. So . . . what? Five days ago?"

"And when was the next time you saw him?" Clay asked.

"The next morning around eight. He came to the station."

"What happened?" Joey demanded.

"Sarge, I know I screwed up. I should've told you what was going on right–"

"Detective Pecora, just answer the question and spare us the excuses."

Pecora grimaced. "He brought his flash drive with him so I could make a copy of the pictures. I did and then gave him his drive back."

"Why did you give it back to him? It was evidence," Clay growled through gritted teeth.

"Well, sir, he, he asked for it. He said he had a bunch of business files on there that he needed."

Joey railed at Pecora, "And of course, you were just practicing good customer service, right?" Before the detective could respond, he continued,

"So, why don't you show us the pictures you copied from the flash drive."

"I, I can't, Sarge," Pecora said, his head dropping.

"Why is that?"

"The file won't open. It got corrupted somehow. I had the IT people try, but they said they couldn't retrieve anything."

Clay sat staring at Pecora, shaking his head in disgust. "Okay, Donnie. You screwed up big time. But you fixed it. Right? You went back to Petersen and got the flash drive. Tell me you did that."

Pecora hung his head, literally wringing his hands. "No, sir," he answered, this time speaking so softly neither man heard him.

"Speak up, Donnie," Clay said.

The embarrassment was evident on Pecora's face. "I didn't get it. I tried, Commander. Honest. He said he wouldn't give it to me unless he got it in writing from the state attorney that his drug case was dropped. He also wanted immunity on any others we try to make on him in the future."

Frustrated, Clay slammed his fist on the desk so hard coffee sloshed out of his cup, splattering budget paperwork he had been reviewing. Uttering a string of curses under his breath, he blotted the liquid with a copy of the upcoming city council agenda as Pecora sat motionless, his eyes wide in alarm.

Struggling to regain his composure, Clay said in a measured voice, "Detective Pecora, do you see how giving the flash drive back to this guy before checking to ensure the copy you made wasn't corrupted was an incredibly stupid thing to do?"

"I do now, yes, sir," Pecora said in a subdued tone.

"You do now," Clay repeated. "You know, this job isn't hard, Donnie. But you make it very difficult when you do stuff like this. You have to think about the consequences of everything you do before you do it. When you don't, this is the kind of crap that happens."

Staring hard at Pecora, Clay continued, "Why did you wait so long to tell us about this?"

"I was hoping I could pull him in and get the drive before . . ." he stopped, his face growing red again.

"Before we found out?" Clay prompted.

"Yes, sir."

"And how did that work out for you?"

"Not so good."

"Obviously," Clay said. "So what's your big plan now to recover the device?"

Pecora peered at Joey for a sign of support but saw a similar expression of disgust. "I don't know, Commander," he said.

"Okay, next question. Where is your snitch?"

"I don't know, Commander."

"You . . . don't . . . know."

Pecora could only shake his head. "No, sir. I've been searching for him. I've gone by his apartment every day, but he's not there. And he's not answering his cell or his home phone."

Clay felt like shaking Pecora until his teeth rattled. "Call the attorney prosecuting the drug case on this guy. Tell him what happened and what this jerk wants. I guarantee you he won't be too eager to do anything that helps your snitch after a stunt like this. Also, ask him if there's anything the state attorney's office can do to force him to give up the pictures. That is, assuming you can find him."

"Yes, sir," Pecora said, getting to his feet. Halfway to the door, he paused. "I'm sorry I screwed this up, Commander."

Neither man responded. Shoulders slumped, Pecora left the office, closing the door quietly. Clay's eyes were drawn to the window, seeing bright sunshine and a deep blue sky. He felt an almost overwhelming urge to get up and walk out the door. Just drop his badge and gun on the desk and say to hell with the job and his career.

Sensing the emotional turmoil in his friend, Joey said, "Clay, I'll keep Pecora on top of this. We'll find his CI and get the pictures."

"Losing that evidence is bad, Joey. Without it, we have no case against this pedophile. And we don't even know who he is, thanks to Pecora," he said, taking a swallow of cold coffee.

"You're right, but I'm betting Petersen is guarding those pictures very carefully. He sees them as his get-outta-jail-free card. He's not going to destroy the best chance he's got to work a deal for himself."

Clay sighed, staring down at the desk. "You're probably right. I hope so. You know, Joey, I'll never understand people like that. This world can be a vile, twisted place. The deaths of innocent people. And good cops. Now, on top of that, we've got to contend with this crap from Thomas

Barclay and Lou Dunlop. And, of course, we don't want to forget the *honorable* Mayor Adams and her sidekick, Deputy Mayor Gordy Cooper. I'm sick of the whole mess!" he ended vehemently.

Taking a deep breath, Clay tried to calm himself. "In the past few weeks, I've been reminiscing about when I first started here, patrolling the streets in uniform with you and then working dope. Runnin' and gunnin' was the most fun I ever had standing up," he said with a short laugh. "Now, it seems like every day brings nothing but more crap to deal with. Endless paperwork. Personnel problems like this thing with Pecora. And now this latest attack from Barclay. I don't know how much more of this I can take, Joey."

"Clay, you have to stop this," Crutchfield said in a firm voice. "Listen to your old FTO while he gives you some good advice."

Clay leaned back in his chair, rubbing his face with his hands before saying in a tired voice, "Okay, coach. Give me a pep talk. I really need it right about now."

Joey sat on the edge of Clay's desk, his leg dangling. "I have two questions for you, and I need you to answer them both honestly. Can you do that?"

"Was that the first question?" Clay asked, arching an eyebrow.

Joey grinned, "Cute, but you're avoiding the issue."

"Yes, I'll be honest."

"Okay. First, in your best judgment, was there anything you *should* have done differently that day at the store with the homeless guy?"

Clay didn't hesitate. "No, nothing."

"Now, second. In your best judgment, was there anything you *could* have done differently?

This time, Clay didn't answer right away. He rocked back and forth in his chair staring at the ceiling as he considered the question. He said, "I guess it's possible there are other things I *could* have done."

"For instance?"

"For instance, I could have told the store clerk to call 9-1-1 and stayed out of it since I was off duty."

"Do you think that was a viable option?" Joey asked.

"No, of course not," Clay responded, shaking his head. "You didn't say the other options had to be good ones. There is simply no possible way I could have predicted or anticipated what happened. I mean, c'mon. What are the odds that the transient would roll into the street at the exact moment the concrete truck came by? Then add to that the chances that Barclay's daughter would pull onto the road just as the truck crashed. They're astronomical. What happened was an unforeseen, tragic event caused by a homeless guy who thought some damn potato chips were worth killing me over."

"Anything else?" Joey pressed.

"The more I think about it, even if I had stayed in the store, the homeless guy would have still rolled out in front of that concrete truck and been killed. So, my answer to the second question is that, while there might have been other things I *could* have done, none of them are better than the actions I *did* take."

"Good. That's what I wanted to hear. You did nothing wrong, just like the chief and FDLE and the state attorney said. Anyone with an ounce of common sense would come to the same conclusion. That is, anyone but Barclay, who is too emotionally devastated to view it objectively. As for Lou Dunlop, he gets paid to be Barclay's attack dog, so his opinion is irrelevant. Now, let's see. Who does that leave? Oh, yes, the mayor, who might be screwing Barclay. She has no credibility. Then there's Deputy Mayor Gordy Cooper. Where can I possibly begin when it comes to that asshole? I'll be brief and just say Cooper's a man whose opinion I value even lower than the mayor's, if that's possible.

"What I'm trying to tell you, my friend, is that it's okay to feel bad about what happened to Barclay's daughter. It's even okay to feel sorry for Thomas Barclay himself. What's not okay is to allow yourself to be dragged down by people whose opinions are based on emotion or self-serving bullshit."

"I agree with what you're saying except for the part about Adams and Cooper. Their opinions *do* matter simply because they have political power."

Joey held up a hand. "Yes, they have power, but they're only two votes. And from what I know of the other five on the council, I doubt they can get any of those to go along with them."

Clay smiled faintly. "I hope you're right." Getting to his feet, he went to the window and gazed at the beautiful day on the other side of the glass. "Thanks, Joey," he said, turning around. "You're a good friend, and I promise I'll think about what you've said. In the meantime, let's get back to the problem our dumbass detective created. We need to figure out how to get our hands on those pictures and identify the guy that has them."

Joey said, "I've got a better idea. You look whipped. Go home and spend some quality time with your sweet wife and daughter and let me take care of it."

With another look out the window, Clay slowly nodded. "You know, I think I'll do that."

An ocean breeze rustled the tops of palm trees lining the driveway of Denise Adams' home, a white stucco two-story located in a cul-de-sac overlooking the ICW. The late afternoon sun was nearing the horizon as Lou Dunlop pulled into the driveway. He stepped from his car, buttoning the jacket of his navy blue suit as he walked briskly to the front door. He rang the doorbell once, hearing the chimes play a Beethoven melody that went on for several seconds. *Pretentious twit*, he thought.

Denise Adams opened the door, an expectant smile on her face. She was barefoot, dressed in white shorts that hugged her hips. A green sleeveless blouse tied in a knot exposed a bare midriff.

Dunlop watched her eyes suddenly widen as she crossed her arms instinctively over her chest. "Good evening, Mayor," he said.

"What are you doing here?"

Dunlop smiled, enjoying her discomfort. "I'm sorry, Mayor. I assume you were expecting Senator Barclay?"

"I was. Where is he?" she demanded in a sharp tone.

"If you don't mind, may I come in? That's what I wanted to discuss with you."

Adams hesitated, her eyes shifting from Dunlop to the driveway and, for a brief second, down at her clothing. "Wait here," she said, closing the door in his face.

Dunlop grinned, pleased at putting her on the defensive. Seeing several padded rockers on the large veranda, he chose the one closest to the door. He eased his heavy body onto the seat and began a slow, back-and-forth motion. Each time he rocked back, his feet lifted slightly off the deck. He knew he was short of stature. He knew he was overweight. He didn't care.

Ten minutes passed before the door opened again. Denise stepped out, dressed in black slacks with a conservative white blouse and a pair of black, open-toed sandals. "Come in," she said curtly, turning abruptly and going back inside.

Dunlop slowly leaned forward and got to his feet, thinking it would have been nice to have stayed a little longer in the comfortable rocker. He went inside, closing the door before turning around. He stood in a large living room, its twelve-foot ceiling giving a sense of openness. The decorating style was a tasteful mix of traditional and contemporary furnishings. Adams sat stiffly on a charcoal gray Montauk sofa, an annoyed expression evident.

Dunlop's eyes focused on a painting hanging behind the couch. The artist appeared to have used various body parts to apply an eye-assaulting shade of crimson paint to the canvas. Dunlop could identify an ear pressed here, an arm and the side of a hip there, the perfect impression of a pair of feet in yet another portion of the canvas.

Following his gaze, Denise said drily, "It's called art, Lou. Stop staring at it like it's a foldout from a skin magazine."

Ignoring the taunt, he said, "That is one of the most interesting and provocative pieces I've ever seen. If you don't mind my asking, who is the artist?"

"Me," she said.

"May I say that I'm highly impressed with your work."

Dismissing his compliment with a wave of her hand, she said, "You were going to tell me why you're here instead of Thomas."

Before responding, he sat on the opposite end of the couch. He unbuttoned his jacket and leaned back, crossing his legs and draping his arm over the back as he turned toward her. "Yes, I wanted to take a few minutes to bring you up to speed on what's happening with the senator. He's been extremely busy these past few weeks taking care of Senate busi–"

She interrupted, "I am well aware of what Thomas says he's been doing and why he hasn't called me. I'm talking about why you're here right now, and he's not. He told me he was coming home for the weekend. In fact, he said he would be here today, Friday. Instead, you're here. Why?"

Irritated at having control of the conversation taken away, Dunlop nevertheless kept his face impassive. "You're correct, Mayor. Would Senator Barclay have preferred to be here? Absolutely. Would canceling meetings with very wealthy donors that have been scheduled for three months piss off those gentlemen and send them and their checkbooks elsewhere? Almost guaranteed. Ultimately, I'll take the blame for the senator not being here. I argued very strongly that he should stay and meet with those supporters, and he reluctantly agreed."

"Then when is he coming back?" she demanded.

"Senator Barclay is in the middle of hearings and campaign commitments that will probably take him to the end of this month and possibly into the next as well. He said he hopes his schedule will allow him a visit home in about three or four weeks. He did want me to convey to you his sincere regrets at not being able to be here, Mayor."

"Oh, I've no doubt he is *truly regretful*," she snapped sarcastically. "So regretful he can't take five minutes to call me and cancel. Instead, he sends his lapdog to do his dirty work."

Frowning, Dunlop struggled to maintain his composure. "Mayor Adams, I can assure you that the senator would have preferred to be here instead of me."

"That's not true, and you know it. He's a powerful politician and is probably going to be the next president. If he had wanted to come, he would have. And those rich donors you're saying would abandon him? That's crap, too. They'll keep dropping their money at his feet because they want what he can give them."

Shaking his head, Dunlop said, "You're wrong there, Mayor. The rules of politics at the highest levels are very different from the small-town variety. Quite frankly, I don't understand why you can't see that. After all, you're an elected official, too."

Shifting on the couch, she tucked her legs under her before answering. "Don't lecture me, Lou. In spite of the fact that I'm a politician of the *small-town variety*, as you so patronizingly put it, I've worked with

Thomas and seen how he operates for almost as long as you have. He and I have had many in-depth discussions about politics, so I feel I have a clear understanding of his needs. However, I'm growing increasingly concerned that he seems to have forgotten about *my* needs. That's why I asked him to come back here so we could have a direct discussion about certain important issues. Issues, by the way, that don't concern you."

"Mayor, I respectfully disagree. Anything that could adversely impact the senator's political future is definitely my concern," he said, shaking his head vigorously.

Denise raised her eyebrows. "I'm confused. What does a private discussion between Thomas and me have to do with his political future?"

"Good question. Let's step back and examine this logically. You're in a relationship with the senator. As such, people, and when I say people, I mean the senator's political opponents, are going to examine that relationship with a magnifying glass, searching for any impropriety. Is Senator Barclay's first responsibility to those constituents who have stuck with him all these years and who now ardently support his candidacy for president? Yes, of course it is. And many of them are people with strong moral values. Does he need those supporters? Yes again, without question."

"But how does my relationship with Thomas hurt him with the voters?" Denise questioned. "When his wife died, that left him free to move on with his life. That's what he's doing. What we're doing. No one is going to criticize him for wanting to find happiness after all the tragedy he's endured."

Dunlop paused before answering. Both his professional future and Barclay's depended on getting this woman to go away. He decided it was time to quit dancing around and slam the door on her dream once and for all.

"What you've said would be true were it not for . . . other issues. The senator has had to ask himself whether the voters will continue to stand by him if it becomes common knowledge that he was having an affair. An affair that began while his wife was fighting cancer. I can tell you unequivocally that many would not," he said, allowing a note of sadness to creep into his voice.

"No one's going to find that out. We were always careful to avoid being seen together except in a group."

"Even if that were true, and I doubt you were always as careful as you claim, there's the other problem."

"What other problem?" she asked.

Dunlop uncrossed his legs and leaned toward the mayor as he spoke in an earnest tone. "I had hoped to avoid bringing this up, knowing how painful it must be to you. Even after all these years."

Denise folded her arms, her eyes narrowed. "What do you mean?"

"I'm referring to that unfortunate bit of legal trouble you had some years back."

Her voice barely above a whisper, she said, "I don't know what you're talking about."

"What I'm talking about is getting arrested for buying prescription diet pills from an undercover cop. Specifically, methamphetamines. Let's face it, Mayor. That wasn't a smart thing to do."

Her eyes wide, she exclaimed, "How did you find that out? My record was expunged!"

Dunlop shrugged. "It's not important how I got the information. What *is* important is that, if I found it, so can others."

Her voice cold, anger pulsing with every word, she said, "I was an eighteen-year-old kid who had just had a miscarriage. I gained a lot of weight and couldn't get it off. My doctor didn't believe in prescribing medications for weight loss, so I did what I had to do. Yes, it was stupid. But I was given deferred adjudication because I didn't have a record. So there was no final conviction. Then, two years later, I hired a lawyer and got my record expunged. There isn't supposed to be any record of my case anywhere."

"As I said, I found it, and that means others can, too. Add your criminal record to the illicit affair, and you're just too great a liability to the senator."

Her face burning, she snapped, "So that's it. You've convinced Thomas to dump me."

"Now, Mayor," he responded, "I wouldn't use such harsh words to describe this unfortunate situation."

"But that's what you did, isn't it?"

"Well, I'll put it to you the way the senator put it to me. He feels it would be best if you gracefully bowed out of the picture."

"I don't believe this!" she exclaimed. "This isn't really about Thomas or what he wants. It's all about you! You want the power his election will give *you*, you self-serving prick!"

"Excuse me," he said, his voice rising to match hers. "I don't appreciate being called names. Let's keep this on a professional level."

"Screw you and your professional level!" she shouted. "I won't be treated like one of Thomas's *constituents*, to be kicked aside by a fat, no-talent piece of crap like you!"

Dunlop lost it. "I don't have to take this from you!" Knowing he was over the edge, but too far gone to stop, he raged, "You're nothing but a cheap whore that Thomas uses to relieve stress! And here's another tip for you. If I have anything to say about it, and I do, the only way you'll ever be called first lady is if you go to court and get your name changed to First Lady Adams!"

Leaping to her feet, Denise screamed, "GET OUT! GET OUT OF MY HOUSE, YOU SON OF A BITCH!"

Dunlop stomped toward the door with Denise following right behind, still yelling. "You tell Thomas Barclay he'd better get his ass back here and talk to me, or so help me he'll regret it the rest of his life!"

Dunlop yanked the door open. As he stepped onto the porch, he turned to glare at Denise. "I'll pass your message along, but don't hold your breath waiting for him. And, since you chose to criticize my appearance, here's a tip for you. That outfit you were wearing when I first arrived? It's blindingly obvious you've chunked up since you smeared your body parts on that canvas hanging on the wall. You might want to consider trying to score some diet pills again," he finished with a smirk.

Without warning, the mayor punched him in the mouth, the force of the blow sending him reeling back. Reaching the edge of the porch, his arms flailed as he tried and failed to regain his balance. He fell hard on his back, narrowly missing the sidewalk.

Shaking his head, he sat up slowly. Blood trickled from a cut on his lip. Wiping his mouth with the back of his hand as he struggled to his feet, he roared, "You'll be sorry for this!"

"Get off my property!" she shouted. "The cops work for me in this town. With one call, I can have you arrested and turn your life into a living hell. You tell your boss I expect a call from him very soon," she said, slamming the door.

15

Dunlop stood there, adrenaline pumping so hard his body shook. Resisting the urge to kick in the door and beat the woman senseless, he turned and walked slowly to his car, his mind racing as he calculated what she might do if Barclay ignored her demands.

Getting behind the wheel, he yanked his tie down and unbuttoned the top button of his now bloodstained shirt. Wincing in pain, he gingerly blotted his lip with a handkerchief.

Dunlop half expected to see her laughing at him from the door as he backed out of the driveway and accelerated away from the scene of his humiliation. Digging his cell phone from his pocket, he hit the speed dial for Barclay's private number.

"Thomas Barclay."

"It's me," Dunlop said, grimacing as the edge of the phone bumped his lip. A mental picture of him smashing the spiteful woman's face with the phone flashed through his mind, producing a brief smile in spite of his discomfort.

"Hey, Lou. How'd it go with Denise?"

"Let's just say it could have gone better."

"What do you mean? Was she pissed about me not coming?"

"You could say that," Dunlop agreed. "Specifically, she said you'll be sorry if you don't call her soon."

"What? Why would she do that?"

Dunlop wavered, trying to find the right words. He opted for a small portion of the truth wrapped around a lie.

"Thomas, I think the woman is mentally deranged. I'm talking *seriously* crazy. She went off when I told her you couldn't make it back until next month. In fact, she was so angry that she punched me in the mouth and knocked me off her porch. I've got blood all over me. It was horrible!"

The shock in Barclay's voice was evident. "Denise hit you?"

"She did," Dunlop responded, immediately slowing down when he spotted a Jacksonville Beach patrol car parked on the side of the road. As he drove past the car, his eyes went to the mirror, watching to see if the officer came after him. He didn't believe the mayor would follow through on her threat to have the cops harass him, but he wasn't certain, given her emotional state.

Dunlop let his breath out with a relieved whoosh when he saw the cop make a U-turn and take off after a car going the other way. He realized with a start that Barclay was talking to him.

"Hey, Lou. You still there?" Barclay asked.

"I'm here. Sorry about that. Guess I was in a dead spot for a second. What were you saying?"

"I asked what caused her to attack you. In all the years I've known her, I've never seen her lose her temper like you're saying. Surely she didn't do it just because you told her I couldn't make it back right away, did she?"

Dunlop knew he had to be careful at this point in the story. "Part of this was my fault. She was so pissed over you not showing up that she started calling me names. I took it for a while, but then it started getting to me. I asked her to treat me as a fellow professional, and that just made her nastier. It got to the point that I simply couldn't take it anymore."

"What do you mean? What did you do?"

Dunlop turned into a shopping center parking lot, pulling to a stop in an empty space so he could concentrate on his story. "I told her I was going to recommend to you that she not be involved in your run for president."

"Okay," Barclay said hesitantly. "And that caused her to punch you? That doesn't sound so bad. You didn't tell her I was dumping her, did you?"

"No, no, of course not. Not in those exact words, but . . ."

"But what. Talk to me, Lou," Barclay said, anger creeping into his voice.

"Uh, well, she might possibly have drawn that conclusion."

"Cut the crap!" Barclay exclaimed. "Tell me exactly what you said, word for word."

Dreading the expected eruption from his boss, Dunlop told Barclay everything, including calling her a whore.

"Lou, I can't believe you've screwed this up so bad! There's no telling what she'll do now. Hell, if she goes to the media, I'm ruined!"

Dunlop bit his tongue to keep from saying that this was what he had been telling Barclay for months. But he knew he had to be careful or risk losing everything. Speaking with a calmness he didn't feel, he said, "I have an idea that may solve the problem."

"Like what?"

"First off, Thomas, I was wrong to let her get under my skin and go off like I did. I criticized her for being unprofessional and then turned around and acted the same way. For that, I'm sorry."

"Fine," Barclay said in a clipped tone. "Apology accepted. So, what's your idea?"

"Now that I've hinted at the possibility she's off the team, so to speak, it should be easier for you to close the deal. It won't be the shock it would have been had you sprung it on her cold."

"That's stupid, Lou. It doesn't solve a thing. If that's the best you can come up with, I'm in deep trouble here, and you are, too."

Dunlop didn't respond right away. A possible solution had been bouncing around in his head for several minutes. One filled with all sorts of risks, yet one that might work if handled just right.

He said, "You're right, Thomas. Dumb idea, but how about this? She demanded you call her soon, as she put it. So you do that. Put the whole mess off on me."

"That's a novel idea. It *is* your fault."

Ignoring the shot, Dunlop continued. "Tell her whatever it takes to get her to calm down. Tell her you'll be down the middle of next week to straighten it all out. It would take you rearranging your schedule a little. Is that possible?"

There was silence as Barclay pulled up his calendar. "I guess I could push a couple of meetings to the end of the week and come in for a day or two," he said, grudgingly.

"Great. That should give me enough time to put together something that will resolve the problem permanently. Then you'll be done with her and can concentrate on your campaign."

This time, there was silence on the other end for almost a minute. Dunlop waited patiently, knowing his boss was evaluating the possible political ramifications.

Lowering his voice, Barclay said, "What's your plan?"

Dunlop shook his head, although Barclay couldn't see the movement. "Senator, this is on a need-to-know basis. If you can get her calmed down for just a little while, I think I can put this all behind us . . . behind you."

"Okay, then what about Randall?"

Will you ever let that go? Dunlop thought bitterly. Gripping the cell phone tightly, he said in an even tone, "Don't worry. I've got a strategy in mind to take care of him, too."

After a brief hesitation, Barclay said, "Okay, Lou. We'll try it your way. But I'm warning you. This had better work. All of it, or I'll find a new chief of staff."

"I'll make it happen, Senator. Just let me know as soon as you get the mayor cooled off," Dunlop said, hanging up before Barclay could say anything else. He stayed in the parking lot for several minutes, drumming his fingers on the steering wheel. His mind furiously weighed the possible consequences of what he was considering.

Dunlop prided himself on being able to make tough, smart decisions in a crisis. This was a crisis, without a doubt, and it was up to him to make the right decision before everything spun out of control. He scrolled through the cell phone's address book searching for a particular name. Finding it, he hesitated, finger poised over the keypad as he asked himself if this was a good idea. Though not entirely convinced, he dialed the number.

16

Detective Donnie Pecora was growing frantic. For the past two weeks, he had searched everywhere for his snitch. He had watched Zach Petersen's apartment for hours on end, periodically going to the door and knocking. Each time, there had been no response.

In desperation, he went to the apartment office and spoke to the manager. She told Donnie that Petersen's rent was two weeks overdue, and she was going to file for eviction if he didn't pay up soon.

Donnie got lucky when he asked if Petersen had given a forwarding address or a contact person at the time he leased the apartment. The manager gave him the name and phone number of a Jan Petersen, listed as his spouse, with a Jacksonville address.

Driving quickly to police HQ, he walked briskly past Clay Randall's office, hoping he wouldn't be asked for a progress report. Closing the door to his office, he grabbed a notepad and pen and dialed the number for Jan Petersen.

On the second ring, a woman answered.

"Is this Jan Petersen?" he asked.

"Yes, who's calling?"

"Ms. Petersen, my name is Detective Donnie Pecora, Jacksonville Beach Police Department. Would it be possible for me to come by to talk to you?"

"What about? What's wrong?" she asked with a note of alarm in her voice.

"I'm conducting an investigation here at the beach, and I need to get some information from you."

"It's Zach, isn't it? Something's finally happened to him."

"What do you mean by that, Ms. Petersen?"

"He's still dealing drugs, isn't he?" she responded in a resigned voice.

"It would be better if we discussed this face to face rather than over the phone. Would that be possible?"

"Are you really a cop?" she asked, sudden suspicion in her voice. "How do I know you're not somebody who wants to hurt me or use me to get to Zach so you can do something to him?"

"Ms. Petersen, I assure you I'm a police officer. If you like, you can call the Jax Beach P. D. and ask for me by name. Detective Pecora."

"Okay, I'll do that," she said, abruptly hanging up.

Donnie pulled the phone from his ear, staring at it in surprise. "And goodbye to you, too," he said.

Two minutes later, his phone rang. "Pecora," he answered.

"Donnie," the detective division admin said, "I have a Ms. Jan Petersen on the line asking for you."

"Put her on," he replied. When she came on the line, he said, "Thanks for calling me back, Ms. Petersen. Are you satisfied now I'm legitimate?"

"Well," she said, the suspicious tone not entirely gone, "I guess you're who you say you are. So, why can't you tell me over the phone what's going on with Zach?"

"There are certain things I believe are better discussed in person. I would deeply appreciate it if you would agree to meet with me. If you don't want me to come to your house, I could meet you in some public place. Like a coffee shop, maybe?"

"When?"

"You say where, and I'll be there in about half an hour," he said, almost holding his breath.

"Are you going to be by yourself, or will you have a partner like on those cop shows?"

Just as she asked the question, Summer Hayes, newly appointed as a detective, walked by Donnie's office. "Ms. Petersen, could you hang on a second?" he asked, putting her on hold without waiting for an answer.

"Summer," he called. "Hey, Summer."

She came back to the door. "Yeah, Donnie, what do you need?"

"Are you working on anything right now?"

She shook her head. "No. Since I've only been assigned to detectives a week, Commander Randall has me reviewing old homicide cases to get a feel for how those investigations are done."

"Great. I need you to come with me. I have to interview the wife of a snitch I'm trying to find, and she's worried about me showing up alone. I figure if I come with another woman she'll feel more comfortable."

Summer shrugged, "Be glad to help. First, let me clear it with the commander."

Donnie didn't want Clay to know what he was doing until he had something solid to report. "That's not necessary. He's up to his ass in paperwork and meetings and stuff right now. It'll be okay."

"Are you sure?" she asked. "Shouldn't I at least tell Sergeant Crutchfield?"

He shook his head, smiling. "I'll clear it with Sarge. Let me tell the lady we're coming, and we'll hit the road."

Tapping the flashing light on his phone, he said, "Ms. Petersen? I'm sorry I had to put you on hold. I wanted to check with another detective to ensure she was available to come with me. Her name is Detective Hayes. So did you decide where you would like to meet us?"

"I guess it's okay to come to my house. Do you have the address?"

"I've got it, and thanks for your cooperation. Detective Hayes and I will be there shortly," he said, hanging up.

Donnie headed toward Joey's office, holding up a hand to stop Summer before she could follow him in. He didn't want her around in case the sergeant went off on him again. "Grab your notebook and meet me at the car. I'll be right there."

Knocking on Crutchfield's door, Donnie said, "Sarge, got a minute?"

Joey put down a report he was reviewing. "I guess. But first, where's your CI?" he growled.

"That's what I wanted to tell you. I've located his wife in Jacksonville, and I'm heading there now to meet with her. I'm hoping she can give me a lead on where he went."

"For your sake, I hope she can, too," Joey said.

"Oh, and I'm taking Hayes with me."

"Why? She's still learning the basics of detective work. I don't think she would be much help to you right now."

"I know, but Petersen's wife acted a little paranoid about me coming to her house alone. I had trouble convincing her I was a cop, so I figured Hayes, being a woman and all, would put her at ease."

"Right, and the fact that Detective Hayes is very attractive isn't influencing your desire to take her with you, I assume?"

"Sarge, I am crushed you would think that of me," he grinned in mock indignation.

Joey smiled thinly. "You can't deny your history of pursuing good-looking women. So, here's a piece of advice that you would be smart to remember. I think a lot of Detective Hayes. I consider her almost like a daughter. Consequently, I wouldn't want anyone to take advantage of her. You get what I'm talking about?"

"Got it, Little Heat," Donnie said with a grin, throwing his sergeant a mock salute as he turned to go.

"Hold it right there, Detective Pecora!" Joey commanded.

"Sir?" Donnie replied, his grin disappearing.

In a cold voice, Crutchfield said, "You haven't earned the right to call me by my nickname. It's Sergeant or Sarge. Got it?"

"Yes, sir," Donnie responded in a humble voice. "I'll just go now. If that's okay, Sarge."

"Get outta here. And don't forget what I said about Detective Hayes."

Donnie fled before his sergeant decided to do something worse than chew his ass out. Summer was waiting for him at the back door, notebook in hand. Donnie led the way to the car, his confidence flooding back as he took quick peeks at Summer. By the time they reached the car, he had already forgotten his sergeant's direct order. Donnie had wanted to date her since the first time he saw her in a uniform, but she never showed any interest. He hoped that was going to change.

"Do you want me to drive?" she asked.

"Naw, I've got it," he said, sliding behind the wheel of a white, unmarked sedan that shouted POLICE.

As Donnie crossed the ICW into Jacksonville, he briefed her on the case, telling her about the flash drive but glossing over the part about letting Petersen get away with the evidence. He kept up a steady patter of conversation, trying to show the woman beside him that he was a funny and engaging guy. Someone she would like to know better.

When they reached Jan Petersen's street, he drove slowly, checking numbers for her address. Summer spotted the place first, pointing to a small, wood-frame house set on a tiny lot.

Donnie pulled to the curb and stopped, killing the engine. He touched Summer's arm as she opened the door. "I'll handle the interview. Don't jump in unless I give you a signal."

"I wasn't planning to say anything," she responded. "I don't want to screw up the investigation."

"You'll be fine, Summer. Let's do this."

17

The door opened as they mounted the steps to the porch. A blond-headed woman in her late twenties, dressed in jeans and a blue cotton tee shirt, asked, "Are you the police officers?"

"I'm Detective Pecora, and this is Detective Hayes," Donnie said as they showed the woman their IDs.

She studied them both closely, saying nothing as her eyes shifted back and forth. When she remained quiet, Donnie said, "May we come in, Ms. Petersen?"

Opening the door wider, she said, "Sure. Come on in." Donnie gestured for Summer to go in first, following behind her and closing the door. They all stood awkwardly in the small, neat living room, no one saying anything.

Jan Petersen broke the silence. "Please have a seat," she said, gesturing toward a worn but spotless couch. "Can I get you anything to drink? Detectives always drink whiskey or something when they're investigating a crime, don't they?"

Donnie and Summer glanced at each other, an unspoken message passing between them: *This woman watches way too much television.*

"No, thank you," he said. "Cops don't drink on duty. At least not real cops."

Dropping her head in embarrassment, she said, "I'm sorry. I didn't mean to offend you."

Donnie smiled. "No apology needed. Most people get their ideas about police and how we do things from what they see in movies and television shows. Real police work is usually the exact opposite of that stuff."

Jan Petersen sat in an upholstered rocker across from the two detectives. "Okay, what's going on with Zach? Is it drugs again?" she asked.

"We need to talk to your husband," Donnie answered. "Can you tell us where he is?"

She responded in a determined voice, "I keep asking the same question, and you keep avoiding giving me an answer. Is Zach involved in drugs again?"

"I'm sorry. We can't discuss the specifics of the case, but we do need to reach your husband, and–"

"Excuse me, Officer . . . what did you say your name was?"

"Detective Donnie Pecora."

"Detective Pecora, you keep referring to Zach as my husband. He's actually my ex-husband. For over a year now."

"Oh, I'm sorry."

"Don't be. I'm happy to be away from him. After five years, I realized I couldn't change Zach Petersen," she responded, giving Summer a look that said, *We women know how weak and pathetic men really are.*

"He's a dope dealer and will be until the day he dies or goes to prison, and one or the other is likely to happen sooner rather than later. Anyway, as for my reason for divorcing Zach, the drugs and the, uh, other stuff finally killed what little there was left of the marriage. I packed up our two-year-old son and left. And I don't intend to go back."

"I'm curious. You said other stuff. What other stuff?" Donnie asked.

Dropping her eyes, she said, "I, I didn't intend to say that. It's nothing."

"Why don't you let me be the judge of that, Ms. Petersen?"

Shaking her head vigorously, she said in a defiant tone, "It's personal, and it's none of your business. If you can't accept that, then this conversation is over right now, and you can both leave."

Realizing he had antagonized her, Donnie tried to steer the interview back on track. "Ms. Petersen, I apologize. I didn't mean to pry into your personal affairs. And I appreciate your candor about Zach's drug use. But it's very important that I talk to him. He's been gone from his apartment for two weeks now."

"And I deserve to know what's going on if for no other reason than he's my son's father. Not that he's much of a father. Is he dealing drugs again?"

Since she didn't immediately deny knowing where her ex-husband was, Donnie began to feel a ray of hope. "I can't give you specifics, but what I can say is that Zach has important information about a crime. And that's why I need to reach him as soon as possible."

"What crime?" she asked, insistent.

"Nothing that involves violence or anything like that," he reassured her. "But it's a serious crime that he has direct information about. Please, can you tell us where you think he might have gone?"

Jan didn't respond right away. Donnie and Summer watched her, guessing she was trying to decide whether to tell them.

"You say he's been gone for two weeks?" She asked.

"That's right, and I've checked his place every day since then. Banged on the door, tried to see in the windows, called him. But there's never been any response. The lights are off all the time. He's not there."

Jan said, "Okay, odds are he's on the west side of Jacksonville. Zach's parents left him a rundown old house out in the middle of nowhere."

"Why do you think he's there?" Donnie asked, starting to get excited.

"It's a familiar pattern," she responded. "He did that every time he pulled one of his drug rip-offs. He'd stay out there until he figured the guys he stole the dope from had given up trying to find him. Then one night, he would come sneaking in the door, wake me up, and have me pack what I could throw in a couple of suitcases. Then it was into the car and off to some new place he'd rented. That happened three times before I said to hell with it and refused to move again."

"Do you have an address for this place?" he asked, gesturing for Summer to open her notebook.

"I think I still have it. I'll be right back," Jan said, leaving the room.

Summer whispered to Donnie, "Do you think she was involved in his drug dealing, too?"

Leaning close enough to catch the fresh scent of her shampoo, Donnie said, "She's not stupid. She had to have figured out his scam after all those midnight moves. But I don't know. The fact she dumped him is a plus in her favor. Remember, though. Always assume the person is lying about something. Don't trust, always verify."

He leaned away as Jan came back into the room. "Here's the address," she said, handing a sheet of paper to Donnie. "Do you need me to write down the directions? It's kind of hard to find."

"That's not necessary. I'll put it into the GPS on my phone. It should lead us right there," he concluded, getting to his feet.

He walked to the door with Summer while Jan remained by the couch. Turning, he said, "I'm curious about something."

"What?" she asked.

"The Zach Petersen I'm familiar with is sort of a nerd. He does financial stuff for people. You know, taxes, keeping people's business books, that sort of thing. On the other hand, the man you described here today is a professional thief. A drug dealer who steals dope from his customers. That takes balls, if you'll pardon the expression. People in the drug trade tend to get violent when someone rips them off. To do stuff like that takes like a whole other mindset. I'm just having trouble squaring the Zach Petersen you've described with the one I know."

She shrugged, crossing her arms over her chest. "Zach's a very smart man. He would have been successful in any legitimate business he tried. But he rejected that life early on."

"Why?" Donnie asked.

"Both his parents were highly successful, driven people. Very wealthy. He once told me they were too busy making money to remember they had a son. Then they died when he was twelve or thirteen. He never forgave them for what he saw as, best case, indifference, and, worst case, outright animosity toward their only child."

"How did his parents die?" Summer asked, glancing at Donnie for confirmation that it was okay to get involved in the questioning.

"Killed in a plane crash flying to some business conference."

"Who got custody of him?" Summer asked.

"That's where things really started going downhill for him. The courts put Zach with his uncle, his father's brother. The guy was the complete opposite of Zach's father. He was an alcoholic, but he also used drugs. Marijuana mostly, but cocaine and meth at times, too. He's the one who taught Zach how to rip off drug dealers."

"And what happened to the uncle?" Donnie asked.

"He was killed doing a drug deal that went bad. Zach was seventeen when it happened. A couple of months later, he turned eighteen, and he was on his own. And the rest is history, I guess," she concluded, sadness slipping into her voice.

"Is there anything else you can think of that we might need to know about Zach or the cabin?" Donnie asked.

When she didn't say anything for several seconds, Donnie said, "I sense there's something you want to tell us. Please don't hold back. It might be really important to what we're investigating. Your ex-husband is the key to getting a very bad man off the street and behind bars where he belongs."

Eyes shining with tears, she said, "It's just . . . Zach always said he would never go to prison. He said if it came down to that or killing himself, he knew which one he'd choose. I'm not stupid, Detective. This is not about Zach being a witness to something, is it? At least not just about that. He's done something bad himself, hasn't he?"

His face revealing nothing, Donnie said, "I'm sorry, Ms. Petersen. I really can't say. So, if there's nothing else?"

Jan Petersen stood mute, tears rolling down her cheeks.

Summer opened the door and walked out with Donnie behind. As they reached the sidewalk, Jan stepped onto the porch.

"Detective," she called.

Both officers turned. "Yes?" Donnie asked.

"Zach keeps guns there at the cabin. I wouldn't let him have them anywhere around where my little boy might find them."

"What kind of guns?"

"I don't know their names or brands or whatever you call them. But there were a couple of pistols and a shotgun."

"Did he ever indicate having a problem with the police? Like, he hated cops or anything like that?" Donnie asked.

Jan shook her head slowly. "I don't remember him ever saying that. He used to say he thought cops were stupid and that they would never catch him dirty. I have a feeling he was wrong about that."

"Well, thanks for taking the time to meet with us," Donnie said. "We may need to contact you again. Is that okay?"

"Of course," she said, "but please do one thing for me."

"If we can," he said.

"Whatever you do, please don't hurt Zach. I don't mean for me. I'm past caring for him, but my little boy still loves his daddy. If anything bad happened to him, I, I don't know . . ." she said, her voice fading away as tears began to fall in earnest.

"We'll do our best, Ms. Petersen," Summer said, stepping forward and hugging the distraught woman.

"Thank you," she answered, stepping back and wiping her eyes as the detectives left.

I

t's funny," Summer said as Donnie drove away from the house.

"What is?" he asked, glancing at his partner.

"How people in the same family can be so different. Zach Petersen's parents are overachievers, but his uncle's a drug dealer. Then his parents die, and he becomes a drug dealer himself. He's above average in intelligence, according to his ex-wife, yet he chooses to use his brains to commit crimes. I just don't understand how people like that think."

"I know, and what about his kid?" Donnie observed. "You'd think being a father would make him want to set an example."

They rode in silence for several minutes before Summer spoke. "Do you want me to get directions to Petersen's place?"

"That'd be good. I'll get on I-10 westbound while you find it."

Summer entered the address into her phone and relayed the route information. "Should we be going to this place without backup, seeing as how Jan says he keeps guns there?"

"It's cool," Donnie said. "We're just gonna check out the place first. If he's there, we'll call Jax SO dispatch and ask them to send a couple of officers. There's no need to bother them unless we're going to take action."

"When you say take action, what do you mean? Arrest him?"

"Right, right," he answered. "You know, incarcerate his ass. Cuff him and stuff him. That sort of thing."

"Donnie, I know I'm new in detectives, but don't we need a warrant to arrest Petersen?"

"Oh, sorry. I forgot to tell you," he responded with a grin. Patting his pocket, he said, "Got it right here."

"What's the warrant for?"

"Sale of cocaine. It's the original charge that started this whole mess."

"Well, if you think it's okay to do it this way," she said hesitantly.

"What? Talk to me. We're partners on this, Summer."

"It's just that I'm nervous about doing anything that gives the slightest impression we're violating policy after the blowup over my officer-involved shooting."

Checking the side mirror, Donnie switched lanes and took the next freeway exit. Pulling into a fast food restaurant lot, he parked and shut off the engine.

Turning to face Summer, he said, "Listen, all that commotion over your shooting was just political crap. The mayor hates the chief and the commander, so she tried to use your shooting to get to them. You did right, and every cop in the department would have done the same thing. We don't get paid to be stupid and get ourselves killed."

She returned his gaze directly. "I know I did the right thing. But sometimes, in spite of that, a cop gets screwed over. You said it yourself. It was political crap, but I might have lost my job if the chief hadn't been strong. I'm just saying that, if my name keeps popping up with people getting shot or killed, the chief is going to find it harder to keep supporting me. That's why I want to be sure I don't do anything that gives the mayor or anyone else any ammunition."

Donnie smiled. "If it'll make you feel better, I'll call Sergeant Crutchfield and tell him what we're doing. I'll ask him to contact the sheriff's office zone commander to let them know we're heading to Petersen's place."

Before he could dial, Summer reached over and put a hand on his phone. "I'm not afraid of Petersen. That's not what this is about."

"Whoa, hold up," he said raising his hands in mock surrender. "I don't think that at all. You're a fearless cop. You proved that to me and everyone else that night at the Seawalk Pavilion."

"No, I'm not fearless. In fact, I was scared because I thought I was about to die."

"But you didn't freeze up and get yourself splattered against the stage. You acted in spite of being afraid. That shows real courage."

"I appreciate that, Donnie."

"No problem," he grinned. "Now, hang on while I talk to Sarge."

Dialing the number, Donnie waited as it rang several times. Just when he thought it would go to voicemail, Crutchfield answered.

"Sarge, it's Donnie. I have an update."

"Did you talk to your snitch's wife?"

"We did, but she's the ex-wife now. She gave us a lead where we might find him out on the west side. We're headed there now."

"Did you call JSO to get them to respond with you?"

"That's what I'm calling about. I was hoping you could talk to one of the higher-ups there to kind of hurry them up. You know how long it normally takes to get an officer to respond. It'll be an hour or more if we call."

"I can do that," Joey said. "Meanwhile, what did the ex-wife have to say?"

Donnie spent several minutes bringing Joey up to speed and giving him the address. "And JSO can serve the warrant when we grab Petersen," Donnie concluded.

"Okay, that sounds good. When you get into the area, stand by until JSO gets there. Don't go to the place alone. You got that?"

"I'm with you, Sarge. Thanks for the help," he said, hanging up.

"Well?" Summer asked.

Starting the car, Donnie pulled out of the lot and jumped back onto the freeway. "It's all good. We're to stand by close until a JSO unit gets there. I just hope this isn't a dry run. If he's not there, we'll need to set up surveillance, and that's a manpower-intensive proposition."

Twenty minutes later, Donnie drove slowly past Petersen's place. A beat-up old Ford sat in the yard with its nose facing the road. The paint, once a light blue, was faded, and primer showed through in several spots on the hood. The house was little better, its cedar siding mottled shades of gray. Full curtains over the windows blocked the view of the interior. There were no signs of life.

"That's Zach's car. He must be there," Donnie said excitedly.

"What should we do? JSO's not here yet," Summer said.

"We'll set up down the road and wait for them," Donnie said, continuing a short distance before turning around and stopping on the side of the road. From that spot, they could still see the front end of the car while remaining hidden from view of anyone in the house.

While they watched, Donnie and Summer swapped stories about cases they had worked and dumb criminals they had arrested. In addition to her fresh, good looks, Summer had a level of maturity that impressed him.

After half an hour, both detectives were getting antsy. "I've never had to wait this long for a JSO officer to respond to me in Jax Beach. Is this normal when you're in their jurisdiction?" she asked.

Donnie shook his head. "It is, sometimes. It all depends on how busy they are. I'll call our dispatch and see if they can get an ETA."

He called and spoke to a dispatcher and made the request. Five minutes later, she called back with bad news. The responding officer, along with every other officer in the zone, had been dispatched to a shooting that had just occurred. Consequently, JSO dispatch couldn't advise how long it would be before an officer could break free to assist them.

Hanging up, Donnie struck the steering wheel with his fist. "Can you believe it? Every cop in this part of the county is tied up."

"What do we do now?" Summer asked.

Before Donnie could answer the question, both detectives heard a car engine with a bad muffler crank up, and the Ford began moving forward, revealing a lone occupant behind the wheel.

Donnie squinted through the windshield. "That's our guy," he said, starting the engine and putting it in gear. They watched as the car reached the road and turned toward them.

"Do we stop him?" Summer asked.

"Absolutely. I'm not letting him get away again. Hang on," he said as he yanked the wheel to the left and pulled across the road in front of the car.

Petersen slammed on the brakes, skidding to a stop a short distance from the unmarked police car.

Donnie jumped out, pulling his pistol and pointing it at Petersen as he yelled, "Kill the engine and step out of the car, Zach! Now!"

Petersen's eyes grew wide as he recognized the detective. His hands squeezed the steering wheel tightly as Summer opened her door and stepped out, her weapon coming up, also. Without warning, he gunned the engine and floored it, roaring straight toward Summer.

She flashed back to her fatal encounter with Len Westcott. Unlike that incident, she realized she wouldn't have time to shoot and then dodge the speeding vehicle. She just had time to think, *Not again!* before diving over the hood of their car. Petersen swerved at the last second, missing the police car by inches as he raced away.

"You okay?" Donnie exclaimed, running to the car.

"Go!" she shouted, diving into the passenger seat and slamming the door barely in time as Donnie spun the car around and took off, tires squealing.

"Switch to the JSO channel and tell them we're pursuing a felony suspect!" he yelled.

Summer flipped to the sheriff's office frequency and called in the pursuit as Donnie mashed the pedal to the floor, his eyes locked on the Ford that was now two blocks ahead. Only one JSO unit came on the radio to advise he was responding, although he wasn't close enough to be of immediate help.

Donnie gritted his teeth in frustration at the possibility he might lose the snitch again. But in seconds, the gap began to close. When they were within a half block of the car, Donnie switched on the red lights and siren. That seemed to rattle Petersen, as he locked the brakes and made a sliding left turn before punching it again.

The gap had widened to a block when he skidded around the corner onto 103rd Street. Traffic was heavy, forcing Petersen to weave from lane to lane on the divided highway to get around drivers oblivious to the dangerous pursuit coming up fast behind them.

Donnie eyed the speedometer and saw they were going almost eighty miles an hour. Tightening his grip on the steering wheel, he said, "The guy's gonna wipe out if he doesn't stop soon."

Summer tore her eyes away to look at her partner. Alarmed, she raised her voice over the wind noise and screaming engine, "You don't have your seatbelt on!"

Not willing to slow down and take a chance on losing Petersen, he said calmly, "Hold the steering wheel straight while I get it on."

Summer exclaimed, "Are you out of your mind? I can't steer from the passenger seat at this speed! We'll both be killed!"

"Seriously," he replied never taking his eyes off the road. "It's okay. I'll hold on with my left hand and put the belt on with my right. You just need to help me keep the wheel steady and straight."

In spite of her misgivings, she did as he asked. Donnie grabbed the belt, flipped his left arm through the shoulder harness, and clicked it closed in less than two seconds.

Grinning at Summer, he said, "Nothing to it."

Shaking her head in disbelief at his calm demeanor, she turned back just in time to see the pursuit come to an abrupt, tragic end.

At nearly ninety miles an hour, Petersen blew through the red light at Chaffee Road, another busy intersection. He almost made it. A large van pulling a trailer loaded with lawn equipment entered the intersection, slamming into the passenger side of Petersen's car. The impact caused the driver's door to fly open, ejecting Petersen, who was not wearing a seatbelt.

Donnie and Summer watched in horror as the man tumbled directly into the path of a pickup truck entering the intersection from the opposite direction. Donnie slammed on the brakes, sliding to a stop a few yards past the pickup.

Leaping from the police car, he yelled at Summer to call for a rescue unit as he ran back toward the crash. Reaching the passenger side of the pickup, he dropped to his knees and peered underneath, fearing the worst. Petersen's body was mangled, arms and legs twisted at unnatural angles. Donnie figured the wounds were more than likely fatal. Leaning farther over, he revised his opinion. Petersen was positively, unquestionably dead. The man's head was gone.

Stomach clenching, Donnie crawled toward the back of the pickup searching for the missing head. Suddenly, a scream caused him to jerk, banging the back of his head on the undercarriage. Staggering to his feet, he rubbed his head as he searched for the screamer.

The pickup driver, a girl no more than eighteen, stood motionless at the front of her vehicle, hands to her face, mouth hanging open, eyes wide in horror and revulsion. Donnie hurried to her, intending to escort her away from the scene before she saw Petersen's body.

Clearing the front of the truck, he stopped in shock at the sight of Zach Petersen's head firmly embedded in the grill. The bumper had struck Petersen's upper body at the perfect spot to remove his head as neatly as if it had been done with an ax. Petersen's eyes were open in seeming surprise at ending up a hood ornament on a Dodge Ram.

19

Summer arrived in time to break the girl's fall as she fainted. Lowering her gently to the ground, she called to a man gawking at the mayhem from a dozen feet away. "Come here! I need your help!"

The man shook his head, backing away. "No way, lady. I ain't gettin' nowhere near that, that thing," he said in a shaky voice, pointing at the grisly head.

She yelled, "I'm a cop! Get over here right now or I'll put your ass in jail!"

The man took a step toward Summer before suddenly taking off in the opposite direction, running so hard his flip-flops came off. Summer watched the fleeing man in amazement as a woman kneeled beside the teenager, informing Summer she was a nurse. The woman quickly took control, determining the teen had merely fainted from shock and was uninjured. After getting her to the sidewalk, Summer asked the nurse to check on the driver of the van that initially struck Petersen's car.

By this time, JSO officers arrived and began trying to unsnarl the massive traffic jam. Satisfied that things were getting under control, Summer scanned the crash scene for her partner. Not seeing him anywhere, she went around to the passenger side of the Dodge pickup. Donnie was on his stomach, his head and shoulders under the truck.

Kneeling beside him, Summer said, "What are you doing, Donnie? You don't need to get his ID right now. We know who he is."

With his head still under the truck, she couldn't hear his reply. "What?" she asked. "Did you say you're trying to find a dumb guy? I gotta tell you, I think you've found him already."

Donnie backed out from under the pickup, his hand bloody. "Keep your voice down," he hissed. "I said I was trying to find the thumb drive."

"Oh, a computer flash drive. Duh!"

"Right. Thumb drive. Flash drive. Same thing. Listen, if I don't get it now, we'll have to wait for who knows how long while the traffic homicide guys process the scene. That means they won't let the body snatchers cart Zach off to the ME's office for hours. Meanwhile, I need to find that drive to get Clay Randall off my ass. Do you understand now why I was getting up close and personal with the headless wonder?"

"Then don't let me stop you. Just don't forget that you're tampering with a crime scene in JSO's back yard. I don't think they'll appreciate you taking anything out of Petersen's pocket and concealing it from them."

Exasperated, he said, "They don't care about the thumb drive. It's not relevant to their traffic case. Petersen was a fleeing felon who was killed during a legitimate police pursuit. The thumb drive has nothing to do with it. If you're so worried, then back away."

Without another word, he crawled back under the truck as Summer watched, conflicted about what she should do. Before she could decide, Donnie slid back out and climbed to his feet, Petersen's wallet in his left hand.

"They'll need his DL for the report, so I'm doing them a favor. Besides, it'll save them from getting their uniforms dirty."

Eyeing him closely, Summer asked, "Well?"

He opened his right hand and grinned as he showed her the flash drive. "Success."

"Where was it?"

"I didn't have to dig for it. His pants pocket was torn open, and it was just laying there beside the body."

"How do you know it's the right one?"

"He told me when this all first went down that he only needed this one thumb drive for everything because it's got one terabyte of storage. This is it."

"Okay, so what happens now?"

Holding up the wallet, he said, "We give this to the traffic officers. Then, we knock out a couple of quick statements and head back to the station to tell the commander and Sergeant Crutchfield about finding the drive."

Summer replied, "You're not going to have to wait to tell them."

Turning, Donnie saw Clay Randall and Joey Crutchfield coming their way, and from the expressions on their faces, they didn't seem happy.

"Sarge, how did y'all get here so fast?" Donnie asked.

"After you called me, I briefed Commander Randall and told him I needed to head your way in case you encountered a problem. He decided to come along," Joey said.

"I didn't want to be forty-five minutes away and have things blow up. It appears to have been a wise decision," Clay said, pointing toward the crash scene.

"What happened?" Joey demanded.

Summer started to speak, but Donnie cut her off. "I'll handle it," he said, quietly. "While I brief them, could you take Petersen's wallet over to the traffic officers?" he asked, anxious to tell them himself about recovering the flash drive.

Summer reluctantly took the wallet from Donnie and walked over to the officer taking pictures of the crash scene.

Holding up the device, Donnie said, "This is Petersen's thumb drive. The one with the pictures on it."

"Okay, let's hope they're still on there," Clay said. "Now, tell us what happened here."

Donnie gave Clay and Joey the details of the surveillance, the confrontation followed by the pursuit, and its tragic ending. When he finished, Clay asked, "You're telling me that Petersen deliberately tried to run over Summer?"

"Exactly."

"And she didn't get hurt?"

"No, she's fine."

"Why did he take off like that?" Clay asked. "Surely he didn't know you were holding the drug warrant, did he?"

Donnie shrugged. "I don't know, Commander."

"I think I know," Summer said as she walked up to them. "I talked to one of the traffic officers just now. When he checked the inside of Petersen's car, he found a pint Ziploc bag on the passenger floorboard containing a white powder. He called for a JSO narcotics officer to respond with a field-testing kit. The guy got here a few minutes ago and tested it."

"And?" Donnie said when she didn't continue.

"It tested positive for cocaine."

"Well, damn!" Donnie exclaimed. "His ex-wife was right. Old Zach was never gonna change."

"Sounds like it turned out okay, Detective Pecora," Clay said. "Now, back to the flash drive. Is there going to be anything on it that tells us the identity of the suspect who had the pictures on his computer?"

"I'm not sure," he replied. "Maybe. But if the information isn't there, can't we get a search warrant for Petersen's house?"

Clay asked Joey, "What do you think, Sergeant?"

Joey scratched his head in thought. "It's possible. We'll have to talk to the state attorney handling the dope case to see what he says."

"Okay. Get it done. The sooner the better," Clay said. "And Donnie, give JSO whatever they need in the way of statements, and then get back to the beach ASAP."

It was nearing five o'clock by the time the detectives made it back to the beach. Entering the detective division, Joey Crutchfield met them at the door.

"About time you got back here," he grumbled. "What took you so long?"

Glancing at his partner, Donnie said, "We stopped by Petersen's ex-wife's place to tell her what happened."

"How did she take it?"

"I'm not sure. After we told her about Zach, she asked to talk to Summer alone. That's when it took a strange turn. I'll let her fill you in on that conversation."

"Okay. Hold that thought. Sounds like Commander Randall needs to hear this. Go in the conference room. We'll be there in a minute," Joey said, heading to Clay's office.

As the detectives went toward the conference room, Donnie suddenly stopped, putting a hand on Summer's shoulder. "Hey, I gotta hit the head before I explode. Grab me a Coke," he said, reaching into his pocket for change.

Summer eyes narrowed. "What's going on, Donnie? At the scene, you sent me on an errand while you briefed the commander and sergeant.

Now, you have me fetching drinks. Do you see a name tag on my shirt?"

Staring unabashedly at her chest, he shook his head, "Nope. No name tag. What are you talking about?"

"You don't see a name tag because I'm not a waitress. I realize I'm a rookie detective. But if I'm going to be your partner on this investigation, then I expect to be treated as an equal."

Donnie cocked his head to the side, a crooked smile on his face. "I heard you didn't take crap off anybody. Guess it's true. I like that," he said, heading toward the locker room.

Before going in, he saw Summer still standing outside the door to the conference room. Winking, he said, "I'll treat you as an equal from now on. And I'll also fetch my own drinks."

"Fair enough. Oh, and while you're at it, I'll take a Diet Coke," she said, stepping into the conference room and closing the door.

Donnie's mouth dropped open in surprise. Laughing, he hurried into the locker room.

Five minutes later, he walked into the conference room right behind Clay and Joey. Putting a Diet Coke on the table in front of Summer, Donnie grinned at her as he sat down.

Clay said, "What do you have, Summer?"

She responded, "I assume you know that Petersen's ex is the one who told us where we could find him?"

"Donnie briefed us on that at the scene," Clay answered. "I understand she wanted to talk to you alone."

"That's right. I was a little uncomfortable at first, but she insisted she had something to tell me that she was too embarrassed to say in front of Donnie."

Joey spoke up. "Summer, you have to be careful about separating from your partner like that."

"I know, Sergeant, believe me. That's why I was hesitant at first. But she suggested we talk on the porch, so I figured it would be okay. She was very emotional. Crying and all. Besides, I'm probably six inches taller and outweigh her by thirty pounds. I could've taken her."

Donnie grinned, "Best two out of three falls?"

Summer laughed at her partner until she saw Clay and Joey. They weren't smiling.

"Sorry, Commander," she said. "Anyway, we went outside, and I asked her what she wanted to tell me. At first, she wouldn't say unless I promised to keep it a secret."

"I assume you didn't agree to that?" Joey asked.

"No, no. I told her I couldn't keep it confidential if it was about a crime. She didn't say anything right away, and I thought she was going to back out. Then she shrugged her shoulders and said okay. She said she guessed it didn't matter anymore since Zach was dead."

Taking a sip of her drink, she continued. "Jan said Zach was into weird sex stuff. B and D. You know, bondage and discipline. He was big into the whole scene and wanted her to participate with him. She said she went along with him on some of the stuff in the privacy of their bedroom, but there were some things he kept trying to get her to do that she absolutely refused."

Clay asked, "Summer, is this relevant to the case?"

"I think so. I just feel sorry for her and hope she can somehow be saved embarrassment. She's not so much worried about herself as she is about the possibility of her son finding out. The thing that led to their divorce was when he took her to a party that he claimed was supposed to be with a bunch of customers and financial people he associated with. Jan said she was suspicious from the start because the people at the party didn't act anything like the way she thought business people would act."

"What did she mean by that?" Joey questioned.

"I asked her. She said she just got a weird feeling. Like the last thing these people wanted to do was talk about taxes and investments. Anyway, after they had been there about an hour and had a couple of drinks, Petersen told her he needed to discuss something privately with some people he was hoping would hire him to do some accounting work. They went off to another part of the house and were gone for like thirty minutes. She started getting pissed and went searching for him. When she opened the door to the room he was in, she got the shock of her life. She wouldn't say specifically what they were doing, but she said it ought to be against the law. That's when Jan decided her husband had to go."

Clay drawled, "O-o-kay. That's interesting, I guess, but I still don't see what this has to do with drug dealing or kiddie porn."

"Nothing as far as drugs go. But she knows about the pictures on the flash drive."

"How?" Joey asked.

"Zach told her about it. He said it was his golden ticket in case he got into trouble."

"Did he show her the pictures?"

"No. He refused. But he did say that if the cops knew who he got the pictures from, they would freak out."

Clay frowned. "He said specifically that the *cops* would freak out?"

"Yes."

"Did she ask him what he meant by that statement?"

"She did, but he wouldn't tell her."

Addressing Donnie, Clay said, "Check the flash drive to make sure the pictures are still there. Also, Petersen was doing the pervert's taxes, so there should be a folder on there with the guy's name and personal information."

"Commander, he did a lot of other people's taxes and stuff, so I would guess there's probably a ton of customer files on there."

"What's your point, Detective?" Clay responded.

Shifting in his seat, Pecora said, "Uh, well, I just meant that it might take me some time to go through everything on there."

"Then you'd better get started."

21

As Donnie Pecora trudged to his desk to begin searching the flash drive, Lou Dunlop rolled his overnight bag out the exit doors of McCarran International Airport in Las Vegas. The hot desert air hit with palpable force, and he quickly stepped back into the terminal. Shrugging off his jacket and loosening his tie, he thought once again about the circumstances that led to this trip.

The face-to-face meeting between Senator Barclay and Denise Adams had been a fiasco. At first, she had blamed Dunlop for trying to sabotage their relationship for his own political gain. However, when Barclay told her it was his decision to end it, she threatened to destroy his presidential hopes by telling the media of their affair that continued even while his wife lay dying.

Barclay went off on her at that point, and the meeting quickly deteriorated into shouting and threats on both sides. As Barclay stormed out the door, she had given him an ultimatum. He had one month to come to his senses. If he refused, she would follow through on her threat. This trip to Las Vegas was the result of the ultimatum she had given Barclay.

After Denise Adams knocked him off her porch, and Barclay had blamed him for screwing everything up, Dunlop had called a man he knew in DC. MacKay was a political fixer well versed in techniques that employed both legal and, sometimes, highly illegal acts to achieve political goals. Dunlop got right to the point, asking MacKay to recommend someone who could take care of a politically sensitive problem.

"What kind of political problem we talking about, Lou?" MacKay asked.

Dunlop played him off, not wanting to say specifically what he needed the person to do. After several minutes of discussion, he said, "I need a *professional*. Someone who can make a problem go away on a more or less permanent basis."

"I gotcha. Why didn't you say so up front, Lou?" MacKay said. "Hang on while I dig up the information."

Dunlop heard MacKay put the phone down followed by footsteps receding. He waited impatiently for several minutes before the man came back. MacKay gave Dunlop a phone number and told him to use a specific name when he called.

"Thanks, Mac. I owe you," Dunlop said, hanging up.

He held the information for several days, not wanting to take such a drastic step in case a better option presented itself. When Barclay ranted to him about his confrontation with Denise and her repeated threats to expose the affair, Dunlop came to the realization that he had no other choice.

Heading to the sprawling St. Johns Town Center in Jacksonville, he purchased a cheap, disposable phone with a hundred minutes of talk time. Back home, he changed into shorts, tee shirt and flip-flops before pouring himself a double shot of whiskey and settling into a chair on his deck facing the beach.

Nervous, Dunlop drained the drink in one swallow, immediately pouring a second double that quickly chased after the first one. Within minutes, as the alcohol hit his stomach and the warmth began to spread throughout his body, he could feel himself beginning to relax.

Pulling the cell phone from his pocket, he thumbed the power button and waited for a connection as he went over his spiel one more time. When he was satisfied, he took a deep breath and dialed the number. The phone rang four, five, six times. As the call continued to go unanswered, his nerves began to jump again.

A computer recording clicked in telling him to leave a number. He thought briefly about hanging up, not sure he wanted a record of his voice left on the person's phone. Shaking his head as he realized he was out of viable options, Dunlop left the cell number. He identified himself as Chester Jones, the name MacKay had assured him would generate a callback.

Twenty minutes later, the phone rang. Noting the number on the screen, Dunlop recognized a Las Vegas exchange.

"Hello," he answered.

"You called me," a deep voice responded.

"I was given your number by a mutual acquaintance."

"And you are?"

"Uh, my name is Chester Jones. I'm interested in obtaining your services to take care of a prob–"

"Stop," the man interrupted, his voice suddenly sharp.

"Why? What's wrong?"

"I don't discuss business over this phone."

Dunlop said, "I'm talking on a disposable phone. Isn't that good enough?"

"On your end, yes. On mine, no. I'll call you back."

Dunlop repeated the number of his cell phone, and the man immediately hung up. Drumming his fingers on the table beside his chair, his irritation grew by the minute. Fifteen minutes later, as he was considering calling again, the phone rang.

Seeing the number was blocked, he figured it had to be the man. "Chester Jones here," Dunlop said.

"Go ahead," the man answered, falling silent.

"I assume you can talk now?"

"That's correct, within reason. First, who gave you my number?"

"The person is a friend of mine. His name isn't important. He told me to say I was Chester Jones, and you would know I was okay. He also said your number was unlisted. I called it, and you called me back. That should be enough."

"If you want to continue this conversation, give me the name right now."

Blowing out a breath in irritation, Dunlop said, "MacKay. Is that sufficient?"

"What is his cat's name?"

"Do what?" Dunlop responded, thoroughly confused.

"You said he's a friend. Answer the question."

Dunlop shook his head, laughing sarcastically. "What kind of game are you playing here? He doesn't own any cats. He's violently allergic to them."

Ignoring the question, the man replied, "What do you need, generally speaking?"

"You haven't told me your name. What should I call you?" Dunlop asked.

"Smith."

"Just Smith?"

"Yes."

Dunlop didn't respond right away. He knew he was about to take a giant leap across a line beyond which there would be no return. No political dirty trick he had ever used would match what he was debating putting into motion.

He said, "I've got a situation that's causing a big problem for, uh, someone, and I need it to go away."

"What's the time frame?"

"As soon as possible," Dunlop said.

"My services are expensive, and my fees are non-negotiable."

"Money is not an issue," he said, shaking his head.

"Okay. I'll expect you to bring ten thousand in bills no larger than a twenty. We'll discuss your specific needs when you arrive. Then I'll decide on my fee."

"Okay, I can do that," Dunlop said. "But there's just one problem."

"What?"

"You said to bring ten thousand with me. That presumes I'm flying out to Vegas. I think it would be more appropriate if you came here, considering I'm the one doing the hiring."

"No."

"No?" Dunlop asked in disbelief.

"No," Smith repeated.

"Well, why the hell not if I'm paying the bill?"

"I don't travel unless an agreement is reached, and money is in my hand."

The conversation was not going the way he expected. However, with timing growing critical, Dunlop swallowed his frustration. "Alright, I'll try to get a flight there by tomorrow. Are you going to be available if I'm flying all the way across the country?"

"What time?"

"How can I know that? I'll have to check flights."

"Do that. Then call back at this number," Smith said, giving Dunlop the new cell number and abruptly hanging up.

Dunlop scowled at the phone. *Who the hell does he think he is?* Fuming, he went online to check flights leaving Jacksonville for Las Vegas. Booking one leaving at noon the next day, he called Smith again.

"Yes?" Smith answered on the first ring.

"This is Jones," Dunlop said. "I'll be there tomorrow at one-fifteen in the afternoon, your time. Where can I meet you?"

"Be at the Tail End Lounge at three o'clock."

"Where is the Trail End Lounge?"

"*Tail* End, not *Trail* End. Take a cab. They know."

"Okay," Dunlop growled. "So, how will you recognize me? Should I wear something like a red ball cap or carry a newspaper in my left hand? Something like that?"

Smith snorted audibly. "Right, like in a spy movie, you mean? No, Mr. Jones. Just walk in the door. I'll know you," Smith said, clicking off.

Dunlop was suddenly anxious. What did Smith mean? How could he know him? He sat without moving for several minutes, his mind tossing around the many ways the plan could go wrong. With a shrug, he reminded himself once again that there was no other real alternative.

Shifting gears, Dunlop turned his thoughts to his plan for Clay Randall. He had no qualms about the hell he was about to put the man through.

Picking up the phone again, he dialed a number from memory. When the person answered, Dunlop asked, "Is it ready?"

"Yep. Good to go. You give me the word, and I'll make it happen."

"Tomorrow?"

"Sure, if you want it."

Dunlop wondered if he should wait until he returned from Las Vegas. He concluded it would be better to be out of town to give himself deniability in the event Randall or anyone else tried to blame him.

"Make it happen," he said.

"You got it," the person answered, hanging up.

"Sir, you need help with your bags?" a porter asked, breaking through Dunlop's reverie. He shook his head, walking out of the airport terminal and heading for the ever-present line of cabs. He had just over an hour before his meeting with the mysterious Mr. Smith. Something told him he shouldn't be late.

S mith sat back in his chair as the cocktail waitress placed a fresh drink in front of him. Leaning over the table to pick up the empty glass, the young woman gave Smith an unobstructed view of her assets. *Can't be more than twenty-one,* he guessed.

He eyed her shapely rear and taut calves as she walked away. An aspiring showgirl, Smith surmised, one of the thousands of hopeful women who trekked to Las Vegas every year, seduced by the twin sirens of fortune and fame, hoping to parlay years of dance and voice lessons into a show business job.

He wondered if she knew how remote her chances were of achieving her dream. How many young women like her grew bitterly disappointed when they failed to make it, taking low-paying waitressing jobs or, for a few, turning tricks to help make ends meet. If she were smart, she'd go running as fast as she could back to Des Moines or Kansas City or wherever the hell she called home.

Just over five-eight, Smith may have weighed one-fifty fully clothed. In his mid-fifties, he kept his hair trimmed short. A face lined with wrinkles attested to years spent outdoors without the benefit of sunscreen. That and almost forty years of smoking added to his skin's leathery appearance. His hands were unusually large, out of proportion to his otherwise small stature.

Smith's wardrobe was rooted firmly in the mid-twentieth century farm belt. Not the overalls, long-sleeved cotton work shirt, and scuffed work boots version. Instead, he wore a Sunday-go-to-meeting suit, as his father had always called them. His preferred suit color was dark blue, with a white shirt, plain, navy blue tie, and black lace-up shoes that carried a high shine.

Lighting a cigarette, he inhaled deeply, savoring the taste. Smith had chosen this bar for the meeting because it was one of a dwindling number that still allowed smoking. Through the tall windows of the Tail End Lounge, he watched a steady stream of people pass by in the sweltering heat that hammered Las Vegas every summer. Although he had lived in Vegas until a few years prior, he would never understand the obsession people had for this city in the desert. He guessed it had to be the belief, although unrealistic, that the next pull of a slot machine's arm or the next throw of the dice would bring riches beyond belief.

People were pathetic. Parents passed along to their children the lies that Santa Claus and the Easter Bunny were real, and most of them never lost that childlike belief in magic and fairy tales. Not Smith. He had no illusions. He believed in himself. Everyone else could go to hell.

He took another drag before crushing the fire between his calloused thumb and forefinger. Unconsciously, from force of habit, he fieldstripped the butt the way his Army drill sergeant had taught him years before. He dropped the filter and bits of paper into the ashtray.

Suddenly, he coughed, feeling thick phlegm in the back of his throat. Grabbing a handful of paper napkins, he spit, frowning at the strings of dark blood in the secretion. The bouts of coughing had grown more frequent over the past few months, but the blood was a recent phenomenon. He wadded up the napkins and tossed them aside. Now was not the time to worry about his health.

Smith instantly recognized the man using the code name of Chester Jones when he stepped through the door. Although he had never met him, the guy had the nervous appearance of someone afraid that what he was about to do might get him in a world of shit. He had seen that same look before.

He appeared to Smith to be an inch or two shorter than himself and about the same age. Smith felt an instant dislike for him even before they spoke, although he couldn't say exactly why. In spite of this feeling, he accepted that the man had a problem and was willing to pay to fix it. Likeability wasn't part of the equation.

When the man turned his way, Smith gave a slight nod and watched him immediately begin making his way toward Smith's table.

As Dunlop approached, he said, "Excuse me. I was supposed to meet a Mr. Smith here. Are you him?"

"I'm Smith," came the response. "Have a seat, Mr. Jones."

Dunlop continued to stand, uncertainty on his face. "I thought the person I was meeting would be . . ."

"What, bigger? Like a biker or a wrestler?"

"I guess. You have a deep voice, so I just figured, well, you know," Dunlop said, clearly embarrassed.

"Let me ask you a question. Do you base your decision on buying a car on the height and weight of the salesman?"

"Of course not," Dunlop said, indignation in his voice.

"How about a realtor?"

Shaking his head, Dunlop scowled, "No. What's your point?"

"Because," Smith said, shrugging his shoulders, "you're doing it to me."

Dunlop sat down across from Smith. "I just thought, considering what you do," he stopped.

Smith wasn't ready to talk business yet. He asked, "What are you drinking?"

Dunlop surveyed the gaudy interior of the bar. "Have they got anything in this place besides vodka?" he asked, pointing at Smith's glass.

Smith waved toward the bar, and the waitress made her way over.

"Hi, what can I get for you?" the young woman asked, leaning a hip against the table as she offered a smile to Dunlop.

"Do you have a wine list?"

"No, we don't. We've got red wine and white wine, but I'm not sure what their names are. Do you want me to check?"

Dunlop grimaced. "No. Do you have Jack Daniels Black?"

"You bet. How would you like it?"

"Up."

As the waitress left, Smith lit a cigarette, saying, "You told me on the phone you needed help with a problem."

Dunlop waited as the waitress placed his drink on the table. When she left, he took a large swallow. Then, glancing around the bar, he said quietly, "Is this a good place to be having this conversation? What if someone hears us?"

Leaning forward, Smith responded, "As soft as you're talking, *I'm* having trouble hearing you, and I'm sitting two feet away. Trust me. People in here aren't interested in our conversation. Not as long as you don't start shouting."

Dunlop tilted his glass again, emptying the Jack in one long swallow. The waitress chose that moment to pass the table. "Would you like another round?" she asked with a smile.

"Absolutely, darlin'. But make this one a double."

Smith waited for Dunlop to continue, but he said nothing, staring at his empty glass until the waitress returned. He took the drink from her hand and immediately drained half of it. Smith noted the abrupt change in the man's demeanor. He had gone from arrogant to anxious in the space of five minutes.

Wiping his mouth with the back of his hand, Dunlop said, "Okay, I have a problem with something, and I'm told you might be able to help me with it."

Smith said nothing, waiting.

When he didn't respond, Dunlop said, "Is that right? Can you help me?"

"Depends."

"On what?"

"On what it is you need."

"But, I thought it was understood. I was told you could help me. I'm confused."

"I don't know what you were told. About me or about what I do. But I don't commit to anything unless and until I have a clear understanding of a potential client's needs. That means, if you wish to employ my services, you should state in plain and simple terms what it is you would like me to do."

Dunlop took another drink. Picking up a cocktail napkin, he began shredding it into tiny pieces.

Smith watched him impassively. He had seen this type of behavior many times before. There was a line most people were afraid to cross, fearing the consequences almost more than they feared doing nothing. He could sense the internal struggle going on behind the man's eyes. He would decide to go ahead. Or he wouldn't. Smith waited, sipping his vodka.

Dunlop eyed the man across the table. "Can I trust you to be discreet?" Smith said nothing.

"I need someone to, uh, to go away," he blurted out in a loud voice, instantly darting his eyes around the bar to see if anyone had heard him.

Smith didn't react to Dunlop's outburst, continuing to watch him calmly through a haze of cigarette smoke. In a soft voice, he replied, "Mr. Jones, remember me telling you no one would pay attention unless you started shouting?"

"I, I'm sorry," Dunlop said. His hands were shaking as he went back to work on the napkin, all traces of bravado gone. "I just, I don't know what else to do. If something doesn't happen quick, I, well, it just needs to be taken care of."

Smith smiled inwardly at the man's nervousness and his noticeable reluctance to speak plainly. He decided to mess with him a little to see how he reacted. "Mr. Jones, if you need someone to go away, try hiring a limo service. Or call a cab. You don't need me for that."

Dunlop scowled at Smith, "I don't mean go away in that sense," he said, dropping his voice almost to a whisper. "I mean make someone go away, you know, *really* go away. And not come back."

Smith blew smoke at the ceiling before fixing his eyes on Dunlop. It was true he made people disappear, just as the man across the table was asking him to do. His appearance belied such an occupation. Movies more often than not cast the character as a guy standing over six feet, maybe two-fifty or so, with massive arms and a chest like Schwarzenegger in his prime. A man people would step off the sidewalk to let pass.

Most people figured him for an insurance salesman or maybe an accountant. Some safe, incredibly boring job. When Smith left a room, no one later remembered seeing him. He was largely invisible, the type of person cops referred to as nondescript. That ability to fade into the background had been crucial to his success over the years.

Smith didn't make snap decisions. Those who did, most notably in his business, usually didn't last long enough to retire.

"Why?" he asked.

"Why?" Dunlop repeated.

"Yes. Why do you want this person to go away?"

Before Smith could finish speaking, Dunlop was shaking his head. "No, no, that's not part of the deal."

"Then our business is concluded," Smith said, draining the last of his drink and picking up the pack of cigarettes as he started to get up.

"Wait. Where are you going?" Dunlop asked, reaching out and grabbing the sleeve of Smith's coat.

Smith didn't respond as his eyes shifted downward to Dunlop's hand, staring at it with such intensity that the man quickly let go.

"I'll tell you. Don't go. I really need your help," he pleaded.

Smith scrutinized the man for several seconds before sitting back down.

"She, uh, the person," Dunlop corrected himself, "has become a huge problem to someone. This person is—"

"It's okay, Mr. Jones," Smith said, amused. "I understand you're referring to a woman."

"Alright. I didn't know if you had any qualms about, well, you know."

"Yes, I know. By the way, what is her name?"

Dunlop scowled. "Why do you need to know that?"

Patiently, he said, "Mr. Jones, if you intend to pay my substantial fee, then you will expect me to make the person of your choosing *really* go away and not come back, as you so eloquently described it. For me to accomplish that task, I must have certain information. The identity of the target is critical. Wouldn't you agree?"

Dunlop laughed shakily. "Yes, yes, of course. I'm just nervous." Leaning forward, he whispered, "Her name is Denise Adams."

"And where does Ms. Adams live?"

"In Jacksonville Beach. That's a suburb of Jacksonville. In Florida," he added.

"Does she have a family?"

"No. She lives alone."

Smith could tell there was a lot more to the story. He was only seeing the very tip of the iceberg, the other nine-tenths still hidden. Dunlop had avoided answering the question of why he wanted Denise Adams killed. But Smith was patient. "What does Ms. Adams do for a living?"

Dunlop grew more nervous, tapping his fingers on the glass. "She, she's a politician. A local politician."

"What type of politician, specifically?"

"She's the mayor of Jacksonville Beach," Dunlop said, his eyes once more flitting around the now crowded bar.

"And what has she done that makes her a candidate for my services?"

"Please, Mr. Smith," Dunlop said in an imploring tone. "I can't tell you. It would mean. I, I just can't. Why is it so important that you know, anyway?"

"It's not, in most cases. However, I tend to be more cautious about taking on a client if solving their problem could cause substantial publicity. Making an elected official disappear has heightened risks that cause me to question whether this is a good idea."

"Are you saying you won't take the job?" Dunlop asked anxiously.

"I'm saying I have to understand why it's so important that your mayor disappear before I agree to take on this task."

Dunlop licked his lips nervously. Coming to a decision, he said, "Denise Adams is causing a huge problem for someone I know. They've had a relationship that, in her opinion, was much more serious than it was to my, to the person I'm helping. When it became clear to her that the relationship was over, she lost it and threatened to go public. This must not happen. It would damage the person's reputation and cause irreparable harm to certain plans he has to . . . well, I'll just say they're big plans that can't be allowed to be destroyed by this *bitch*," he snarled, grabbing his glass and gulping the rest of his drink.

"You keep referring to this person who will be harmed. Who is he?"

His eyes widening, Dunlop said, "No. That's definitely not part of the deal."

Smith considered whether the person's identity was crucial right then. He decided it wasn't. Besides, he knew he could find out everything he needed from MacKay.

"Mr. Jones, I'm not going to push the issue at this point, but don't delude yourself into thinking I'm some drug-addled flake you ran across in some dive and decided after half a dozen tequila shots to hire me to fix your problem. I'm a professional. That means I do my homework by learning as much about my client as I do about the person he wants to make go away. Do you understand that?"

As Smith was talking, Dunlop continued shredding the cocktail napkins, creating a growing mound on the table in front of him. He said, "It's just that you threw me when you wanted to know the man's name. He needs to be kept completely out of this situation."

"Does he know you're meeting with me and what you want done?"

Shaking his head vigorously, Dunlop said, "Absolutely not. As his chie–, his employee, it's my job to make problems go away. To smooth the path in front of him so he doesn't stumble, so to speak. He doesn't know and can't ever know."

Lighting another cigarette, Smith said, "Are you still interested in employing my services?"

Dunlop didn't answer for several seconds. When he did, his voice had a slight tremor. "I am, but you have to guarantee me that nothing will go wrong with this. Also, that my boss won't under any circumstances be connected to it. If you can't give me that, then I think we should forget we ever had this meeting."

Smith shrugged. "Someone once said that life is full of uncertainties. I can't guarantee you that the sun will come up tomorrow, although I would bet serious money that it will do just that. However, a guarantee that nothing will go wrong? I can't give you that. And as far as your boss never being connected to the good mayor's demise? That one's a little less certain in my mind simply because I don't have total control over all aspects of the situation."

"What are you saying? That it might come out? A connection between them?"

"You told me they already have a connection. I assume it's common knowledge?"

"Well, yes, but I was talking about a connection between him and her death."

"I see. Once again, while there are no guarantees in life, I can assure you that I have been very successful in keeping a wall between my clients and the people who become, shall we say, the recipients of my particular talents."

Dunlop muttered, "I don't have any other choice. The problem with the mayor is almost to the point of being out of control. I guess I'll have to trust you to keep it contained."

Smith considered everything Dunlop had told him. He said, "Okay, as I see it, there are a couple of issues I have to consider before I can determine my fee. First, the potential negative consequences of a politician being killed are greater than, for example, some store clerk getting shot during a robbery. Second, the fact the mayor is female raises the stakes higher. Killing a woman will just naturally generate more media coverage and a higher degree of sympathy for the victim. The difficulty in ensuring these issues don't cause you and your boss any problems means my fee will not be cheap."

Dunlop didn't flinch. "I told you yesterday that money won't be a problem. But I do have one more request."

"And that would be?"

"There is a certain other person who has caused my boss substantial pain and anguish. I mean that literally and not figuratively. So bad that the man needs to suffer the worst sort of retribution short of dying."

Smith waited, curious where this was going.

Dunlop continued. "What I'm getting at is that I need you to arrange it so that this man is blamed for the mayor's death."

"You mean as in planting some type of evidence that would result in this man being charged with a homicide?"

"That's exactly what I mean," Dunlop said.

Smith said nothing, staring until the man's eyes dropped in discomfort. A smile tugging at the corners of his mouth, Smith spoke, "Mr. Jones, you've been reading too many murder mysteries, I think. But before I give you my answer, tell me who the man is and his connection to your boss."

"I can tell you his name, but I can't be more specific about his connection to my boss for the same reasons as before."

"Okay, let's start with the name of this bad guy."

"It's Clay Randall," Dunlop whispered.

"And what does Clay Randall do for a living?"

Observing the other patrons before speaking, he leaned forward and said softly, "He's a cop."

Although the response surprised Smith, he kept his face expressionless. He had never been asked to incriminate someone else for a murder he had committed. While he wasn't necessarily opposed to the idea, the thought of setting up a cop was a little disconcerting.

Smith said, "Mr. Jones, are you sure you know what you're asking?"

Dunlop said, "Absolutely."

"Before I decide, paint me a picture of this Clay Randall. What does he look like? How old? Where does he work?"

"I'd guess he's in his early forties, probably six feet tall, light brown hair. He's a commander in the Jacksonville Beach Police Department."

"Okay, and you're certain this Randall has done something so bad that he deserves to be blamed for a murder?"

Nodding vigorously, Dunlop said, "Yes. No question about it."

"To make this happen, I would need something that will conclusively link this man to the death."

"I've already thought of that, and arrangements are being made to get you what you would need."

Smith said nothing as he considered the possibilities.

Desperation creeping into his voice as the silence lengthened, Dunlop said, "You can do it, can't you?"

Smith still didn't respond as he continued to mull over the idea. "How old is Ms. Adams?" he asked.

"In her early to mid-forties, I think," Dunlop responded.

"Any physical ailments or disabilities?"

"Not that I'm aware of."

Smith leaned forward, saying, "Okay, Mr. Jones. Taking into account these latest special requirements, my fee will have to be increased."

Dunlop cleared his throat, wiping the back of his hand across his mouth. "Increased by how much?"

"You said money was no problem. Remember?"

"I know, but there is a limit to what I have immediately available. What kind of number are we talking about?"

Smith always based his price first on the difficulty of the assignment and second on the individual's ability to pay rather than a specific amount. He wasn't running a grocery store selling milk and cereal for a set price.

"It will be fifty thousand dollars."

"Fifty thousand!" Dunlop exclaimed. Immediately lowering his voice, he said, "I don't understand. Why so much?"

"Because of everything I've already detailed. Would you like me to go over the list again?"

"No, no. But still, that much money?"

"Mr. Jones, let me make this clear for you. My fee is not negotiable. If you're not satisfied, we have nothing further to discuss."

Smith watched as Dunlop's face went from anger and disbelief to reluctant acceptance. His shoulders sagged, and he nodded. "Okay, fifty thousand."

"That's half up front, with the remaining twenty-five due upon completion," Smith said.

"I don't have that much," Dunlop protested. "I only brought ten with me. That's the amount you told me to bring."

"I did. I also told you I would determine a fee after we talked. Now that we've decided on the price, and taking into account you only brought ten thousand with you, I'll help you out," he smiled. "I'll take the ten now and give you twenty-four hours to come up with the other fifteen. If you don't, I'll keep the money to cover expenses associated with this meeting."

Dunlop glared. "That's outrageous! This meeting didn't cost you a damn dime! Maybe I should just walk out of here right now. What are you going to do then? You'll have nothing."

"True," Smith said, still smiling, "but then that would result in *your* unfortunate death."

"What?! Why?"

"Two reasons," Smith noted. "One, allowing you to walk away after you've agreed to a deal is bad for my business. It sends the message to potential customers that I'm easy, and that pisses me off. And two, you're an asshole, and I don't like you."

"Yet you'll take my money?" Dunlop asked, a bewildered expression on his face.

The killer shrugged. "It's just business."

Smith watched Dunlop's eyes, seeing fear awaken as he realized the man sitting across from him would not hesitate to follow through on his threat if he backed out.

"I, I accept your terms." Removing a thick envelope from the inner pocket of his jacket, Dunlop slid it surreptitiously across the table as his eyes darted around the bar. As Smith reached over to take it, Dunlop pulled the envelope back slightly.

"Remember. You have to do it in a way that implicates Randall. Okay?" Dunlop said.

Smith took the envelope without comment and slipped it into his coat pocket. "I'll expect the other fifteen within twenty-four hours, as agreed. Call this number when you have it," he said, handing Dunlop a napkin with a cell phone number scribbled on it.

As Smith stood to leave, Dunlop said, "Wait. You didn't answer my question. What about making sure Randall is blamed for it?"

"Mr. Jones, it's likely you'll be satisfied with the results. Now, if that's not good enough for you, I'll be on my way," he said, starting to walk away.

"No, wait, that's okay," Dunlop said, hurriedly. "MacKay told me you were the best, so I guess I have to accept it. One more question, though. When is it going to happen? Timing is critical."

"When I have the rest of my upfront fee in hand, we'll talk," Smith said, walking away.

Leaving the Tail End Lounge, Smith strolled toward the parking lot where he had left his car, threading his way through the throngs of people crowding the sidewalks. At most intersections along the Strip, men holding stacks of colorful cards slapped them against their palms to attract the attention of tourists. Whether the mark was a man or a woman, they tried to hand each one a card depicting scantily clad women promising personal companionship for a price.

He had lived in Vegas for a while when he first came to Nevada. Long enough to know that avoiding eye contact was the easiest way to get past the gauntlet of raunchy literature. Merely on principle, however, he always gave them a cold stare, which invariably caused the card men to turn away hastily in search of a less intimidating customer.

Smith had a specialized talent, one that people were willing to pay large sums to employ. Cash only, of course. He had a reputation in the insular world he occupied as a highly skilled professional who always got the job done, leaving nothing behind to link him or his clients to the deed. His customers were wealthy; they had to be to afford his fees.

He employed no one particular method, the better to confuse cops and forensics experts who had grown adept at identifying patterns that could ultimately lead to the capture of a killer. Given optimal circumstances, his preferred method involved a scoped rifle, the better to keep some distance between himself and his target. He almost never used a firearm more than once, dismantling and discarding the pieces in multiple locations to avoid the possibility that the cops might trace one of his jobs to a particular weapon. And then to him.

He utilized handguns, knives, and even poisons when a situation called for it. In one diabolically inspired kill, he used a rattlesnake to dispatch his victim.

As he reached his car, Smith thought about the meeting he had just left. About the man's demand that nothing go wrong. Early on, he learned two valuable lessons he had never forgotten. Remembering those painful lessons took his mind back to his first job as a professional killer.

Growing up in Lawton, Oklahoma, Smith joined the army right out of high school and spent several years learning how to shoot a rifle better than most people. However, an incident during Operation Desert Storm in Iraq in the early nineties led to a dishonorable discharge and years spent in a military prison as a guest of the government.

When the military discharged him from prison, he returned to his hometown, full of anger and resentment. Unable to hold a job for more than a few months at a time, he was unemployed the night he took an empty stool next to a man in a bar in downtown Lawton. Over beers, they struck up a conversation about the Dallas Cowboys and the odds of them making the playoffs that year.

Eventually, the talk turned to a local murder trial. The story was on all the TV stations about how a disgruntled wife hired her lawn service guy to kill her husband after she discovered he was cheating on her with the bookkeeper for his small car wash chain. To cover herself, the wife wanted the murder to appear to be a robbery gone bad.

The killing went off without a hitch, but the robbery story soon fell apart when police discovered emails between the woman and the lawn guy discussing the scheme. Using the emails, it was but a short trip to the prosecutor's office before police arrested and charged both of them in the murder for hire plot.

Smith and the man downed several more beers as they talked about how stupid the lawn guy was to agree to kill someone for money. As the intoxication level rose, Smith began saying he could have done the deed and never been caught. His bar mate, by then pretty hammered himself, challenged Smith to explain how he would have done it.

Smith told him it was simple. He would have made sure there was nothing recorded. No emails, no telephone messages, nothing the cops could use to point the finger at him. Bleary-eyed, the man bobbed his head up and down as if Smith had just explained the meaning of life to him.

When the bar closed, they staggered down the street to an all-night diner where, over coffee, the man poured out his story of woe to Smith. He married a woman who had become wealthy through shrewd investments of alimony payments from a previous husband, the CEO of a multinational corporation.

He described a loving marriage filled with travels all over the world, a huge home, and an active sex life. As the man talked, Smith felt a twinge of jealousy, recognizing the stark loneliness of his own life.

Everything was great until the man's wife reached her late forties when she developed severe rheumatoid arthritis. The disease began in her fingers and hands and eventually spread to both knees and ankles, leading to unremitting pain, swelling, and discomfort.

The man said it almost killed him to watch his wife turn from a beautiful, sexy creature into a haggard and broken woman who looked years older than her true age. With tears streaming down his face, he said she told him she wanted to die rather than go through the rest of her life in such terrible pain. He convinced her to go to a counselor, but she stopped after a few visits, telling him it hadn't helped.

The week before, as the pain grew worse, he said she asked him to help her commit suicide. He was shocked and refused to discuss it with her, but she persisted, begging him to help her end the pain. As he listened to the man's story, Smith began to feel genuine sympathy for the woman. There had been many nights since he got out of prison when depression threatened to overwhelm him, when his only relief was a fifth of vodka.

Smith asked the guy what he was going to do. After some hesitation, he told Smith he was a coward and that he could never take the life of the woman he loved. As fresh tears fell, he asked Smith if he would do it for him. For her.

Smith was drunk, although not so far gone that he hadn't begun to realize what was going on. He told the man he was crazy for even thinking he would help him kill his wife. They talked for another two hours as the man continued to try to convince Smith that it was the only humane thing to do.

As he began to sober up, Smith's thoughts turned from total rejection of the idea to how he could do it while ensuring he wouldn't spend the rest of his life in another prison cell. The turning point came when the man offered him twenty thousand dollars in cash. Smith did a quick mental calculation and found he had less than three hundred dollars to his name, no job, a twelve-year-old car with two hundred thousand miles on it, and a rundown apartment he was about to lose if he didn't pay his rent by the end of the month.

He decided he could live with the idea of a mercy killing, as he came to think of it. It was simply the right thing to do. After all, the woman wanted desperately to die, and her husband didn't have the guts to do it. He, on the other hand, had killed before. In Iraq.

As they discussed various methods for ending the woman's pain, Smith suggested a gunshot to the head, made to appear self-inflicted. But the man objected strenuously. In a horrified voice, he said he couldn't bear the thought of his wife's beautiful face being mutilated by a bullet. They talked a while longer but failed to come up with a method that seemed acceptable to the man. Smith left the restaurant after agreeing to meet him later that day to discuss the proposition further.

That afternoon, his head still pounding from a hangover, Smith met him in a parking lot near the Comanche National Museum and Cultural Center. Sitting in the man's new Mercedes, the smell of leather upholstery enveloping him, he continued to express reservations about taking the job.

The man reached over the seat and grabbed a paper bag, dumping the contents into Smith's lap. He handled each of the banded stacks of twenties, more money than he had ever seen at one time in his life. The sight was mesmerizing. Fanning one of the stacks, Smith quickly decided he wouldn't offend the man by counting it in front of him. He shoved the money back into the bag and cradled it in his lap.

"Since you didn't count it, there's ten thousand there. I'll give you the other ten as soon as you take care of my sweet wife," the man said sadly.

He agreed to take the job. However, Smith, unschooled in the business of killing for hire, was not yet aware of two cardinal rules. Never guarantee a successful outcome. And everyone lies.

A fter considering and rejecting several methods, Smith settled on a drowning in the Olympic-sized swimming pool in the secluded back yard of their two-acre estate, a choice the husband quickly embraced. Because of her arthritis, the man said his wife used it every evening for gentle exercise to ease the relentless pain. A slip and fall, striking her head on the pool wall as she went in, seemed a reasonable way to go that would arouse no suspicion.

On the night it was to take place, the husband said he needed an alibi, so he arranged to be at a business function with several dozen people. Smith left his car in the parking lot of a condominium complex several blocks away. Cutting behind the buildings, he slipped through thick woods separating the complex from the gated community where the man lived. He arrived in the late afternoon while the wife was taking her daily, drug-induced nap. Large oak trees and hedges surrounding three sides of the house provided visual cover from neighboring homes.

Smith positioned himself behind the pump house and settled in to wait. An hour later, as the sun neared the horizon, the wife came hobbling out the door, using a walker to help her maneuver across the flagstone path to the pool. She wore a two-piece bathing suit that revealed little of her pre-arthritis figure. Her hair was blond and cut short, framing a face that still retained traces of her former beauty.

Smith watched her slowly maneuver the walker as she approached the shallow end of the pool adjacent to the pump house. As the woman turned to face the water, Smith eased out from his hiding place and moved toward her, covering the ten feet of pool apron quickly and silently.

Without hesitation, he grabbed the woman, placing one hand over her mouth and the other around her emaciated waist. Sweeping her off her feet, he shoved her lower body toward the water while dropping her upper torso straight down. The back of her head struck the edge of the pool with a sickening crunch, knocking her unconscious.

Smith pushed the woman away from the side of the pool and watched as her body floated for a second or two before sinking to the bottom. The walker had fallen into the water when he grabbed her, and it came to rest a couple of feet away. Smith kneeled on the pool apron, breathing rapidly from tension and excitement at what he had done. As he watched, the water turned pink from the gash on the back of her head.

Her fingers twitched several times, and he was afraid she was going to regain consciousness. He worried that he would have to get into the water to finish the job. He didn't want to risk the chance of being stopped by a cop and having to try to explain his wet clothing. After a couple of minutes, seeing no air bubbles from her mouth or nose, he was satisfied she was dead.

Smith watched as the woman's body began to drift slowly toward the deep end of the pool. He had never killed anyone other than in the military, and those had been enemies. She wasn't. A feeling of remorse passed quickly as he realized he should bear no guilt over killing the woman. He had simply done for her what she so desperately wanted, an end to her suffering. Rising to his feet, Smith turned to leave, intending to cut back through the woods to his car.

"Hey, wait up," a voice called from the direction of the house.

Smith wheeled around, startled. The woman's husband was striding toward him, dressed in a tuxedo. In the fading light, he saw a dark object in the man's hand. As he drew near, the object became clear. It was a black semi-automatic pistol pointed directly at him.

Startled, Smith said, "What are you doing?"

"You mean this?" the man replied, brandishing the large handgun and grinning. "It's the means by which I intend to bring this little incident to a successful conclusion. Of course, *you* might not call it successful, but, after all, it's never been about what you wanted. It's always been about resolving my problem in a way that will give me full access to my wife's millions and not have to worry about someone like you hitting on me for more money to stay quiet."

Smith was in shock. He realized the man had been conning him from the moment he first encountered him in the bar. He took a quick look over his shoulder, wondering if he could make it into the woods before the man could shoot him.

"I wouldn't do that if I were you," the man said. "Running will only get you killed sooner."

In spite of the danger he was in, Smith laughed. "You're joking, right? You set this whole thing up. You wanted your wife dead but didn't have the balls to do it yourself. That's why you hired me to do it, and now you plan to kill me so I can't come back on you. But you're forgetting a couple of things."

"Really?" the man smiled, the gun held steady. "And what would that be?"

"If you kill me, you've lost ten thousand dollars. You were dumb enough to give it to me upfront. Since you have no idea where I've got it, you'll never see it again."

The man's smile remained. "I pay my lawn guy more than that just to cut the grass. Now that you've taken care of that bitch," he said, glancing quickly over his shoulder at the body of his dead wife, "I've got thirty million to play with, so a measly ten thousand is nothing. Hurry up. What's your second point? And don't insult my intelligence this time."

"I thought you said you loved your wife. You sat in that place and cried like a baby."

"I did, didn't I?" the man laughed. "My job requires me to act a part at times. One of my many talents has been the ability to cry on cue. Pretty convincing, huh?"

Still playing for time, Smith said, "Aren't you supposed to be at some event so you'll have an alibi?"

"You mean the tux? I was there for a short while and made sure plenty of people saw me. Then I slipped out when the program started. I got back here and sneaked in the house while my wife was changing into her bathing suit. I was inside enjoying a martini and watching the whole thing. I have to say your plan to make it seem like an accident worked perfectly. My congratulations on that. Now quit stalling. I have things I have to take care of," he said, gesturing over his shoulder at the pool as the pistol remained pointed at Smith's chest.

His confidence shaken, Smith kept trying. "You should know that I didn't trust you from the start, so I documented our whole conversation. I went into great detail about your request for me to kill your wife and about you giving me ten thousand dollars with a promise for ten more after I did it. That document, along with all of the money, is in a locked briefcase that I gave to my lawyer with instructions to open it if I don't call him by ten o'clock tonight."

"Nice try," the man responded sarcastically. "But that's sounds like pure bullshit. Tell me, who's your lawyer?"

Smith racked his brain for a name to give the man. Then he remembered seeing a billboard advertising a law firm as he drove to the house. "Johnson, Davis, and Turner."

"Really?" the man responded, eyebrows raised. "And which partner has the briefcase?"

"Johnson," Smith said, watching the man's eyes closely to see if he was buying the story.

"Interesting. Now I know you're lying, so let's bring this little drama to a conclusion," he said, raising the gun to point at Smith's head.

"Wait!" Smith exclaimed, raising his hands. "I'm not lying! It's the truth!"

"Well, unless there's another law firm in Lawton named Johnson, Davis, and Turner, I know you're lying. Because that's my firm, and I'm Johnson."

"You're, you're a lawyer?"

Johnson smiled, "Yep. I'm the senior partner in the firm. So you see, I know you haven't documented anything." His voice suddenly hard, he said, "Turn around! Put your hands behind your head and lock your fingers together. Do it now!"

Smith, his mind whirling, did as Johnson ordered. Panicked now and in fear of his life, he asked, "Would it make any difference if I told you the money is in my car? I'll take you there and give it to you right now. Then I'll leave, and you'll never hear from me again."

"Um, no, don't think so," Johnson replied, a smile back in his voice. "We're going on a short trip into the woods where you came from. Now walk. Slowly!"

Smith started walking toward the woods behind the house, his mind feverishly considering and rejecting one desperate plan after another. Johnson stayed several steps back, making it impossible for Smith to turn and grab the gun before he could pull the trigger.

He entered the woods, his elbows brushing the bushes and low hanging limbs as he kept his fingers laced behind his head. By now, the sun had dropped below the horizon, leaving their surroundings in deep gloom. As they moved farther into the woods, the path became harder to follow, and Smith found himself having to force his way through thick brush.

A plan began to form as he maneuvered through the heavy vegetation. Noticing a tree root protruding from the ground, he purposely tripped over it, falling forward. Throwing out his left hand to break his fall, he slipped his right hand into his pants pocket and pulled a lock-blade knife in one fluid motion.

"Get up!" Johnson demanded, not seeing the quick move in the dim light.

Smith climbed slowly to his feet, the knife cupped in his hand as he stood. "I didn't fall on purpose. It's getting hard to see in here."

"I don't want excuses," Johnson said. "Turn around and get your hands behind your head. Then start walking again."

Smith did as he was told, carefully pressing the knife against the back of his head with the palm of his hand as he started forward.

When Smith calculated they were about halfway through the patch of woods, Johnson told him to stop and turn around. Smith turned, careful to keep his hands behind his head.

Johnson stood six feet away, the gun still pointing at him. "This is as good a spot as any to conclude our business," he said.

"Mr. Johnson, is there anything I can do to convin–", Smith stopped, his breathing suddenly labored. Staggering forward a couple of steps, he dropped his hands to his chest and pressed them together, wheezing loudly.

"I, I've got a heart condition," he gasped. Smith bent over at the waist, still holding his chest and coughing repeatedly. Suddenly, he lunged forward, snapping the knife open and slashing at Johnson. The blade cut deeply into the man's wrist, slicing nerves and tendons. Johnson screamed as the gun dropped from his hand. Without hesitation, Smith drove the knife to the hilt in the man's throat. Johnson fell to the ground, grunting as he tried to speak. Smith picked up the gun and stood back to avoid the blood that continued to pump from the severed artery in Johnson's neck.

In less than a minute, it was over. Smith stepped around the spreading pool of blood and started to check for a pulse. Quickly realizing there was no need, he turned and jogged to his car. An hour later, his few belongings and the ten thousand dollars stashed in the trunk, Johnson's gun under the seat, he headed for Interstate 40.

Getting hungry, he stopped at a truck stop a few miles down the road. He went into the restaurant and ordered the special, a sixteen-ounce Porterhouse steak and a fully loaded baked potato, chased down with several cups of coffee and a large piece of pecan pie. Feeling stuffed, Smith got into his car and pulled to a far corner of the lot. Climbing into the back seat, he slipped off his shoes and curled up, planning to get a few hours of sleep before hitting the road again.

He thought about the two people he had killed. He felt a sliver of guilt about Johnson's wife. He went back over everything Johnson had said about her. After hearing the man describe his wife as a bitch and bragging that he only wanted her money, it was clear that she didn't want to commit suicide. About Johnson, he had no more remorse over killing him than he did the Iraqi soldiers he shot.

As he began to drift off, Smith's last conscious thought was that he had always wanted to see Las Vegas. Now seemed like the perfect occasion.

Dammit, Clay, back off!" Chief Wilson exclaimed.

Clay Randall stood over Jack Hargraves, the patrol division commander, fists balled up, his whole body shaking.

"You heard the man. Better back off," Hargraves drawled, his relaxed posture in stark contrast to Clay. Draping an arm casually over the back of his chair, Hargraves continued, "You know, Randall, you really ought to see somebody about your anger issues."

"Shut the hell up, Hargraves!" Wilson roared. Standing abruptly, he stalked to the door and slammed it, causing his administrative assistant to jump with alarm at her desk.

Wilson turned to see Clay still standing over Hargraves. "Commander Randall, sit down! Now!"

Giving Hargraves a final, contemptuous glare, Clay dropped into the chair beside him.

Wilson sat, pointing at both commanders, "I want the two of you to keep quiet and listen carefully because I don't intend to have this conversation again."

Hargraves frowned as he opened his mouth to protest. Wilson cut him off. "Which part of keep quiet and listen carefully did you miss, Commander? I don't want to see your lips moving unless I ask you a specific question. You got that?"

"Yes," Hargraves said, slumping back in his chair.

"Fine. Now, Commander Hargraves," Wilson said, holding up a folded sheet of paper, "as to the allegations in this note that have been made against Commander Randall, I want to know who wrote it."

Hargraves acted surprised. "You're asking me, Chief?"

Wilson's eyes narrowed. "Cut the crap. Answer my question."

Hargraves shook his head. "I'm sorry, Chief. Your question confuses me. It sounds like you think I know who wrote it, and I don't. Somebody obviously left it on my unmarked after I parked in my driveway last night. I found it when I came out to go to work this morning."

Clay snorted at the statement. He and Hargraves had disliked each other for years, going back to the time when Gordy Cooper was the police chief. Hargraves, a lieutenant at the time, had been the man Gordy tasked to make life miserable for employees that questioned any action of the chief.

In return for his loyalty, Cooper promised Hargraves that he would be the new chief when he retired. However, Gordy's termination during a difficult serial killer investigation, coupled with Hargraves' unquestioning loyalty to Cooper, ensured the job would not be his.

Mike Wilson's first order of business as the new chief was to promote Clay to the rank of commander over Hargraves. That was a decision that only increased the man's animosity toward Wilson and added Clay to the list of people he detested.

However, Hargraves was smart enough to keep his mouth shut and play the game, which eventually led to his elevation to the rank of commander, also. But he never forgot the perceived slight, and he tried in various subtle ways to undermine both Mike Wilson and Clay Randall every chance he got, although never going quite far enough to be demoted or lose his job.

Wilson asked, "Why would someone just happen to pick *your* car to leave this note?"

Hargraves shrugged, "You got me, Chief. I can't imagine. Unless they thought I was the one most likely to report it instead of covering it up."

Clay's hands clenched the arms of the chair so hard his knuckles turned white.

With a warning look at Clay to keep his cool, Wilson said, "I see from the stains on the paper that an evidence technician tried to lift prints."

"He did. The tech said whoever handled it was wearing gloves, probably latex."

"Considering the allegations against Commander Randall contained in the note, why did you allow a civilian access to the note? This should have been held in the strictest confidence while we investigated it."

"Chief, what was I supposed to do? I didn't want to take the chance of destroying any prints that might be on there. Quite frankly, considering Randall and I aren't exactly best friends, I didn't want to accidentally put my prints on there and have anyone think I wrote it. The accusation in the letter is pretty serious, Chief, as I'm sure you'll agree. Of course, if it's true ..."

"I can tell you with complete confidence," Mike said, waving the paper in front of Hargraves, "that the crap in this letter is totally false."

"But, Chief," he protested, "how could you know that? Shouldn't someone at least investigate it before you write it off as unfounded?"

Wilson stared scornfully at Hargraves until the man dropped his eyes. "Okay, Commander Hargraves, I'll tell you what. Let's do that. We'll go through this letter and see what truths it contains. You good with that?"

Hargraves shrugged. "Whatever you think, Chief," he muttered.

Wilson scowled as he cleared his throat. In a monotone, he read:

Attention Jacksonville Beach Police Department,

There is a man working for the Jax Beach PD that is a criminal and should be in jail. Instead, he's still walking around with a badge and a gun. His name is Clay Randall, and he's breaking the same laws he's supposed to enforce.

I'm sure you want to know how I know this. Because I saw it myself. I was taking a walk on the beach last night, July 16th, at eight o'clock. By sheer coincidence, I was walking past where Randall lives on the oceanfront. Something drew my attention to the second floor deck of his house. Imagine my shock when I saw him sitting in a chair, all kicked back, his feet up on the table, and he was smoking what was clearly a crack pipe!

I'm sure you're wondering how I could see this since his house is on the other side of the dune line. It's because I always carry binoculars with me in case I see something interesting out in the water, like sharks and dolphin and such like.

When I realized he was smoking crack cocaine, I absolutely couldn't believe it! I started to call 9-1-1 and report this serious crime, but I stopped when I realized they might be able to identify me by my phone number. Randall has killed at least two people that I know of, so one more wouldn't make any difference when killing me would allow him to continue abusing such a horrible drug. People expect police officers to be role models for our children. Wake up! Randall is NO ROLE MODEL! The example he's displaying to this community is one that neither I nor the rest of the law-abiding citizens of Jacksonville Beach want our children to copy.

I'm concerned that you will try to cover this up, so I've made sure you can't by sending this letter to all the TV stations and the newspaper.

A Concerned Citizen

The silence stretched out as Wilson finished reading. He regarded the two men sitting across from him. Clay's mouth set in an angry line, his hands clenching and unclenching repeatedly. Hargraves meanwhile had regained some of his cockiness, a thin smile playing across his face.

"Now, let's add up the facts in this piece of, in this letter. Fact, Clay Randall works for this police department. Consequently, he carries a badge and gun. Fact, he lives in a house on the oceanfront and has a second-floor deck overlooking the beach. Fact, he has previously been put into the unfortunate position of having to use deadly force against a criminal. Those are the only, and I stress *only*, facts in this piece of garbage. Everything else written here is a *total and complete lie*," Wilson said, jabbing the paper with his finger as he emphasized each word.

Pointing directly at Hargraves, he said, "Commander, this false accusation has to be one of the lowest, most vile things I've seen pulled on an innocent man in my entire life."

"Wait a minute, Chief," Hargraves protested. "I didn't accuse Randall of anything."

"No, you didn't specifically accuse him, I'll give you that. But you came very close."

"But, Chief," Hargraves started to object.

Holding up a hand, Wilson said, "Stop talking and listen."

Wilson continued, "For me to accept this accusation as true, I would have to believe that Commander Randall is certifiably crazy."

"What do you mean?" Hargraves asked.

"What I mean is that a man in his position would have to be nuts to sit in the wide-ass open on his deck smoking crack cocaine in full view of anyone who happened to pass by on the beach. Knowing full well that Commander Randall is *not* crazy is in and of itself sufficient reason for me to say the allegation is false."

Hargraves opened his mouth to respond, but the chief kept talking. "Also, there's another reason that carries even more weight."

"And what would that be?" Hargraves asked, disbelievingly.

Mike said, "It seems you're having trouble accepting what I'm saying, so I'll simply repeat myself. The allegations against Commander Randall are false."

Hargraves stood up abruptly, his face contorted in anger. "This is bullshit! You're covering for Randall! Why?! Does he have something on you? He's been your favorite for years even though everyone knows I'm a better cop than he'll ever be! In fact, I should have been the chief instead of you!" Hargraves yelled, his eyes wide and his breath coming in gasps.

All during the man's rant, the chief sat calmly watching him. Now he stood and pointed a finger at Hargraves, speaking in a deadly quiet voice, "You've stepped over the line, Hargraves. You are officially relieved of duty as of right now. Go home and stay there until I call you."

Stunned, Hargraves didn't speak as his mouth opened and closed like a fish out of water.

"MOVE!" Wilson yelled, pointing at the door.

Hargraves glared incredulously at the chief. "You're relieving me of duty for expressing an opinion?" he demanded, his voice rising.

Wilson's tone was pitiless. "Contrary to your insinuations about Commander Randall's character, you've *directly* accused me of unethical acts. And all without a shred of evidence. You've committed serious policy violations. Now, do what I directed you to do, or I'll add additional insubordination charges."

The hostility was evident on Hargraves' face, but he kept his mouth shut as he walked to the door and opened it.

He turned and started to speak when Wilson growled, "Do you really want to test me, Hargraves? Get your ass out of my sight."

The man wavered, struggling with his desire to lash out. Instead, he shot a look of pure loathing at Clay before going out the door.

C lay waited until the door closed behind Hargraves before speaking. "Mike, I'm sorry I blew up."

Wilson said, "Don't worry about it. He's never gotten over me getting the chief's job instead of him. I've come to regret making him a division commander, and I intend to rectify that soon."

"Getting accused of something like this is so bad that I can't think of words strong enough to express my anger. What's most upsetting about it is that some people will believe it no matter what the truth is. And now I have to figure out a way to tell Dana before she hears it on the news."

"It's going to be okay," Wilson said, reassuringly. "You've got my full support."

"Thanks, Mike, but you've got your own problems, what with the mayor and now Cooper putting pressure on you to get rid of me."

The chief shrugged, leaning back in his chair. "If they get my job, I'll kick back on my deck and sip a cold one and tell the whole world to kiss my ass. Starting with Denise Adams and Gordy Cooper."

Clay laughed in spite of his frustration. His smile quickly faded as he said, "There's more stuff going on I haven't told you."

Mike frowned, "More?"

Clay nodded. "Not as bad as this, of course. More of a huge irritation.

Someone's been ordering pizzas in my name and having them delivered to the house. I've had three in the past week from different places that I've had to tell I didn't order anything. With one of them, I got a call from the manager demanding I pay anyway since the pizza was made and delivered. I told him it wasn't me and that I wasn't going to pay for something I didn't order and didn't eat. He was pissed but finally gave up."

Before Mike could respond, Clay continued. "Then there was the load of dirt dumped in my driveway a couple of days ago."

"Dirt? What are you talking about?"

"Someone ordered five yards of dirt to be delivered to my house. A truck dumped it on my driveway and left the bill in the mailbox. I called the company and told the manager I hadn't ordered it. The guy was even more pissed than the pizza dude, as you can imagine. I had to tell him I was a cop and that someone was screwing with me. He backed down then and sent a truck out to haul it off. He said he'd never heard of that happening before, but he was going to start getting payment up front, just in case."

Mike shook his head. "Any ideas who's doing this?"

Clay's eyes narrowed. "Lou Dunlop."

"Dunlop? You're not serious, are you?"

"I'm very serious. Think about it, Mike. I've never had anything like this happen to me in my entire career. Then one day, a powerful senator's daughter is killed in a freak accident. Now, suddenly, I'm the devil."

"I don't know, Clay," the chief said, shaking his head. "That seems like a real stretch to me, accusing a man of something as bad as this," he said, tapping the letter with his finger. "I'm not sure even Barclay would stoop that low."

"I'd like to think the man has more integrity, but Lou Dunlop doesn't have any idea what the word means. He all but admitted to me that he spun up Mr. Westcott into attacking us at the city council meeting. I'd bet my paycheck Dunlop's behind all this."

"You know you've sent a lot of people to prison over the years. Some of them would probably like to get back at you. Don't you think it could be someone like that instead of Dunlop?"

Clay had started shaking his head before Mike could finish. "Nope. To accept that, I'd have to believe that Jack Hargraves is tied in with some ex-con. Otherwise, how would a guy like that know that Hargraves would run straight to you with that letter? No, it's someone he knows very well. And that someone is Dunlop."

"Hargraves and Dunlop?"

"They've been tight for years. I did some checking and discovered they were fraternity brothers in college."

"Really? I never knew that," Mike said. "That does shed a little different light on this. So, any suggestions?"

"I don't know what's going to come out of this latest attack," he said, gesturing at the letter. "Dunlop or whoever wrote it said the letter had been given to the media, so I figure it's just a matter of time before the parking lot is full of TV vans and people trying to stick microphones and cameras in my face or yours."

"You're probably right that they'll show up here," Mike agreed. "But don't worry. I'll handle the media myself."

"Mike, you don't need to do that," Clay objected. "You and I both know I haven't done anything wrong. I can look them all in the eye and say every word of it is a total lie."

"I know you can, but I don't want you put into that position. No matter how strongly you profess your innocence, they can twist your statements to fit the spin they want to give the story. Face it, a cop, and a high ranking one at that, accused of smoking crack? It'll be like throwing raw steak to a pack of hungry dogs."

"I understand, but—"

"No," Mike said, holding up his hand. "I'm not going to hang you out there to face this. I've got it."

"Wait, listen to me, Mike," Clay protested, his voice rising. "If I don't defend myself, it's going to seem like I'm not denying anything only because I'm guilty."

"I hear what you're saying, but I don't agree. You're going to have to trust me on this. I'll handle it. You keep a low profile until we can figure out who's behind it."

"I'm telling you, it's Dunlop. Probably helped by Hargraves."

"Dunlop. Hargraves. Whoever it is, we'll find out. And they'll pay the price."

"What about the mayor?" Clay asked, dejection evident in his voice. "She'll jump on this even harder than she did on Summer's shooting. If that happens, you're going to face the real possibility of being pushed out the door yourself. I can't stand by and let that happen to you. I think the best thing for me to do is resign. That'll give Barclay what he wants. Then everything will quiet down."

"You said you didn't do anything wrong, and that's the truth. I don't intend to stand by and watch you throw away an honorable career over people with no honor at all!" Mike exclaimed.

Clay dropped his eyes, overcome by the chief's impassioned support. "Thanks, Mike," he said softly. "I'll wait to see what the fallout is before I decide what to do."

Wilson stood and extended his hand. "I can't stop you if you decide to resign, but I'm telling you that would be a huge mistake. Give me a chance to clear up this crap before you do something dumb. I don't intend to let an innocent man be attacked without kicking some serious ass first."

Clay's eyes filled with tears as he returned the chief's handshake, his voice breaking, "I can't tell you how much I appreciate your support and your friendship, Mike."

"Get outta here. Go home to Dana. She needs you, and you're going to need her," Mike said gruffly, his voice quavering with emotion.

With a nod, unable to speak, Clay left.

C hief Wilson," the TV reporter said loudly, thrusting his microphone toward Wilson's face as the cameraman stood to his left with video rolling. "What can you tell us about this letter accusing Commander Clay Randall of smoking crack cocaine?"

Mike gazed around the patrol squad room. Packed with TV, radio, and newspaper reporters from Jacksonville, there were also media people from outside the area sprinkled throughout the room.

There was nothing like a perceived scandal to bring out the media horde, all of them anxious to be first to air the dirty details. Alleged bad behavior by public sector employees was a juicy target for them. However, when the assumed behavior involved a law enforcement official, that was generally considered the crown jewel of scandal reporting.

Mike had scheduled the news conference in response to a flood of calls from media outlets that had received the anonymous letter. He had delayed the inevitable until Clay could tell Dana about the letter and what they could expect. She wanted to call the media people herself to tell them the letter was a lie. But Clay convinced her it was best to let Mike handle it, and, although outraged at the allegations, she reluctantly agreed.

Holding the press release, Mike addressed the group. "Please take a seat while I read a prepared statement. After that, I'll respond to a few questions."

He stood silently as the reporters vied for chairs closest to the podium, hoping to increase their chances of getting their questions asked first. When the room grew quiet, he perched his glasses on the end of his nose and began reading.

"Last night, an unknown person reportedly placed a letter, a copy of which many of you have received, on a city vehicle assigned to a police commander with this department. The vehicle was parked in the driveway at the commander's residence. That commander advised me that he discovered the letter when he came out of his residence this morning. After reviewing the contents, the commander then brought it to police headquarters, where it was eventually delivered to me. I have read the letter in its entirety, and I can state unequivocally that the allegations against Commander Clay Randall contained in it are completely and totally false. I–"

"Chief," the TV reporter who had first spoken, interrupted, standing up as he signaled for his cameraman to keep him in frame. "How have you determined the allegations are false?"

Mike raised his head, struggling to hide his irritation at the interruption. "As I previously stated, I will read the prepared statement and then answer your questions. If you'll just be patient, you'll find that most of them will be answered."

He waited until, with a curt nod, the reporter sat down. "In case anyone missed what I said, let me read that last sentence again," Mike said, giving the room a quick scan. "I have read the letter in its entirety, and I can state unequivocally that the allegations against Commander Clay Randall contained in it are completely and totally false."

Raising his eyes from the statement, he paused to see if anyone else would interrupt. When no one spoke, he continued.

"I have direct, irrefutable knowledge that Commander Randall did not commit the alleged acts attributed to him in the anonymous letter. I have had the honor and privilege of serving with Commander Randall for almost twenty years. I know for a fact that he is a man of the highest integrity, and, further, that he is innocent of these despicable allegations."

Pausing to remove his glasses, he said, "That concludes my prepared statement. I'll now take a few questions."

The room erupted with numerous reporters shouting questions. Mike pointed at the TV reporter in the front row. "Now, sir, what was your question again?"

The reporter lunged to his feet. "Yes, Chief. Channel 13 News. Your statement makes it clear you don't believe the allegations. So, can you explain why a concerned citizen would make a false accusation against Commander Randall?"

"Why someone would fabricate such an accusation against an outstanding officer like Commander Randall is beyond my comprehension. All I can say is that this person, whoever he or she is, must either be mentally disturbed or someone with a personal vendetta against Commander Randall."

Pointing next to a reporter he recognized from a local radio station, he said, "What's your question?"

"WYSS, 99.9 FM News," she said with a nod at Wilson. "Chief, you said you know for a fact the allegations are false. How do you know that?"

"Good question. The person who wrote this letter stated it happened, quote, *last night on July 16th at eight o'clock*, unquote. It just so happens that on July the sixteenth at eight o'clock, Commander Randall and his wife and daughter were at my home for dinner. They arrived at 6:00 p.m. and didn't leave until shortly after 11:00. Consequently, it couldn't possibly have happened."

"A follow-up, if I may?" she asked.

"Go ahead," Mike responded as her fellow reporters clamored to ask their questions.

"Could the letter writer have been confused on the date or the time of day?"

Mike kept his face impassive as he spoke. "The person was adamant about both the date and time. So my answer is an emphatic no."

Turning to the other side of the room, he pointed to a short, heavyset man. "Your question?"

"Beaches News. You described the person who wrote the letter as, quote-unquote, either mentally disturbed or someone with a personal vendetta against Commander Randall. Several months ago, the commander was involved in an incident in which United States Senator Thomas Barclay's daughter was killed and his granddaughter severely injured. It's been rumored that the senator has accused Commander Randall of causing the accident resulting in that tragedy and has encouraged you to terminate his employment. Could you speculate as to whether this accusation that you have determined to be false could in any way be connected to the senator?"

The room grew still as the assembled reporters leaned forward in anticipation of the answer. Mike didn't hesitate. "I have spoken previously to Senator Barclay and expressed my condolences to him for his family's tragic loss, as has Commander Randall. The incident involving the senator's daughter and grandchild was thoroughly investigated not only by the Florida Department of Law Enforcement but also by members of the state attorney's office for the Fourth Judicial Circuit. The clear conclusion drawn by both agencies was that Commander Randall acted lawfully at all times and was in no way responsible for what happened to Senator Barclay's family members. To address your question specifically, there is no evidence nor is there any indication that Senator Barclay had anything at all to do with writing this letter."

"Chief Wilson, I would like to say something," a voice called out.

Hearing the familiar voice, the chief saw Deputy Mayor Gordy Cooper standing in the back of the room. "Go ahead, Mr. Cooper," he said, keeping his voice neutral.

Cooper strolled to the front of the room, stopping to shake hands with a couple of reporters he knew personally. Reaching the front, he nudged the chief aside as he moved behind the podium.

With a big smile, he gripped the sides of the podium as he spoke. "Ladies and gentlemen, I want to thank you all for coming here today. Mayor Adams wanted me to let you know that she had a prior engagement that prevented her from being here with you. She asked me to express to you on her behalf her absolute horror at these allegations against a member of the city's police department. She also wants you to know that the accusations raised will be investigated to the fullest extent. To accomplish that, the mayor has asked me to chair a committee comprised of one council member, which will be me, and will also include an attorney, a high-ranking member of the police department, and two residents of our fine community. This committee will have one goal, to discover the truth. And if the accusations are proven to be true, we will present our findings to the state attorney for consideration of criminal charges against Mr. Randall."

The room erupted with shouted questions as Gordy Cooper stood placidly watching the chaos he had created. Mike Wilson was shocked into silence by Cooper's words.

A reporter shouted a question, "Councilman Cooper, who are the members of the committee besides yourself?"

Gordy smiled as the crowd quieted down. "As I said, I will be chairing the committee. Our city attorney will provide expert legal advice. The police department representative will be the patrol division commander, Jack Hargraves. And our citizen representatives will be Mr. Wayne Westcott and Mr. Louis Dunlop."

The chief stepped back to the podium, crowding Cooper as he glared at him. "To you, Mr. Cooper, and for the media representatives here, let me be clear. Neither you nor the mayor has the authority to appoint members of my staff to any council committee. You mentioned Jack Hargraves being appointed a member of this so-called committee. That's impossible since Commander Hargraves has been relieved of duty pending possible disciplinary action for serious violations of departmental policies. As for your citizen representatives? Mr. Westcott and Mr. Dunlop are directly connected to incidents involving this police department. They are not and cannot be objective by any reasonable definition of that word," he concluded.

During his impassioned response, Cooper stood calmly by, the smile never leaving his face. He said, "Chief, it sounds like the mayor and the city council need to conduct an emergency session to discuss your attempts to thwart the will of the elected representatives of this city. I'll be conferring with the mayor shortly."

Ensuring the cameras were recording every word of the exchange, Gordy said, "Thanks again for coming. You all will receive a notice shortly of the council's next steps to get to the bottom of this." With that parting shot, Gordy Cooper strolled out of the room.

Chief Wilson was blazing with anger at Gordy Cooper and Denise Adams. "That concludes this press conference," he snapped, exiting the room as reporters continued to shout questions at him.

29

Smith stepped off the plane onto the jetway in Jacksonville, the humidity reminding him why he enjoyed living in the desert. Over the years, his profession had taken him all over the country, but he had always returned to Nevada. There was something about the place that appealed to him, more so than just the dry desert air. It wasn't the gambling, although he occasionally enjoyed playing poker in some of the smaller casinos. He guessed it was a general feeling that was pervasive throughout the state. If you were good enough, or lucky enough, you could be a winner. He knew he was a winner.

Dragging a small carry carry-on, he retrieved his suitcase from the baggage carousel and made his way to the car rental counter where he paid cash for a week's rental. Ten minutes later, he was heading south on I-95 for the short trip to the beach. He punched in the speed dial number for Dunlop as he drove.

Dunlop answered, "Chester Jones."

"Mr. Jones, I'm here and heading to Jacksonville Beach," Smith responded.

"I expected you hours ago. What's the deal?"

"The flight was delayed in Atlanta with mechanical problems. Where can we meet?"

"Do you have a map?"

"The car has GPS. Give me an address, and I'll get there," Smith answered, pulling to the side of the road in the breakdown lane to enter the location.

Dunlop said, "Meet me in the parking lot at the Jacksonville Zoo. It's on your way from the airport. I don't have the address, but you can—"

"Enter the destination, I know," Smith interrupted. "I'm doing that now. Do you have the equipment?"

"You mean the—"

"Stop," Smith said. "You know what I require. There's no need to run through the list on this phone."

"Okay, okay. Aren't you being a little paranoid?"

"No, and you *should* be," Smith said with an edge in his voice. "I'll be at the zoo in about fifteen minutes. When can I expect you?"

Dunlop answered, "I'll be there in about forty-five minutes. I've got to pick up the equipment, as you refer to it, and then I'll be on my way."

"I'm in a white Acura with Georgia plates. I'll pick a spot toward the back of the lot and call you with the location."

"Okay," Dunlop said, hanging up.

Ninety minutes later, Lou Dunlop pulled into the zoo parking lot, driving slowly until he reached the back row where he observed Smith's rental car backed into a parking space. As he pulled into a vacant slot directly across the lane, Smith stepped out of the Acura and walked to Dunlop's car, climbing into the passenger seat.

"You said forty-five minutes."

"Give me a break," Dunlop said. "I got hung up in traffic. I'm here now, so can we get down to business?"

"Where's the equipment?"

Dunlop retrieved a black, zippered bag from the back seat and dropped it in Smith's lap. "Everything you asked for is there," he said.

Smith unzipped the bag and visually checked the contents. Reaching inside, he picked up a small, black revolver with brown wooden grips. Keeping his hands in the bag, he gripped the weapon with his right while hitting the cylinder release with his left. The cylinder dropped open, revealing five, twenty-two caliber shells. He dumped the rounds into his palm, carefully examining each one. The hollow point bullets were new, as he had specified. The cylinder spun freely, and the smell of gun oil was strong, an indication the weapon had recently been cleaned.

He saw a large scrape on the barrel. "Did you do this?" he asked Dunlop.

"Yes, I did. You told me you wanted a gun with the serial number obliterated, so I filed it off. Why?"

Smith shook his head. "Don't attempt things you know nothing about. A crime lab can pull that number right back up the way you've done it."

"Do you want me to file on it some more?"

"No, I'll take care of it," Smith replied.

Reloading the gun, he set it aside and picked up a folding, lock-blade knife. He flipped the blade open and tested the edge for sharpness. Satisfied, he said, "Okay, Mr. Dunlop, the equipment is–"

Stunned, Dunlop interrupted, "Wait. How do you know my real name?"

"I told you when we met in Las Vegas that I make it my business to learn everything I can about my clients."

"I know, but, but," Dunlop stuttered, "how did you find out?"

Smith shrugged noncommittally.

"Wait. MacKay must have told you, didn't he?"

Smith didn't answer.

"Dammit, I told him not to use my real name."

"Mr. Dunlop, in every case, I learn the true identity of my client to ensure I'm not being set up by the cops. I knew who you were within a day of our meeting in Las Vegas. And by the next day, I knew the identity of your boss."

"You did?"

"U. S. Senator Thomas Barclay, senior senator from Florida. Being talked about as a potential candidate for president."

Dunlop leaned forward, putting his head in his hands, "Oh, man, this is not good."

"Mr. Dunlop, calm down. The fact I know your real name and who you work for is information that will remain confidential. Let's move on."

Dunlop sat back after a few seconds and wiped his brow. "You hit me cold with that. So you're still sure my boss won't get dragged into this, right?"

"I've explained my position before. I see no reason to go over it again," Smith said, cocking an eyebrow at Dunlop. "As I was saying, the tools are satisfactory, with the exception of the serial number, which I'll handle. However, you were supposed to provide me with a personal item belonging to the police officer. There's nothing in the bag."

Dunlop removed a clear plastic baggie from his jacket pocket and passed it to Smith. The baggie contained an object roughly the size of a silver dollar.

Smith examined the item without removing it. "You're telling me this will be immediately recognizable as belonging to the officer?"

"Absolutely, according to my source."

Smith slipped it into the black bag without further comment. Placing the bag on the floor between his feet, he said, "Let's discuss timing. How soon?"

"As I told you in Vegas, the sooner the better."

Smith watched a man and woman and three teenage kids as they exited the zoo and walked to a van one aisle over. "Do you have her schedule?"

"You mean like a work schedule?" Dunlop asked.

"Work schedule. Play schedule. Dating schedule. I need to know everything about her. When she's at home. When she goes to work or shopping or out to dinner. That sort of thing. You do realize that I can't move forward until I have a clear pattern of her movements, don't you?"

"I'm not sure how I could get most of that stuff. I know she goes to city hall most every day, and I understand she plays tennis with some woman several days of the week. Beyond that, I wouldn't know when she goes to the store or out to dinner and other places unless I started following her around. I have a lot of skills, but tailing someone like in the movies isn't one of them. Isn't that part of what I'm paying you to do?"

Smith considered what Dunlop had said, then offered a rare smile. "You're right. Give me everything you have. I'll take care of the rest."

"I'll get it to you by this evening," Dunlop said. "Where are you staying?"

"I'll find a place and call when I'm checked in."

"Okay," Dunlop said, pulling a piece of paper from his jacket pocket and handing it to Smith. "This is her address here. There are houses on both sides, but the lots are wide, so there's plenty of privacy."

Slipping the paper into his pocket, Smith opened the door and started to get out. Looking over his shoulder, he said, "You take care of the schedule, and I'll take care of the problem." Starting to walk away, he stopped and leaned back down. "You do remember the payment arrangements."

"Of course. You make the problem go away. Actually, both problems, and I pay you the rest of your fee."

"Just checking."

O ver the next three days, Smith developed his plan as he carefully tracked the movements of Mayor Denise Adams. Each morning promptly at six, she drove to the beach in her red Lexus convertible and went for a two mile run at a brisk pace. Afterward, she stopped at a coffee shop and had a small glass of orange juice followed by a cup of coffee and a cigarette. She always sat alone at an outdoor table. Twice, people who obviously knew her stopped by to chat briefly.

Driving back home, she would go inside, coming back out promptly at nine, showered and dressed each day in slacks and a silk blouse. She tossed a gym bag into the trunk before lowering the top on her convertible. She then drove directly to the Jacksonville Beach city hall, where Smith assumed she had an office used to conduct business as the city's mayor.

At ten, she exited city hall and drove to the Ponte Vedra Inn & Club, where she played two sets of tennis with a woman similar to her in age and conditioning. At one o'clock, the two women sat at a table on the shaded patio of the restaurant eating lunch and sipping white wine. By three-thirty each day, she was back at home, where she stayed until the next morning when the routine repeated itself.

Smith was curious that her daily schedule showed no evidence of a social life. At first, he thought she might be in a relationship with her tennis partner, but he quickly dismissed that theory since they were never together except for the daily match and lunch.

Nearing seven o'clock, Smith returned to his hotel room after dinner at a nearby restaurant. He sat at the tiny desk and added the day's activities to the detailed notes he had already taken on the mayor's movements. As he reviewed the information, his cell phone rang. It was Dunlop, demanding to know what he was doing and why it was taking so long.

Smith responded in an icy tone, "I *told* you I had to establish a pattern of movement before I could finalize my plan. Which part of that have you forgotten?"

Dunlop sighed into the phone. "I know. It's just that I'm getting nervous she's going to do something stupid if this doesn't get resolved quickly."

"I'll do the job you hired me to do, but it'll be done my way and on my timeframe. Stay out of it, and you'll be satisfied with the results," he said, hanging up.

Smith went back to his notes and began writing out a strategy. He put together a timeline and a series of actions that would all but ensure he could do the job successfully without detection. An hour later, after numerous changes, he sat back and read through the plan. Satisfied there were no glitches, he committed the steps to memory, then tore the sheets of paper into small pieces and flushed them down the toilet. He climbed into bed, set the alarm for 9:30 p.m., turned on his side, and quickly fell asleep.

As Smith drifted off to sleep, Denise Adams gaveled the closed-door session of the Jacksonville Beach City Council to order. All seven members of the council were present along with the city attorney.

The mayor began the shade meeting by explaining to the assembled members her reason for wanting to create a committee to investigate the allegations raised in the anonymous complaint against Clay Randall.

Before she could finish, Councilman Peter Daniels interrupted her. "Mayor, everyone here has heard the comments from the police department news conference. Surely you don't expect this council to approve representatives for this committee of yours that have previously expressed animosity toward Commander Randall, do you? And before you answer, I have the same question about Commander Jack Hargraves. According to Chief Wilson, Hargraves has been relieved of duty for improper conduct and may face serious disciplinary sanctions because of that."

Denise waited until Daniels finished before she spoke. "I don't intend to discuss specific members of the committee since I have sole authority to appoint each one. Suffice it to say I have complete faith that each member will exercise good judgment and will make a recommendation that will be in the best interests of this city."

Daniels said to the city attorney, "I'm not a lawyer, but I cannot find any legal justification that gives the mayor unilateral authority to appoint a committee such as this."

Glancing at the mayor, the city attorney said, "You're partially correct, Councilman Daniels. Under normal circumstances, the mayor does not have that authority. However, in an emergency, as determined by a majority vote of the full council, that authority could be vested in the office of the mayor."

Denise frowned at the city attorney. "Are you certain about that?"

"I am absolutely certain, Mayor," he responded.

"Well, then," Daniels said. "It seems you need at least four votes to move forward with this railroad job against Commander Randall."

"I'll thank you to keep your comments at a respectful level, Mr. Daniels," she angrily replied.

Daniels shrugged. "I'm sorry you take offense to my comments, Mayor, but I stand by them. I wonder what my fellow council members think about this committee idea," he said, turning to the other members. With the exception of Gordy Cooper, each of them expressed unanimous disagreement with the idea of the committee.

Clearly disgusted, the mayor addressed the city attorney. "Okay, let's move on. As I understand it, the city council has no authority to terminate Commander Randall from the police department. Is that right?"

"That's correct," the city attorney responded. "The charter is specific in that regard."

"I guess it means in order to ensure that our citizens are protected from this, this *individual*," she spat, "Chief Wilson has to be the one to terminate him. And if he refuses, our only option is to get rid of the chief and hire someone who will do what we direct."

"That's the bottom line, Mayor," the attorney responded. "But I–"

"Hold on," Councilman Daniels interrupted. "Once again, with all due respect to your position, Mayor, I don't think this is a good idea at all. In fact, it reeks of petty politics. You're talking about destroying the careers and reputations of two honorable men over allegations that have already been proven to be false. In my opinion, you're overstepping your authority, and I for one am not going to stand back and watch it happen."

Gordy Cooper leaned forward, pointing his finger at Daniels. "Counselor, you're full of crap," he said sternly. "Everybody here besides you knows what needs to be done. Randall is a cancer on this city. He's a hothead and needs to go. And Mike Wilson is right there with him. In fact, it wouldn't surprise me one bit if it comes out that Wilson is as dirty as Randall. Can you just see the headlines if that gets out?"

Daniels stood, his face red. "Gordy, you have no right to criticize anyone. As we all know, the previous mayor terminated you as the police chief for highly unprofessional conduct of your own. You have no credibility to challenge the integrity of anyone, much less Mike Wilson and Clay Randall!"

Cooper stood up, his face redder than Daniels's, shouting, "Screw you, Daniels! I was fired for no good reason! All so Wilson could get my job! You hear me?"

The mayor banged her gavel repeatedly on the table, yelling herself, "Gentlemen, please! Let's have order here!"

Both men slowly sat down, though they continued to glare at each other across the dais.

Her voice shaking, the mayor said, "I realize this is a very emotional issue, but we can't have these outbursts. Please control yourselves."

Addressing the other four council members and deliberately ignoring both Cooper and the mayor, Daniels said, "I apologize to you for allowing my emotions to get out of control."

Denise Adams nodded stiffly, missing the fact that he did not include her in his apology. Catching Cooper's eye, she raised an eyebrow in an attempt to elicit an apology from him. However, the deputy mayor stayed silent, continuing to shoot hostile looks at Daniels.

When it became clear that Cooper wasn't going to offer an apology, the mayor said, "I would like to hear from any other council member who hasn't expressed an opinion about what we should do."

The longest-serving member of the council, a man with over twenty years in office, said in a soft voice, "I've known Clayton Randall since he was a teenager, and I have to say I've never seen or heard even a hint of any activity such as what this anonymous person claims to have seen. His mama raised him right, and I just don't believe he would do something like that. I say we do nothing."

The councilman continued. "As for you, Gordon, I've been around this beach long enough to know how you operate. I've seen you do some things that I thought slipped very close to the edge of being unethical if not downright illegal. I respect the vote of our citizens that put you in office, but I can't say as I have a lot of respect for you personally. I believe we should put our trust in Chief Wilson to do the right thing by his department."

As Gordy Cooper glowered at the councilman's words, the other three members expressed their agreement with the recommendation.

Peter Daniels stood up. "Five council members don't support your position, Mayor. Or yours, Mr. Cooper," he said. "There will be no committee, and we have nothing further to discuss here tonight."

Chairs scraped back as everyone but Denise Adams and Gordy Cooper stood and exited the room.

31

I t was almost nine o'clock by the time Clay and Dana finished their usual nighttime chores and got their daughter tucked into bed. As they settled into their chairs in the family room for some mindless television, the phone rang. "You wanta get that?" Clay asked.

She laughed, "Why? You know it's for you. Nobody calls me this late at night."

Grumbling under his breath, he saw the name on Caller ID. "Aw, crap."

"Who is it?"

"Denise Adams. What could she possibly want?"

"I guess the only way you're going to know is if you answer it, my love," she said teasingly.

"I guess," he said with a huge sigh, picking up the receiver and answering.

"Clay?" the mayor said.

Startled that she called him by name after her insistence on the use of formal titles, he said, "Yes, Mayor. What can I do for you?"

"I was wondering if you could come to my house. I need to talk to you."

Caught off guard by the request, he said, "Uh, Mayor, it's almost nine o'clock, and Dana and I were planning to head to bed in just a few minutes."

"I understand, and I apologize for such a late call, but it's important that I talk to you tonight."

"Can you tell me what this is about?"

"I'd rather not discuss it over the phone. Just know that I wouldn't bother you if it weren't really important."

"Okay, I can be there in fifteen or twenty minutes. Is that good?"

"That's perfect. Thank you, Clay. I appreciate it."

"No problem," he said. "See you shortly."

He sat with the phone in his hand trying to decipher the mayor's motive. He had never been in her home before, and the lateness of the hour seemed unusually strange.

"Clay," Dana said. When he didn't answer, she took the phone out of his hand and put it on the table. Kneeling beside his chair, she said, "What was that all about?"

He shrugged. "I have no idea. First off, she called me Clay rather than Commander. As you know, she went off on me when I called her Denise recently. She's been a stickler for formal titles ever since she became mayor. She sounded like she's had a few drinks, also."

"Really? In all the years I've known her, I've never seen her drunk. But maybe you have since you know her so much better than me," she said with a sly wink.

"That was like twenty years ago, and, besides, I don't remember any woman before you," he said, grinning.

Clay had dated Denise Adams while both attended the University of North Florida. They even talked about marriage after graduation. However, it always felt to Clay as if something was missing in the relationship. Although he couldn't pinpoint what it was, that missing something made him reluctant to make a lifetime commitment to Denise.

Then, after a violent incident in which he came to the assistance of a police officer fighting a huge assailant, he realized his true calling. Dropping out of college, he joined the Jacksonville Beach Police Department and quickly began making a name for himself as a smart, dedicated cop.

One day, while conducting a follow-up investigation of a residential burglary, he met the victim, Dana Cappella, a dark-haired, green-eyed beauty, and his life changed forever. The relationship with Denise Adams soon ended, and, within a year, Clay and Dana married.

"Well, I guess I'd better go see what she wants," Clay said, getting to his feet.

Dana stood, wrapping her arms around him tightly. "Just be careful. You've seen how vindictive she can be. Don't let her trick you into doing or saying anything that will give her ammunition to use against you or Mike."

"I know. I'll listen to what she has to say, but I won't make a commitment on anything. Believe me, I don't trust her at all."

"Okay," Dana said, kissing him softly. "I love you, Clay."

"I love you, too, babe," he said, stroking her hair gently. "Wait up for me. I'll be back shortly."

Clay pulled into the mayor's driveway, killing the engine. For several moments, he sat behind the wheel mentally preparing for what he expected to be an unpleasant meeting. Getting out, he walked up on the porch and was reaching for the doorbell when Denise opened the door.

"Hi, Clay. Please come in."

As he stepped inside, Clay noticed her bloodshot eyes and flushed face. "Mayor, you don't look well. Are you okay?" he asked.

"I'm fine. Can I get you anything? You always liked Bud Light, as I recall. Is that still your drink of choice?"

"No . . . yes, I still drink Bud, but no, I don't want anything. Thanks," he said.

"Well, just so you know, I'm having a glass of wine myself," she said, sitting on the couch and taking a sip of red wine.

Clay sat across from her in a comfortable wingback chair. He debated asking her what she wanted but decided to let her initiate the conversation.

Denise swallowed the rest of her drink and sat twirling the empty glass by the stem, seemingly ill at ease.

As the silence lengthened, Clay finally spoke. "What did you want to talk to me about?"

Continuing to spin the glass, she said, "I've been doing a lot of thinking lately."

When she didn't continue, Clay asked, "About what?"

"About this whole business with you and the senator's daughter getting killed. I've been thinking that I was a little too quick to criticize you. To . . . go along with blaming you for her death."

Surprised, Clay said, "What made you change your mind?"

"Oh, I don't know. Just thinking," she said, avoiding his gaze.

Clay could tell she wasn't being honest with him, but, knowing how volatile she had been recently, he didn't want to antagonize her unnecessarily. He simply responded, "Well, thank you. I appreciate that, Mayor."

"Clay, there's no need for formality. We're not working. Denise is fine."

"Okay. Denise."

She smiled. "Are you sure I can't get you anything to drink?" she asked, holding up her glass.

"Thanks, but I'll pass. Now that I've gotten older, I find a late night drink screws up my sleep."

She laughed, "I remember a time when several drinks late at night didn't bother you at all."

Clay wondered where she was going with this. "I did a lot of things years ago that I don't do anymore. I guess with age comes a certain amount of maturity."

"I guess," she said, lapsing into silence.

As the quiet stretched out, Clay decided he had to take control of the conversation. "Denise, was there something else you wanted to discuss?"

Sighing, she said, "Hold that thought while I refill my glass."

When she went into the kitchen, Clay debated whether he should leave. It was clear something was bothering her, but he didn't care enough to try to pull it out of her. He just wanted to get out of there without having to endure another meltdown. In addition, the veiled reference to their long-ago relationship bothered and confused him as he tried to decipher her meaning.

While those thoughts rolled around in his head, Denise came back in, wine glass in hand. Sitting on the couch again, she took a sip and set the glass carefully on the end table.

"Okay, now where were we?"

Hiding his growing frustration, Clay said, "I asked you what else you wanted to discuss."

"Oh, right," she said. "I'm not sure exactly how to say this, but here goes. Tomm–, *Thomas* Barclay and I, which you alluded to recently, have had a relationship for a while. As you're aware, he was devastated by what happened to his daughter and granddaughter, and he's not gotten over it. He's totally convinced that you are directly responsible."

"I know. He's made that very clear to me and to anyone who'll listen."

"Right. So he asked me to do whatever I could to get you fired, to make you pay for the pain he believes you caused him and his family. And, to my deep regret, I agreed."

"But why, Denise?" Clay asked. "What have I done to you that would justify going along with Barclay and trying to destroy my career and my reputation?"

Shaking her head, she said, "Nothing. You've done absolutely nothing. And don't for a second think you leaving me all those years ago for Dana had anything to do with it. As I said to you that day in my office when we both got out of control, I don't want to live the rest of my life in this little town. I dreamed of going to Washington and becoming a member of Congress myself, and maybe even higher. You actually did me a big favor. Because if I had stayed, we probably would have gotten married, and I would have grown to resent you for keeping me here.

"I realize it sounds irrational to blame you for my life decisions, but that's the way I would have felt. So you see, it was a good thing for both of us. You found a woman you love and who loves you. And Dana isn't interested in leaving here. Consequently, by you breaking up with me, you gave me the freedom I needed to pursue my goals."

"Okay, my question still stands. Why did you do it?"

Nervously twisting a bracelet on her wrist, she seemed to struggle with what to say. Taking another swallow of wine, she said, "He and I were going to be married. At least he *told* me he wanted to marry me. Then, when he was elected president, I would be the First Lady. I would be at the center of power in this country. It was an intoxicating thought. But that wasn't my ultimate goal. I had a bigger dream. Of being the first woman president. And I thought Thomas Barclay was the man to help me get there."

Her confession fascinated Clay. In the years they dated, he knew she was ambitious. But this? He had no idea just how driven she was. "I understand how you could see Barclay as a powerful ally who could help you. What I don't understand is why you're telling me this now. And why you seem to be saying that it's all changed."

"Clay, I'm telling you because I'm ashamed of myself. Of the way I've acted toward you and Chief Wilson. I've always believed an elected official should have uncompromising integrity. That there really are honest politicians who make decisions they actually believe are in the best interests of their constituents and not simply to be reelected or to gain power, money, or prestige. I've tried to comport myself that way since I've been in office. Until now, anyway.

"That's what has been so devastating to me. Treating you and Chief Wilson the way I have is just dirty politics." Seeing the surprise on Clay's face, she continued, "Yes, you called me an unethical politician that day in my office. At the time, I hated you for it. However, I've come to realize that the shoe fits, so to speak. As for circumstances changing, you're right. Thomas dumped me."

"Why?" Clay asked.

"Because I became too insistent on making our relationship public and eventually getting married. Ideally, before he made his formal run for president. Only too late did I realize that he viewed marrying me as a negative to his campaign rather than a positive. It has also become painfully clear that he used me only to satisfy his, shall we say, needs, if you know what I mean. I can see now that he never had any intention of marrying me."

"Listen to me, Denise. You're very talented. You have all the brains and drive it takes to succeed. You don't need Barclay to get you where you want to go."

With a sad smile, she replied, "Thanks for the kind words, Clay. Considering how I've treated you, that makes me feel even more ashamed if that's possible. And I hope you will accept my sincere apology for my actions."

"Of course I accept your apology, and don't feel ashamed. We're all human, and we all make mistakes. God knows I've made my share," Clay said.

Getting to her feet, she extended her hand. Clay stood, covering her hand with both of his.

"Thanks again for coming by so late and for accepting my belated apology," she said. "I intend to meet with Chief Wilson tomorrow and try to make things right with him. I also owe apologies to the city attorney and the other members of the city council, so I'm going to be busy over the next few days."

"I've always heard that the things we say in anger are almost always words we later wish we could take back. I was wrong to attack you the way I did that day, and I apologize to you for that. While I can't take the words back, I want you to know that I'm proud and honored to serve with you."

Tears rolled down her cheeks. "Thank you, Clay. You're a good man. I mean that. And Dana is a lucky woman to have you."

Reddening, he said, "Dana would probably argue with you about that sometimes, but thank you for saying it. And if I can help you in any way, please let me know."

Clay went to the door and was about to open it when Denise touched him lightly on the arm. "Do you think Dana would mind if I gave you a hug? One friend to another?"

He smiled. "She wouldn't mind. One friend to another." Taking Denise in his arms, he hugged her, kissed her lightly on the cheek, and went out the door, heading home to the woman he loved.

Smith awoke two minutes before the alarm was set to go off. He quickly dressed in the extra suit he had brought with him, dark blue with a white dress shirt and a navy and white striped tie. Donning the suit jacket, he slipped the small revolver Dunlop had provided into his pants pocket. The knife went into an outside coat pocket.

Examining himself in the bathroom mirror, Smith saw no bulges indicating the two weapons. He checked his watch. It was 9:45. Time to go. He carefully remade the bed, fluffing the pillows and smoothing the top spread to give the appearance it had not been disturbed. Smith scanned the room to ensure he had left nothing that could identify him. After the job, he would check into another hotel nearer the airport. Satisfied, he left the room and headed to the parking lot.

Thirty minutes later, as Clay was telling Dana what happened in his meeting with Denise, Smith drove past the mayor's house. He noted lights on in the living room. Parking down the street from her residence, he locked the doors and walked quickly back. There was no moon, and streetlights provided little visibility to anyone who might be peering out a window as he walked past.

Reaching the house, he turned up the walkway without hesitation, mounted the steps, and rang the doorbell. Soft light shined through the leaded glass insert in the front door, allowing him to see someone approaching. The porch light came on, and a second later, Denise Adams opened the door.

Standing in the entryway, she observed the man's unusual choice of clothing for the beach and for so late at night. "Can I help you?" she asked.

Smith reached into the breast pocket of his jacket and retrieved a black leather case. Flipping it open to reveal a gold badge and identification card, he said, "Yes, ma'am. I'm Special Agent Jeremiah Smith, Federal Bureau of Investigation. Are you Mayor Denise Adams?"

Denise stood without speaking, her left hand on the door handle as her eyes shifted between the badge and Smith's face. "May I examine your identification?" she asked.

"Yes, ma'am," Smith said, extending the case toward her.

Denise took the identification and studied it closely, reading the wording on the badge and the card itself. Squinting at the tiny picture, she held it up and tried to compare it to the man standing at her door. "I can't tell if this is you. Do you mind if I take this over to my reading lamp so I can see it better?"

Smith said, "No, ma'am, not at all. I apologize for coming so late in the evening, but if you could allow me a few minutes, I can explain everything."

With a piercing look at Smith, she said, "Hang on," and closed the door. Smith heard the lock engage and saw her distorted figure through the etched-glass sidelight as she moved away from the door. He figured she would find the badge and identification to be genuine. Two thousand dollars had bought facsimiles that would fool even a real FBI agent.

When she didn't return right away, he grew concerned. It would be a problem if she called the local FBI office for verification of the identity of the man standing at her door. A quick check of the agent's name on the ID and the ruse would fall apart.

As the seconds passed without her returning, Smith began thinking he would have to abandon the plan and go to his backup. Just as his hand closed around the knife, she came back, unlocking the door and opening it.

Noticing the empty driveway, she hesitated. "Where's your car? Did you walk here?"

Laughing softly, he said, "No, ma'am. The Bureau has had its share of budget cuts, but they haven't reduced us to walking. Not yet anyway." Glancing toward the street, he said, "To be truthful, I had trouble spotting your house number, so I parked my car down the street and walked along checking each house until I saw the numbers over your door."

The intense inspection Denise gave Smith made him wonder whether she could read his mind. Keeping his face expressionless, he waited.

"I apologize for making you wait, Agent Smith." Handing him the leather case, she continued, "I also had a phone call that I had to take. Please come in."

Pocketing the ID, Smith smiled as he stepped past her into the house. "That's absolutely not a problem, Mayor Adams. Once again, I apologize for coming so late, but I was given this assignment two hours ago and was told it was a high priority."

Following her into the house, Smith quickly scanned the living room and what little he could see of a library. Across the room, he noted an arched doorway leading into the kitchen. To the left of the front door, stairs led to the second floor. Although there was no indication of anyone else present in the house, he nevertheless assumed nothing.

Denise sat down in the wing chair recently vacated by Clay, a glass of wine on the end table beside her. Smith sat on the couch across from her. From his jacket, he retrieved a pen and a small, leather-bound notebook.

She said, "It seems highly unusual that an agent with the FBI would be given a high priority assignment to speak to the Jacksonville Beach mayor at this late hour. I can't imagine what information I would have that would be of interest to the federal government, and particularly the FBI," she said, setting the glass down as she lit a cigarette and blew smoke toward the ceiling.

The smell of her cigarette wafted across to him, tempting Smith to ask if she minded if he joined her. He quickly dismissed the idea, adhering to his ironclad rule about leaving no evidence at a scene that police could link to him.

Instead, he smiled as if in agreement with her comment about the visit. "Yes, ma'am, I agree it's somewhat unusual. However, I don't question my assignments. I'm sure you can understand that, considering the fact you also work in the public sector."

"Yes, I guess I do. So, what can I do for you, Agent Smith?"

"Mayor, first, I need to know if you're alone here."

Tensing, she asked, "What possible business is it of the FBI whether I'm alone?"

"I apologize for asking such a personal question," he said. "The information I'm about to give you is classified, and it has been authorized for release to you only. That's why I asked about anyone else being here."

Her shoulders visibly relaxed. "Okay," she laughed. "It's just that this whole thing is a little disconcerting, if you know what I mean."

"I understand completely, and I hope we can get this all cleared up in a few minutes."

"That's fine."

Appearing to consult his notepad, Smith said, "Mayor, WFO–," he stopped, seeing the confused look. "I'm sorry. The Washington Field Office of the FBI received an anonymous call a few hours ago from someone claiming to be you."

"Me? That's impossible."

"Ma'am, I've read the transcript of the call myself. The woman clearly stated her name was Denise Adams and that she was the mayor of Jacksonville Beach in Florida."

"I don't understand. I haven't made any call to the FBI. Here or to your Washington office. What did this person say?" she asked, reaching for the wine glass and taking a drink.

Smith responded, "You see, that's the part that's confusing. As I said, the person referred to herself as Mayor Denise Adams. Then she went on to make a threat against a high-ranking official in the government."

"A threat?!" she exclaimed. "I would never do such a thing, and I'm offended that someone would use my name like this!"

Holding his hands up in a placating manner, Smith said, "Please, Mayor Adams. I'm not accusing you. The call was made from an unlisted number that we are in the process of obtaining right now. I'm reporting this to you to elicit your help in identifying the actual person who made the call."

Somewhat mollified, Denise asked, "Did this person say who the high-ranking official was?"

Smith shook his head. "No, not by name. However, she said the official was a United States Senator who was considering a run for president. Would you have any idea who that might be?"

Denise's eyes grew wide, and she shook her head vigorously. "No, I don't. I mean, I know that Senator Thomas Barclay has been talking about running, but, as far as someone making threats against him, I can't imagine."

Smith said sternly, "Are you certain you don't know anything about this? We've checked your background and learned that you know Senator Barclay very well."

Denise was indignant, spilling a few drops of wine from her glass as she leaned forward. "Yes, I know Senator Barclay. He's been my political mentor since I got into politics. You said you weren't accusing me, but your words and your tone certainly sound like it to me."

"Mayor, I'm just here gathering information that hopefully will lead to the identity of the person who made a threat against a member of Congress."

Figuring the charade had gone on long enough, he suddenly coughed and cleared his throat. "I apologize, but I've been having a bout of allergies. Could I trouble you for some water?"

"Sure," she said, getting up and heading toward the kitchen. Pausing, she asked, "Would you like a glass of wine instead?"

Smith smiled, "No, thank you. Water will have to do until I'm off the clock."

"Suit yourself," she said as she disappeared into the kitchen.

Smith pulled the small pistol from his pocket and stepped noiselessly to the doorway. Denise reached into the cabinet to retrieve a glass as he slipped up behind her, raising the gun as he approached.

Sensing a presence, Denise turned suddenly, a glass tumbler in her left hand. Her eyes flared as she saw the gun aimed at her chest. She reacted instantly, slamming the tumbler into the gun. The glass shattered, scattering shards across the tiled kitchen floor. Smith fired at the same instant, but Denise's swift move caused the round to deflect, punching a hole in the refrigerator door.

Still holding the jagged base of the broken tumbler, Denise savagely struck at the gun again, causing Smith to drop the weapon. Screaming, she bolted for the living room.

"You bitch!" Smith exclaimed, leaping after her as he drew the knife from his pocket, popping open the blade with a practiced flick of his wrist. As Denise raced toward the front door, she grabbed the end table by the sofa and overturned it behind her. Smith tripped over the table and went sprawling across the floor. Leaping to his feet as pain ripped through his lower leg, he caught Denise just as she reached for the door handle, driving the four-inch blade deep into her back.

She fell, her head slamming against the hard tile floor, temporarily stunning her. Before she could recover, he limped to the kitchen and retrieved the gun where it had slid under the counter. Coming back, he saw her feebly reaching a hand behind her back attempting to reach the knife.

Smith jammed the gun against her right temple and squeezed the trigger twice in rapid succession, sending two hollow point bullets into her brain. Kneeling beside her, gun at the ready, he watched her life drain away as he cursed in a low voice. She had surprised him in the kitchen, something that never would have happened a few years before. Pulling up his pant leg, he saw a large scrape on his shin from tripping over the end table. "I'm getting too old for this shit," he muttered.

Ignoring the pain, he went to the window and eased the curtain aside. The street was dark. A light glowed from a second floor window in the house directly across the street. Seeing no movement after a couple of minutes, he dropped the curtain and moved back to Denise's body. The broken base of the tumbler lay on the floor inches from her left hand.

Picking up the piece of glass, he felt a burning sensation on the back of his right hand. Shaken at seeing a jagged, one-inch cut, he drew in a sharp breath as drops of his blood hit the floor next to the body. Pressing his left hand over the cut, he hurried back to the kitchen. He dropped the broken glass into the sink as he turned on the faucet, thrusting both hands under the flow. The water hitting the open wound stung, but he barely noticed it as his mind raced. He would need to find and clean up every spot of his blood.

He would have to move quickly. The longer he stayed, the greater the chances someone might call or come by in spite of the late hour. He wasn't sure how often someone from the police department contacted her about some serious event that had just occurred, but he had to assume it happened occasionally. He didn't want this to be one of those times, at least before he could clean and set up the crime scene and get the hell far away.

Checking the cut closely, Smith saw it was shallow. He figured a couple of butterfly bandages would suffice. He dried his hands with paper towels and pulled a latex glove from his coat pocket. Slipping one on the left hand, he wrapped the towels around the cut. He hurried through the living room and up the stairs, ignoring the body as he passed. In the master bath, he went immediately to the medicine cabinet, where he found a roll of gauze and paper tape. He bandaged the cut and then slipped the other latex glove over the injured hand. Shoving the extra wrapping and tape into his pocket, he hurried downstairs to the kitchen.

Smith rummaged through a cleaning supply closet until he found a bottle of bleach. Taking the roll of paper towels and a plastic garbage bag, he checked the kitchen floor, finding several blood drops on the tiles where they were standing when the woman cut him. He poured bleach directly on the blood to obliterate his DNA, then carefully wiped up all traces and stuffed the paper towels into the garbage bag. Next, he thoroughly bleached the glass base. Then he deliberately smashed it onto the tile floor where it shattered into several pieces, joining other fragments of the tumbler scattered around the kitchen floor.

Stepping closer, he peered at the small hole in the refrigerator door to the right of the pull handle. He opened the door and saw the bullet had not penetrated into the interior. Smith debated digging out the bullet before deciding the metal door would have damaged the small projectile enough to make a match with the gun all but impossible. The same would hold true for the two rounds he fired into the mayor's head.

Checking carefully throughout the rest of the kitchen, he found no additional blood drops. Getting down on his hands and knees, he crawled slowly toward the front door, his eyes inches from the floor as he searched for the smallest speck of his blood. Finding none until he reached the body, he repeated the cleanup process, being careful not to smear any of the mayor's blood. He knew if the cops realized an attempt had been made to clean up the scene, they would search even harder for trace evidence left behind.

After removing three small drops where he had stood at the window, he moved back to the body. Grasping the knife, he tried to pull it out of

Denise's back, but it wouldn't budge. *Damn knife must be wedged between her ribs,* he thought.

As he pulled harder, her upper body began to lift from the floor. Easing off, her body settled back to the floor with an audible sigh as the lungs compressed. Smith repositioned himself, straddling her and placing his left hand on her back, curling his fingers into a fist for better leverage. Ignoring the blood coating his glove, he grasped the handle again, pushing down with his fist while he heaved upward. This time, the knife came free with a faint, sucking sound. Grabbing a wad of paper towels, Smith wiped the blade and handle free of blood, closed the knife, and dropped it into the garbage bag along with the gloves and bloody paper towels. Stepping away, he checked to ensure the soles of his shoes had not left a pattern in the blood.

Smith pulled on a clean pair of latex gloves and retraced his path upstairs. Five minutes later, the bathroom counter and sink carefully wiped clean, he came back down. Taking the plastic bag from his pocket containing the object Dunlop had given him, he scanned the room, searching for the best spot to place the incriminating item. It needed to be positioned in such a way that it gave the impression it landed there in the midst of a struggle, yet be sufficiently hidden that investigators would assume Randall had missed seeing it after killing the mayor.

Choosing the wing chair where the mayor had sat, he opened the bag and upended it, allowing the object to drop to the floor. It struck the tile and rolled across the living room, coming to rest against the baseboard. Frowning, Smith went over and carefully picked it up, holding it by the edges. *Should have done this to start with,* he thought, placing the object behind one of the wide claw feet of the chair. In that position, the cops should easily see it.

Satisfied, he stripped off the second pair of gloves and dropped them into the garbage bag. He checked the living room and kitchen one more time to reassure himself there was nothing left that would enable cops to identify him. With only a brief look at the body of Denise Adams, Smith went through the kitchen and slipped out the back door.

He walked at a leisurely pace down the street to his car, where he placed the bag in the trunk and climbed behind the wheel. Taking a moment to light a cigarette, Smith took several drags before putting the car in gear and driving away.

33

The mayor's assistant didn't think it strange when Denise Adams failed to show up at city hall the next morning. The mayor had told her the day before that she had no appointments scheduled and probably would not stop by the office. However, when she didn't make the ten o'clock tennis match, her regular partner called city hall, assuming she was still in her office.

Curious when told the mayor had not planned to come in, she called Denise's home and cell phones, getting voicemails on both. The lady grew concerned, being aware of much of the drama surrounding Denise's relationship with Thomas Barclay. She quickly changed out of her tennis clothes and drove to Denise's residence to check on her.

Pulling into the driveway, she stared at the house. Everything appeared normal. With the garage doors closed, she couldn't tell if Denise had gone somewhere and just forgotten about their match. She went to the door and rang the bell. After getting no response, she tried a second time, again without success.

She called the home number then and almost immediately heard muffled ringing inside the house. After several rings, Denise's recording came on telling the caller to leave a message. Hanging up, she tried the cell phone for the second time. To her surprise and growing unease, she heard the ring tone faintly begin playing one of Denise's favorite songs, once again from inside the house.

Standing at the front door, she debated calling the police to come check the house. She could tell them about her concern for the mayor's welfare while not mentioning Denise's recent unhappiness about her relationship with Senator Barclay. But she knew Denise would be livid with her if she did and officers arrived only to discover she was in the shower.

For years afterward, the woman wondered what made her reach out and try the door that day. Maybe she sensed something terrible had happened. The house seemed so quiet, as she described it later to Sergeant Joey Crutchfield. Too quiet.

She grasped the decorative handle and pressed down, and the door swung open several inches. She paused, still gripping the door handle as she debated what to do. Should she go in? Should she call the police now? After all, people stopped leaving their doors unlocked long ago.

She decided she was being silly. Leaning close to the opening, she called out for Denise in a loud voice. As she drew a breath to call again, she got a whiff of something odd coming from inside. A sickly smell that caused her to step back involuntarily, letting go of the door handle. A breeze ruffled her hair as it slowly pushed against the door, swinging it open.

She screamed.

An hour later, neighbors stood in small groups talking quietly as they watched police officers cordon off the edges of the property with barricade tape. Television crews jammed the street as they filmed the house, the police cars, the knot of uniformed officers and plainclothes detectives in the front yard; in short, anything that might attract viewers to the six o'clock news.

Neighbors were interviewed by TV reporters. Each one was asked how well they knew Denise Adams and was she a good mayor, and, most important, how did the tragedy make them feel.

Clay Randall and Joey Crutchfield stood on the porch in quiet discussion as Mike Wilson approached.

"Morning, Chief," Joey said. "Helluva way to start the day, huh?"

"Isn't it?" the chief said with a huge frown as he saw the TV cameras pointing their way.

"Let's go somewhere the cameras can't reach us. How about inside?" he asked, reaching for the door.

"Not here, Chief," Clay said quickly, putting a hand on the chief's arm. "She's right inside the door. We need to go around back and come through the kitchen."

"Okay, lead the way," the chief said. As they approached the back door, Mike spoke to an officer standing at the foot of the steps, clipboard in hand. "Are we clear to go in?"

"Yes, sir. I'll make a note for the crime scene log that you and the commander and sergeant are entering the crime scene."

"Good," he responded, patting the officer on the shoulder as he stepped into a short hallway leading to the kitchen. Stopping at the doorway to the kitchen, the chief could see detectives and technicians going through the painstaking process of the crime scene investigation. An evidence technician was taking pictures of broken glass on the kitchen floor. Mike noticed a marker taped beside what appeared to be a bullet hole in the refrigerator door. Without going into the kitchen, he craned his neck forward, seeing the mayor's body sprawled face down on the living room floor, blood soaking the back of her blouse.

Turning around, he asked Clay, "Okay, what's the story?"

"We have a witness. Actually, not a witness to the homicide, but a friend who found her. Joey talked to her here at the scene and then had her transported to HQ for a formal statement."

Clay had Joey relay the information the tennis partner had given him about how she came to be at the house checking on Denise.

Concluding the friend's story, Joey said, "The lady panicked when she saw the mayor's body and ran to her car and called 9-1-1. The first officers arrived within three minutes and immediately locked down the scene."

"What's your take on the sequence of events?" Mike asked.

Clay said to Joey, "Tell the chief our theory."

With a nod, Joey stepped just inside the kitchen and pointed in the direction of the front door. "First, there's no sign of forced entry into the house. The front door is unlocked, so we believe whoever did this is someone the mayor knew."

"Either knew," Clay interjected, "or at least felt comfortable inviting the person into her home."

"Right," Joey agreed. "I'm not sure you can see it from here, but there's a glass with about an inch of red wine in it on a table beside a wing chair in the living room. The chair sits directly across from the sofa and is about ten feet away from the body. There are also several sections of yesterday's newspaper beside the glass. It appears she was reading the paper and having a glass of wine when the killer arrived."

"What's the significance of the broken glass in the kitchen?" Mike asked.

Clay took up the narrative. "From the larger pieces, I would guess it's one of a set of drinking glasses that are kept in the cupboard to the left of the sink. We think maybe the killer asked for a drink of water or something to get Denise to go into the kitchen. Why did the killer want her to go into the kitchen? We're not sure, unless it was to get her farther away from the front of the house so the gunshot would be less likely to attract attention."

"Okay, that sounds reasonable so far," Mike said. "But the bullet hole in the refrigerator, the broken glass, and the mayor's body all the way in another room would seem to indicate something went wrong with the killer's plan."

"That's what we think, too," Clay replied. "Joey and I are speculating that Denise may have had her back to the killer as she got the glass out of the cupboard. She turns around, sees a gun, and just reacts. Maybe the killer said something that caused her to turn around. Who knows? But she must have either thrown the glass at the shooter or actually held it and hit the gun with the glass at the same time a shot was fired, causing the bullet to be deflected into the refrigerator door. Then, we think she took off running for the front door in an attempt to escape."

"So, the killer shot her in the back as she was trying to get away?"

Clay shook his head. "We don't think so. It looks like the shooter caught her before she reached the door and stabbed her in the mid-back. We won't know until the autopsy, but we believe from the location of the wound that the knife may have punctured her heart."

"But why a knife when the guy or the woman, I guess I need to qualify it, had a gun and had already fired one shot?"

"It's possible that Denise knocked the gun out of the killer's hand with the glass. Then, when she took off running for the door, maybe the killer didn't think there was time to retrieve the gun before she escaped. So he, or she, used a knife. Of course, it's always a possibility that there were two."

"Two?" Mike asked.

"Two killers. One armed with a gun and one with a knife. That's just speculation right now, but we don't want to discount it until we see where the investigation goes."

The chief didn't respond right away, his eyes taking in the broken glass, the bullet hole, and ultimately the mayor's body. Massaging the back of his neck, he said, "This is bad."

"Tell me about it. And it's especially tough for me."

Curious, Mike said, "I understand you didn't want anything bad to happen to her, but, considering how nasty she's been toward you, why is it so tough?"

"Did Denise happen to call you? Like last night?"

Shaking his head, Mike said, "No. Why?"

"Because she called me at home and asked me to come over to talk to her."

"What did she want?"

"Funny. That's the same question I asked myself all the way over here. It seems Denise had a change of heart about you and me. She admitted she and Barclay were seeing each other when his daughter was killed. She said she felt sorry for him over what happened to his family, and, of course, she was ultimately hoping to marry the guy. So, when he demanded she force you to fire me, she went along with it. But Barclay just recently dumped her, and that's when she realized he had just been stringing her along the whole time. For the sex, as she indicated to me. And believe it or not, she apologized to me."

"Really?" he said.

"Denise said she was ashamed of the way she acted toward me. And she said she was going to go see you and try to make things right with you and the rest of the city council for the way she's been acting."

"I have to admit I would have been very surprised to hear Denise Adams be critical of herself," Mike said.

"One more thing. I've never told you this, but did you know that Denise and I dated in college?"

"No, I didn't. Add that to the list of surprises this morning."

"We met in our freshman year and went together for a while. Denise was different back then. She was always driven to succeed, but she was a fun person to be around. Never had anything bad to say about anybody.

Always upbeat. We even talked at one time about getting married. Then I quit school and joined the police department. She told me I was stupid to give up a college degree to be a small town cop. We argued a lot about that, so things were already pretty rocky when I met Dana. Not too long after that, I broke it off with Denise. She mentioned me breaking up with her while we were talking last night, but not in an angry or hostile way. Anyway, the conversation ended on a good note. She gave me a hug as I was leaving, and–" he stopped, suddenly turning away, unable to continue as he looked at her body on the floor only a few feet away.

Mike squeezed his shoulder. "I'm glad to hear that you two cleared the air."

Clay nodded, walking away as he struggled to get his emotions under control.

Joey stepped in at that point and continued the briefing. "I interviewed the neighbors on both sides and across the street. No one saw anything except an elderly lady directly across the street. She's a retired schoolteacher. Taught at Fletcher Senior High. She was closing her living room shutters when she saw Commander Randall leave the house."

"How did she know it was Clay?"

"Because she recognized me," Clay said, coming back. "I took three years of English and English Lit from her at Fletcher. She's a nice lady."

"Okay. Anything else?"

Before either man could answer, Andy Markousky, the lead evidence technician, stepped to the door, a strange expression on his face. "Sorry to interrupt, Chief, but could I talk to you a second? Privately?" he asked, glancing nervously at Clay.

With a curious look at Clay, Mike said, "Sure."

Going through the kitchen, careful to avoid the areas marked off with evidence tags, Markousky stopped just inside the living room. A second technician and two detectives watched them intently, the mayor's body temporarily ignored.

Mike asked, "What's so important that you couldn't say it in front of Commander Randall and Sergeant Crutchfield?"

"Well, sir, it's not so much Sergeant Crutchfield as it's, um, the commander."

"What do you mean?"

"I found something that you need to see," Markousky said, pointing at the foot of the wingback chair.

"What is it?" Mike asked, bending down and squinting.

"The object behind the right front leg of the chair."

Mike kneeled and peered closely at the object. "Okay, I see it. It's a law enforcement challenge coin, a Saint Michael's medal, the patron saint of law enforcement. Are you thinking this was dropped by the killer?"

"I'm not sure, Chief. I photographed it in place and then picked it up to get a shot of the other side. That's when I saw the inscription. After I read what it said, I took a picture and put it back in the same position. That's when I came and got you."

"So, what does it say?" Mike asked, growing impatient.

Holding up his camera, Markousky said, "Here's the shot I took of the other side."

Mike took the camera and examined the picture, his eyes narrowing as he read the inscription, "*Clay, may the Archangel Michael watch over you each day as you serve and protect. Love, Dana.*"

"Damn," the chief muttered, taken aback by the potential significance of the piece of evidence. He studied the investigators, seeing both confusion and suspicion on their faces.

He kept his face neutral as he asked the evidence tech, "Can you process this for prints and DNA?"

Markousky shook his head. "We can do one or the other but not both."

"Why not?"

"Because doing either one eliminates the ability to do the other. Using fingerprint powder or superglue will contaminate any DNA on the coin, and the same thing the other way if we take swabs for DNA first."

The chief considered the two options. "Do you think you can lift usable fingerprints off of it?"

"I would say probably not. There are not enough flat surfaces on the object large enough to lift a print with enough points to be able to match it to someone."

Mike said, "Okay. Swab it for DNA."

Heading for the kitchen, he stopped suddenly. Turning around, he pointed a finger at the group, none of whom had moved. "Don't make assumptions, and don't jump to conclusions. It'll bite you in the ass every time. Got it?"

"Yes, sir," they answered in chorus.

Looking sternly at each one in turn, he went back to the kitchen.

Clay and Joey were still in the same place, discussing the next steps to take in the investigation.

"What's up, Mike?" Clay asked.

"Sergeant, give us a minute. Commander, let's take a walk," Mike said, going out the door without waiting for a response.

Joey mouthed at Clay, "What the hell?"

"I have no idea," Clay shrugged. "While I talk to Mike, check on where they are in processing the living room. We need to get the ME's people in here as soon as they're done so they can get the body . . . so they can get Denise loaded up and out of here."

"You got it," Joey responded.

Clay caught up to the chief at the rear of the property near the marsh. Mike was sitting on a bench in a bright yellow gazebo, his arms folded as he gazed off into the distance.

"What's going on?" Clay asked, sinking onto the bench across from his boss.

Mike kept his eyes on a large pleasure boat cruising by on the ICW a quarter of a mile away. "You know, sometimes I regret coming back after I retired. It was nice not having to deal with all this crap. I slept until I was ready to get up. Every day, I did pretty much what I wanted to do, not what somebody told me I had to do. Except, of course, for the honey-do lists that Tanya always seemed to make for me," he said with a wry smile.

"Why the down attitude?"

Ignoring the question, Mike said, "I have to ask you something, and I want a straight-up, no BS answer."

"You've never gotten anything else from me," Clay said. "So, ask away."

"Where is your Saint Michael's challenge coin?"

"My Saint Michael's coin? What's up with that?"

"Just answer the question."

Shaking his head, Clay said, "I don't know."

"Why not?"

"Because someone took it out of my locker over a week ago."

"What do you mean?"

"I've always kept it in my locker on the top shelf. At least I have since I got promoted and quit going out on patrol regularly. But every morning when I get to work, the first thing I do is stop by my locker and pick up the coin. I always read the message on the back. It's something Dana had inscribed for me. I know it probably sounds corny, but it just makes me feel, I don't know, safe, I guess. You know, the whole Saint Michael watching over me thing. The last thing I do is wipe it with a rag to keep a shine on it and then put it back on the shelf. But when I came in last Monday and went by my locker, it was gone."

"Don't you lock your locker?" Mike asked.

"C'mon, Mike, it's the police department. I've left money and jewelry in there for years and never given a thought to it not being there when I came back. No one goes in the locker room but other police officers. If I can't trust my fellow cops, then I can't trust anyone."

"Apparently you can't if someone took it out of your locker."

"I'm lost here. Why all the questions about my challenge coin?"

"Because that coin, specifically *your* coin, is currently resting under a chair a few feet away from the mayor's dead body."

"Are you shitting me?!" Clay exclaimed, jumping to his feet.

Mike shook his head. "Calm down, Clay. That's what Markousky wanted to show me. It was either dropped or deliberately placed there."

"Damn it, Mike! I'm being set up. Whoever killed Denise must have planted it there to try to frame me."

"Clay, this is very important. Have you told anyone else about it being taken?"

"Joey knows. I told him the same day. I was bitching about it being gone and thought maybe he had taken it as a prank. But he was adamant he hadn't done it. In fact, he thought it could be connected to Barclay and company. But I couldn't see how stealing my challenge coin would help them get to me." Pausing, he scowled. "I guess I was wrong."

Mike said, "You realize what this looks like, don't you?"

"Of course I do. I was here last night. Then Denise is found murdered this morning, and my coin is discovered near her body. That's a lot of circumstantial evidence, all of which points right at me. This just gives

Barclay more ammunition. The facts won't matter, either. Of course, he won't be doing it alone. Lou Dunlop will be right in there with him."

As Mike remained silent, Clay asked, "You do believe me, don't you?"

Before he could answer, Joey came out the back door, hurrying across the lawn to the gazebo. Visibly agitated, he spoke rapidly, "Chief, I was just talking to the guys inside, and they showed me Clay's challenge coin under the chair. It was stolen out of his locker last week. He told me about it the morning he found it missing. This is a setup! You can't believe that Clay had anything to do with–"

Mike held up his hand. "Calm down, Sergeant. Clay and I have just been talking about it. And no, I don't believe he had anything to do with this."

"Oh," Joey said, relief in his voice. "Well, I just wanted to make sure you knew. And I told the guys about his coin being stolen because I could tell they were kind of freaking out thinking all sorts of stuff they shouldn't."

With a troubled expression, Joey said, "I know you don't want to imagine this, Chief, but it's possible that the killer may be one of our own."

"Why do you say that?" Mike asked.

"Because Clay's coin was stolen over a week ago, and it suddenly shows up at the crime scene today. Nobody outside the department has access to the locker room. The only logical conclusion I can draw is that it had to have been taken by a cop, and that cop killed the mayor," Joey concluded.

Clay spoke up. "Unless."

"Unless what?" Mike asked.

"Unless someone inside the department took it and gave it to someone else."

"Who are you suggesting took it?"

"How about Jack Hargraves, our suspended patrol commander, for example?" Clay suggested. "And the obvious person he would have given it to is Lou Dunlop."

Joey said, "I'm convinced Hargraves knows exactly where that alleged anonymous letter about Clay came from, so I think it's worth investigating, Chief."

"I've about come to the conclusion that Hargraves is someone who doesn't deserve to wear the badge," Mike said. "But in spite of that, I don't want to think he would knowingly involve himself in a murder. As for Dunlop, Clay and I were just talking about him as a possible suspect. However, I can't see him in any sort of physical confrontation. Not even with a woman."

Clay said, "I agree. Dunlop wouldn't want to get his hands dirty, but maybe he has connections to people who would do it for a price. It's even possible that if Hargraves took it, he didn't know what my challenge coin was going to be used for. Since the anonymous letter didn't work, this may have been a fallback tactic."

"Maybe you're right, Clay," the chief said. "I'm going to talk to Hargraves about all of this. In the meantime, who else did you tell about it disappearing from your locker?"

"Dana, of course. I told her when I got home that night. Why? Does that matter?"

"It should be obvious to you, of all people. It matters because there are going to be people who will think Crutchfield and your wife are covering for you."

"I would never do that," Joey responded.

"Hear me out. Denise Adams has been on a very public campaign against Clay. Suddenly, she ends up dead, a victim of a homicide. Some people are going to think Clay had a motive to kill her."

"Excuse me, Chief, but I'm not buying that," Joey protested. "Just because the mayor was trying to get him fired is no reason for him to want to kill her."

"That's the logical response, but there will be people viewing this emotionally. And there are some who would love to hurt him."

"Nice to know I'm so well thought of," Clay growled.

"You can't be everyone's best friend. You've got the reputation of being a by-the-book cop. That pisses off some people to the point that they would love it if someone managed to knock you off your pedestal."

"Dammit, Mike! I don't put myself on a pedestal."

"I'm not saying you do, but that *is* your public persona, and there's nothing you can do about it. Nor should you."

Clay shook his head in disgust. "Can we get back to why we're here? And for the record, I didn't have anything to do with her murder."

The chief clapped Clay on the shoulder. "You don't have to defend yourself to me, but, at the same time, I don't want you getting blindsided."

"Fine," he said, stalking back to the house as Joey and Mike followed, concern on their faces.

When they entered the house, Markousky was waiting for them. Avoiding eye contact with Clay, he addressed the chief. "I've got some more evidence you need to be aware of. First, in addition to the stab wound to the back, there appear to be two gunshot wounds to the mayor's head."

"Show us," Clay ordered quickly.

Looking anxiously at Clay, he said, "Commander, I'm sorry if I offended you when I asked to speak to the chief a little while ago. I didn't know what to do about the, uh, the coin. Sergeant Crutchfield told us about somebody stealing it out of your locker, so I wanted you to know that I never doubted for a second that you had anything to do with, well, you know," he ended, his face getting redder by the second.

Clay waved his hand in a dismissive gesture. "Forget about it, Andy. I probably would have done the same thing."

Visibly relieved, Markousky led the men into the living room, indicating they should stand to the right side of the body. Kneeling, he used a metal pointer to lift the mayor's hair carefully away from the right side of her face. He then pointed out two small holes about one-half inch apart slightly above and behind her ear.

"As you can see, there is heavy stippling around both wounds, indicating the barrel of the gun was held in very close proximity to the head when it was fired."

"I guess the killer didn't want to depend on the knife finishing the job," Joey said.

"You have good documentation of the bullet holes as well as the knife wound?" Clay asked.

"We do. Of course, we'll get better pictures from the autopsy."

"Okay. What else do you have for us?" Clay prompted.

"Right," he said. "We need to go back to the kitchen."

Following Markousky through the living room into the kitchen, they watched him pull a long-handled pair of tweezers and a flashlight from his pocket as he crouched in front of the refrigerator. "You'll have to get down low to see it," he said.

They kneeled in a semi-circle around the evidence tech as he lit up the underside of the refrigerator. In the midst of several dust bunnies, a small piece of broken glass glistened in the flashlight beam.

"I've already taken pictures of this, so I'm going to remove it now," Markousky said.

Carefully grasping the broken glass with the tweezers, he pulled it out and held the sliver up for them to see.

"That looks like blood along one edge," Joey observed.

"I'm pretty sure it is," Markousky agreed. "I'll submit it to the crime lab with a rush request to have DNA testing done."

With rising excitement, Clay said, "If our assumptions are correct about what happened here in the kitchen, this is likely the killer's blood."

"You're right," Joey said. "Andy, when you said you'd put in a rush request for DNA testing, how soon are we talking about getting a response?"

Markousky shrugged. "Sergeant, rush is a relative term. Most DNA testing takes months because of the huge backlog of requests. But some cases can get pushed up in the order if they've got an extremely high profile, like the victim is someone rich or famous or something like that."

"I think the murder of an elected official would certainly fit that definition," Joey said.

"Probably," Markousky agreed. "That said, though, it could still take a few months."

Clay asked the chief, "What about using that private lab in Tampa? We used them several years ago during the serial killer investigation. As I recall, it cost the city a couple thousand dollars, but we got results back really fast."

"You're right," Mike said. "I'll authorize the expense. Call the state attorney and get her approval to send it to the Tampa lab. Then contact the company and find out how long it will take for results once they have the evidence in hand."

"Yes, sir," Markousky said, carefully sealing the piece of glass in an evidence container.

"Oh, and about Commander Randall's challenge coin. I've changed my mind. Don't swab it. Keep it bagged and send it to the private lab along with the piece of glass. We'll have them do DNA testing on everything."

Gesturing for Clay and Joey to follow him out the back door, he started to speak when Clay held up his hand. "Hang on, Chief. I've been thinking about the glass with the blood on it. Obviously, the killer was cut, right?"

"I'd say that's fairly obvious," Mike said, wryly.

"I want pictures taken to prove that I don't have a single cut on my hands, wrists, arms, chest, back. Nowhere. Just in case certain people try to blame me for Denise's death."

The chief looked off toward the marsh as he considered Clay's suggestion. "Do you really think that's necessary?"

"It most *definitely* is necessary," Clay insisted. "We can't afford to have this investigation sidetracked by Barclay or Dunlop raising a bogus accusation."

Mike nodded. "Okay, you're right. Joey, when you finish up here, get back to HQ and take the pictures, but don't put them into the official file. Lock them up separately. I'll use them only if things get ugly."

"Thanks, Mike. I appreciate it," Clay said.

"In the meantime, keep your guys moving on the investigation. Around the clock if you have to. This is the highest priority. Understood?"

Clay and Joey both nodded.

"Okay," the chief said as he slowly headed toward the front of the house where the throng of reporters and cameras still waited. "In the meantime, I'll go give a sound bite to the media that'll tell them nothing in a hundred words or less."

At two o'clock that afternoon, Clay, Joey, and Summer Hayes stood in an autopsy room waiting for the medical examiner to arrive. The mayor's body lay on a stainless steel table, covered up to the neck in a sheet.

Summer pressed her hand over her nose trying unsuccessfully to block the smell of beginning decomposition. Leaning over, Joey spoke in a low voice, "I heard the mayor got her perfume straight from Paris. What do you think?"

Gawking at him in surprise, she whispered, "I can't believe you said that, Sergeant."

He chuckled. "Listen, Detective Hayes. When you've been in this job as long as I have, and you've seen as much crap as I have, you find whatever works to help you cope. You tell jokes. You talk hunting or fishing or shopping or whatever. If you don't, you can get wrapped up in the emotions of violent death and lose focus. When that happens, you're going to miss something that can make the difference between solving the crime and letting the bad guy get off."

Clay turned from the body. "Joey, I don't ever remember hearing you explain the job quite that straightforward."

"Just trying to educate our new detective on the finer aspects of criminal investigation, boss."

Clay said, "So, Detective Hayes, what did you learn from Sergeant Crutchfield's coping mechanism?"

She seemed to weigh her words. "I think he means the best way to handle a crime like this," she gestured toward the body, "is to bury my emotions while I'm working so I can do the job the right way."

"Alright, I think she's got it!" Joey said with a grin.

Clay said, "Just be careful you don't bury them so deep that you lose your ability to feel. That's what gets cops in trouble. Those are the ones who turn to alcohol or drugs to help them cope with bad stuff like . . . like this," he said, pointing at Denise's body.

"I understand," Summer replied.

The medical examiner came walking briskly into the room followed by one of her assistants. The ME was a short, energetic woman in her early fifties, dressed in green hospital scrubs with her hair tucked under a tight-fitting cap. A mask dangled around her neck, ready to be lifted into place when the autopsy got underway.

"Commander Randall, nice to see you," she said, shaking Clay's hand with a firm grip. Turning to Joey, she shook his hand, also. "Sergeant Crutchfield, aren't you about ready to retire?"

"Not yet, Doc. My wife says she's not prepared to have me hanging around the house every day."

With a smile, she turned to Summer. "I don't believe I've met you."

"No, ma'am. I'm Detective Summer Hayes."

"Summer Hayes," the doctor said with a quizzical expression on her face. "Why is that name familiar?"

"I don't know, Doctor."

She snapped her fingers. "Got it. You're the officer who killed the young man that was trying to run you down. What was his name? Let's see. Endicott? No, that's not quite right. It's . . . Westcott. Leonard Westcott," she said with a satisfied smile.

Seeing Summer flustered at being reminded of the traumatic experience involving her ex-boyfriend, Clay jumped in, "That's right, Doc. You've got a good memory considering how many customers you have."

She shrugged in response. "Just part of the job, Commander. Regardless, I know you're not here to dredge up old cases. You want to know exactly how this lady died," she said, pointing at the body.

"Right," Clay said.

"Then, let's get this done." Turning to her assistant, called a diener, she directed him to prepare for the autopsy.

As the procedure began, the doctor dictated each step of her forensic investigation into a mic hanging above the table. Initially, she scrutinized the mayor's body thoroughly, turning it to one side and then the other. She took particular care examining the knife wound, measuring the length, width, and depth of the cut.

When she got to the extremities, she first removed the protective bags Andy Markousky had secured over both hands to preserve possible DNA evidence the killer might have left behind. Then she took extra time inspecting each finger and fingernail. As she viewed the middle finger of the left hand, the doctor suddenly stopped, bringing her face down to within an inch of the nail. "Give me more light here," she directed her assistant.

When he focused a powerful overhead spotlight at the hand, the ME requested a pair of untoothed forceps. Taking them in hand, she painstakingly removed a tiny object from under the nail, holding it up to the light.

"What is it, Doc?" Clay asked.

"Skin," she answered.

"Hers?"

"No. I've checked her body thoroughly, and there are no breaks that would be consistent with a piece of tissue lodged under her fingernail. Considering this person was the victim of a homicide, I can say with a fairly high degree of certainty that this belongs to the person who killed her."

"Is there enough to get a DNA profile?" Clay asked.

"I believe so," she said.

Securing the piece of evidence for processing, she directed her assistant to begin the actual autopsy. The diener made a long, Y-shaped incision that ran from the shoulders, curving around both breasts and ending just above the pubic bone. He then took a scalpel and carefully peeled the skin, soft tissue, and underlying muscles away from the ribs.

The next step involved the use of a bone cutter to snip through the rib cage to provide clear access to the internal organs. Within minutes, he had the organs cut free and removed. After weighing and visually examining each organ, he excised thin slices from each one for further lab tests.

As the autopsy proceeded, Joey kept a close eye on Summer, curious to see how she would react.

After a few minutes, she noticed him watching her. "Am I doing something I'm not supposed to?" she whispered.

Shaking his head, he went to the other side of the room, gesturing for her to follow. In a hushed voice, he said, "I wanted to make sure you were okay with this. Some people end up running out of the room and puking their guts up in the hallway."

Summer arched an eyebrow. "Well, thanks for caring about my welfare, but I'm fine."

"No upset stomach? Not feeling faint or anything," he asked, starting to grin.

"Not at all," she answered with a sigh.

"Good. Wanta grab a steak when this is over? Say, medium rare?"

Summer rolled her eyes. "Sure, Sarge, only I like mine rare. Now, are we done here so we can get back to the autopsy?"

Joey continued to grin. "You bet. I like your style, Detective Hayes. Nothing fazes you."

During their discussion, the diener had made a cut starting behind the right ear and going over the crown to a point behind the left ear. Using a scalpel, he peeled the front half forward over the face and the back half down below the base of the neck.

As Joey and Summer moved back over to observe, the diener used a Stryker saw to cut through the cranium and remove the top of the skull, exposing the brain.

"This is the only part I don't like," Joey whispered to Summer. "The smell of burnt bone from the saw cutting through the skull is bad," he said as he put a hand over his nose.

It was clear that Summer agreed as she did the same. They both noticed Clay didn't seem affected by the smell.

"This isn't bothering you?" Joey muttered.

"Yes, it's bothering me," Clay murmured, "but not because of the smell."

"Denise?" Joey asked, softly.

Clay nodded but didn't speak, keeping his eyes on the ME.

Before proceeding, she examined the CT scan and observed nine bullet fragments scattered throughout the brain. Using the scan as a guide, the ME began the tedious process of cataloging the locations and removing each fragment.

After ninety minutes, the job was finished. The ME stripped off her gloves and mask and tossed them into a biohazard waste container. "Okay, preliminary thoughts," she said, "pending toxicology and DNA results, which will not have a bearing on cause of death. The knife blade punctured the right upper lobe of the lung, collapsing it. This wound would not necessarily have been fatal. Almost certainly not if she had received prompt medical attention. Taking into consideration the angle of the wound, it appears the deceased was in an upright position, bent slightly forward at the waist."

"Doctor, we believe she was trying to run away from the killer," Joey said.

"That would fit with the angle of the wound path, which indicates the person wielding the knife was right handed. In addition, the location and trajectory of the bullet wounds support the conclusion that the person was right handed. As for the specific cause of death, I attribute that to the gunshot wounds to her head, either of which would have been fatal. In this case, death was for all practical purposes instantaneous."

"Thanks, Doc," Clay said.

"You're welcome. I'll have my report dictated and forwarded to you as quickly as possible," she responded.

"Okay," Clay said, pausing to consider what additional investigative steps he needed done. "What about DNA processing of the piece of skin?"

"I'll take care of transmitting it to the FDLE crime lab."

Clay was shaking his head before she finished. "No, Doc. That will take too long. Chief Wilson has authorized us to use a private lab in Tampa for other pieces of evidence in this case. We would like to send this to the same place. They can give us a quick turnaround."

The doctor eyed the sealed container holding the evidence before responding. "Okay, how do you want to handle it?"

"Can you hold it here until we make the arrangements with the state attorney and the lab? Then we'll pick it up and transport it directly there."

"That's fine, if that's what you want to do."

"Thanks again, Doc. We'll be in touch soon," Clay said, shaking her hand. With a wave to Joey and Summer to follow, Clay headed for the door, mentally going over an increasing list of tasks as he went.

37

What the hell happened?" Senator Barclay demanded, glaring at his chief of staff.

Lou Dunlop's face was dripping with sweat. The handkerchief gripped tightly in his hand was damp from his unsuccessful attempts to stem the tide. He shook his head. "I don't know, Senator. I really don't. I called my contact in the police department, but he doesn't know anything. Since Wilson suspended him, he's sitting on his ass at home, completely out of the loop."

"So you're telling me you have no idea?"

"Some woman was supposed to play tennis with Denise. When she didn't show up at the club for their match, she went to her house and found her dead. That's all I know right now."

"You're not telling me anything I haven't already heard from watching the same newscasts as you. What I want to know is whether you had anything to do with this."

Dunlop had been expecting the question since he walked into Barclay's office, figuring the man's concern was solely for his political future and not for the fact his lover was dead.

Adopting a wounded look, Dunlop said, "I can't believe you'd think I would be involved in killing someone. Most of all, her."

"Well, it sure as hell seems coincidental, don't you think?"

"What do you mean, coincidental?"

"Don't go all stupid on me, Lou. You told Denise it was over between us, which, by the way, you did directly contrary to my instructions, and–"

"But, Senator," Dunlop interrupted, "I told you she assaulted me. I didn't tell you this before, but I'm pretty sure I hit my head on the sidewalk when she knocked me off the porch. I believe as I've thought back on it that I may have suffered a slight concussion, and that's why I told her it was over."

"That's a load of crap, and you know it!" Barclay raged. "You were pissed, and that's why you said it."

Dunlop decided it would be to his benefit to keep his mouth shut in the face of Barclay's escalating anger.

The senator kept ranting. "Because of what you did, she threatened to go to the media in retaliation. Then you tell me you have an idea that will convince her to go away. The next thing I hear, she's dead. Murdered! I think that's one hell of a coincidence, don't you?"

Dunlop shrugged, spreading his hands in a placating gesture. "Thomas, what can I say? Strange coincidences sometimes happen."

Barclay stood abruptly and began pacing around his office. Suddenly, he turned and barked, "Lou, I pay you a lot of money to handle problems, and you've screwed this thing up with Denise from the get-go. I never wanted her dead. I just wanted her to go away. What do you suppose will happen to my campaign if it gets out that I had a relationship with her while I was still married, and she ends up murdered? People are going to think I had something to do with it!"

"Thomas, that's not going to happen."

"You don't know that!" he yelled. "There are dozens of people digging into my life all the way back to the day I was born. Probably *before* I was born!"

Dunlop was unemotional in the face of Barclay's fury. "With all due respect, Senator, and maybe I shouldn't say this, but isn't it possible you should have given more consideration to the potential consequences before you began your relationship with Mayor Adams?"

Barclay stopped his pacing, glaring at Dunlop. "I hadn't made up my mind to run for president when Denise and I got together. Besides, don't you dare lecture me, Lou. What I do with my personal life is *my* business. Understand?"

"I do understand, and I apologize, Senator. I know this is very disturbing to you. It is to me, too. But I'm just trying to help."

Dunlop kept his voice soft, his face a mask of concern. "And on my word of honor, I promise you I did not have anything to do with her death. But," he paused.

Barclay snapped, "But what?"

"I would hate to accuse an innocent person, but is it just possible that Clay Randall might have had something to do with this? I personally think it is. Maybe even *likely* that he killed her."

In a doubting voice, Barclay said, "I'm not saying you're wrong, but why would he kill her?"

Dunlop shrugged. "The most obvious motive is her ongoing attempts to get rid of him. I don't know, maybe he cracked under the pressure. Or maybe the chief told Randall he was going to terminate him to keep the mayor off his own back. I mean, we know Randall is a hothead with a well-documented violent history. There are at least two people we know of that he's killed."

"But he was cleared in both of those incidents."

"Sure," Dunlop said, "he was cleared, but his own department did the investigations, I believe. Really, how objective could they have been? You know cops are always going to stick together."

Barclay considered what Dunlop had said. "Regardless of who killed her, this could be a real PR problem for me."

Dunlop was relieved that Barclay had shifted his attention to how the mayor's death could affect himself politically. This was his arena, his area of expertise. He ran with it. "Thomas, I'm confident you're covered there. If Randall is the killer like I suspect he is, her death can be attributed to bad blood between the two of them."

"How?"

"Easy. Only three people know for sure about you getting her to go after Randall. Well, there's just two now, you and me, since Denise won't be doing any talking," he said, chuckling.

Barclay cringed. "Knock it off, Lou. I was done with Denise, but I still cared about her. Show a little respect."

"Sorry about that, Senator. You're right. Anyway, I found out something interesting about the mayor and Randall a couple of days ago as I was doing some research on his background trying to find something we could use against him."

"Really?" Barclay said, perking up. "What is it?"

"It seems he and the mayor dated back in college. The word I got was they were pretty serious. Then Randall met his current wife, and the next thing you know, he dumps Denise and marries her instead. That could explain the mayor's attitude against him. You know, the old *woman scorned* thing. So maybe Randall killed her in a fit of rage over that instead."

Barclay stood up and began pacing again as he searched for loopholes in Dunlop's scenario. Stopping suddenly, he said, "Hang on. You said this all happened back when they were in college. That had to be close to twenty years ago. Why would it suddenly become an issue after so many years?"

Dunlop smiled. "How about a mix of truth and spin? The rumor gets floated out to the media that the two of them were having an affair. You know, picking up where they left off in college. Then she starts pressuring Randall to leave his wife and marry her. He refuses, so she goes on the attack like she's been doing. Randall still refuses to leave his wife, so Denise threatens to tell Randall's wife what's been going on between the two of them. That sends him over the edge, and he kills her."

Barclay nodded slowly. "I guess that might work. But what if Randall isn't the one who killed her?"

"If it turns out she pissed off one of her constituents and that person killed her, then you're still in the clear. But I'm betting the cops are going to find that Randall did it."

"Okay, so how should I address her death? It's common knowledge that Denise and I knew each other. She and her consulting firm have done work for me during my Senate campaign. Also, I helped get her elected mayor."

"I think it would be appropriate to issue a press release expressing shock and outrage over her murder and your pledge to use the power of your office to ensure that the killer is brought to justice. You could even say you intend to contact the local U.S. Attorney and the FBI to ask that they monitor the investigation in order to guarantee it receives the highest priority."

"Should I say anything about Randall?"

Dunlop shook his head. "Not at this point. You don't want to give the impression you believe he was involved. I'd say let the investigation go forward and see what it shows. You'll have a chance to say something about Randall when they arrest him for her murder."

"Lou, you seem very confident that Randall did it."

"I just don't see any other likely suspect," he said, keeping his expression blank.

"Okay, good," Barclay responded. "Put together the press release for my review. I want to get something out to the media as soon as possible."

"You got it," he said, leaving the office. As he walked to his car, Dunlop felt a sense of relief at having managed to allay Barclay's suspicions. *If Smith followed instructions, the word should get out soon about Randall being arrested,* he thought. With a satisfied smile, he drove away, his mind already composing the senator's press release.

At four that afternoon, Mike Wilson approached the closed door to the detective division conference room. Knocking once, he stepped inside and closed the door, acknowledging the three detectives as he sat down.

Crime scene photos littered the conference room table along with graphic shots of the mayor's body. Written reports by responding officers lay in piles before each detective. His eyes were drawn to the wall behind Summer where someone had taped a diagram of the floor plan of the mayor's house.

Clay poured a cup of coffee and handed it to the chief. Eyeing the jet-black liquid in the cup, Mike held it close to his nose and sniffed. Jerking his head back quickly, he said, "Whew! What is this stuff? It smells strong enough to stand on its own without a cup."

"That's primo stuff from my personal supply," Clay said. "It's gen-u-wine Dark Roast Seaport coffee from the Texas Coffee Company in Beaumont, Texas, Joey's hometown. He knows I like it strong, so he had some shipped to me a couple of months ago. You like it?"

Cautiously sniffing it again, Mike said, "I drink my coffee black, but I don't know if I can handle this without support."

"Don't screw it up with a bunch of cream and sugar. The most you should add is one teaspoon of sugar. Otherwise, you dilute the taste," Clay cautioned.

Staring at the liquid suspiciously, Mike added one teaspoon of sugar and, as Clay went back to reviewing a report, quickly slipped a second spoonful into the cup. After a couple of stirs, he took a sip.

All three detectives watched, waiting in anticipation for his reaction. Saying nothing, he took another swallow, and then a third.

As he continued to drink in silence, Clay said, "Well?"

Mike cradled the cup in both hands as his eyes traveled around the room, coming to rest on his division commander. "Well, what?"

"C'mon, Chief. What do you think? You love it, don't you?"

"I'll have to say it's probably the best coffee I've ever tasted."

Clay grinned at Joey. "Told you he'd like it."

Joey shook his head. "That's only because the stuff he usually drinks has the flavor of used motor oil. Anything would taste good to him."

"Now, Sergeant, just because you don't drink coffee is no reason to knock those of us who can't get through the day without a pot or two of the stuff," Mike said.

"Give me a case of Diet Coke, and I'm good to go," Joey declared as he took a long drink from his fifth can of the day.

Mike leaned back in the chair and crossed his legs. "Okay, what's the ME's verdict on cause of death?"

Clay answered, "The knife wound punctured her right lung, but the doc said it probably wouldn't have been fatal if she had received prompt medical attention. The shots to the head are what did her in."

"Did the ME have an opinion on the caliber?"

"The fragments weighed the equivalent of two, twenty-two caliber bullets."

"Anything else?"

"She found a small piece of tissue under a fingernail that she believes is enough for DNA testing."

The chief perked up at the news. "She thinks it's from the killer?"

"She does," Clay confirmed.

"Did you talk to her about releasing the evidence to us so we can submit it to the private lab?"

"Yes, and she's fine with us sending it there since we're using them already. I figured you would want to handle this the same way."

"Absolutely. Let's get the evidence down there as soon as possible."

"We've already contacted them," Joey spoke up. "Summer is driving everything down there first thing in the morning."

"What's the turnaround time?" Mike asked.

"They said two to three days if we're willing to pay extra."

"I'll pay whatever it costs," he said as he picked up the cup, gazed at the remaining liquid, and set it down without drinking.

"Detective Hayes, I need to discuss a few things with Commander Randall and Sergeant Crutchfield. I assume you have paperwork to get done?" he asked, eyeing Summer.

"Yes, sir," she said, gathering up her files and leaving the conference room.

As soon as the door closed, Mike asked, "Anything you've found that points to a specific suspect?"

Before Clay or Joey could answer, the sound of loud voices erupted outside the conference room. Gordy Cooper suddenly came barging into the conference room followed by Summer Hayes.

She said, "Chief, I told Councilman Cooper you were in a meeting and couldn't be disturbed."

Cooper ignored her as he came over and stood in front of the chief. In a condescending voice, he said, "We need to talk." Pointing at Clay and Joey, he jerked a thumb toward the door. "Out. That means you, too, young lady," he growled at Summer. "Now."

As Joey started to get up, Clay put his hand on his arm and pulled him back down, never taking his eyes from Cooper. "Councilman Cooper, what part of the chief being in a meeting did you not understand?"

Cooper's nostrils flared in anger. "You arrogant prick. You clearly don't know who you're talking to, Randall. I'm the mayor now, and you damn well better show me some respect. Get your ass out of that chair, take your detectives with you, and hit the door running."

Clay asked, "Chief, would you like me to escort *Mr.* Cooper out of the building?"

A brief smile crossed Mike's face. "I appreciate the offer, Commander, but no. I'll take Councilman Cooper to my office. You stay here and keep working. I'll check back in a few minutes."

Getting to his feet, Mike pointed at Cooper. "Come with me." Without waiting for a response, he left the room.

Glaring at Clay as he left, Cooper said, "You're done, Randall."

Mike stopped at his admin's door and told her to hold his calls except for an emergency. Leading the way in, he shut the door and sat at his desk, gesturing to a chair. Cooper ignored him, continuing to stand.

"What can I do for you, Gordy?" the chief asked in a neutral tone.

"You can start by referring to me as Mayor Cooper since I'm now your boss."

"Oh? I wasn't aware the council met and voted to appoint you mayor. I believe there has to be a public notice issued before any meeting of the city council, and I've received no such notice."

Cooper leaned forward, putting both hands on the desk. "You know something, Wilson? It's easy to see where Randall gets his cocky attitude."

Mike waved his hand. "Gordy, cut the crap, and just tell me what you want."

"Okay," he said, abruptly straightening up and pointing his finger at the chief. "I want Randall arrested for the murder of Mayor Denise Adams."

Mike leaned back in the chair. "On what grounds?"

Cooper sat down and crossed his legs, running his hands back and forth over the leather arms of the guest chair. "Nice furniture you got here," he said. "Better than the crap I had to put up with when I was the chief. I don't know what you did to convince Denise to spring for real leather, but you're going to find money a lot tighter in my administration."

Mike ignored Cooper's attempt to deflect the question, leaning forward and tapping his index finger on the blotter as he emphasized each word. "Answer. My. Question."

With a contemptuous smirk, Cooper said, "There are people who think I should still be the chief. They talk to me. And they tell me that Randall was at the mayor's house late last night."

"Whether or not Commander Randall might have been at the mayor's residence last night is not something I intend to discuss with you unless and until you're formally approved as the mayor."

Cooper's smile grew wider. "Then you better start discussing. Under my authority as the deputy mayor, I sent out a press release to the media two hours ago announcing an emergency meeting. I was voted in as mayor by a three to two majority. Of course, I abstained to avoid the appearance of a conflict of interest. You know, voting for myself and all that," he ended with a self-satisfied chuckle.

Mike was disturbed but not surprised by the news. Gordy Cooper had shown an uncanny ability over the years to get what he wanted. He tried one more delaying tactic. "Can I assume the meeting on your annoint–, uh, appointment was recorded and minutes were taken for the public record?"

"Of course. Now quit stalling and answer my question," Cooper demanded, turning red at the veiled slight.

Clenching his jaw, Mike said, "What's your question again?"

"I want to know how soon Randall is going to be arrested and charged with killing Denise Adams."

"He's not going to be arrested, and he's not going to be charged with anything," Mike answered calmly.

"And why not?"

"Because he didn't kill her."

"So you say," Gordy said sarcastically. "But I have it on good authority that a witness saw him coming out the mayor's front door last night around nine or after. I also know the ME put the time of death between nine and midnight last night. I'd say that makes Randall a prime, make it *the* prime suspect."

"Dammit, Gordy," Mike exclaimed, "you're way out of line! Clay Randall didn't have anything to do with her murder."

"How do you know?"

"Okay, what I'm about to say is confidential, criminal investigative information, and it cannot, it must not be repeated by you. Do you understand that?"

"Cut the crap, Wilson," Cooper snapped. "I was a cop for forty years. I know the drill."

Rubbing his face, Mike paused to gather his thoughts. He would give Cooper the basic information, but he wouldn't share the details with a man he despised and wouldn't trust to tell the truth if his life depended on it.

He said, "Mayor Adams was shot and killed with what we think is a small-caliber handgun."

When he didn't continue, Cooper said, "And? I know all about that. Shot twice in the head with a twenty-two. She was also stabbed in the back. Her body was found in the living room a few feet from the front door."

Astonished, Mike demanded, "Who gave you that information?"

Cooper shrugged, "As I said, I've got informants. But, just to show how cooperative I can be, I'll tell you. I got a call from Lou Dunlop."

Scowling at the mention of Dunlop's name, Mike said, "How did that son of a bitch get it?"

"It seems his boss is personal friends with the ME. He called her when he heard the news and asked what happened, and she told him. So he told Dunlop to contact me, figuring you would be less than cooperative in sharing information."

Shaking his head in disgust, Mike leaned back in his chair. The fact the medical examiner shared confidential case information with Barclay didn't surprise him. She was also an elected official, and he had observed over his long career how political considerations often trumped doing the right thing.

Cooper said, "So, when can I expect the call telling me Randall has been arrested?"

Speaking in a low voice, Mike said, "I've told you. Clay Randall had nothing to do with her murder, so don't sit by your phone waiting. If I do call, it will be to tell you we've arrested the real murderer."

"Tell me something, Wilson," Cooper said in a conversational tone.

"What?"

"How can you be so sure that Randall didn't do it?"

Shaking his head, Mike responded, "Suffice it to say that I *know*, beyond a shadow of a doubt. As to what led me to that conclusion, I'm not going to discuss specifics of the investigation with you, Gordy. Now, please show yourself out. I have work to do."

Turning his back, Mike began shuffling through a stack of papers on his credenza. After several seconds, he realized Cooper hadn't left. Spinning around, he was surprised to see the man grinning at him. "What is it?"

Cooper got to his feet and casually walked to the door before answering. With his hand on the knob and the grin still in place, he said, "You are one arrogant son of a bitch, Wilson. You know that?"

"Ask around, Gordy. Most people believe you wrote the book on arrogance."

Cooper's eyes narrowed, and the grin faltered before quickly returning. "Watch yourself, Wilson. I only need three other votes to send your ass packing, and with Senator Barclay's political connections, I believe I can get them. As for Randall, I'm directing you to suspend him from duty immediately."

"In spite of your belief that you and the council have supreme power, Gordy, one thing you don't have is the authority to direct the operations of the police department."

"You're right. We don't. At the moment, anyway. Just imagine, though, how it will play in the media if it turns out Randall had something to do with her death. When they find out I told you to remove him from duty, or at least from active involvement in the murder investigation, and you refused both requests? Let's just say it won't be pretty. You're putting your job and your whole career on the line to cover for that lowlife. You'd do well to keep that in mind," he said, walking out the door.

The chief gazed at the closed door without moving, his thoughts racing. He had purposely withheld from Cooper the fact that the pictures Joey took of Clay confirmed he had no marks or wounds of any kind on his body. He figured if he opened the door to sharing information on the case with Cooper, the man would try to insert himself fully into the investigation. That was something Mike wasn't going to let happen.

He knew Gordy Cooper was capable of doing almost anything to get what he wanted. In this case, he wanted Clay Randall's head, whether to please Thomas Barclay for some political gain, or simply because Clay refused to bow before the man's massive ego, it didn't matter. Mike was potentially in a position to pay a heavy price for refusing to go along with Cooper's demands.

Sighing heavily, he picked up the phone and dialed the extension for the detective conference room.

"This is Detective Hayes."

"Summer, are Commander Randall and Sergeant Crutchfield still there?"

"Yes, Chief, they're here. Did you want to talk to one of them?"

"Ask them to come to my office, please."

"Yes, sir. Do you need me there, too?"

"No, just them. Thanks," he said, hanging up.

Minutes later, Clay and Joey came into the chief's office, concern on their faces.

"Have a seat," Mike said.

As they sat down, Joey opened his notebook and pulled a pen from his shirt pocket.

"You won't need that, Sergeant," the chief said.

"Can we assume the meeting with Gordy Cooper didn't go well?" Clay asked.

"Let's just say I've had more productive conversations with my dog," Mike said. "Cooper is demanding that I have you arrested for the mayor's murder."

"Imagine that," Clay replied with a lopsided grin.

Joey said, "This is a joke. Right, Chief?"

"Does it sound like a joke?" he countered. "But you don't seem surprised, Clay."

"I'm not. Considering everything that's happened, I expected something like this. Since you didn't have Sergeant Crutchfield cuff me when I came in, can I assume I'm not about to be arrested on murder charges?"

Joey snorted, "Gimme a break, Clay. He's not going to do that. Right, Chief?"

The somber expression on the chief's face caused both men to drop the banter and sit back uneasily.

"I've made a decision that probably neither of you will like, but I believe it's the right thing to do under the circumstances," Mike said.

"Whatever you decide, we'll support you. You know that," Clay assured him.

"I hope you still feel that way after I tell you what it is. In light of all the ongoing crap with Barclay, and with Detective Hayes' shooting stirring things up even more, now we have to deal with the mayor being murdered. Consequently, I've decided it will be in the best interests of the department and the solving of this crime that I remove you, Clay, from overall supervision of the investigation."

Both men began protesting loudly. The chief let them vent a while before holding up his hands, saying firmly, "Stop. Both of you."

"But–" Joey started to protest.

"That's enough, Sergeant," Wilson said sharply.

Still visibly angry, Clay said, "Can you at least tell me why?"

"It's simple. A couple of hours ago, the city council voted in Cooper as the mayor. His first order of business was to direct me to have you arrested. When I refused, he demanded that I suspend you without pay. I declined to do that, also. But, considering everything that's happened, I think it's a good idea that you not be directly involved in the investigation."

"Chief, I respectfully disagree. I'm the detective commander. It's my responsibility to ensure all crimes are investigated properly, especially one as big as this."

"I accept that you don't agree. However, this is way more than some drive-by or domestic violence homicide. The citizens have to have confidence in our ability to investigate crimes objectively and go wherever the evidence leads. Unfortunately, we now have a new mayor who I'm convinced will push the story that your active involvement is a deliberate attempt to delay or deter the investigation from finding the killer. I'd say it's likely he would leak the fact you were at her house shortly before she was murdered and that your coin was found at the scene. All to imply that the mayor's killer is the one in charge of investigating her death. You and I know that's bullshit, but we can't afford to get into a pissing contest in the media. All that will do is distract from our focus from finding the real killer. I'm sorry, but that's my decision, like it or not. Joey will assume overall supervision of the investigation."

Clay slumped in the chair, shaking his head in frustration. "Joey, give us a minute," he said. "Get with Summer and keep going through the paperwork."

With a nod to both men, Crutchfield left the office, easing the door closed behind him.

Clay sat in the chair without speaking, his eyes focused on the wall behind Mike. The chief said nothing, giving him time.

He looked his boss in the eye. "You know I have great respect for you, both personally and professionally. You always try to do the right thing, no matter how hard it is sometimes. But I just don't believe it's right to take me off the case. If that happens, there'll be people in the department and the community who will assume you're doing it because I'm guilty.

Removing me is going to make it much harder to do my job," he said, his voice cracking.

"No, it won't!" Mike said heatedly. "I won't let it." Getting to his feet, he paced from one end of his office to the other, head down, hands clasped behind his back.

Going back to his desk, he said, "I have an idea. Putting Crutchfield in charge might make Cooper back off from wanting to get you at all costs. However, knowing him, he also may assume you're still pulling the strings in the background, so I'll assume command of the investigation."

"You?" Clay asked in surprise.

"Me. What about it?"

"It's just that it's been, what, ten years or more since you investigated a major crime?"

"Of course not," Mike objected. "It's been less than that since I was the detective commander. Besides, I've probably investigated more serious crimes than you and Crutchfield put together in my thirty-plus years here. Listen, this will work, Clay. Most people are going to be so focused on the fact that an elected official has been murdered that they're not going to pay attention to who's in charge. When I'm the face everyone sees on TV and the one giving all the updates and quotes for the newspaper, trust me on this, Cooper won't have any leverage to bring your name up at all."

Clay thought about Mike's proposal before responding. "I don't like it, but I guess you're right. Does this mean I'm going to be out of the loop?"

Mike shook his head. "Of course not. I'll be overall in charge of the investigation. Crutchfield will handle witness interviews and the day-to-day stuff, but you and I will communicate regularly every step of the way."

"Okay. I appreciate it. I know you don't have time to get tied up on a murder investigation, but this is better than cutting me out entirely. And at the same time giving Cooper what he wants."

Mike squeezed Clay's shoulder. "Don't worry about Gordy. I'll handle him. Let's just find the killer."

Joey Crutchfield suddenly burst into the room. "Sorry for interrupting, Chief. I heard what you said, and I think we may have done exactly that."

Before Clay or Mike could react, Joey pointed over his shoulder at Summer, who was standing behind him. "Summer just got off the phone with a neighbor of the mayor. You gotta hear this."

The chief waved them into the office. After sitting down, Mike gestured for Joey to explain.

"I'll let Summer tell it if that's okay."

"Sure. Go ahead, Detective Hayes," the chief said.

Summer cleared her throat, excitement clear on her face. "A call came in through dispatch about thirty minutes ago and was transferred to me. They said a guy was on the line wanting to talk to someone about the mayor's murder, so I took the call. His name—" she stopped, glancing down at notes she had typed on her computer tablet. "His name is Richard Michael Forsyth, but he goes by Mike. He lives across the street and five houses down from the mayor.

"Mr. Forsyth said he has trouble sleeping sometimes. He's seventy years old, by the way. When that happens, he goes outside and sits on his porch. He claims the breeze helps relax him. So he's out there in his rocking chair when he sees a man walk by his house."

"What time was this?" the chief asked.

"Between ten-fifteen and ten-thirty by his estimate. He said he thought it was strange that the guy was dressed in a suit."

"Why did he think that was strange?" Clay questioned.

Summer shrugged. "I asked him that. First off, he said because of the time of night. And also," she paused, reading from her notes, "he said nobody wears a suit at the beach unless they're going to church or they're stretched out in a casket."

They all laughed at that, bringing a grin to Summer's face. She continued, "Mr. Forsyth said he was thinking about calling out to the man and asking him what he was doing when the guy went up to a car parked on the opposite side of the street and two houses past his. He watched him open the trunk, and that's when he noticed the man was carrying a black garbage bag. Mr. Forsyth said he put it in the trunk and then seemed to make an effort to close the lid quietly without slamming it. The man then got into the car and sat there for about a minute, Forsyth guessed. He said he started getting suspicious, so he went over and stood behind a palm tree at the edge of his yard to try to see what the guy was doing. He watched the man moving around like he was searching for something in his pockets. Then he said the guy lit a cigarette, started the engine, and drove off."

Summer stopped. "Questions so far?"

"Can he identify the man?" Clay asked.

"Possibly. Mr. Forsyth said it was dark where the car was parked, but he got a good look at him when he passed under the streetlight as he went by his house. He described him as a white male, average height, about five-eight or so. Short, grayish-white hair, probably in his early- to mid-fifties. He said the man was wearing a dark-colored suit with a white shirt and a tie, either dark navy or black."

"That's a pretty comprehensive description. A lot of people can't remember what they saw five minutes ago," Mike said.

"It's probably because of what he did for a living before he retired."

"And that would be what?" Clay asked.

"He was a cop for twenty-five years in Ohio, so he knows the drill."

"That's great," Clay said. "You said he might be able to identify the guy if he saw him again?"

"He wasn't positive, but he thought so. And there was one more thing. Mr. Forsyth said he was limping like he was favoring his right side."

"It sounds like he may have been injured during the attack," Clay said.

"Could be," Joey agreed. "A good question to ask when we find him."

"Okay, well, this is helpful," Clay said. "Any chance he got the license plate number on the car?"

"He did. He saw it when the man cranked the engine and the lights came on."

"This guy is good. He could teach some of our young cops a few things about being observant."

Summer referred to her notes again, and then quickly continued. "The plate came back to Coastal East Car Rental at Jacksonville International. I called and talked to the manager at the airport. She said a man named Jeremiah J. Smith rented it five days ago using a Las Vegas address."

"Did you run the name?" the chief asked.

Joey jumped in. "We ran it along with the Nevada driver's license number the guy gave the clerk. It came back to a Jeremiah Jonas Smith with the same address as what he put on the rental agreement. But–" he stopped.

When he didn't continue, Clay prompted him, "But, what?"

Crutchfield leaned back in his chair, an expectant look on his face. "Summer did an Internet map search to see where the address was located in Vegas. And guess what? It's a cemetery called Desert Rest Memorial Gardens. So unless Mr. Jeremiah Jonas Smith is a dead man who crawled out of his grave and flew to Florida to kill the mayor, I'm thinking we've got a fake ID here."

"Interesting," Clay said. "Anything else?"

"Yeah, I told Summer there was something familiar about the guy's name. Do either of you remember hearing about an undercover FBI agent who was killed out in Vegas maybe eight or ten years ago?"

The chief shook his head. "I don't. Do you, Commander?"

Clay's brow furrowed in concentration as he searched his memory. "I remember reading something a while back about an FBI agent who infiltrated an outlaw motorcycle gang out there. His investigation led to several of the top guys in the gang being arrested and charged with the murder of a federal judge in Las Vegas. As I recall, though, the agent was killed before any of the gang members went to trial, and the feds had to drop the charges since he was the primary witness."

"Good memory," Joey said. "The undercover agent was stopped at a traffic light on the Strip when the shooter pulled up and popped him through the passenger window. They never identified the killer, although the feds were convinced the biker gang was behind the hit."

"You've lost me, Sergeant," the chief said. "What does this have to do with anything?"

"Maybe nothing. Maybe everything, Chief. You see, Jeremiah Jonas Smith was the agent's name. I think you'll agree it's not exactly what you'd call a common name."

Clay spoke up, "Alright, Joey, let's assume it's not just a wild coincidence that the name of the murdered agent and our possible, and I stress the word *possible*, murder suspect, are the same. What's the link between the two Jeremiah Jonas Smiths?"

"I don't have an answer to that, but the other connections make me think there might be something there."

"Like what?" Mike asked.

"First," he replied, ticking the points off on his fingers, "an FBI agent named Jeremiah Jonas Smith infiltrates a motorcycle gang and gathers evidence that they killed a federal judge. In Las Vegas. Then he's shot and killed shortly after the gang members are charged. Again in Las Vegas. Second, our mayor is stabbed and shot to death in her home. Four days before Denise Adams is murdered, a man named Jeremiah Jonas Smith flies into Jacksonville from Las Vegas and–"

"Hang on," Clay interrupted. "Have you confirmed this Smith guy came here from Vegas?"

"Not yet, but considering he showed a driver's license with a Vegas address at the car rental place, I think it's a pretty safe assumption that's where he came from. Anyway, it's on our list of things to check out. Okay, so Mr. Smith flies into Jacksonville from, for now, an unknown city. He rents a car at the airport using a Nevada driver's license in the name of Jeremiah Jonas Smith. Finally, you add to this the fact he's got a fake address on his driver's license, and I'd say that's too many coincidences to ignore."

Before the chief could respond, Clay spoke up, "You know, Joey may have something there, Chief. How about this? What if our killer is also the one that took out the FBI agent, the *real* Jeremiah Smith? Maybe he's a pro. A contract shooter. And maybe using the name of a previous victim as an alias could be his twisted way of keeping score of kills. Like putting notches on the butt of his gun."

"Couldn't have put it better myself," Joey said with a gratified smile.

Clay continued. "And if the guy really is a hired gun, this fits in with what we were talking about at the crime scene concerning Barclay and Dunlop. Especially Dunlop."

"The man's a dishonest prick, no doubt about it," Mike said. "But I'm having trouble seeing him hiring a professional hitman to kill the mayor. What's the motive? What could she possibly have done to Barclay or to him that would be so bad they would want her dead? It just doesn't make sense to me."

"Let's think about this a minute," Clay said. "Last night, Denise told me she and Barclay had been seeing each other. She also said that he dumped her very recently."

"If that's the case," Mike said, "then why kill her?"

"Denise didn't tell me she threatened to expose their relationship, so this is all supposition. Let's say she threatened Barclay with going public. Imagine what that would do to his presidential ambitions. That could be sufficient reason to want her dead."

Shaking his head, the chief said, "That's a possibility, I guess, but I'm still having trouble believing a man running for president would have someone killed because he thought it might hurt his political career."

In a low voice, Joey said, "Probably what Marilyn Monroe thought, too."

Summer said, "Marilyn Monroe? Oh, never mind. I get it. Also, Sergeant Crutchfield and I have one more piece of information we haven't told you about."

"Okay, and what is that?"

"We know what Smith looks like."

"How did you get it?" Clay asked.

"During my conversation with the car rental manager, she mentioned they had recently installed a video security system. They put it in because they were having problems with employee thefts from the register. It's programmed to start recording whenever the register is opened. It was our good luck that Smith paid cash for a week's rental."

"Do they still have the recording?" Clay quickly asked.

"They do," Joey said, "and they've been told to hold it for us."

"Has the car been turned in yet?"

"We don't know right now. Customers can just leave their car in the rental lot and drop the keys and paperwork in a box as they head into the terminal. The manager told Summer they're running behind on processing returns because they recently fired two employees they caught stealing using their new security camera system."

Clay got up and started pacing as he talked. "Okay, several things need to get done right away. Tell the manager to make it a priority to check their records and find out whether Smith's car was turned in. If it has been, tell them not to touch it so we can process it. While we're there, we'll pick up the video of Smith at the car rental counter. Also, we have to check the airlines for a passenger named Jeremiah Smith. Does he have a return flight scheduled or has he already left? My guess is he's already hauled it out of here. We'll get the airport police to check their security videos for the guy anywhere in the terminal. We want to be able to track him through the airport from the second he stepped off the jetway."

Clay stopped his pacing, cutting his eyes at Summer Hayes. "Are you getting all this down, Detective?"

"Yes, sir," she said, starting to type quickly.

"Okay, what am I forgetting?" Clay asked.

The chief said, "First, Detective Hayes, you did a great job on this. Go call the manager and tell her someone will be heading out there shortly to pick up the recording. Then contact the airport police and get the ball rolling on the other videos. If they give you any crap, let me know, and I'll talk to their boss."

"I'm on it, Chief," she said, leaving the office.

Mike drawled, "Clay, to answer your question, what you're forgetting is the fact that I've taken over the lead in this investigation."

Clay grimaced. "C'mon, Mike. You can't leave me on the sidelines on this."

"I can, and I am. For all the reasons I gave you before Crutchfield and Hayes came barging in here."

"Mike, listen. I know what you said before, but the fact our suspect is likely to be from Las Vegas puts a completely different light on things. If you send Summer with Joey out there, he'll essentially be working alone. Hayes is sharp, but she's a rookie detective with zero experience investigating homicides."

Wilson moved several stacks of paper to the credenza before answering. Addressing Crutchfield, he said, "While you were gone, I decided I would take personal charge of the investigation to blunt our new mayor's hate campaign against Clay. You'll still be doing the legwork. Considering the fact a public figure was killed, it's the right thing to do."

"Okay," Joey replied. "So, you want me to head out to Vegas depending on what we find on the airport videos?"

"That's right."

"Will it just be Summer and me?" he asked, glancing at Clay.

The chief thought about the ramifications of the decision he was making. "I may regret this, but I want the three of you going. Assign Donnie Pecora to handle the day-to-day investigative stuff, and have him report directly to me."

"Thanks, Chief," Clay said, getting to his feet. "I appreciate you sticking your neck out for me."

"Just find the guy before Gordy Cooper decides he needs to appoint himself chief of police," he grumbled.

At 10:30 a.m., the man known as Jeremiah Smith approached the airlines ticket counter where he purchased a one-way ticket to Las Vegas. From there, he endured the tedious process of going through the security checkpoint. He had no worries the TSA employees would find any prohibited items.

The gun and knife were long gone, pitched into the black waters of the St. Johns River as he drove over the Dames Point Bridge. Before heading to the airport, he had stuffed the suit along with the blood-soaked gloves and towels into a dumpster behind a convenience store.

Clearing security, Smith walked slowly toward his gate, his mind going over once again the botched killing. He miscalculated the woman's ability to react so quickly upon seeing the gun pointed at her. He hated making mistakes, and even more so because of the prominent status of his victim. The crime scene investigation would include an exhaustive search by police of every square inch of the house, he knew. The initial struggle in the kitchen followed by the final, deadly confrontation in the living room increased the possibility that he might have missed some minute piece of evidence that could eventually lead back to him. Smith dismissed the thought immediately. It was not in his nature to worry about things he couldn't control. If it happened, he would use one of his false IDs and simply disappear.

Stopping at one of the airport shops, he bought a newspaper and a bottle of water. As he handed money to the clerk, he noticed a television monitor mounted in the corner. A blond-headed reporter was standing in front of the mayor's house pointing toward police officers stringing crime scene tape around the property as she spoke. Smith casually walked over to the monitor, reading the crawl at the bottom of the screen as he approached, "**JAX BEACH MAYOR FOUND DEAD; POSSIBLE FOUL PLAY INVOLVED**".

As Smith drew near, he heard the reporter saying, "*-are not giving out any details at this time. The only information Jacksonville Beach police have provided so far is that the city's mayor, Denise Adams, was found deceased in her home shortly after ten this morning. I've spoken to a neighbor who lives across the street who said she heard a loud scream coming from the direction of the mayor's house a short while ago. When she went outside to see what was going on, she saw a woman running away from the mayor's front door. The witness, a retired Duval County schoolteacher, said she saw the woman get into a car in the driveway and start talking on a cell phone. Shortly afterward, two police officers arrived. The witness said they talked to the woman, who was reported to be hysterical, and then they went into the house. Right after that, one of the officers came back out and started talking on his radio. Within minutes, numerous police officers, a rescue unit, and detectives showed up along with Police Chief Mike Wilson and Detective Commander Clay Randall. About ten minutes ago, the woman was driven away in a police car by a detective.*

"I attempted to get a statement from Chief Wilson, but he went around to the rear of the residence with Commander Randall and another detective before I could get his attention. Police have stretched barricade tape around the mayor's property, preventing this reporter from getting any closer. As this investigation continues into the death of Jacksonville Beach Mayor Denise Adams, we will-"

Smith turned away before the reporter finished, strolling out of the shop and heading for his departure gate. Taking a seat across from the gate, he kept his hat pulled low as he flipped casually through the newspaper and drank the bottle of water.

Little more than twelve hours had passed since the murder. He figured the cops were still at the house conducting their investigation. They probably didn't know yet exactly how she died, but that would change when an autopsy was done. By then, he would be safely back home awaiting the remaining twenty-five thousand dollars Lou Dunlop owed him.

Hearing his flight called, Smith joined the throng of passengers headed for the jetway. Thirty minutes later, the plane lifted off, leaving the beaches of Jacksonville as it headed for the desert sands of Las Vegas.

The following two days were busy for the detectives, filled with both successes and frustrations. From the car rental records, they knew the date and approximate time Smith's flight arrived. With the assistance of airport police, they used that information as a starting point to review security videos from various points in the airport. They were then able to scan through the footage and locate the suspect as he exited a Delta Airlines jetway. From there, they followed his movements using various camera locations as he made his way through the airport terminal.

The man wore a light-colored suit with a wide-brimmed Panama hat as he rolled a small, black carry-on behind him. He kept his head down at all times, effectively shielding his face from security cameras. However, at the car rental counter, he removed the hat as he talked to the clerk, allowing a clear view of his face.

Locating those pieces of video was easy. The harder task was trying to determine whether the suspect had flown back out. The man's itinerary showed he had purchased a one-way ticket to Jacksonville. Using the ME's estimated time of death as a starting point, Joey worked with airport and Delta officials to search for a Jeremiah Smith purchasing a return ticket to Las Vegas. That search came up empty.

He reported back to Clay with the information, and they discussed the possibility the suspect was still in the area. Doubting the man would have hung around after committing a murder, Clay told Joey to check other airlines for a Jeremiah Smith. Once again calling on the airport police for help, they checked all airlines offering flights to Las Vegas and got a hit. Jeremiah Smith had purchased a ticket on Southwest Airlines that left at 11:45 the morning after the murder.

With that information, it was an easy task to locate the man on video. He appeared to be wearing the same clothing as the day he arrived. As before, the Panama hat sat firmly on his head in such a way that his face was never clearly visible.

Joey watched as he went into a store and came out with a newspaper and a bottle of water. Heading to his gate, he took a seat off to himself and proceeded to flip through the pages of the newspaper while he occasionally took a sip of water. He never removed the hat and managed to drink the entire bottle without ever raising his head far enough to show his face.

Joey noticed several interesting things on the video. Although the man finished drinking the water, he didn't pitch the empty bottle into a trash can as most people would do. Instead, he crumpled it up and slipped it into his carry-on bag along with the newspaper, as if he didn't want to leave anything behind that had his fingerprints on it. Joey also saw what looked like a bandage on the man's right hand when he raised the bottle to drink. In addition, Smith walked with a conspicuous limp on his right side, a limp he didn't have when security video captured him upon his arrival in Jacksonville.

Joey shared the observations with Clay, who was most interested in the latter two. "The ME said she felt certain the killer was right-handed from the angle of the knife wound and the bullet entries. I know Denise was left-handed, so it's probable that she had the glass tumbler in that hand. She struck the gun and the back of his right hand with the tumbler. It broke when it hit the gun, and the blood on the piece of glass must have come from the back of his hand. Therefore, the bandage."

Joey said, "That makes sense. Now, think back to the scene. The end table that was knocked over. Did it sit at the end of the couch closest to the kitchen?"

Clay thought about it a moment and nodded. "It did. Denise sat there, and I was across from her in the chair. She put her wine glass on the end table."

"I wonder if Denise knocked it over as she ran by and then Smith banged into it. That could explain why he was limping on the security video the day he flew out. Also, remember our witness, Forsyth, who said he saw the man walking to his car with a limp."

Clay and Joey briefed Chief Wilson on what they had discovered and also told him of their discussion with an assistant state attorney about issuing an arrest warrant. After reviewing the evidence, the ASA told them there wasn't sufficient probable cause to justify the issuance of a warrant. They argued their case, but he held firm.

The false address on the driver's license failed to impress him. He suggested it could simply be a typo committed by a careless clerk at a driver's license office. When Clay pointed out that Smith had entered the same address on the car rental application, he said it could be because he was mindlessly entering the information without noticing it was incorrect.

Clay then showed the prosecutor several photos of his challenge coin with its inscription. Even after he explained that someone stole it from his locker the week before the murder, the attorney wouldn't budge. He said with a hint of sarcasm that a smart defense attorney could argue that Clay himself committed the killing and had dropped his own coin inadvertently at the scene. He would only concede that the item was interesting. Still, it was insufficient to establish probable cause.

The attorney grew more attentive when they told him about finding the bloody shard of glass and the bit of skin under the mayor's fingernail. Joey showed the prosecutor the airport video revealing Smith's limping gait and his bandaged hand, and then shared his speculation as to what those things meant.

The ASA wasn't too excited over Joey's theory about the reason for Smith's limp, but he focused on the man's bandaged hand. He asked whether the evidence had been submitted for DNA testing. Clay assured him the items were already at a lab in Tampa, although the results were not expected back for another day or two.

The best they could get from the prosecutor was a promise to reconsider their request for an arrest warrant in the event DNA could be extracted from one or more of the samples and a match with a known person could be established. His final word was that their case against the man known as Jeremiah Smith was entirely circumstantial at that point and would never hold up to judicial scrutiny.

Frustrated, Clay asked what it would take to get him to authorize an arrest warrant. He laughed and said a complete confession along with the murder weapon and a DNA match would tie it up neatly. Turning serious, the ASA said, assuming they could find the man, they should try to convince him to sit down for an interview. If he agreed, the attorney said they should ask him to give a voluntary sample of his DNA, which they could then use to test against the sample.

Further, he instructed them to ask the man to explain why he came to Jacksonville and why his address was incorrect on his identification. He agreed the man's ID, if they could prove it was an intentional fake, might justify federal charges since he used it to obtain the airline tickets. He suggested they discuss that issue with the appropriate federal law enforcement agency.

They came away disappointed but determined to keep pushing forward.

S mith's flight arrived in Las Vegas thirty minutes late. Violent storms over the Dallas-Fort Worth area caused the pilot to take a detour to avoid a plane full of airsick passengers. He retrieved his checked bag and headed out of the terminal, catching a shuttle to the offsite parking lot where he had left his vehicle. He placed his luggage in the back, then removed his Panama hat and jacket and laid them carefully on the front passenger seat. Wiping sweat from his brow, he climbed behind the wheel, cranked the engine, and turned the air conditioner to the coldest setting. Five minutes later, he hit the freeway heading out of Las Vegas.

As he drove, Smith tuned the radio to an all-news station. He doubted there would be any news of his handiwork outside the Jacksonville market considering the low news value of a local politician's murder. Twenty minutes later, as a panel of financial analysts continued to pontificate on the state of the economy, he switched to a station that played seventies rock, drumming his fingers on the steering wheel in time to songs from his teenage years.

An hour later, he turned off the highway into a quarter mile long, crushed rock driveway that wound around several large boulders, ending at an expansive, three-bedroom ranch with a stone and stucco veneer. The house sat on five acres of sand and cactus trees and not much else. His nearest neighbor was almost two miles away, which had been a key selling point when he purchased the property years before.

Exiting the car, a rush of hot air and blowing sand hit him, causing him to turn away and close his eyes. When the gust passed, he retrieved his bags and headed for the house. He unlocked the door and stepped inside as the alarm system began chirping. Opening the security panel, he entered the disarm code, then stood unmoving, listening carefully to the silence of the house. Checking each room, Smith saw that everything was exactly as he had left it days before.

In the master bedroom, he entered the walk-in closet and hung his jacket on the rack. On the rear wall, he pressed a small button near the floor with the toe of his shoe. With a soft click, a section of the wall swung open, revealing a large safe standing over five feet tall.

Smith spun the dial several times and entered the combination. Pulling open the heavy door, his eyes scanned more than a dozen handguns and three shotguns. Smith then admired the five, scope-mounted rifles in their racks, his preferred choice of firearm.

He had never used his personal weapons in his job. A firearm used more than once had sent many a man either to his death or to life in a cage when cops were able to link it to crimes through ballistics. Smith always used a pistol or rifle he didn't mind dumping in a river or the ocean after a job. Those in his safe were too valuable for that fate.

He lifted one of the rifles from its rack and carried it to the bed, sitting down and cradling the weapon across his lap. It was his favorite, an M82 Barrett sniper rifle in a desert camouflage finish with a Leupold Mark 4 telescopic sight. With the attached bipod legs and carrying handle, the big rifle weighed more than thirty pounds with ten rounds of .50 caliber ammunition loaded into the magazine.

Running his hand along the barrel, his thoughts drifted back to another Barrett sniper rifle, one that was almost identical to the weapon he held in his hands.

———————————

It was January 1991, and he was a sergeant in the Army, stationed in Iraq during the Gulf War. Trained as a sniper, he was a damn good one.

Smith had just completed a three-day deployment under harsh conditions. High temperatures each day had topped out at five degrees, with lows dropping below zero. He and his spotter spent most of that time hunkered down trying to keep from freezing. Arriving back at the base, he headed straight to his tent. All he wanted to do was to drop into his bunk and sleep around the clock. That was not to be.

Smith had no sooner sat down on his bunk when his staff sergeant stepped in and ordered him to report to the base commander. When he asked what he had done, the staff sergeant shrugged his shoulders and told him the major hadn't seen fit to take him into his confidence and to get his ass moving on the double.

With a mumbled curse under his breath, Smith headed over to the major's quarters. As he approached, the adjutant stepped out and told him to enter, holding the tent flap open. Smith ducked inside and immediately came to attention, announcing himself and saluting the major, who was sitting at a folding table reviewing a document.

The major continued reading the document for several seconds before returning a perfunctory salute and telling him to stand at ease.

Smith wondered nervously what he could have done to get on the man's radar screen.

After finishing his review, the major initialed the last page and tossed the document into a basket marked OUT. Taking a cigar from a box on his desk, he snipped the end with a pair of clippers and took his time lighting it, taking several puffs until he had it going to his satisfaction. Leaning back in the chair, he put his feet up on the table as he watched his sergeant through a cloud of smoke. He said nothing for almost a minute, his eyes never wavering from Smith.

As Smith grew increasingly uncomfortable under his commander's gaze, the major asked, "Sergeant, how many confirmed kills do you have to date?"

"Nine, sir," Smith responded.

"And I understand a few of those are at ranges over half a mile. Is that correct?"

"Two of nine, yes, sir."

The major took another puff of his cigar before continuing. "Would I be correct in saying that you don't have a problem with killing the enemy?"

Although the question confused him, Smith answered promptly, "No, sir. I don't have a problem doing my job."

"So, if I were to give you an order to kill an enemy, you're telling me you would follow that order without question. Do I understand you, soldier?"

"Yes, sir," Smith answered, curious about the direction the conversation was going.

"I, or to be more accurate, *we* have a problem that requires your skills."

When he didn't elaborate, Smith said, "Yes, sir?"

"Sergeant, what I'm about to tell you is highly classified. If you ever reveal this conversation, you will be court martialed and spend the next few decades in the United States Disciplinary Barracks at Fort Leavenworth. Do you follow what I'm saying to you?"

Smith's mind raced as he tried to figure out what the man was talking about. He nervously replied, "Yes, sir."

"Okay, you say you understand. Tell me what I said, and what it means. *To* you and *for* you."

His mouth so dry he could barely speak, Smith cleared his throat and then said, "Sir, you intend to share highly classified information with me. And if I ever reveal what you tell me, I could maybe spend the rest of my life in the stockade."

"That's exactly right," he said, gesturing toward a chair in front of him. "Sit down, Sergeant."

Smith dropped into the chair, sitting ramrod straight, his knees together, hands gripping the arms of the chair. Then he waited. For what, he didn't know.

Taking another drag on the cigar, the major dropped it into an ashtray, leaned forward, and pointed a finger at Smith. "Alright, Sergeant, this is what's happening. We have a man on this base who has betrayed our country."

Smith frowned, "Sir, you mean one of our guys?"

"No. I mean a Jordanian national who's been working for us since shortly after Desert Shield operations commenced. The guy's name is Jamir Hassab. He's been gathering intelligence on our troop strength and weapons capabilities and passing it to Saddam's Republican Guard."

Confusion passed fleetingly across Smith's face as he tried to figure out the reason for such secrecy as well as the threat of military imprisonment over a traitor. He asked, "So, this Hassab guy was caught passing intelligence, sir?"

"Not caught, Sergeant. Observed."

"Yes, sir. Is he on the base now?"

"He is, but he'll be leaving in a couple of hours."

"Well, sir, I don't understand. Is there a reason why we can't go get him right now and lock him up?"

"You remember my caution about this conversation, soldier?"

"Absolutely, sir. Never repeat it."

"Right. There are two reasons why we can't take that option. First, Hassab is the son of a high-ranking Jordanian official. Any action we take must be one that will never point back at the United States."

Smith said, "I understand, sir."

"Second, and equally important, the reason we haven't moved against him before now is because a man . . . let's call him Jim, has been feeding Hassab false intel to pass to the Republican Guard."

"Jim?" Smith asked, perplexed. "Is he military assigned to our unit?"

The major hesitated before answering. "It's above your rank, sergeant. Let it go."

"Yes, sir," Smith responded.

"Jim has an informant who provided evidence that Hassab has been playing both sides. So, a month ago, he had his informant start passing false intel to Hassab."

Suddenly dawning on Smith that Jim must be a CIA operative, he said, "Sir, may I ask a question?"

"Go ahead, Sergeant."

"Is there a reason Jim doesn't want to continue feeding this Hassab false information? I mean, it seems that the more bad intel we can funnel to the Republican Guard, the easier it's going to be to take them down."

The major shook his head. "That's a fair question. Jim has advised me he believes Hassab is starting to get suspicious. We can't afford to take the chance that he'll take off before we get him."

"And, sir, I understand specific questions about Jim are off limits. But why can't he take care of the problem himself?"

"Because he's been called away on another assignment, so it's our responsibility now."

"Then, sir, I'm your man."

"Good, that's what I wanted to hear."

"Sir, what is the guy's description, and where can I find him?"

"Hassab is short and skinny, maybe five, five and a hundred and twenty pounds. The usual full beard. You can't miss him. He always wears a black and white checked keffiyeh. He's the only one here who wears that color, so he'll be easy to spot. As for his location, he's on the base right now, but he'll be heading out at 2100 hours. He and another Jordanian are assigned to meet an Iraqi who supposedly has intelligence on Saddam's troop movements. The Iraqi will meet them on the main north-south road ten klicks from here. Hassab will be riding shotgun in a Humvee with the informant driving."

"Is the other Jordanian a bad guy, too, Major?"

"No, he's actually the man who has been feeding Jim the intel on Hassab." Glancing at his watch, he stood up. "It's 1900 hours now. I need you to move out quickly so you'll have time to locate the pickup point and get yourself into position."

"Sir, I have a few more questions, if that's okay."

Sitting back down slowly, he asked, "What else do you need to know?"

"Well, sir, I want to be certain I take the right shot. How accurate is the information that the other guy will be driving the Humvee instead of this Hassab? I would hate to pop the wrong one."

"Good question. First off, he's about the same age and size as Hassab. He also has a dark beard, but the key difference is his keffiyeh. It's red and white. That should make it easy to differentiate between them."

"Yes, sir, but we're talking about taking a shot in extreme low light conditions. The ability to identify colors through a night-vision scope will be impossible. I'll only be able to distinguish patterns. Do their keffiyehs have different designs?"

"I don't believe they do, but don't worry about it, Sergeant. I guarantee the informant will be driving. Hassab considers himself the other man's superior because of his family connections, so he will demand a driver."

Smith said, "Yes, sir. In that case, I only have one more question, Major."

His voice growing impatient, he said, "What is it? I've got to get to a meeting."

"Will I be using my regular spotter?"

He shook his head. "No spotter. You're doing this job solo."

Smith frowned. "Sir, I've never taken a shot without a spotter. My training specifically requires one."

"Sergeant, I don't give a rat's ass what your training requires. I told you this operation was highly classified. It's on a strict need-to-know basis, and no one else needs to know. Are you telling me you're incapable of doing your job without someone there to hold your hand?"

Smith felt a flush of anger, but he kept his face impassive as he thought, *You prick. You want me to put my ass on the line, but I bet you'd never do it.*

"No, sir," he answered. "I don't need anyone to hold my hand. I just need to be clear that I'm being ordered to conduct an operation without a spotter."

"You have your orders, Sergeant. Now, if there's nothing else, I suggest you get moving," he said handing Smith a map with the coordinates where the two men intended to meet their contact.

Standing and coming to attention, Smith saluted, saying, "Yes, sir," and left.

Heading back to collect his gear, Smith worried that this operation was going to turn out to be a disaster.

As Smith gathered his weapon and gear, his spotter, a corporal, stepped into the tent. Seeing Smith loading up, he asked, "Where you headed, Sarge?"

"Got a mission," he answered, continuing to pack his gear.

"No way! We've been back, what, half an hour? The staff sergeant said we had the next forty-eight hours off. Surely, they're not sending us out now, are they?"

"First, the major outranks the staff sergeant. And second, it's not us. Just me."

"What's going on? There's no solo sniper team," the corporal objected.

"I can't talk about it. Orders from on high. I'm heading out solo. Period."

"Did you tell–"

"Yes, I told him our training requires a sniper to have a spotter. He basically called me a coward for wanting one. I gotta go," Smith said, carrying his bag and rifle and heading to the motor pool to check out a vehicle.

Twenty minutes later, his gear loaded in a Humvee, Smith drove off following the map coordinates the major gave him. Night-vision goggles enabled him to see the road clearly as it headed straight into the desert.

The greenish cast the goggles gave to the landscape always made him feel like he was traveling across a desert on some alien planet.

Smith reached the rendezvous point and did a visual evaluation. The intersection with the highway was flat in all directions, which would give him a clear line of fire. Turning around, he backtracked to a low hill he had passed earlier that he believed would give him cover as well as a good angle to the target.

Concealing the Humvee on the far side of the mound, Smith grabbed his gear and hiked the short distance to the top. He arranged his shooting platform and loaded three, fifty-caliber rounds into his rifle. For a single target, Smith always used three rounds, in spite of the magazine's ten-round capacity. He was superstitious about putting more rounds into the magazine than he felt he needed. If he filled a full mag, he believed it would make him overconfident and possibly cause him to miss his target. He knew it was irrational, but he didn't care. It worked for him.

Smith went through his pre-shot routine, checking the distance to the target first. It was just over a thousand yards, not much of a challenge for his skill level. The wind was blowing at eleven knots from east to west. Smith noted the ambient temperature and relative humidity as well as the fact he was positioned approximately thirty feet above the location of his intended target. When he finished entering all the data, he sighted through the tactical scope. He was ready.

Within fifteen minutes, Smith spotted the Humvee heading toward his location. He shifted the rifle to focus on the interior of the vehicle. He could see two men in the front, both wearing keffiyehs. It was just as he told the major. The night vision scope didn't enable him to differentiate the colors of the headwear, and the patterns appeared very similar.

As the Humvee continued past him, Smith worried again about the order to take out the passenger. The commander had been adamant that the traitor, Hassab, would not be driving. What if that information was wrong, he wondered? He would be killing the informant instead of the bad guy.

Smith settled in behind the scope of his rifle and began tracking the Humvee as these thoughts continued to swirl. When should he take the shot? If Hassab stayed in the Humvee, it would necessitate shooting through the side or front window. That would be okay as long as the informant was not in there, also. There was a high potential for injury to the informant with shattered glass and bits of metal flying around as the bullet penetrated the interior of the Humvee.

It would be easier if one or even both men got out of the vehicle, as long as he didn't lose track of which one was the passenger. The question was answered seconds later when the Humvee stopped a hundred feet short of the meeting point. The driver stayed behind the wheel as the passenger opened his door, climbed out, and stood for several seconds appearing to stare off into the distance toward Baghdad.

The man fit the physical profile, which didn't help him since the major's description of both men had been essentially identical. Smith watched as the man walked a dozen steps away from the Humvee and relieved himself. Coming back to the vehicle, he opened the passenger door and appeared to say something to the driver. The man then walked back to the front of the vehicle and leaned against the bumper, his arms folded.

Smith knew it was time. He would have to trust the intelligence he was given. The man standing outside the Humvee was Hassab. The informant was still inside the vehicle.

Focusing the aim point based upon all his calculations, Smith relaxed as he slowed his breathing. Curling his index finger softly onto the trigger, he took a breath, eased it halfway out, and began gently squeezing.

The Barrett bucked against Smith's shoulder as the fifty caliber round exploded out of the barrel. In little more than a second, the round impacted the man's head just above the base of his neck, nearly decapitating him. The body dropped straight down in front of the vehicle.

Smith didn't need to check on Hassab's condition. He knew. Instead, he focused the scope on the informant, who was still sitting behind the wheel of the Humvee. For several seconds, the man sat motionless as if in shock. Then, he suddenly gunned the big engine and drove straight forward, running over the body. Reaching the highway, the Humvee turned toward Baghdad and raced away.

Smith watched in surprise and confusion. Why had the informant gone that way? Why didn't he turn around and head back to the American base? As those questions pounded through his brain, he quickly gathered up his gear and rifle and ran to his vehicle.

Jumping behind the wheel, he took off, covering the distance to the man he had killed in less than a minute. He slid to a stop twenty feet away from the body and leaped out, pulling a small flashlight from a pocket of his BDUs as he ran.

Shielding the light with his hand, he gasped in horror at the sight. The right front and rear wheels of the Humvee had passed over the man's lower torso, crushing and twisting the body grotesquely.

But that wasn't what caused his heart to race. It was the blood- and brain-spattered keffiyeh beside the body. The keffiyeh that, in spite of the gore covering most of it, was clearly red and white.

"Son of a bitch!" Smith exclaimed. "It's the informant!"

He now thought he understood why Hassab was driving the Humvee. The man named Jim was right. Hassab must have learned that the Americans suspected him of being a spy. He had to have figured that someone wanting to target him would assume he wouldn't be driving considering his insistence on being chauffeured wherever he went. That was why he had taken off toward Baghdad. He was heading there because he knew Saddam's military would protect him.

Staring at the keffiyeh, Smith knew he was in a world of shit. Hurrying now, he ran to the Humvee and pulled it beside the body. Opening the hatch, he wrestled the body into the cargo area and tossed the red and white keffiyeh inside, also. Jumping behind the wheel, he took off in a swirl of dust, heading back to the base and an uncertain future.

————

Smith blinked as he came back to the present. His eyes drifted down to the Barrett rifle and saw sweaty handprints on the barrel and receiver. He retrieved a gun cleaning rag from the safe and carefully wiped the rifle clean. He stored the weapon in its padded slot before closing and relocking the safe.

Slowly undressing, his mind turned again to that terrible time. He had been court-martialed. The major had denied ever telling him that Hassab refused to drive himself. The military prosecutor presented several witnesses who swore they had seen Hassab driving other people on multiple occasions. Smith had no doubt that the major had convinced the witnesses to go along with his story.

In the preparation of his defense at the court-martial, Smith told his military attorney about the anonymous "Jim" that the major claimed was involved. The attorney later told Smith that he had been unable to find anyone who admitted to knowing a man named Jim. Smith realized at that point, before the trial had even begun, that he would be the sacrificial lamb for the colossal screw up.

The bottom line was that he found himself convicted and sentenced to fourteen years in the Disciplinary Barracks at Fort Leavenworth. The only thing that kept his sentence from being much longer was the army's desire to keep publicity about the killing to a minimum.

Smith's face cracked in an embittered smile. He had always been proud to say he was a soldier. He had considered it an honor to serve his country. Yet his pride and his honor had been wrongly taken from him while the major had suffered no damage to his career. He thought it was funny, or maybe ironic, how life sometimes favored one person over another. Funny. Ironic. It didn't matter. All he knew was that he intended to spend the rest of his life taking care of himself, and to hell with everyone else.

T he plane bounced and shook its way through the last remnants of a strong thunderstorm, breaking into bright sunshine and smooth air en route to its cruising altitude of thirty-five thousand feet. The first leg from Jacksonville to Atlanta had been easy, with no turbulence to disturb the crowded passenger cabin. Then storms moved in as they awaited their connecting flight, and the takeoff had proven to be a white-knuckle ordeal for many of the passengers, including Joey Crutchfield.

Clay grinned at his seatmate. "You can let go of the armrests. I think you may have cracked one already."

Joey grimaced. "I *told* you I hate to fly. I still don't understand why the chief wouldn't let us drive to Vegas."

"Because," Clay said patiently, "it's twenty-two hundred miles one way. If we're lucky enough to get a confession from the guy, the last thing we want to do is drive back with him handcuffed and stuffed in the back seat. I'm sure Detective Hayes wouldn't like to ride that far sitting beside him, anyway."

Summer, sitting in the window seat beside Joey, shook her head. "Uh-uh, absolutely not. I get carsick if I sit in the back seat. So, if we had driven, I guess you would've had to babysit him on the way back, huh, Sarge?"

Joey sighed, throwing his hands up, "Okay, I give. It's just that I don't like to fly. Did I mention that?"

Clay laughed. "I think you may have once or twice. But it's okay, Joey. We're out of the bad weather now, so you can kick back and enjoy the rest of the ride."

Lowering his voice, Clay said, "Let's review what we know so far and go over the plan for finding our suspect."

"Okay," Joey responded, reluctantly releasing his grip on the armrests and retrieving a notebook from the seat pocket. Flipping through several pages, he scanned what he had written. Glancing occasionally at his notes, he summarized the investigation to date.

"First off, we have the DNA report back from the private lab," he said, holding up a sheaf of papers. "They classified the blood from the glass tumbler and the piece of skin under the mayor's fingernail as well as your challenge coin, Clay. All we need now is a comparison sample from our suspect."

"Next, today is August 3rd. We've established that our man flew out of Jacksonville International at 11:45 a.m. on July 30th. He was on Southwest Flight 45, arriving in Las Vegas on a connecting flight from Atlanta. We got a copy of the flight manifest and confirmed that he was on the flight."

Turning to the following page, he continued. "Now, jumping back to July 26th when the guy flew in to Jacksonville, he came in on Delta flight 1235 from Las Vegas, arriving at 2:18 p.m. At approximately 3:00 p.m., he was captured on video renting a car from Coastal East Car Rental, paying cash in advance for one week. Detective Hayes and I got with the airport cops and shared the car rental video with them. They scanned their security tapes for all of the gates going back one hour before he arrived at Coastal East and saw him entering the terminal from the Delta flight.

"They then checked the footage from all the cameras between the jetway and Coastal East. He made a stop at the first restroom he came to. He was in there three minutes and twenty-seven seconds before coming out. From there, he went to the baggage carousel where he retrieved one checked bag and then went straight to the car rental counter."

"Go over again about the car and how the print was found," Clay prompted.

"When Summer and I went to the airport, we asked the Coastal East manager if the vehicle was still there, and we got lucky. When our suspect brought the car back, it was taken out of service because it was due for scheduled maintenance. But instead of being moved to the section of the lot where they put cars that need servicing, a new employee got confused. He parked it in the section where they store their older rentals that are being removed permanently from service and sold at auction. At first, the manager thought the car was stolen, but she found it when she walked the lot herself."

"So nobody rented the car in between when our suspect brought it back and it was found parked in the wrong place."

"That's right," Joey said. "And no one else had driven it except the employee who stuck it in the wrong lot."

"Okay, you took elimination prints from the employee that were matched to the steering wheel and the driver's door handle inside. But you also found another print."

"We did. The evidence tech found an almost perfect thumbprint on the glove box release button. The button is smooth metal, and that print was shinin' like a diamond in a goat's ass."

Clay leaned forward and looked at Joey. "That expression is just wrong on every level."

"You're obviously one of those people who can't truly appreciate the visual simplicity of such an expression. But I still like you, anyway," Joey said with a grin. "So, about the print. We checked Florida records and came up dry, but we got a hit in Nevada."

"How did you get a fingerprint records search done so quickly out there?"

"I know a supervisor in the Nevada Department of Public Safety Records and Technology Division. I met him a few years ago at a conference, and we got to be good friends. We still stay in touch, so I called and told him what we had. He said to send a copy of the print, and he'd see what he could do. I'll admit I was very surprised when he got back to me less than three hours later with the information on our suspect."

"His name is Von Slater?"

Glancing around to ensure no one was paying attention to their conversation, Joey said in a low voice, "Right. Von Edward Slater. Born January 8, 1960, in Lawton, Oklahoma."

"Why does Nevada have his prints on file?"

"He was arrested twice for simple battery. Once in 2006 and again in 2007. Both incidents occurred in Vegas and were handled by Las Vegas Metro PD. In both cases, the charge was dropped due to insufficient evidence."

"What are the details?" Clay asked.

Joey shook his head. "Don't know right now. My records buddy contacted Vegas Metro, and they told him it would probably take a couple of days to pull up the reports. They've got a huge backlog of public records requests they're having to process right now."

"By the way, any arrests elsewhere?"

"Well, that's an interesting question. His criminal history through NCIC shows the two in Nevada. And then there's an arrest and conviction for homicide while he was in the Army."

"Really?" Clay said. "Charged in a local jurisdiction?"

"No. Through the Uniform Code of Military Justice, or UCMJ for you non-military types. Von Edward Slater was a sergeant in the Army during Desert Storm back in '91. He was a sniper with nine confirmed kills."

"The number of kills was listed in his criminal history?" Clay asked, surprised.

"No, after I got this information, I did a little more background and found a website that tracks military snipers and their kill totals going way back. Anyway, it seems Slater had a tenth kill that wasn't counted because it didn't go well. He was convicted under UCMJ and did fourteen years in the military prison at Fort Leavenworth, Kansas."

"Can we get the specifics on the incident and the charges?" Clay asked.

"Summer is working on that," Joey said.

"Okay, good. I'm not sure whether there's any connection to the mayor's murder, but it bears investigating. Keep me posted on that, Summer," Clay said.

She nodded as he digested the information. "Did you find any record under his alias, Jeremiah Smith?" he asked Joey.

"There are several Jeremiah Smiths in the database, but none with a middle name of Jonas and none that match the approximate age and physical description of Slater."

"You have mug shots from the Nevada arrests?"

"Yep," Joey said, pulling two pictures from the inside flap of his notebook and handing them to Clay.

Holding the mug shots side by side, Clay shifted his eyes back and forth, closely examining first one, then the other. Slater was forty-seven years old at the time of his first arrest and forty-eight at the second. In both pictures, the man looked the same.

"Do you have a screenshot of the guy with his hat off at the rental counter?"

"Right here," Joey said, pulling out an eight-by-ten black and white shot lifted out of the video.

In the years since the second arrest, Slater's hair, still cut short, had gone from salt and pepper to mostly white, and the lines in his face aged him well beyond his years.

"Which picture did you use for the photo spread you showed our retired cop, Mr. Forsyth?"

"This one," Joey said, tapping the screen shot.

"And he picked out Slater?"

"As soon as he saw the man's face, Forsyth pointed at it and said, 'This is the man I saw that night.' There was no hesitation at all."

"How could he be so sure, taking into account the fact it was night time and under less than ideal lighting conditions when he saw him."

"Forsyth said he's got twenty-fifteen eyesight without glasses. I asked him what that meant, and he said he can see at twenty feet what most people can only see at fifteen feet. For someone his age, that's rare. The bottom line is he's positive this is our suspect."

"Well, that's good, but you can bet if we get Slater into court, he'll have some smartass attorney try his best to discredit Forsyth's identification."

"No doubt," Joey agreed. "But the man's law enforcement career gave him lots of practice testifying and dealing with lawyers who try to put the cops on trial when they know their clients are guilty."

"Okay. Do we have an address for Von Edward Slater?"

"We do, and it's not the Desert Rest Memorial Gardens that he listed on the driver's license. According to my DPS buddy, the real address is about sixty miles west of Vegas outside the Town of Pahrump."

"What kind of name is that?"

"There are several theories on its origin. One source suggested it's a takeoff from Indian names for water and rock. Hundreds of years ago, the Southern Pauites named the place, Pah Rimpi. Pahrump somehow derived from that, although I'm not clear on exactly how."

"And where did you find this interesting bit of trivia?"

"Where else? On the Internet, of course. Also, while I was checking out Pahrump, I ran across a place not too far outside the town called the Cherry Orchard," Joey smirked.

"Let me guess. They don't grow cherries there," Clay said.

"Not exactly. Although I'd say it's a good bet that most of the employees would have lost their cherries before they went to work there."

Summer rolled her eyes at the two men as Clay responded, "Okay, let me just say, unless Mr. Slater is working at the Cherry Orchard, I doubt we'll be visiting a brothel."

"But, Clay, think about it. We could stop by there and pick up a tee shirt for the chief. We could tell him the place has the best cherries in at least five of the Western states. I'll even pay for it," Joey grinned.

"Yeah, right," Clay said. "And when he found out what it really was? Let's just say we won't be making that little side trip."

T he plane nosed up to the gate just after noon, Las Vegas time. When he felt the aircraft come to a stop, Joey muttered, "I'm gonna need something stronger than diet soda before I get on another one of these deathtraps."

"Sorry, Joey. If we get lucky and catch our suspect, you'll be sticking to non-alcoholic drinks until we get back," Clay said as he retrieved his bag from the overhead bin. "My goal is to arrest him, convince him to waive extradition, and take him back with us."

Strolling through the terminal toward baggage claim, the dings of slot machines drew their attention as they passed.

"Can you believe people are still playing slots while they wait for their flights?" Summer asked. "You'd think they would have had enough for one trip."

Joey shook his head. "They're hoping they'll win back some of the money they donated to the Las Vegas economy."

"I take it you're not a gambler, Joey," Clay said.

Shaking his head, he said, "I only bet on sure things."

"For instance?" Summer asked as they started down the escalator toward baggage claim.

"For instance, that I'm never going to ride a bicycle a hundred miles like our intrepid leader here," he said, poking Clay on the arm.

"Humph," Clay grunted. "The only problem with that is everyone knows your pathological aversion to physical exercise of any kind, so you'd never get anyone to bet against you anyway."

Half an hour later, their bags loaded into the rental car, Joey called his tech friend with Nevada DPS, who informed him the two battery reports involving Slater had yet to be pulled. Passing the information along to Clay and Summer, they discussed what they should do first.

Summer asked, "Should we drive on over to Pahrump and contact the local police department to see if they have any information on Slater?"

Clay said, "That's a good idea, Summer. However, according to Joey's research, the town is unincorporated, so I doubt they have a local PD. Is that right?"

"Yes," Joey answered. "They're covered by the Nye County Sheriff's office. And as long as I can get a six pack of Diet Coke for the trip, I'm good with heading over there right now."

Ninety minutes later, and one bathroom break for Joey after consuming three Diet Cokes, they arrived at the Nye County Sheriff's office. Entering the lobby, all three presented badges and police identifications to a uniformed receptionist. An assistant escorted them back to the administrative section where they waited while the sheriff finished a telephone call.

Ten minutes passed as they discussed how they would present the information to the sheriff.

"By the way," Joey said, "did anyone get the sheriff's name?"

"I saw it on a pamphlet in the lobby," Summer answered. "His name is D. F. McDougle."

"Ah, and maybe he's a wee Irishman," Joey said in a mangled attempt at an Irish brogue.

"And maybe you should confine your attempts to do accents to your Texas roots," Clay said with a grin.

"Well, I thought it was pretty darn good. Didn't I sound like a true Irishman, Summer?"

Not for the first time, Summer rolled her eyes at Joey. "I have to tell you it sounded more like a Texan with a bad head cold trying to do a south Alabama accent."

Before Joey could respond, a woman in a crisp uniform walked up to them. In her early fifties, with short, brown hair that framed a deeply tanned face, she exuded a quiet confidence as she said, "Good afternoon, I'm Sheriff Faye McDougle." She gave each of them a firm handshake as they introduced themselves in turn and handed her their business cards.

Seeing the surprise on their faces, she said with a smile, "I assume you were expecting a male sheriff."

"We saw your name on your department literature," Clay said with a smile, "so we just assumed with the initials that you were a man. Sorry, no offense, Sheriff."

The sheriff laughed. "None taken. It's a common mistake. Some people still have difficulty with the idea of women in law enforcement, and particularly as an agency head. I've found that using my initials tends to prevent people who have never met me from developing preconceived notions. Please come in," she gestured, leading the way into a spacious office.

Prints of majestic western scenery covered the walls. Behind the dark mahogany desk, there were framed photos of the sheriff smiling with various state and national political figures.

"Can I get any of you something to drink? A cup of coffee or water?" Sheriff McDougle asked as she sat down.

Clay and Summer declined as all three settled into comfortable armchairs covered in a cowhide print.

Joey said, "I could take a Diet Coke if you have one."

"I'm more of a Pepsi fan myself," the sheriff responded with a smile, "but I'm sure we can find one for you." Picking up the phone, she asked her administrative assistant to get a soda for Joey.

They spent a few minutes discussing differences in policing between Florida and Nevada until the assistant brought Joey his drink. When they were once again alone, the sheriff inspected the business cards lined up on her desk blotter. Addressing Clay, she asked, "Commander Randall, what can the Nye County Sheriff's Office do for our law enforcement partners in Florida?"

"First, thanks for agreeing to see us without an appointment. We just flew in to Las Vegas and drove straight here. We're following up on a suspect in the murder of our city's mayor, and we have information that the man possibly lives in this area."

"You say your mayor?"

"Yes. Mayor Denise Adams was attacked in her home. The assailant stabbed her and then shot her twice in the head."

Sheriff McDougle said, "That has to be tough. What evidence do you have that the suspect lives here?"

"With your permission, I'll have Sergeant Crutchfield and Detective Hayes summarize the case for you."

Over the next half hour, Joey and Summer took turns detailing the evidence they had gathered against Von Slater. As they spoke, the sheriff took notes on a legal pad, occasionally interrupting to clarify a point and to ask for particulars on Slater's age and Nevada address. When they finished, she leaned back in her chair, processing the information.

She said, "Your case sounds pretty solid, but I agree with your prosecutor that you need this Von Slater's DNA to close the loop. Do you have any thoughts about how you're going to convince Mr. Slater to give you a DNA sample? If he's guilty, I can't imagine he'll agree to do it willingly."

Clay said, "We talked about that on the plane coming out here. We figure it's a given that he'll tell us to pound sand if we ask him straight up for a sample. So, we thought we would try to trick him into giving us one."

"Trick him how?" the sheriff asked.

"First, can you tell us how far it is to Slater's place from here?"

Turning to her computer, the sheriff pulled up a search engine and entered Slater's address. Within seconds, a satellite map appeared with a flashing dot over a tiny image of a house surrounded by desert.

Spinning the screen around so they could see, she pointed to the flashing dot. "This is a satellite view of the man's place. It's about eight miles from here."

Clay said, "Here's what we would like to do. We make contact with him at his residence. We'll ask him to come here for an interview. Assuming he agrees, during the interview, we'll offer him something to drink. When he touches the bottle or coffee cup, we'll seize it and get it processed for DNA."

The sheriff shook her head. "If he's your killer, I would guess he'd be smart enough to know what you want and would refuse to touch anything that would leave his DNA."

"We figured it was a long shot, but we wanted to try," Clay said. "Regardless, we need to interview him. He flew to Jacksonville using a fake ID, and that's a federal violation that we'll try to have filed with the U. S. Attorney in Jacksonville if we need it."

"Okay," Sheriff McDougle said. "What do you need from me and my people?"

"Could we have one of your deputies accompany us since we have no legal jurisdiction here?"

"Sure. In fact, I'll go with you. Your case intrigues me, and I like to get out of the office occasionally anyway."

Clay nodded. "Also, I haven't discussed this with my detectives, but, in an abundance of caution, it seems to me that we shouldn't let Slater see all three of us."

Joey spoke up, "Sorry, Commander. I don't understand."

"I'm just trying to think of every contingency. In the event the interview doesn't work out the way we hope, we'll need to start surveillance on the guy, which could involve personal contact with him. If that becomes necessary, it needs to be someone Slater has never seen before."

"Makes sense," the sheriff agreed.

"Okay," Joey said, "which one of us do you want to stay back?"

Clay responded, "Joey, you gave a statement to the media the day the mayor was found dead, and it ran on a couple of the TV stations. We have to assume that Slater would have seen the clip and could remember you."

Turning to Summer, he said, "I want you to stay in the background. I have a feeling Slater is going to tell us to go to hell, assuming we make contact with him at his place. If that happens, I need you available in case we have to go to plan B, whatever that is."

"I understand, Commander," Summer said. "What do you want me to do while you're gone?"

Before answering, he asked the sheriff, "Could you have someone recommend a hotel so Detective Hayes can get rooms for us while we try to contact Slater?"

"That's no problem," Sheriff McDougle replied. "My admin assistant can help her with that."

"Okay," he said, turning back to Summer. "After you get checked in, call Chief Wilson and brief him on our plan."

"Are you wanting to visit Mr. Slater today?" the sheriff asked.

"The sooner the better," Clay said. "In fact, right now, if you're available."

"Let's do it. I'll get my car and meet you in the parking lot. If you like, you can ride with me so Detective Hayes can take your car to the hotel."

Twenty minutes later, Sheriff McDougle turned into the driveway of Slater's property. A shiny black Ford Expedition sat in the turnaround in front of the house. The sheriff ran a license check and confirmed the car belonged to Von Slater at the same address.

Before they reached the door, it opened, and the man they now knew to be Von Slater, alias Jeremiah Smith, stepped out, closing the door behind him. He wore a dark blue suit and white shirt that appeared similar to the clothing the retired cop described the man wearing as he walked past his house the night the mayor was killed.

"Afternoon, ma'am," Slater said calmly, showing no sign of nervousness or concern. "What can I do for you and, I assume, your fellow law enforcement officers?" he asked, gesturing toward Clay and Joey.

"Good afternoon," the sheriff said. "Are you Von Edward Slater?"

"I am," the man nodded.

"I'm Sheriff D. F. McDougle, Nye County Sheriff's Office. And," she said, turning to indicate Clay and Joey, "these are police officials from Florida. They would like to ask you some questions, if you don't mind."

Slater's eyes cut toward Clay and Joey at the mention of Florida before returning his attention to the sheriff. "Sheriff McDougle, under normal circumstances, I would be happy to help you, but I'm afraid I have an appointment. I was just leaving when I saw you pull up."

"I see. I'm sorry we caught you at an inconvenient time, but these officers are on a tight schedule, and the questions they have shouldn't take a lot of your time."

"Well," he said, "I guess I can postpone my meeting. If you're sure this won't take long."

Clay spoke up. "Mr. Slater, I'm Commander Clay Randall with the Jacksonville Beach Police Department, and this is Detective Sergeant Crutchfield. We shouldn't need more than a half hour to get this cleared up."

Slater's eyes lingered on Clay before he responded, "Anything to help our law enforcement community."

Opening the door, Slater led the way into a great room with floor-to-ceiling windows highlighting a spectacular view of the desert that seemed to go on forever. Settling into a straight-back rocker beside a massive stone fireplace, Slater indicated a large sectional that faced the windows.

As they took their seats, Clay asked, "Do you need to call someone to let them know you'll be a little late?"

Slater waved his hand, "It's not necessary. I'm sure this is more important than my appointment. What can I do to help you?"

Slater's cell phone abruptly rang. He pulled the phone from his pocket and viewed the screen. He stood, saying, "I'm sorry, but I have to take this call. I'll only be a moment." The man went into an adjacent room, closing the door behind him.

Clay said softly, "Did anyone see a bulge like he was packing a weapon?"

"I didn't," Joey answered. "Sheriff?"

"As small and thin as he is, I don't think he could hide a sharp pencil anywhere."

Clay said, "Did you notice how he cut his eyes at us when the Sheriff said we were from Florida?"

"Definitely," Joey said. "Doesn't it seem odd that he's not curious why Florida cops have shown up at his door wanting to ask him questions? His whole demeanor is not how you'd expect a normal person to act under the circumstances," he added, as Slater opened the door and came back into the living room.

"My apologies," he said, settling once again in the rocker. "So, I had just asked how I could help."

Clay spoke up. "Mr. Slater, we would appreciate it if you could accompany us to the sheriff's office for the interview."

"I'm sorry, but that would take too long. I still need to make my appointment, even if I'm a little late. I'm comfortable talking to you here."

Clay nodded, expecting that answer. "Okay, I understand." Retrieving his cell phone, Clay said, "Mr. Slater, do you have any objections to this interview being recorded?"

Slater hesitated as he looked at the three cops arrayed in front of him. Shaking his head, he said, "Of course not. I have nothing to hide. Turn on the recorder."

Clay set his phone to record and put it on the coffee table so it would pick up both their questions and Slater's answers.

"Mr. Slater," he began, "before we ask you any questions, I need to advise you of your constitutional rights."

"Really? Why would you need to do that? Am I suspected of some crime?"

Ignoring the question, Clay said, "It's just normal police procedure. Please listen while I explain your rights."

Clay read from a rights card each of the points set out in what is commonly known as the Miranda warning. When he finished, he asked, "Do you understand each of these rights I have explained to you?"

Slater smiled. "Sure."

"Second question. Having these rights in mind, do you wish to talk to us now?"

"Sure," he said again, still smiling.

"Alright. Thank you," Clay said. "Now, Mr. Slater, have you been to Florida lately?"

Slater squinted his eyes as if searching his memory. "I don't recall exactly how long it's been since I was there last. A beautiful state, though. I love the beaches along the west coast of Florida around Sanibel Island."

"When was the last time you were in Jacksonville?"

"Oh, my, I couldn't really say. It's an interesting place, though. Used to be named Cowford, wasn't it?"

Disregarding Slater's attempt to deflect the line of questioning, Clay shifted gears. "Who is Jeremiah Jonas Smith?" he asked, watching the man's face closely for a reaction.

Slater blinked rapidly, twice, then responded in a casual tone, "You got me. Who is Jeremiah Jonas Smith?"

"We thought you could tell us since you presented identification with that name when you purchased a plane ticket to Jacksonville, Florida. You also used a Nevada driver's license with that name to rent a car at the airport shortly after arriving in Jacksonville."

"Interesting," Slater responded in a neutral voice.

When he didn't continue, Clay asked, "Do you have any response other than *interesting* to the information I just shared with you?"

"No."

Clay kept going. "Did you have occasion to visit the residence of Denise Adams on or about July 29th?"

"Who is that?"

"She is, or was the mayor of Jacksonville Beach."

"Was? What happened, did she get voted out of office?"

"No, Mr. Slater. She was murdered in her own home."

Slater shrugged. "Life's tough for everyone. Tell me, officer. Sorry, I don't recall your name. What does all this have to do with me?"

Clay pressed on. "Where were you starting on July 26th and ending on July 30th. Specifically?"

Before answering, Slater picked up a pack of cigarettes and a lighter from the table beside the rocker. He tapped out a cigarette and offered the pack to the officers. Seeing three heads shake, he shrugged and dropped it back on the table. Lighting the cigarette, he took a deep drag, holding the smoke deep in his lungs before letting it out slowly.

Again screwing up his face as if trying to remember, he responded, "Well, let's see. What were those dates again?"

"July 26th through July 30th. Considering today is August 3rd, it shouldn't be too hard to remember where you were only four days ago," Clay said, keeping his voice composed in spite of his growing frustration.

All pretense of courtesy gone, Slater snapped, "Officer, why don't you cut through all this horseshit and tell me what this is about."

"Sure, let's do that," Clay answered. "On the night of July 29th,

Jacksonville Beach Mayor Denise Adams was murdered in her residence. On July 26th, a man named Jeremiah Jonas Smith flew in to Jacksonville from Las Vegas. On July 29th, around the time the mayor was murdered, a man fitting your physical description, wearing a suit that matches what you're wearing right now, was seen walking to a car a few doors down from the mayor's house. On July 30th at 11:45 a.m., a Jeremiah Jonas Smith flew out of Jacksonville and arrived in Las Vegas later that same day. What is your response to this?"

Smith drew on his cigarette again before answering. Stubbing it out in the ashtray beside him, he immediately lit another.

Then he said, "What does some guy named Jeremiah Jonas Smith have to do with me? Just because he might resemble me physically and owns a dark suit? That has nothing to do with me. My name is Von Slater, not Jeremiah Smith, so what's your point?"

Clay smiled. "The point is that Jeremiah Jonas Smith and Von Edward Slater are one and the same."

Slater's expression didn't change. "So you say. What evidence do you have to support that?"

"On July 26th, we have you on video when you arrived from Las Vegas. You were recorded at various points throughout the terminal from the time you stepped onto the jetway until you left the airport with the keys to your rental car. We also have you on video on your departure date, July 30th. And we have you giving the false name of Jeremiah Smith at the car rental place. Your address listed on the fake driver's license is a cemetery in Las Vegas. It's clear you're not dead and buried there, considering you're sitting here talking to us."

With a quick glance at Slater's right hand, Clay said, "Mr. Slater, what happened to your hand?"

Slater's eyes flicked to his right hand holding the cigarette before shrugging. "I don't know what you're talking about."

"You have a cut on the back of your right hand that appears to be several days old. How did that happen?"

Slater held his right hand in front of his face. "Are you speaking of this scratch?"

"I wouldn't necessarily call it a scratch, Mr. Slater. It looks to me more like a cut from, say, a broken piece of glass."

"Interesting conjecture on your part. Wrong, but interesting. Actually, I received this scratch from my cat. He sometimes gets a little aggressive when I'm playing with him."

"A cat, huh? Where is he right now?" Clay asked, making a show of looking around.

"Oh, he's here somewhere," Slater said with a vague wave of his hand.

"I noticed you're not limping like you were in the airport video. Would you mind pulling up your right pant leg?"

"Look," Slater said in a condescending voice. "You seem to think I've done something wrong. Something that brought you all the way across the country just to find me. And that would be what? That I killed your mayor? If you've got all this so-called evidence, then why am I not in handcuffs being transported back to Florida?"

"We haven't left Nevada yet, Mr. Slater."

Getting to his feet, Slater said, "It's unfortunate that you've traveled such a long distance on a fruitless errand. I am an innocent man. I don't know who this person is you claim to be me, but I'd like to meet him. It's said everyone has a twin somewhere, so I guess mine resides in Florida."

Turning to the sheriff, he said, "Sheriff McDougle, I voted for you. Twice. However, considering your part in this attempt to assassinate my character, I'm afraid you've lost me as a supporter. If I'm guilty of anything, it's being too courteous by inviting you into my home and wasting my time on this whole charade. While it's been mildly stimulating, unless one of you has an arrest warrant in your pocket, it's time for you to leave. I really have to go to my appointment."

As they stood, Clay said, "Since you claim you're innocent, how about giving us a DNA sample so we can eliminate you as a suspect?"

"I don't think so. You see, I don't trust my government to do right by its citizens."

"Is that because of the time you spent in Fort Leavenworth for killing a guy when you were in the military?" Joey suggested.

Anger flashed in his eyes as Slater snarled, "We're done here. Get out of my house."

T hey discussed the interview with Slater on the drive back to the sheriff's office. By the time Sheriff McDougle dropped them off at their hotel, the only thing they had decided was to meet again the following morning to discuss possible schemes for obtaining Slater's DNA.

At the hotel, they met Summer and got keys to their rooms. After dropping off their luggage and freshening up, they headed out for dinner at a steak house one of the deputies had recommended to Summer. Over drinks, Clay and Joey briefed Summer on the aborted interview with Slater.

"Without his DNA to compare with what we have from the crime scene, we just don't have enough to satisfy our state attorney," Joey grumbled.

"I know, Joey, but the prosecutor is right," Clay said. "This guy's a pro. He's not going to admit to anything, even if we have a dozen witnesses who all say they saw him kill the mayor. We've got to have his DNA. We get that, along with all the circumstantial evidence, and we'll lock this case up so tight no defense attorney will be able to beat it."

Summer spoke up. "Commander, I did some digging on the Internet searching for any public documents on Slater, and I got some hits."

"Anything of value?" Clay asked.

"Possibly," she said. "I found three marriages for Von Edward Slater. The first one was in Georgia, and the last two were here in Nevada."

A solemn expression on his face, Joey asked, "What are you saying, Summer? You're not thinking of being wife number four, are you?"

Unable to resist rolling her eyes, she said, "No, Sergeant, I don't think a professional killer offers great marriage potential for me. Okay?"

Joey grinned. "Got it. Then, what's your point? So what if he's been married three times?"

"I'll get back to that in a minute. First, though, did either of you happen to notice the décor in Slater's house?"

Baffled, Joey said, "Uh, Summer, I feel certain I speak for Clay when I say that we're not really into *décor*. Not unless it's a ninety inch flat screen TV and a built-in bar in the recliner. That, we can get behind!"

Laughing, Clay said, "Okay, Summer, I'll bite. What about the décor?"

"I don't know," she shrugged. "It's probably nothing."

"No, go ahead. Ignore our Texas Neanderthal here. What's your point?"

"Did the style seem somewhat masculine? Like the crazy stuff Sergeant Crutchfield was talking about?"

"Ouch, that hurts," Joey laughed.

Clay thought back to the short time they had spent in Slater's house. "We weren't there that long, and we only saw the entryway and the main living area. But from what I recall, I'd say it was masculine. Dark furniture. Pictures of western scenery. An antique rifle over the fireplace. I don't recall seeing flowers or frilly throw pillows or other things I would consider feminine. You've been in my house, Summer. Dana is the decorator, so it definitely has the feminine touch. Except for my office of course. She gives me one room to deck out with my stuff. And, of course, the garage is mine," he grinned.

Summer said, "Based on what you described, I'd say it's likely he lives alone."

"I'm lost. So what if he lives alone?" Joey asked. "What does that prove? And what does any of this have to do with us getting his DNA?"

"I've been thinking about how we might be able to do just that. Now, unless he's at an age where sex is no longer important, he's either got a girlfriend who doesn't live with him or . . ." she paused.

"Or what," Clay and Joey said, simultaneously.

"Or he's getting it somewhere else."

Joey looked blankly at Summer. "Still not getting it. And don't you dare roll your eyes at me, young lady!" Joey said in mock outrage.

Summer laughed. "I'll try to control it, Sarge, but you make it so hard."

"I have an idea where you're going with this, Summer. Keep talking," Clay said.

"He won't provide his DNA voluntarily, so we have to get something containing it that he's discarded. Right?"

"Right," Clay said, smiling.

"I was wondering if it would do any good to try to find out if he visits a brothel."

Joey said in a hushed voice, "That's a potentially brilliant idea, Summer."

Clay gave her an approving nod. "I thought that's where you were going. Joey, on the flight out here, you mentioned a brothel called the Cherry Orchard."

"I did. If you recall, I suggested getting the chief a tee shirt, but you shot that down."

"So I did," he admitted. "It's probably a long shot, but we'll discuss it with Sheriff McDougle in the morning. One of her detectives may know someone who works at the Cherry Orchard. If so, we might be able to find out if he's a customer."

Joey raised his glass of Diet Coke and said, "A toast to Detective Summer Hayes. I taught her everything she knows!"

"You also wanted to tell us something about Slater's three marriages," Clay reminded her.

"Right. The first two ended in divorce, but his third wife died. This was eight years ago."

"What were the circumstances?" Joey asked.

"According to the death records, she committed suicide. This reportedly happened in Las Vegas where they were living at the time."

"What was the cause of death?" Clay asked.

"The police report indicated she shot herself. Her body contained a large amount of barbiturates. Not enough to kill her, but certainly enough to knock her unconscious. I called Vegas PD and was lucky to get one of the detectives who responded to the call. She told me she was suspicious as hell of Slater. She said he called it in, using the main number rather than

9-1-1. She listened to the recorded call and said he showed no emotion at all. She said he was so matter of fact that he could just as easily have been calling to report an illegally parked car."

"I assume they weren't able to prove a homicide as opposed to suicide," Clay surmised.

"That's right, but the detective has never forgotten that case. She believes Slater shot his wife and then put the gun in her hand to make it appear self-inflicted."

"Interesting information, but it doesn't sound like it will help us nail him for Denise's murder," Clay concluded. "Good job of digging, though."

At eight-thirty the next morning, Sheriff McDougle listened intently as Summer explained her idea for getting Slater's DNA. "That's our proposal, Sheriff," she concluded.

"It seems a bit of a long shot," the sheriff speculated, "but it's worth a try. Let me check with one of my detectives who works vice and see what he can tell us."

By five that afternoon, when they had not heard from the sheriff, they went back to the same steak house for dinner.

"I'm here to tell you," said Joey. "The filet is almost as good as back home, and that's saying something."

"You mean back home in Florida, don't you?" Clay asked with a grin.

"Now it's *my* turn to do a Summer Hayes eye roll," Joey said. "You *know* I'm talkin' about Texas."

Two hours later, their stomachs full, Clay's cell phone rang as they headed into the hotel lobby. It was the sheriff.

"Commander Randall, I believe we might be in luck. According to my detective's informant, Mr. Slater is a regular visitor at the Cherry Orchard."

"Outstanding! How did he get that information?"

"He downloaded Slater's real Nevada driver's license and enlarged the picture. When he showed it to his CI, she positively identified Slater. She said he visits a couple of times a month and always asks for the same girl, who happens to be her best friend. The CI said she has talked to Slater a few times while he waited for his appointment with her friend. He told her he was a salesman. She said he was always polite, and her girlfriend told her he never wanted anything kinky, just straight up sex."

Excited, Clay asked, "Does he just show up or make an appointment every time?"

"He always makes an appointment so he can be sure he gets the same girl. Now, I guess you'd like to know when his next visit will be."

"You bet."

"It's tomorrow afternoon at four."

"Sheriff, this is great news," Clay said, giving a thumbs up to Joey and Summer, who were impatiently waiting to hear what the sheriff was saying.

"Will there be any trouble getting the girl to cooperate on getting his DNA?"

"Not according to my detective. He said when he told his CI that the man was a killer, she guaranteed him she would make sure her friend got what you needed."

"Thanks very much, Sheriff. Now, one more favor, if you don't mind."

"Name it."

"Do you have access to a private lab that will expedite processing of a DNA sample?"

"How quickly do you want it back?"

"Any time before the first commercial break like on those cop shows would be perfect," Clay laughed. "Seriously, though, we used a private lab for the DNA from the crime scene, and they turned it around in three days."

"I believe there's one in Las Vegas. I'll check on it and get back to you."

They hung up after agreeing to meet the next morning. After Clay briefed Joey and Summer on his conversation with the sheriff, they headed off to their rooms, excited at the prospect of arresting Von Slater very soon.

At nine the next morning, they were ushered into Sheriff McDougle's office. They could tell immediately that something was wrong.

"I have some bad news," the sheriff said as soon as they sat down.

"What is it?" Clay asked, glancing at Joey and Summer.

The sheriff shook her head in disgust. "Detective Sergeant Kent Hastings just left here a few minutes ago. His CI called last night and told him her friend refused to cooperate when she found out what you needed her to do. Hastings went out to the Cherry Orchard and met with his CI and the woman. I'm told her professional name is Jasmin, by the way. He assured Jasmin she wouldn't be in any danger. That all she had to do was gather a little of Slater's DNA. But he said she was frightened out of her mind. She has two young children and lives alone. She's scared for them, worried that Slater would kill her if he found out she was working with law enforcement to gather evidence against him."

"Oh, man, this screws up what was a great plan," Clay said. "Is there anything we can do to convince her otherwise?"

"Apparently not. Hastings tried to reach her this morning at work and was told she called in sick. He's called her cell several times, and it just goes to voicemail. He and his CI went by her apartment and said the blinds were all shut and no one would answer the door. I think at this point you're going to have to consider other options because it's clear she's not going to cooperate."

"Sheriff, what are the chances we could get the CI to hook up with Slater as an alternative?"

Sheriff McDougle shook her head. "I already thought of that and had Hastings ask her if she would do it. She said she would be glad to, but she's not Slater's type. When he first visited the place, he told her he wasn't interested in women who were half a foot taller than him. I understand she's about six-two while Slater is around five-eight."

Clay eyeballed Joey, ready to squelch a wisecrack about short people, but he remained quiet.

He said, "We know Slater is planning to be there at four o'clock today. When he finds out his regular girl is unavailable, there's a chance he might pick someone else. If not, I guess our best bet is to start following him as Summer suggested. Maybe we'll get lucky and grab something he touches."

"I'm sorry the plan didn't work out," the sheriff said. "Is there anything else my department can do to help?"

"We could use a couple of your undercover people and cars to help with the surveillance, if that's possible."

"That won't be a problem," she assured Clay, getting to her feet. "Let's go talk to Sergeant Hastings and his team. They'll be at your disposal as long as you need them."

B y three o'clock, Clay, Joey, and Summer were in place in a police surveillance van marked to resemble a Nye County electric utility vehicle. Sergeant Kent Hastings shared the van with them while four members of his team positioned themselves in two unmarked cars in the immediate vicinity of the Cherry Orchard.

At five minutes until four, one of the detectives contacted Hastings on their secure radio channel and advised that Slater's black Expedition had just passed his vehicle. Thirty seconds later, Slater drove into the lot and came to a stop several rows back from the entrance.

He remained behind the wheel for a minute or so before killing the engine and climbing out. They watched as Slater, smoking a cigarette, scanned the parking lot. When his eyes fell on the surveillance van, he remained motionless for several seconds as he studied it. Apparently satisfied it was legitimate, he turned and headed for the building.

Just before going in, he crushed the cigarette out between his thumb and forefinger. Then he pulled the remaining tobacco and paper away from the filter and tossed it on the pavement. As he ground it into a fine powder with his foot, he slipped the filter into his pocket and went inside.

Clay said, "Did everyone see the little trick with the cigarette butt?"

Joey answered, "He fieldstripped it, like when he was in the Army. But he wasn't policing the area, as we called it in the military."

"Yeah," Clay said. "He wasn't going to toss the filter because he knew it had his DNA on it. The guy is smart, I'll give him that."

They watched the front door, half-expecting Slater to come out immediately upon learning Jasmin was not there. However, when he had not come back out after fifteen minutes, their hopes rose that he had decided to go with someone else.

Clay asked Hastings, "Assuming he's in with another girl, do you think you can get her to help us out?"

Hastings shrugged. "I don't know for sure. It all depends on which one he's with. Several of them have been busted on minor drug offenses in the past. If it's one of them, they probably won't be in a big hurry to help out law enforcement. And of course, the guy running the place might balk. I'm doing this sort of through the back door with my CI."

Minutes later, Slater came out the door. He kept his eyes straight ahead as he walked hurriedly to his vehicle. He grabbed the door and yanked it open, slamming it hard as he sat behind the wheel. Starting the engine with a roar, Slater put the big SUV in reverse and sprayed gravel as he backed up. Shifting into drive, he twisted the wheel and floored it, the rear end slewing around as he accelerated out of the parking lot.

Hastings immediately alerted his team to be ready to start a rolling surveillance on the Expedition. As soon as Slater roared out of sight, Hastings cranked up the van and pulled to the rear of the building. Calling his CI, he told her to come out the back door to meet him.

Two minutes later, a very tall, good-looking blonde stepped out the door and approached the van. Hastings opened the back door, and she stepped inside. She was wearing a crop top and a leather miniskirt with high heels that pushed her height almost to six and a half feet.

Folding herself down onto a low bench, the CI acknowledged them with a nod before turning to Hastings. "I only have a couple of minutes. What do you need to know?"

"What happened when Slater found out Jasmin wasn't there?"

"The whole blowup went on in the reception area, so I heard it all. At first, the guy was cool, complaining all polite-like to Denny. He's the manager," she clarified. "Denny offered the guy a discount for his trouble if he wanted to choose another girl, but he said no. He just kept asking where Jasmin was and why no one had called to save him a trip out here. Then he started in about wanting her phone number, but Denny, of course, refused. He demanded her address, but that brought a big 'no way, no how' comeback from Denny. He just kept insisting to know where she lived and her phone number, and Denny kept playing him off. I'm telling you there's something very creepy about him. Most guys get louder the madder they get. But not him. He kept talking softer and softer the more times Denny told him no. After a while, it got kinda frightening."

With a slight shiver, she continued, "And the look in his eyes scared the living hell out of me."

"What do you mean?" Clay asked.

"I'm not sure exactly. I guess the best way to describe it is that if I saw him coming toward me all wild-eyed like he was, I'd be running for my life."

Just then, Hastings' cell phone rang. Answering, he listened briefly and told the caller they would meet up shortly. Clicking off, he said to his CI, "We have to go. You'd better get back inside before Denny catches you out here talking to us. I'm sure he wouldn't be too thrilled to know one of his employees is a CI for the sheriff's office."

Smiling, she stood and went to the door. "It's okay. All he cares about is the bottom line. As long as we bring in the customers, he's a happy man."

As Hastings drove off, he told Clay and the others that the two surveillance teams had followed Slater to a strip center several miles away. They set up at opposite ends of the expansive parking lot and watched Slater as he parked the car and went into a Mexican restaurant. Through the windows, they could see a hostess leading Slater to a table. They reported the restaurant was about a third full at that time. Two of the detectives went in and got a table on the opposite side near the restrooms where they could surreptitiously observe Slater.

"What's their plan for getting something he's touched?" Clay asked.

"Actually, they're waiting for you and your guys to tell them what you want to do," Hastings responded.

"Okay, first, we need some other vehicle besides this one. If this electric utility van shows up at the restaurant after being on the street in front of the Cherry Orchard, he'll make us instantly for cops," Clay said.

"I thought about that. We're going right past the office, so we'll dump this thing and head over there in one of our undercover cars. Once we get there, how do you want to work it?" Hastings asked.

Clay put the question to Joey and Summer. "Any thoughts short of going in there and grabbing his fork in mid-bite?"

For several minutes, they kicked around ideas, but none of them seemed likely to work.

As they pulled into the police lot to switch to the UC vehicle, Summer's eyes suddenly lit up. "I don't know if this will work, but I've got a suggestion. I would need Sgt. Hastings to pull it off, though."

"Please. It's Kent," he grinned.

"Okay, I'll need Kent to help me in case Slater gets suspicious."

When she explained her idea, Clay asked Joey for his opinion.

"I think it has a real chance of working. I say we go with it," Joey said.

"Kent, are you okay with it?"

"Absolutely, Commander. It's a great idea," he said, eyeing Summer.

The decision made, they took two undercover cars instead of one. Hastings led the way while Clay, Joey and Summer followed. Ten minutes later, they parked several rows away from each other where they all had a clear view of Slater's SUV.

Clay stopped Summer as she started to get out of the car. "Are you sure you're comfortable with this?"

"I'm good, Commander."

"Okay, Kent just texted his detectives inside the restaurant so they know what's coming down. They'll cover your back if it goes south. But don't forget for a second that we're dealing with a killer. And I doubt that the mayor was his first victim."

"Commander," she said, "I'm cool with this. I'm a rookie as a detective, but not when it comes to using deadly force." She stepped from the car and headed across the parking lot.

"Damn!" Joey exclaimed. "That is one gutsy cop."

"I never doubted it," Clay responded with a smile. "Okay, here she goes. She's approaching his car."

Summer walked slowly past the Expedition, pausing as if she had seen something. Then she continued on, brushing her hand against the pistol in its concealment holster at her waist. She glanced down quickly to reassure herself that the shirt she was wearing completely covered the weapon without printing its outline.

Reaching the restaurant, she stepped inside and stopped, making a show of scanning the patrons in the restaurant as if searching for someone. She purposely avoided eye contact with Slater, seated twenty feet to her left facing the entrance. Out of the corner of her eye, she saw Slater scoop up a forkful of refried beans and take a bite, which he chased with a swallow from a half-full mug of beer. She quickly looked over the rest of the dining area, spotting the two detectives, who studiously avoided making eye contact with her.

A man dressed in traditional Mexican garb approached and asked how many were in her party. She quietly told him she wasn't there to eat. Ignoring the puzzled expression on his face, Summer took a quick breath as she got ready.

Speaking in a voice loud enough to carry throughout the dining area, Summer said, "Does anyone in here own a black Ford Expedition?"

She turned toward the right side of the restaurant first. When no one responded, as expected, she looked toward the other side. Out of the corner of her eye, she could see Slater watching her, his fork paused halfway to his mouth.

By now, everyone in the restaurant was gawking at her as the silence stretched out. She continued. "I just saw a guy scrape the side of the car with a knife. It's pretty bad. Anyway, I guess it doesn't belong to anyone in here."

Slater said nothing as he continued to watch her, his only reaction to place his fork carefully on the plate.

Summer turned to leave, catching a glimpse of Slater rising from his table as she went out the door. He caught up to her as she stepped off the curb into the parking lot.

Surprising her with his deep voice, he asked, "Who are you?"

She turned, startled by how close Slater was standing to her. Quickly taking a step back, she replied, "Excuse me?"

Slater's eyes bored into hers. "I asked who you were. It's a simple question requiring a simple answer."

"Is the Expedition yours?" she asked.

Slater snapped, "Yes."

"I'm just somebody trying to do a good deed. The way you're coming at me, I guess I should have kept driving."

"I apologize," he said, his voice softening. "You just caught me off guard."

"Okay, well, anyway, I have to go."

"Thanks for getting involved," he said, smiling now. "Would you mind showing me what the man did to my car? Also, can you tell me where he went afterwards?"

Summer peered quickly at her watch. "I'm sorry, but I really don't have time. I'm already late for an appointment," she said, starting to move away.

"Hang on. Surely you can at least give me the guy's description."

"All I can tell you is the guy was a little taller than you. He was dark like maybe he was Hispanic. I never saw his face, though, so I'm not sure."

"Did you see him get in a car?" Slater asked, looking over Summer's shoulder in the direction of his SUV.

"I didn't watch him that close afterwards. I'm sorry, Mister, but I really have to get going now."

Slater stepped up close to Summer, his eyes narrowing. "How about coming with me to my car so you can show me exactly where he scratched it? It's already got some on it, so I want to make sure which scratch you're talking about."

"No, I can't. I'm sorry," Summer said, starting to turn away.

Slater took two quick steps and grabbed her by the arm, squeezing hard. "I don't think so. Something tells me you're trying to con me. You're coming with me to my car," he said, starting to pull her in the direction of his vehicle.

Summer jerked her arm out of his grip. "Don't touch me! What is your problem?!" she exclaimed.

Slater whirled around at the sound of a car screeching to a stop behind him. Hastings jumped out, yelling, "Hey, you! Get your hands off my wife!"

Ignoring Slater, Hastings ran straight up to Summer and spun her around. "So, this is your new boyfriend, huh? I finally caught you, you bitch!"

"Wha, what?" Summer stammered. "He's not my–"

"Shut your mouth!" Hastings continued to yell. "Everything you say is a damn lie! Get your ass in the car right now!" he demanded.

Slater said nothing as Hastings dragged Summer to the car and forced her inside. He thought it seemed likely the woman was going to get an ass whipping from the big man. He watched the guy peel rubber as he raced away and then walked on to his vehicle to check the damage.

As Hastings and Summer exited the parking lot, she looked back in time to see Slater approaching his SUV. She wondered how long it would take him to realize what had happened.

One minute later, after thoroughly inspecting both sides, Slater knew. "That bitch," he muttered. "She set me up."

Suddenly, he turned around. "I'll be damned!" he exclaimed, taking off at a run for the Mexican restaurant.

―――――

Ten minutes later, Summer's cell phone rang as she and Hastings waited down the road from the restaurant.

"Slater just pulled out of the lot heading the other direction. Meet us back at the sheriff's office," Joey said.

Summer relayed the message to Hastings, and they took off, arriving a couple of minutes behind Clay and Joey.

Back in Hastings' office, Joey grinned at Summer. "We heard everything he was saying over your body mic. That was one hell of an acting job. I'll make a detective out of you yet."

"I couldn't have pulled it off without Kent here," she said, patting Hastings on the shoulder.

"I'm glad I got there when I did," Hastings said. "I thought the guy was going to grab you by the hair and drag you off like a caveman."

"Wait a second, Kent," Joey said, holding up his hand. "What you don't understand about this woman here," he grinned, pointing at Summer, "is that she's an expert in mixed martial arts and could have kicked Slater's ass up between his shoulder blades."

"Uh, thanks, I think," Summer said with a bemused expression.

Clay said, "Summer, I really have to give it to you. You predicted he wouldn't trust your word about his car and just let you walk away. He was going to force you over there if he had to just in case you were lying to him. And having Kent here acting like a pissed-off husband was brilliant. Great job. Both of you."

"Thanks, Commander. One question. Were Kent's guys able to get anything from Slater's table?"

"Yep. A beer mug and a fork," Clay replied.

"Outstanding!" she reacted. "So what happens now?"

"You sit at that computer over there and type up a detailed supplement, Detective Hayes," Joey said. "This is what's known as the unfun part of the job."

While Summer and Kent Hastings worked on their reports, Clay called Sheriff McDougle and gave her a report on the successful operation. After hanging up, he briefed them on the timing for getting the DNA processed. "The sheriff contacted a lab in Las Vegas that can handle it. They said processing the evidence and preparing the report will take at least two days."

Turning to Hastings, he said, "How soon can we get all the evidence to the lab in Vegas?"

Kent picked up the phone and called the detectives. He instructed them to see the sheriff to pick up a hard copy of the Tampa results and the evidence from the restaurant and then hit the road right away.

Hanging up, he said, "Quick enough?"

"That'll do," Clay laughed.

Slater reached the restaurant and yanked open the door, out of breath from sprinting across the parking lot. He was fuming over not seeing through the ruse the woman and the man, probably another cop, had pulled on him. The woman was obviously not some bimbo caught by her husband, he realized.

His internal radar had been on high alert ever since the sheriff and the two Florida cops had shown up at his house. Their visit had shaken him, although he felt he had handled the situation well. But the fact that they had so quickly identified him by his real name, coupled with finding his military prison record, was disturbing.

Going straight to his table, Slater saw an employee wearing a white apron pushing a cleaning cart toward the kitchen. It had been cleaned, and new silverware and napkins were already in place. He smiled. The cops had screwed up. They hadn't gotten the eating utensils he had used. But then an alarming notion came crashing into his mind. What if they had help? Someone else in the restaurant pretending to be a customer, waiting for him to leave in a hurry.

His heartbeat quickened as he approached the man with the cart. "Hey, I have a question," he said, tapping the employee on the shoulder.

The young Hispanic man turned around in surprise. "Qué pasa?" he asked.

"Do you speak English?"

"Muy poco," he shook his head, meaning very little.

"May I help you, sir?" a hostess asked as she approached Slater.

"I hope so. I was seated over there," he said, pointing toward his table. "I was eating when a young woman came in and asked if someone was driving a black Expedition."

"Yes, I heard her as I was coming back from the kitchen. Was it yours?"

"It was," he said, "but that's not what I wanted to talk to you about. I was wondering if you or your employee here noticed anyone coming to my table after I went outside. Maybe picking up my beer mug or possibly my knife or fork?"

"I did not, but let me ask Raphael. He does not speak English very well."

"I gathered that," Slater said, sourly.

The hostess asked several questions of the man in Spanish, who responded quickly, pointing at Slater's table as well as another table on the other side of the restaurant. Then he pointed toward the restrooms at the rear of the building.

When he stopped, the hostess turned back to Slater. "Raphael said that right after you left, two men who were seated over there," she gestured toward the table the employee had indicated, "got up and went to your table. One of them picked up your beer mug and a fork and carried them into the restroom. He was in there only a short time, maybe a minute or less. When he came out, he was carrying a black bag, but he did not have the mug or fork that Raphael could see. Both men then left the restaurant. Raphael said he thought it was strange, but he assumed they were friends of yours playing a joke on you."

Slater's heart pounded as his suspicions were confirmed. He had definitely been set up. Holding his anger under iron control, he smiled at the hostess. "Did Raphael say what the two men looked like?"

The hostess had another brief conversation with the employee. "He said there was a white man and a black man, but that is about all he noticed except for one thing."

"What's that?"

"He said they looked like policia . . . policemen."

Slater's big smile didn't reach his eyes. "Okay, I know who they are.

They're a couple of buddies of mine, and they were pulling a prank on me."

Reaching into his pocket, he pulled out cash and handed it to her. "I didn't get a chance to pay for my meal. Here's twenty dollars. That should more than cover the meal and a tip."

With a nod to the hostess, Slater left the restaurant. Walking hurriedly across the parking lot to his car, he cursed himself for his lapse in judgment.

She and the guy were connected to the two Florida cops, as were the two men inside the restaurant. He could barely contain his rage as he visualized creative ways of killing them all. Climbing into the vehicle, he cranked the engine and drove straight home, knowing what he had to do.

He guessed they must have found a drop of blood at the mayor's house that he missed. Probably when the bitch hit his gun hand and shattered the glass. The Florida cops wouldn't have asked him for a sample if they didn't have something to match it with.

Timing was going to be critical. Slater knew they would try to get the items from the restaurant processed as quickly as possible. When they matched, their next step would be to get an arrest warrant against him. He briefly wondered if he was being paranoid but quickly dismissed it. He had been successful in his post-prison career by being suspicious of everyone. Now was not the time to get careless.

Arriving home, Slater pulled into the garage, hitting the button to close the overhead door as he killed the engine. He went inside and retrieved the disposable cell phone he used to communicate with Lou Dunlop. Dialing the number, he waited impatiently as it rang half a dozen times.

Dunlop answered, "Is this Mr. Smith?"

"It is," Slater replied.

"What do you need? I'm kind of busy right now."

"Mr. Dunlop. I've done the job I was hired to do. Now you need to complete your end of the bargain. You owe me twenty-five thousand dollars."

"I know, I know. I'm having trouble moving that amount of money around so I can access it. It's going to take me a little time."

"That wasn't our agreement," Slater said, his voice icy. "Once the job was complete, you were to pay me immediately."

"Well, see, now that you mention it, there's a little problem with that. The job isn't exactly complete."

"What are you talking about?" Slater said, his temper rising.

"Part of what I paid you for was to ensure a certain person was charged with the crime. That hasn't happened."

"I can't help that. Maybe the cops are incompetent. I positioned the coin you gave me in such a way that it could be found by someone with minimal eyesight. If it wasn't, that's not my problem. And if they found it but can't tie it to your police official, that's on you. It must not have been sufficient to throw suspicion on him."

"All I know is that Randall hasn't been arrested, and until he is, the job's not complete. So, should I pay you for a job half-done? I don't think so."

"You're making a big mistake, Dunlop," Slater growled, breaking the connection.

He went into the living room and pulled a bottle of vodka from a shelf under the bar. Pouring a healthy amount into a glass, he downed it straight and immediately poured a second shot. Carrying the glass, he walked into the bedroom and sat in a chair by the window, staring out at the sunlit landscape of late afternoon as he considered what to do.

It didn't take long to realize that his options were limited. If he did nothing, the cops from Florida would get their lab report back and be at his door within a day or two, arrest warrant in hand. The idea of spending the rest of his life in a Florida prison, however long or short that might be, was unacceptable. He had been there and done that and had no intention of repeating it.

It seemed he had no other choice, though he regretted leaving. Slater had grown to love the barrenness of the Nevada landscape. He had heard it described years before as mile after mile of nothing but mile after mile. He liked that.

He began mentally cataloging the steps he needed to take. During the next hour, he finished the drink and smoked another half dozen cigarettes, enduring several more coughing fits and more bloody sputum.

Slater guessed it would be safe to fly if he left no later than the following morning. He had several false identifications he could select from in addition to Jeremiah Smith. Two of those, he rejected immediately as they were names from earlier kills. It was at least possible that the cops had figured out the name connection to the FBI agent he killed. No use taking chances, he thought.

He would use an identification he had always held back in the event he ever needed to do what he was about to do. Run. The decision made, Slater went to the closet to select the weapons he would need, knowing he was unlikely to be back.

Then it hit him. He couldn't fly. He needed to keep his firearms close at hand, most notably the Barrett sniper rifle. Packing a single handgun into a locked container inside checked baggage wouldn't attract much attention. Trying to get his Barrett along with handguns and ammo through the security checkpoint, even sending them in checked baggage, would almost guarantee scrutiny he didn't need. He didn't want anyone to have reason to remember him, even with the false identification.

He would have to drive, but the Expedition was out of the question. The cops knew the car and no doubt had noted the license plate. If things were going bad as he expected, the big SUV's description would be broadcast all over the country along with his face and name. He needed another ride. Slater added that to his list of things to do.

Opening the concealed door at the back of the closet, he entered the combination to the gun safe and swung open the heavy door. The sweet smell of gun oil wafted out from the weapons he viewed as extensions of himself. They had never let him down, and it was going to be hard to leave most of them behind. He pulled the sniper rifle from its rack and put it on the bed. He selected a Glock semi-automatic in forty-five caliber along with boxes of ammunition for both weapons and put them beside the rifle.

Pulling open a drawer, Slater removed the driver's license he intended to use. He read the name and smiled. Frederick Eugene Barrett. A word association off his love for the sniper rifle. The address was from a brothel up near Reno, Nevada he had once visited.

He emptied stacks of hundreds and twenties from a second drawer. Riffling through the bundles, he did a quick count in his head. Eighty-seven thousand dollars. Not bad, but not enough when he knew he was going to have to start over, which included buying another vehicle. There was no way he was going to steal one and hope he wasn't caught.

Slater closed the safe and spun the dial several times, then shut the door to the hidden compartment. There was always a slight chance he could be back, and the idea of leaving the safe unlocked to make it easy for the cops to get their hands on his precious guns was unacceptable.

Clothing and toiletries went into a suitcase. The money, handgun, and ammo went into a specialized gun bag with sewn-in holsters for up to four firearms. The Barrett he packed lovingly into a hard case along with the box of fifty-caliber ammunition. He changed from his suit into jeans and a short-sleeved cotton shirt. Taking the suitcase and gun bags into the garage, he loaded them into the back of the SUV.

The two drinks had worked their way through his system. Having eaten no breakfast and only a few bites of his dinner at the Mexican restaurant, Slater was feeling a little lightheaded. He checked the refrigerator and found a pack of cheese slices. Taking a skillet, he melted butter and made himself a grilled cheese sandwich. He stood at the counter eating the sandwich slowly and washing it down with a beer as he wondered if his string of successes over the years was about to come to a screeching halt.

The first order of business was to acquire another vehicle. He would have to dump the Expedition somewhere and catch a cab to a used car dealership. His best bet was to drive to Vegas to make the transaction.

He turned in a circle, letting his eyes drift over the comfortable furniture, the picture window with the fabulous view, the breakfast nook where he enjoyed a cup of coffee as the sun eased out of its bed each morning. This was a place he had grown to love. It was actually more than just a house. It was his home.

He set the alarm and locked the door. Two minutes later, he was on the road.

Slater stashed the Expedition in a parking garage off the strip and took a cab to a used car dealership. Using his clean Frederick Barrett identity, he paid cash for a five-year old Lexus. Driving back to the parking garage, Slater transferred his luggage and firearms to the Lexus, then switched license plates on the Expedition with another car several rows over. He took the vehicle registration papers from the glove box and locked the SUV. He figured the cops would eventually discover his vehicle, even with the switched plates. By the time they did, he would be long gone.

Slater's next stop was an all-night pharmacy where he bought disposable gloves and hair dye. At a nearby novelty shop, he purchased a pair of fake, horn-rimmed glasses with plain, plastic lenses.

Staying off the Strip, he checked into a cheap hotel that catered to customers wanting an hour or two of privacy to conduct their personal business. There, he donned gloves and proceeded to dye his hair a dark brown. With the fake glasses to complete the effect, Slater was surprised to see that he now looked at least ten years younger.

By this time, it was approaching midnight, and he was tired. He called the front desk and told the surly clerk he would be staying until the morning. The man demanded an additional twenty dollars for staying overnight. Slater agreed, all the while imagining putting a bullet in the man's head. His patience with assholes was running low.

Early the next morning, he left Las Vegas. He was a man on a mission.

O ver the next two days, as they anxiously awaited the report from the lab, Clay, Joey, and Summer surfed the Internet for hours and made dozens of phone calls searching for any scrap of information with which to build a comprehensive profile of Von Slater.

Las Vegas Metro had at last located the two battery cases against Slater and faxed the reports to Sheriff McDougle. They both turned out to be relatively minor incidents that occurred at a couple of lower rent bars far off the Las Vegas Strip. Other than confirming Slater's personality as being prone to violence, they found nothing useful to help nail the man.

Late on the afternoon of the second day, Clay got a phone call from the supervisor at the Las Vegas lab. She confirmed conclusively that Slater's DNA was a match to the sliver of glass as well as the piece of skin recovered from under the mayor's fingernail.

Clay asked about the test results on his challenge coin. She advised him the Tampa lab had obtained sufficient DNA to type and had included the profile; however, it did not match Von Slater.

After asking the lab supervisor to fax the results to him, Clay hung up, a thoughtful expression on his face.

"What is it?" Joey asked.

"I guess you could call it good news and bad news."

When he didn't continue, Joey said, "Don't keep us hanging, Clay. Give us both."

"Well, the good news is the glass and the piece of skin are positive matches for Slater."

"Alright!" Joey exclaimed, turning and high-fiving Summer. Then he stopped, his grin fading. "Okay, that's the good news. So, what's the bad?"

"The DNA on my challenge coin was not a match for Slater."

After a slight hesitation, Joey said, "That must mean Slater put the coin behind the chair without transferring his DNA. Wearing gloves, I would bet. So the DNA must belong to the asshole who stole it from your locker."

"That's one possibility. Jack Hargraves. Or it could belong to the person who passed it to Slater," Clay suggested.

"Lou Dunlop?" Summer interjected.

"Lou Dunlop," Clay agreed. "I need to call the chief."

By this time, it was eight at night in Florida. Clay called the chief at home, giving him first the news of the DNA matches on Slater. Mike told Clay he would have Detective Donnie Pecora head to the state attorney's office first thing the next morning to obtain an arrest warrant. Clay told him he would fax the lab report directly to Mike's office so he would have it when he came in to work.

After passing along the chief's congratulations to Joey and Summer, Clay shared the information about the unknown DNA on his challenge coin.

"What's your take on it, Clay?" Mike asked.

"We've talked about that. I think Jack Hargraves stole it out of my locker. Knowing his close relationship to Dunlop all these years, I believe Hargraves gave it to him. Then Dunlop gave it to Slater to plant at the crime scene."

"That makes sense considering Dunlop doesn't have access to the locker room. But hold on. Is it possible the DNA is yours? After all, you said you picked it up every day and read the inscription."

"Right, I did, Mike. What you're forgetting is that I wiped it with a rag each time before I put it away. The odds of any of my DNA still being on it are slim."

"I remember that. It sounds like we need to find out if Dunlop's DNA has ever been typed. If I had to guess, it hasn't."

"What about Hargraves? Can you order him to give a cheek swab for DNA?"

"From a legal standpoint, I'd say no, right off the top of my head. However, I can certainly *request* one from him. If he agrees or refuses to give the sample, either way, that tells us something. I'll talk to our attorney first and get his advice before I call him in. In the meantime, I'll get Pecora to check with FDLE to see if Dunlop's DNA might be on file there. It's doubtful, but you never know until you check."

"Thanks, Chief. Have Donnie call me tomorrow as soon as he has the arrest warrant for Slater in hand. Sheriff McDougle with Nye County SO has been a big help and will give us as many deputies as we need when we go pick up Slater. I'll keep you posted."

Hanging up, his cell phone rang immediately. Sheriff McDougle advised she had the report in front of her. Clay gave her Chief Wilson's fax number, and she said she would have her admin send it off right away. Clay offered to treat the sheriff and Sergeant Hastings to dinner as a small repayment for her department's assistance. She readily agreed and said she would bring the sergeant with her. At Joey's urging, they arranged to meet at his new favorite steak house.

As he hung up, Clay said, "I want you to know how proud I am of both of you."

"Aw, thanks, Commander. It was nothing," Joey grinned.

"You're right, Joey. Summer is the one who deserves most the praise."

Summer laughed as Joey acted irate. "Now hold on there. As I've said many times, I've taught this young lady everything she knows about police work. I deserve a pat on the back, too."

"Fine," Clay countered. "You want praise? Good job. And since you feel such an overwhelming need for approval, you can repay my kindness by buying a bottle of champagne to celebrate."

"But, but, I don't drink!" Joey sputtered.

"And your point?" Clay asked as they headed for the restaurant.

Over dinner, they talked about the case and discussed strategies for taking Slater into custody without having to use deadly force. They concluded it would ultimately be up to the killer himself and how he reacted to what would be an overwhelming police presence.

Hastings volunteered to prepare the probable cause affidavit for a search warrant on Slater's house to seize the handgun and the knife used to kill the mayor. Enjoying the camaraderie, they stayed until the restaurant was about to close. As they went to their cars, they agreed to meet the next day as soon as Hastings obtained the search warrant.

At six the next morning, Clay was awakened to the insistent ringing of his cell phone. Rolling over, he answered with a yawn.

"Commander, this is Donnie Pecora. You awake?"

Clay peered at the clock and said, "I am, now, Donnie. You got the arrest warrant?"

"Yes, sir. I filled in the ASA on your interview with the suspect and gave him the DNA reports from Tampa and Las Vegas. He reviewed it all and then took it to the state attorney for her review. He said she wanted to personally review what we had because of the high profile nature of the case. She was satisfied and authorized the arrest warrant."

"Have you entered the warrant into NCIC?"

"Yes, sir," Pecora replied.

"Good. Tell Chief Wilson we're meeting this morning with the sheriff to put together a team to serve the arrest and search warrants."

"Will do, Commander, and there's one more thing I need to tell you before you go."

"What's that?"

"You remember the Zach Petersen case?"

"Donnie, I'm not getting senile," Clay said. "What about it?"

"Sorry, boss. It's just that with so much that's been happening, I thought . . . well, anyway, it took me a while to open the thumb drive. It had a security program that required a password to get into it. I asked the IT people if they had the capability to bypass the requirement, and they just laughed. I plugged it into my computer and started trying all sorts of possibilities. None of them worked, of course. So I decided to call Zach's ex-wife, Jan, to see if she had any ideas."

"And did she?" Clay asked.

"Yes, sir. She told me he had used a password on their home computer that always embarrassed her, and she suggested I try that. It was,

'ILoveKinkySex69'," Pecora said, spelling it out for Clay. "He also put dollar signs before and after the phrase."

"And it worked?"

"It did. Now here's the interesting part. After reviewing all the customer files, a name popped up that I think you may know."

Sitting up quickly, Clay said, "Yeah? Who would that be?"

"Lou Dunlop," Pecora said.

"How do you know it's *that* Lou Dunlop? I realize it's not a very common name, but how certain are you?"

"I'm positive, Commander. I opened the folder and saw all the personal information associated with his tax files. You know, full name, address, occupation, that sort of stuff. It's definitely him."

"But wait," Clay said, his initial excitement dimming. "You told me Petersen had a large number of legitimate tax clients. Did you find a connection between Dunlop and the pedophile's pictures?"

"Yes, sir, I was getting to that."

"Sorry, go ahead."

"It turns out Zach Petersen was a very cautious man. I think he knew we would question how he could prove that the pictures belonged to Lou Dunlop. When I opened the folder named 'BabyGirls', in addition to the disgusting pictures, I found three more. They were shots Zach must have taken with his cell phone. They showed a computer sitting on a desk with a bunch of thumbnail shots of the little girls on the screen."

"Why would he take a picture of the pictures?"

"He must have done it to identify Dunlop as the owner of the computer."

"So how did he prove it was Dunlop's computer?"

"If you check out the desk to the left of the monitor, you can see a framed photo of two men."

"And?" Clay asked, getting impatient at the way Pecora was stringing out the information.

"The photo clearly shows our current senator, Thomas Barkley, and his chief of staff, Lou Dunlop, standing shoulder to shoulder at some function."

"That's pretty damning, Donnie, but maybe not enough to convince the state attorney that it's a picture of Dunlop's computer. Any others that can support it being his?"

"There are. There's a second photo that shows the same screen with Petersen holding Lou Dunlop's checkbook open beside the monitor with the pictures. And one more. Petersen took a panoramic shot of the large office showing various pictures on the walls. Most of them were of Dunlop with Barclay and various other politicians. It's really small, but one of them I swear is Dunlop standing with Bill Clinton. I recall reading somewhere that he worked in the Clinton administration way back when. If we can get these pictures enlarged without losing the resolution, I believe this is enough, even if we can't get an arrest warrant, to get a search warrant for Dunlop's house and computer."

Getting excited, Clay began pacing the room as he talked. "Donnie, this is some great detective work. Have you shared this with the chief?"

"Not yet. I wanted you to know first."

"Okay, as soon as we hang up, go give him the news. Then get started on a search warrant for Dunlop's house and computer. If you need anything, tell the chief, and he'll make sure you get it. Make this a high priority."

"Yes, sir. I'll go see the chief right now," Pecora said. "I'll call you back as soon as I know more."

"Okay, and Donnie, before you go, one more thing."

"Sir?" he asked, apprehension creeping into his voice.

"You are officially out of the doghouse," Clay said, hanging up.

By noon, after meeting with the sheriff and members of her tactical team and detectives for over two hours, Clay was comfortable with the plan for taking down Slater. Detectives had been conducting surveillance on the house since shortly after Clay notified the sheriff about the arrest warrant. So far, they had reported seeing no activity.

Kent Hastings had the search warrant for Slater's place in his possession, which they would execute as soon as the tactical team cleared the house and took Slater into custody. Clay, Joey, and Summer rode with Hastings as they followed the team's van.

Arriving at the location, they staged on the curved driveway out of sight of the house. Considering they were dealing with a vicious killer, the judge had authorized a no-knock warrant. The tactical team would approach the house at a fast pace and force entry, announcing themselves loudly as they entered.

When everyone was in place, the tactical team commander gave a signal, and the team moved in and broke through the front door. The alarm began beeping as team members cleared each room in the house. When the, "All Clear", was given, Clay and his detectives went inside with Hastings. By this time, the security alarm siren had begun wailing, so Hastings sent a detective to cut the power to the alarm panel.

"The Expedition's not in the garage," Hastings said. "And some clothes are missing from the master bedroom closet. Shaving gear and stuff are gone from the bathroom, too. I have a feeling he's taken off. Even though the warrant has been entered into NCIC, we can send out a special regional broadcast in Nevada and the surrounding states for him and his vehicle. I can't imagine he would have gone far. Most of the local bad guys that run only go as far as Vegas. They figure there's so many people there we'll never find them."

Clay was frustrated that they hadn't caught Slater so they would have the chance to interrogate him, this time with direct evidence of his involvement in the mayor's death.

"I'm hoping the search warrant will turn up additional evidence that will help tie him to the mayor's murder," Joey said. "Kent's detectives were given what little information we have on the caliber of weapon and the approximate size of the knife blade. They also know to search for any documents that might contain notes or other information about his trip to Florida. Who knows? Maybe he kept a diary. Wouldn't that be sweet?"

"Fat chance of that," Clay answered.

Just then, a detective came into the living room to give a progress report. They had found Slater's hidden compartment containing the large safe. The detective led the way back into the master bedroom and pointed out the safe.

"Is it locked?" Clay asked.

"Locked tight," the detective confirmed. "It's a high quality combination gun and fire safe. We'll need a competent safe company to open this baby. It'll require drilling through the door to access the interior mechanism."

Clay turned to Hastings, "Can you contact someone to get it done?"

"Sure. It may take a little while, but we'll get it open. What do you want to do in the meantime?"

"We'll wait here until the search is done and then decide."

Two hours later, the search complete, they were disappointed that nothing was found linking Slater to the mayor's murder.

Clay got with Joey and Summer and asked for suggestions. Summer waited for Joey to speak.

"I think we've done everything we can here. It's probably time to head home," he said.

"I'm still new at this, Commander," Summer added. "But I agree with Sgt. Crutchfield. The warrant is in the system, including the description and license number of the Expedition. We still have a lot of follow up we can do back home."

Clay turned to Hastings. "Kent, can you get someone to take statements from the employees of that Mexican restaurant and your CI at the Cherry Orchard? We'll also need reports from your detectives who grabbed the items that Slater handled. And, of course, the search warrant return paperwork."

"I'll personally take care of it and send everything via overnight mail. You should have them no later than the day after tomorrow."

Within an hour, Clay, Joey, and Summer were back at their hotel. Joey booked a flight out of McCarran International Airport leaving Las Vegas at ten p.m. and arriving in Jacksonville at four a.m. with the three-hour time difference. Clay called Mike Wilson and brought him up to date while Joey drove them to the airport. They bypassed the security checkpoint with their police IDs and grabbed a late dinner in the terminal.

As they ate, Clay shared the news he had received from Donnie Pecora. Joey's mouth dropped open in shocked surprise.

He put down his fork, the food forgotten. "Lou Dunlop? We all know he's a world class prick, but he's into child porn, too?"

"I know. It sounds crazy, doesn't it? Can you imagine what Barclay's reaction will be when we do a perp walk with his chief of staff? This is definitely not going to help his run for president. I can almost hear the stampeding feet of his supporters running for cover."

"If nothing else, this should get the man off your case," Joey said.

"Who knows? He's been so obsessed with me that he may just double down. Barclay might even accuse us of setting up his poor, hard-working chief of staff by planting that stuff on his computer. I would imagine that's likely to be Dunlop's defense."

As they continued eating, the topic shifted back to the murder case, as each of them speculated on where Slater might have gone.

Summer said, "Kent told me he would have some people check all the flights leaving Vegas since we saw Slater leaving the Mexican restaurant. They're checking on both the Slater and Smith identifications."

"That's okay," Joey said, "unless he has multiple false IDs. If he does, it'll be a helluva lot harder to find him."

"Any thoughts on where he might go?" Clay asked.

Joey shrugged. "Could be anywhere, including out of the country. But it would probably be a good idea to notify Lawton, Oklahoma police since that's his hometown."

"Good thought. Summer, would you check on that first thing tomorrow? See if you can locate any relatives he might have in that area. Also, try to find his first two ex-wives and ask if they've heard from him or might have some idea where he would go."

"Got it," she said, typing notes into her phone.

Clay asked, "Any chance he would go back to Jacksonville?"

Joey shook his head emphatically. "I seriously doubt it. He took care of business in Jax Beach. He's got no reason to go back there again."

Their meal finished, they left the restaurant and strolled down the concourse. As they approached their departure gate, Joey suddenly detoured toward the rows of slots, attracted by the ringing of machines paying off small amounts of coins here and there.

Drawn to a progressive slot machine that advertised a maximum two million dollar payoff, Joey said, "We have a few minutes before they call our flight. I might as well take a chunk of the Las Vegas economy with me before I go. If I win, I'll hire a limo to drive us back home. That way, I don't have to get in another flying death trap."

"Joey, you have a better chance of winning The Players Championship than you do winning two million dollars on that machine. And you don't even play golf."

"What are you talking about? I used to play, and I shot par all the time. Don't listen to him, Summer."

"Summer, the only par Sergeant Crutchfield ever shot was on a miniature golf course," Clay said.

"Sergeant," she spoke up, "I feel compelled to point out to you your statement the day we got here as we passed these very same machines."

"What statement was that?"

"The one about you only betting on sure things."

"That was specifically for your benefit, Detective Hayes. Being young and less experienced than the commander and me, I wanted to ensure you didn't get so mesmerized by all the blinking lights that you would immediately lose all your money."

"Of course, you did," Summer said, mockingly.

"Whatever," he muttered, pulling out a five dollar bill and sitting down at the machine, which featured lions, tigers, hippos, elephants, and giraffes.

Grinning at Summer, Joey said, "I'm going to ignore the negative energy pouring off of you. Now pay close attention, and watch and learn, Detective Hayes. Watch and learn."

Joey slid the bill into the machine. He cracked his knuckles, shrugged his shoulders as if to relieve tension, and gently pulled the handle all the way down. He held it in that position briefly before releasing it.

"Holding it down for a second and a half increases the odds by twenty-one per cent," he said, winking at Summer. The wheels spun for several seconds before stopping on five different animals. The machine emitted a shrill raspberry.

Laughing out loud, Summer walked away, saying over her shoulder, "Thanks, Sergeant. I watched. And I learned."

A t the same time Joey was making his five dollar donation to the Las Vegas economy, Von Slater was sitting in a hotel room in downtown New Orleans, cell phone in hand. He had just finished another conversation with Lou Dunlop about the money he was owed. Dunlop continued to argue that he shouldn't have to pay unless and until Clay Randall was charged in the mayor's death. Slater was beginning to think that Dunlop intended to stonewall him until he was forced to take care of the Randall issue himself.

Tossing the phone on the bed, he got up and paced the room, stopping at the large windows facing downtown New Orleans. From his vantage point ten stories above the street, he could see late-night crowds of people strolling along the sidewalks. For a moment, Slater imagined he was down there, walking hand-in-hand with a wife or girlfriend. A guy who worked with his hands. Only not with guns and knives. Maybe someone who built high-end homes. Or a successful landscape architect.

While his eyes continued to roam over the crowds, his thoughts went back to Dunlop. The man was a sorry piece of human garbage. After the initial meeting with Dunlop in Las Vegas, Slater had called MacKay wanting to know more about the man's background and his real name, not the false Chester Jones name he used.

MacKay told him at that time all about Dunlop and his boss, Senator Thomas Barclay. But when he divulged Dunlop's fantasies about young girls, Slater's anger knew no bounds. His initial reaction upon learning of Dunlop's twisted sexual desires was to refuse any further dealings with him. As he thought more about it, however, he decided to meet the man. Who knew? He might take the job Dunlop planned to offer. On the other hand, he might kill him.

Slater's feelings about people like Dunlop were rooted in a horrific incident from his past. He had married a young woman shortly after joining the army. He met her at a bar outside Fort Benning, Georgia where he was undergoing training. It was love at first sight, or so both of them believed. But life as an army wife wasn't what she expected it to be, and they spent a large portion of their married life arguing and fighting over everything. In a desperate but ultimately failed attempt to heal their growing rift, they decided to have a child.

Within a year, Slater and his wife welcomed a beautiful little girl into their lives, and, for a while, their relationship improved. However, the underlying problems never went away, and, when their daughter was three, they divorced. It was an extremely difficult decision for Slater because he loved his daughter with an intensity he didn't know he was capable of feeling.

His army career took him overseas and to other military bases across the country over the next few years. His visits with his daughter grew sporadic, sometimes only once or twice a year.

The week before his daughter turned six years old, Slater's ex-wife remarried. He met her new husband once and took an instant dislike to him, although he couldn't identify a specific reason. There was just something about the man that got under his skin.

By the time his daughter turned thirteen, Slater was serving his sentence in the USDB. When he called from the prison to wish her a happy birthday, his ex-wife told him their daughter didn't want to talk. He asked why, and she broke down and told him their child had just informed her that the second husband had been sexually molesting her for years.

Slater almost lost his mind. He demanded she call the police and have the bastard arrested, but his ex-wife refused. She said the young girl was so traumatized by what she had been through that she wouldn't put her through the further pain of having to testify against the man. She said she had kicked him out and that they were moving in with her parents back in Georgia.

No matter what Slater said, he couldn't convince her to pursue charges against the man. While still talking to his ex, his daughter picked up the extension. Although he didn't question her about what the man had done, he assured her she had done absolutely nothing wrong and that he loved her more than anything in the world.

A week later, Slater's daughter took a handful of her mother's pain pills and went to sleep forever. She left a letter for Slater that he still kept and read each year on her birthday.

As he thought of his daughter, he pulled out his wallet and removed the letter. It had been folded and refolded so many times that the paper had begun to tear in a few places, and the ink had started to fade. Smoothing it out carefully, he read:

Daddy
I'm sorry it has to be this way but I just can't take the hurt any more. That man Mama maried I refuse to use his name started touching me on my 6th birthday. And he kept on doing it for years. Bdays were always worst. Every year he would find something bad to do to me on what was supposed to be a happy day. You know? HAPPY Birthday! So many times I wish I had the courege to take a butcher knife and stab him right in the heart while he was asleep but I was always to scared. I can't pretend any more that everything is okay, because its not and it never will be. So I'm doing the only thing I can do so I won't hurt or feel any more. That's a good thing, I think. I will always love you Daddy and I hope you will forgive me for doing this.

Krissy

Slater's remaining time in prison was a nightmare. He blamed himself for his daughter's death. If only he had sucked it up and stayed with her mother, Krissy would still be alive. An adult with a real life. Married, maybe. Kids. His grandkids? He shook his head at that. With the life he had led since getting out of prison, he would be ashamed to have his daughter see what he had become.

Years passed after Slater left prison. He became a professional killer and proved to be very proficient at it. Yet he never forgot the man who molested his daughter and drove her to commit suicide. Eventually, the time came when he knew what he had to do. He searched the Internet for information about the man and eventually found him in a little town northeast of Atlanta called Dahlonega. He checked local records and confirmed the man lived alone.

One day in late autumn, Slater flew to Atlanta and rented a car. Early the next morning, he drove to Dahlonega and located the man's rundown trailer on a dirt road a few miles outside of town. He hid the vehicle in a thick stand of trees a hundred yards down the road and stepped out, patting his hip to ensure his gun was secure. As he slipped through the underbrush approaching the trailer, he was startled to hear the distinctive sound of a rattlesnake nearby.

He spotted the six-footer about ten feet away, coiled and visibly disturbed by his presence. Keeping the snake in sight, he considered a change of plans. He saw a broken limb with a fork at the end that gave it the appearance of an oversized slingshot. He picked it up, tested it for rot, and found it still solid. Without hesitation, he moved slowly toward the snake. When he was within reach, he drove the fork of the limb down, pinning the rattlesnake's head on the ground. Then he grabbed the reptile firmly behind the head and picked it up.

Two minutes later, seeing no activity around the trailer, he deposited the agitated snake in the mailbox and slammed the door closed. Slater moved back into the tree line and watched until he saw the man come out to check for mail. When he opened the door to the box, the rattlesnake lunged out, striking him in the right eye.

The man screamed so loud, Slater wondered if he could be heard back in Atlanta. He calmly watched as the man he had hated for so long writhed on the ground in agony. Slowly, his screams turned to moans, then silence. Slater approached slowly, his hand on his pistol. There was no need. The snake's bite had punctured the eyeball, and fluid had run down his grotesquely swollen face. A quick check for a pulse revealed none.

Slater was a little surprised he had died so quickly. Considering the man was easily a hundred pounds or more overweight, he guessed he must have suffered a heart attack. He walked back to his car and sat down. Taking out his daughter's letter, he read it again.

Then, folding it carefully and slipping it back into his wallet, he said aloud, "I still miss you, baby. I didn't get paid for this one, but that's okay. It was a labor of love."

S haking his head, Slater came back to reality in his tenth floor room in New Orleans. He was none of those people down there on the street, and he would never be. His life had taken him down dark roads most people had no understanding of what it was like. No one cared whether Von Slater lived or died. And that was okay. He had himself. That was enough.

Slater assumed the cops had gotten a warrant for his arrest by now, and it was likely his driver's license picture had been passed along to police agencies across the country. He would have to drive carefully. Even with his altered appearance, the last thing he wanted to deal with was being stopped by some state trooper.

Early the next morning, he left New Orleans heading east. Within two hours, he was on Interstate 10, cruise control set exactly at seventy miles per hour. He passed two Louisiana State Troopers monitoring traffic with LASER radars, but neither gave him a second look. Even if they had already found his Expedition back in Las Vegas, which he doubted, he felt confident the cops would not have discovered his purchase of the Lexus.

By eleven, he was well into Mississippi, heading for the Alabama state line when he decided to stop for lunch. Spotting an exit that listed several fast food places, he pulled into the parking lot of a restaurant near the entrance ramp to the freeway.

Before going inside, Slater called Dunlop again, resulting in another argument and one more refusal to pay up. This time, Dunlop hung up on him, which brought on a growing case of heartburn and indigestion for Slater. He had begun chain smoking, lighting a fresh cigarette off the butt of another. The coughing and bloody sputum were steadily increasing, also.

Slater went into the restaurant and ordered a chicken-fried steak smothered in flour gravy with a side of fries. Considering the stuff he was coughing up, he figured the extra cholesterol and fat weren't going to make things any worse.

Thirty minutes later, he was back on the road. A sense of urgency was growing. He wanted to reach Jacksonville, get something resolved, and then get the hell out of the country. Go somewhere safe where he could see a doctor for medicine to kill the crap coming up from his lungs.

As the sun was setting in his rearview mirror, Slater took the exit onto Interstate 95 in downtown Jacksonville. Southbound traffic was heavy as drivers negotiated the ever-present construction barrels and cones. Seeing the exit for the beaches, he managed to squeeze in front of a trucker, who blasted his air horn at him and rode his bumper for a quarter of a mile until Slater exited onto Beach Boulevard.

For the last two hundred miles, he had debated how he was going to resolve the issue with Dunlop. If he killed Randall, he figured Dunlop might freak out a little but then pay up. There would no longer be a need to worry that Randall might walk on a murder charge. Problem permanently solved. On the other hand, if he continued to put the Randall issue on Dunlop's back, it was obvious that the man was not going to pay the rest of his fee.

One of the things Slater prided himself on was his ability to make a decision under pressure. He had waffled on this too long. He knew what he had to do.

He stopped at a small hotel in Jacksonville a few miles from the beach, paying cash for one night. As he started out of the lobby, he spotted a newspaper rack beside the exit. The headline screamed in large, black type, **POSSIBLE CONNECTION BETWEEN U. S. SENATOR AND MURDERED JAX BEACH MAYOR.**

Slater fished in his pocket for change and fed it into the machine. Removing the paper, he tucked it under his arm as he went to the car and moved to a parking space near his room. Ten minutes later, his gear piled on the bed, he sat down at a tiny desk beside the TV cabinet and opened the paper, lighting a cigarette as he leaned back to read the article.

Written by an investigative reporter for the newspaper, it was the lead story, beginning above the fold and continuing on A-5. It began with a summary of the violent death of the mayor, including specifics on how she had been murdered. A friend of the mayor was listed as the person who found her body.

The article then shifted to the reason for the sensational headline. The reporter claimed a confidential source had stated unequivocally to her that that current Florida Senator and rumored presidential candidate Thomas W. Barclay had been having an affair with the mayor.

It went on to say that Senator Barclay's wife of almost forty years had succumbed to cancer less than a year ago. However, the source claimed the senator and Mayor Adams were seeing each other prior to his wife's death. The reporter's source claimed Mayor Adams had confided in the source about the relationship, which allegedly had been going on while the senator's wife battled the cancer that eventually took her life.

The reporter stated she reached out to Senator Barclay for a comment about the allegations; however, his office staff in Washington said he was unavailable for comment due to pressing Senate business.

Reading on, the reporter said she contacted Louis Dunlop, Senator Barclay's chief of staff, and received by email a brief press release. It stated, *Senator Barclay is deeply saddened by the death of Mayor Denise Adams. She was a strong supporter of the senator's efforts to make Congress more accountable to the citizens of this great country. Further, he is angered and appalled by the allegations that have been made against the character of such an outstanding and dedicated public servant.*

Slater smiled at the press release, which said nothing of substance in general and, in particular, failed to express a denial of the allegations.

The rest of the article was a summary of the political careers of Barclay and Denise Adams. When he finished the article, Slater wondered if Dunlop's career as Barclay's fixer was in jeopardy.

55

At eleven p.m., Slater was ready. Dressed in black BDUs, he carried his gear down to the car. Taking Beach Boulevard into Jacksonville Beach, he turned right on Third Street.

The traffic was still heavy at that time of night. He wondered why so many people were still out on the roads that late. It was a Wednesday, not a Friday or Saturday night. Traffic ten times this large cruised the Las Vegas Strip even at four in the morning, but this was a small town beach community, not Vegas. He guessed even people who lived in small towns liked to party. He didn't. Maybe he was just getting old.

He drove slightly below the posted speed, not wanting to be stopped for any reason. If a cop saw his clothing and searched him, the handgun and other items he was packing would be trouble. Except as a last resort, he didn't want to kill some street cop just trying to do his job.

Slater continued for several blocks before turning toward the beach. He stopped just short of the street that ran parallel to the shoreline. He killed the engine and checked in all directions. Everything was quiet. The closest streetlight was half a block away. He had previously removed the car's interior light, enabling him to step out into darkness.

Easing the door closed, he walked to Ocean Drive and turned right. Five minutes later, he was in front of the house. Using an Internet search engine, he had easily located the place. It stood three stories tall with a rear deck that extended the width of the house.

The place was dark. The doors to the three-car garage were closed, and the driveway was empty. It appeared no one was there, but he had to confirm it. Going up to the front door, he pulled the Glock from his pocket before ringing the bell, concealing it behind his back. Then he waited.

When no lights came on that he could see, he tried the doorbell once more. Still getting no response, he sighed in frustration. He would have preferred a straight-on encounter. That didn't appear to be happening, so he made his way back to the car.

He hit the trunk release and retrieved the gun case containing his rifle. Through habit, he had already loaded three, fifty-caliber rounds into the magazine and racked one into the chamber. The weapon was ready to go. Locked and loaded as he used to say, in another time and another place.

He held the rifle case vertically by his side to help conceal it as he closed the trunk and retraced his steps to Ocean Drive. This time, instead of turning, he went straight toward the beach.

The roar of the surf got louder with each step he took. As he neared the beach walkover, he paused and visually searched the area carefully. There were no lights on in the house to the left of the walkover. To the right, an empty lot gave him a cushion.

He considered and promptly rejected taking the walkover. Anyone leaving the beach after a late-night stroll would be coming right at him. His goal was to meet no one. He slipped to the side and climbed the low sand dune, stepping carefully through the sea oats.

As he neared the top of the dune, Slater crouched down and took a night-vision device from a pocket of his BDUs. Slipping it over his head, he hit the power button and watched as the dark night turned into green-tinted day.

He ensured it was clear in all directions before moving over the crest and down onto the beach. Slater stayed on the ocean side of the dune line as he moved quickly in the direction of the house again, counting each block until he drew even with the rear of the property.

Easing up to the crest of the dune, Slater noted the driveway was still empty, and the house was dark. He took a black tarp from a pouch on the rifle bag and spread it on the sand. He then removed the weapon and placed it on the tarp, being careful not to bump the scope. Dropping to his stomach, he took the rifle in hand, getting a sight picture to the house. The distance was negligible, just over one hundred yards. If he had to, he could take a shot at that distance with his eyes closed. The target would completely fill the scope. He could probably count the hairs in the guy's nose.

Slater checked his watch and saw it was eleven-thirty. As he debated what to do, a car pulled into the driveway and rolled to a stop beside the garage, its front facing the beach. As soon as the headlights cut off, Slater raised the rifle to his shoulder and sighted in. The driver's face was clearly visible, and he was obviously angry about something. As Slater watched, the man yanked his tie down and loosened the top button of his dress shirt. He appeared to be talking to someone. Slater assumed he was on his cell phone until he saw the man toss it on the dash and continue talking. He decided to wait to see what developed.

Lou Dunlop was in fact talking to himself, more accurately raving to himself. "I can't believe this! If I could find out who snitched to the newspaper about Barclay and the mayor, I'd choke the shit out of them! Everything is falling apart just as we're starting to get real traction going for the election. And Smith! That bastard keeps calling me wanting his money. I'm not paying him another damn dime! He PROMISED me he would take care of Denise Adams and get that prick Randall blamed for it. And he swore that nothing would point our way. NOTHING! This was my big chance to make it to the top. Barclay was the perfect candidate when I signed on, and what did he do? Damn Barclay! He SCREWED IT ALL UP because he couldn't keep his freaking cock in his pants! We were getting so close. So close!"

Picking up his cell, Slater typed a quick text and hit the Send button.

He watched through the scope as Dunlop grabbed his cell phone off the dash and stared at the message, *Last chance. Answer the phone!* Slater saw him scowl. He waited ten seconds and then hit the speed dial.

Dunlop kept staring at the phone as it began ringing, his eyes getting wider as his anger grew. He answered, "What do you want, you prick?!"

Slater said nothing, curious to see Dunlop's reaction.

"Don't play games! I asked you what you want!" Dunlop yelled.

"You know."

"I've already told you a hundred times! You guaranteed you could do the job and give me the results I wanted! Which included Randall getting arrested for her murder! You blew it!"

"As I've told you repeatedly, I never make guarantees because these things don't always work out exactly as planned. Like that old saying about a war plan never surviving first contact. And I specifically *never* promised you that Randall would be arrested. You're delusional, Dunlop."

"YES YOU DID! YOU DID! You told me you'd put that medal or coin or whatever the hell it is in a place so the cops would be sure to find it and know it was his and then they would arrest him and charge him with her murder! YOU DID, YOU SORRY BASTARD!" Dunlop screamed, pounding the dash with his fist. "You've screwed me royally!"

"Try looking at yourself in the mirror. You screwed yourself."

"No, I didn't! You're an incompetent asshole!"

Enjoying the man's total meltdown, Slater couldn't resist taking a personal shot. "Speaking of assholes, does Barclay know about your, shall we say, abnormal appetites?"

Slater watched through the scope as Dunlop blinked rapidly. He said nothing for several seconds before responding in a strained voice, "What are you talking about?"

Slater said softly, "I think you know exactly what I'm talking about. Your taste for young girls?"

"What? I, I, how did you—"

Slater interrupted him. "I told you early on that I make it my business to learn everything about potential clients. But let's set your perversion aside. My problem, or, I should say *your* problem, is that you've failed to meet your commitment. And that's something you need to do. Right now!"

"You've ruined everything!" Dunlop yelled. "I'm done with you!"

His patience gone, Slater asked, "Are you sure you want to do that?"

"Oh, yes! I'm hanging up now! Go crawl back in your hole, and don't ever call me again!"

"Wrong answer," Slater said, easing the trigger back until the rifle bucked. Traveling over two thousand feet a second, the fifty-caliber projectile punched through the windshield, ripping into Dunlop's head just above the right eye. Blood and brain matter splattered the interior. The slug, by this time starting to tumble, shattered the rear window as it exited. As the cell phone slipped from his lifeless fingers, Dunlop's body slumped against the door, blood from the gaping head wound weaving gory tracks down the window.

Slater watched through the powerful scope as Dunlop's body twitched once and then grew still. He scanned the windows and surrounding grounds. Seeing no movement, he nodded in satisfaction.

He thumbed the END button on the cell phone and dropped it into his shirt pocket. Removing the spent shell casing from the firing chamber, he slipped it along with the rifle into the black nylon case.

Slater checked the area carefully to ensure nothing remained that could be tied to him. He then scuffed the sand in random patterns to disguise the imprint of his body where he had lain.

Satisfied he had taken every precaution, Slater walked quickly along the dune line, putting distance between himself and his deadly handiwork. He left the beach at the same walkover, pausing in the shadows to check for traffic and late-night revelers. The streets were empty.

Reaching his vehicle, he stowed the rifle case in the trunk before sliding behind the wheel. Cranking the engine, he lit a cigarette, drawing the smoke into his lungs and holding it before letting it out slowly.

He flicked ashes into an empty coffee cup as his thoughts turned to the man he had just killed. He felt no remorse. It was just business. Actually, it was as much about the man's sexual attraction to young girls as it was about his refusal to honor his obligation. Slater's daughter flashed into his mind, but he quickly stifled the memory.

He took another drag before putting the butt out and dropping the filter and bits of paper into the coffee cup.

He felt another coughing jag coming on. Hacking worse than ever, he was finally able to get the mucus up, spitting it into a drink cup left over from a fast food meal consumed hours before. Holding the cup up to the pale glow cast by a nearby streetlight, he grimaced at the strings of dark and bright red blood in the secretion.

He had been hoping the bleeding would somehow magically stop on its own, but, staring at the stains, he acknowledged he was deluding himself. It was only going to get worse, and soon.

He laughed at the absurdity of worrying about his health. His core belief was simple; let nothing stand in the way of accomplishing the mission. It was the guiding principle that had made him successful.

Out of long habit, he touched the Glock at his waistband, drawing comfort from its familiar feel. Then, putting the car in gear, he drove away.

J ax Beach 9-1-1. Is this an emergency?"

"You bet it is!" the voice exclaimed.

"Please state the nature of your emergency."

"A guy's just been killed!"

"Say again?" the communications officer said.

"I said a man has been killed! Shot in the head! Are you going to send somebody?! I don't know if whoever shot him is still around here!"

"Sir, please stay calm. Where are you calling from?"

"I'm standing in the driveway of 3101 Ocean Drive. I was walking my dog and I heard a loud bang as I was going past the house. Then the back window of a car in the driveway exploded. I walked up there and saw a guy inside with basically the top of his head gone."

What is your name, sir?"

"Steve Burtchell," he answered.

"And your address?"

"Do you really need all this information? Can't you just send somebody?"

"Sir, we've already dispatched officers, and they should be there very shortly. In the meantime, please give me your address."

"Okay, I'm just a little freaked out, you know what I mean? I live at 3210 Ocean Drive."

"Alright, sir. Officers are on the way. They'll want to talk to you, so don't leave. I'll stay on the line with you until they arrive. In the meantime, please don't touch anything."

"Trust me. The inside of the car is a mess. That's the last thing I want to do," Burtchell said.

Within two minutes, the first patrol officer arrived. Putting Burtchell in her headlights, she further lit him up with the car's spotlight. She stepped out of the marked vehicle, her hand on the butt of her pistol.

"Sir," she said in a commanding voice. "Keep your hands where I can see them."

Burtchell spread his arms wide, his cell phone in one hand and the lead to his Yorkie looped around his other hand. "I'm the one who called. I'm talking to your dispatcher right now," he said, as the little dog cowered behind his leg.

The officer approached cautiously, hand still gripping her pistol. She radioed the dispatcher, who confirmed she was talking to the man. The officer relaxed slightly as she approached and examined his identification.

"Sorry, Mr. Burtchell. Can't be too careful nowadays."

"I hear you, officer," he said, "and I don't blame you one bit."

Satisfied he was legitimate, she directed him to wait beside her patrol car while she approached the vehicle. Standing back a couple of feet, she shined her flashlight at the man's head, noting the grievous wound. "Damn, what size bullet does that much damage?" she murmured under her breath.

The officer made mental notes of the body's position and the condition of the interior for the detailed reports she would be writing later. More patrol officers arrived and quickly began stretching crime scene tape around the perimeter.

As the witness stood watching the growing number of police, he felt a tap on his shoulder. He turned and saw a woman in plain clothes with a gun and badge on her hip.

"Sir, I'm Detective Hayes. I understand you called this in to the police department."

"I did. I was walking by and–"

"Hold that thought a minute. The street is about to get very crowded with more emergency vehicles. Let's move so we won't be in their way."

Burtchell scooped up his dog and followed Summer toward her unmarked car as Clay and Joey arrived. "Detective Hayes, is this our witness?" Clay asked.

"Yes, Commander. This is Mr. Steve Burtchell. He lives down the street."

Shaking hands and introducing himself and Joey to the witness, Clay said, "Can you tell us what happened?"

Burtchell said, "I always take Maxie for a walk before bedtime. As I was passing by," he said, gesturing toward the house, "I heard a loud bang, like a rifle shot."

"Could you tell what direction the sound came from?" Joey interjected.

"I'm pretty sure it came from the beach."

"Go on," Clay said.

"About the time I heard the shot, the back window of the car blew out. Then I heard another pop or crack; I'm not sure how to describe it. It could have been the bullet hitting something else," he said as they all turned to look at Dunlop's car.

"Detective Hayes, would you check the area around the vehicle? See if you can find any indication of where the round ended up," Joey said. "And get some people down on the beach to start checking for any tracks or evidence of someone in the sea oats."

Summer pulled two patrol officers off the perimeter guard and sent them to the beach with strict instructions to step carefully to avoid destroying any marks or other evidence that the shooter had been there. She then went to the back of the car and shined her flashlight through the shattered rear window. Locating the entry hole in the front windshield, she turned around and visually surveyed the driveway and yard checking for any obstacle that might contain the spent round.

Focusing on a palm tree twenty feet away, Summer walked over to check. The trunk had a hole about an inch wide and five feet off the ground. Stepping up close, she shined the light directly into the hole, catching a glimpse of metal.

"Sergeant Crutchfield," she called. "Can you come take a look at this?"

Joey came directly over. "Did you find the round?"

"I'm not positive, but I'm seeing what I believe is a piece of metal in the tree trunk here," she said, holding the flashlight so Joey could see.

He eyed the hole and then looked toward the rear of the car. "It appears to line up with the trajectory. Get an evidence tech over here to take pictures and retrieve the thing. And be sure he knows to cut far enough around it so that it doesn't get damaged any more than it already is just in case this is the bullet."

Summer called for one of the evidence techs working at the vehicle as Joey went back over where Clay was still interviewing the witness. After Summer showed the technician the hole in the tree and passed along Joey's caution, she went to the car to do a cursory examination of the body. Shining her light on the dead man's face, she recoiled in surprise.

Clay's cell phone rang, and he stepped away to answer it as Joey continued to interview the witness.

"Commander, this is dispatch. We have the registration information on the vehicle."

"Go," he responded.

"It's registered to a Louis J. Dunlop, 3101 Ocean Drive, South, Jax Beach."

His voice registering shock, Clay said, "Did you say Lou Dunlop?"

"Well, Louis J. Dunlop is what's on the registration."

"Okay, thanks," Clay said, hanging up.

"Mr. Burtchell, could you excuse Sergeant Crutchfield and me for just a minute? In fact, I would appreciate it if you could go to the station so we can get a formal statement from you. Is that possible?"

"No problem," Burtchell said. "I'm wide awake now, that's for sure."

After quickly making arrangements to have an officer transport the witness to the police department, Clay called Summer over.

"What's up, Clay?" Joey asked.

"You'll never guess who the victim is," he said.

Joey eyed the car as Summer said, "I was just about to tell you both. It's Lou Dunlop."

"WHAT!" Joey exclaimed. "Oh, hell no!"

"She's right," Clay spoke up. "That call was from dispatch. The vehicle is registered to a Louis J. Dunlop at this address. I knew he lived somewhere along here, but I didn't know exactly where."

"Well, this is really going to stir things up. What do you think? Is Slater behind this?" Joey asked.

Clay shook his head. "I don't know. Dunlop's personality has probably earned him a small army of haters over the years."

"But how many of those hate him enough to do this?" Joey noted, pointing toward the car.

Clay shrugged, "No way of knowing. We can't eliminate Slater, though. We know for sure that somebody hired him to kill Denise. Who that person is–", Clay stopped as Summer's radio sounded a loud alert tone.

"Any units available, respond to 101 Hopson Road on a reported home invasion by an armed intruder."

As Slater drove away, he passed several police cars with lights flashing and sirens blaring, barreling in the opposite direction toward Dunlop's house. That was good. Every cop in town would probably be at the house soon, leaving the neighborhood where he was going uncovered. Turning onto Beach Boulevard, he drove toward the Intracoastal Waterway, his mind going through various scenarios for gaining entry into his objective. Just before the bridge, he turned left onto Hopson Road, a small neighborhood comprised of expensive homes abutting the ICW.

Slater was searching for an address near the end of the street. Checking the house numbers on each mailbox, he cut his lights as soon as he saw 101 Hopson Road. It was a five thousand square foot, white stucco house set back from the road almost two hundred feet.

Slater didn't need to check the pistol he carried to ensure there was a round chambered. He laughed to himself as he thought of how Hollywood movies were so far removed from reality in the way they portrayed the handling of a firearm. No cop or criminal with an ounce of common sense would carry a gun into a potential firefight without first ensuring a round was in the chamber. He figured Hollywood directors had actors rack the slide back strictly for dramatic effect, but it was still stupid, in his estimation.

He backed the car into the driveway and killed the engine. If all went well, he would take care of business and be out of here before Dunlop's body got cold. Before getting out, he checked his pockets for the extra items he knew he would need. Finding everything in place, he got out, shut the door quietly, and walked quickly toward the side of the house. There were no lights showing to the front. As he rounded the corner approaching the back, he stayed close to a large hedge that made him almost invisible in his dark clothing.

A screened-in patio faced the back of the property that extended almost a hundred feet back to a black wrought iron fence. Table lamps cast a soft glow throughout the room. Slater saw his objective sitting in a rattan chair with his feet up on a matching ottoman, legs crossed, wearing a pair of cargo shorts and a cotton shirt. He was drinking from a Martini glass as he read a newspaper.

As Slater watched, he debated how he could get into the house before the man could react. He peered closely at the patio and smiled. The large room had tall, horizontal-sliding windows covered by screens. The windows on the back side were open. Slater guessed the man had opened those particular windows to take advantage of the fresh breeze.

Coming to a decision, he turned and retraced his steps to the front of the house. He took a lock-blade knife from his pocket as he walked boldly to the front door. Taking a couple of deep breaths, Slater pressed the doorbell three times very fast. Then, he turned and ran flat out around the side of the house to the rear, arriving just as the man pushed the ottoman away and looked over his shoulder toward the front of the house.

Suddenly, Slater felt a coughing jag coming on. He buried his face in the crook of his arm to muffle the sounds of the hacking that he feared would alert the man to his presence. As the coughing eased, Slater watched the man stand up, a frown on his face. He seemed irritated at the idea of a visitor arriving after midnight.

Slater tensed as the man dropped the newspaper beside the chair and went into the great room adjoining the patio. Knowing he had only a few seconds, Slater went swiftly to the nearest open window and made a long slit in the screen. Spreading it, he climbed inside, pulling the Glock from his belt and pointing it in the direction the man had gone.

He went to the doorway and peered around the corner in the direction of the front door. Although he couldn't see the man, he heard the front door open. After several seconds, it slammed shut.

Slater moved behind a sectional couch and crouched down, listening for the sound of footsteps returning. After a couple of minutes had passed, he grew concerned. Getting to his feet, he heard a toilet flush and water running. He crouched back down, waiting.

Seconds later, the man came walking into the room, a quart bottle of vodka in his hand. Slater stood up abruptly, pointing the gun at him. The man yelled, "SHIT!" Dropping the bottle, it crashed to the tile floor and shattered as he took off running back through the house.

Slater ran after him, slipping and almost falling as he crunched through the gin and broken glass. By the time he got into the great room, the man was already racing up the stairs, taking the steps three at a time. Slater sprinted after him, reaching the second floor in time to see his target dashing into a room at the end of the hall. As Slater ran down the hall, he heard a door slam. When he reached the doorway, he peeked into the master bedroom suite. The man was nowhere in sight.

Keeping the Glock ready, Slater went quickly past the king size, four-poster bed to the large bathroom. No one. Sweeping the gun in both directions, he checked to his right and saw two doors on the opposite wall set ten feet apart.

Easing up to the first door, he threw it open. It was an enormous, walk-in closet filled with dozens of suits, dress shirts, and an electric tie rack stuffed with at least two hundred ties of varying colors. Then there were shoes. Dozens of pairs of wingtips in blacks and browns as well as loafers of every style, again primarily blacks and browns. He ducked and looked under the clothing, confirming the man wasn't hiding there.

Frustrated, Slater backed out of the closet and moved to the second door. There was something odd about it that he couldn't place at first. When he touched the surface, he realized what was different. Although it had the appearance and texture of wood, it was actually metal, unlike the hollow-core door to the closet.

There was another difference. Instead of a knob like the closet door, this one had a lever handle made of heavy gauge stainless steel. The realization that he was staring at a reinforced steel door leading to a safe room hit him hard. He grabbed the handle and jerked downward. It didn't budge.

Slater's anger at losing control of the situation was almost unbearable. Taking deep breaths to calm himself, he noticed the keypad for the first time. It had been right beside the doorframe, but he had been so intent on the door itself that he had missed it. The lever handle had no keyhole, which meant a code was required to open the door.

In the distance, Slater heard a siren. Actually, multiple sirens. The cops were no doubt speeding in this direction. Slater guessed the man must have contacted the police somehow, either with a cell phone or from a wired phone inside the safe room. Feeling the first stirrings of panic, he yanked open the drawer of the bedside table hoping to find something with the code written on it. Pawing through the contents, he saw nothing that would help.

Then a thought suddenly stuck him. He should have heard the beeping sounds of a combination being entered into the keypad before the man made it into the safe room. Instead, he had heard nothing except the door slamming shut. He pressed a couple of buttons on the keypad and heard a loud beep each time.

Slater scanned the keypad and the door for some other means of opening it. As he ran his hand over the top edge of the door facing, he heard the screeching of tires coming from the front of the house. Suddenly, he smiled as he felt a tiny button on the top left edge of the door facing. He pressed it and grinned as the door popped open with a soft click.

Slater stepped into the safe room, pointing the Glock directly at his target's chest.

"Sgt. Von Edward Slater reporting for duty, Major Barclay," Slater said as he pulled the door closed.

59

J oey, you and Summer stay here and handle the investigation," Clay said as he headed for his car. "I'll respond to the call on Hopson Road."

"You sure you don't want one of us to go with you?" Joey asked.

"No, it's okay. There's plenty of units headed that way. I need you and Summer here. The media coverage that's going to hit with Dunlop's murder will be massive coming so close after the mayor's death. We can't afford a single mistake."

As Clay drove toward Hopson Road, he called communications to get more information. A dispatcher answered, telling him the other dispatcher was on the phone with the caller.

"Who is the complainant?" Clay asked.

"Commander, it's Thomas Barclay, the senator," she said in a hushed tone.

Shocked, Clay said, "You're telling me she's talking to Barclay right now?"

"Yes, sir. He's on a cell phone inside a safe room in his house. He told her someone rang his doorbell a few minutes ago, but there was no one there when he went to check. Then when he walked back into his screened-in patio, he saw a guy standing in there pointing a gun at him. He said he took off running and made it upstairs and locked himself in his safe room."

"Did he describe the guy with the gun?" Clay asked as he swerved around a pickup that was slow to get out of the inside lane.

"He said it's a white male, late forties or so, dark brown hair, medium height, wearing military- or law enforcement-type black BDUs. And he exhibited a semi-automatic handgun."

That sounded like Slater except for the hair, Clay thought. "Okay, call out the SWAT team and have them respond ASAP. We don't know exactly what we've got, but I'd rather have them and not need them than the other way around. Also, tell them to get a couple of hostage negotiators heading that way just in case."

"Hang on, Commander," the dispatcher said. Clay waited impatiently as he turned off Beach Boulevard and raced to the end of the street where he joined three patrol cars with flashing lights flanking Barclay's house. As he jumped out of the car, the other dispatcher got on the phone.

"Commander, I was talking to Mr. Barclay when I heard something strange, and then he hung up. I called him back, but he's not answering now."

"What do you mean by strange?"

"Mr. Barclay was telling me that nobody could get into the safe room unless he opened the door for them or unless they knew the code for the keypad. Then, all of a sudden, I heard someone else in the background saying something. It was definitely a man's voice, very deep, but it was kind of faint. He must have been standing some distance away from Mr. Barclay. But it sounded like he said, 'Sergeant something, something,' and then possibly a last name, 'Sable' or 'Sater,' I couldn't tell for sure. Then he clearly said, 'Reporting for duty, Major Barclay.'"

Clay squeezed the phone tightly. "Call out the dispatch supervisor and ask her to start reviewing the 9-1-1 recording. I want her to try to clean it up so we can hear exactly what the man said. Also, call Chief Wilson and ask him to respond to the scene here on Hopson Road. And give me Barclay's cell number."

After relaying the number, the dispatcher said, "Commander, we have a problem with the hostage negotiators."

"What now?" he growled.

"Detective Hayes is still at the homicide scene on Ocean Drive, and the other two negotiators are in Orlando at a training seminar. Do you want me to have Detective Hayes respond?"

Clay thought a moment and then said, "No. Sergeant Crutchfield needs her at the homicide scene. I'm a trained negotiator. I'll handle it."

As he hung up, Clay grimaced at the realization that Slater was holding Barclay hostage. He must have figured out a way to get inside the safe room and locked himself in there with Barclay. Clay wondered how it could get any worse.

A patrol sergeant ran up. "Commander, I checked the back of the house and found a screen cut leading into a patio room adjacent to the main part of the house. No one has gone inside at this point, but I've got officers covering it."

"Let's keep it that way for now, Sergeant," Clay said. "Make sure officers are covering all sides of the house, and tell everyone to keep their eyes open and their heads down. We've got a hostage situation with an armed man who is more than likely the suspect who just killed Senator Barclay's chief of staff as well as Mayor Adams."

60

H ang up, Major. Now!" Slater demanded, harshly.

His eyes on the gun in Slater's hand, Barclay broke the connection to the communications officer. He barked, "Who the hell do you think you are?! You've just broken into the house of a United States Senator, and you're pointing a gun at me! That's a federal crime!"

Slater glared at the man who was the catalyst for his career as a professional killer. He raised the gun a little higher, aiming it at Barclay's left eye. "Sit down in the chair behind you. Do it now, or I'll put a bullet in your head, and you'll go to hell never knowing why."

Barclay's confidence and bluster melted away in an instant, and he collapsed into the chair.

"Now, put your cell phone on the floor and kick it over here to me. If you try anything stupid, it will be the last thing you ever do."

Barclay bent forward and placed the phone on the tile floor. He shoved it with his foot, sending it skittering toward Slater where it stopped within his reach. He bent down and felt around for the phone until he found it, placing it on a table beside him, never once taking his eyes or the gun off Barclay.

"You know something, Major? You mouthed all that stuff at me about being a United States Senator and blah, blah, blah. Let me enlighten you. You have this perception of power, but that power you're so proud of disappeared, just like that," Slater said, snapping his fingers. "You see, I'm the one pointing a gun at you. And he who holds the weapon holds the power. See how that works?"

Slater sat across from him in the only other chair as he studied the safe room. He noted an apartment-size refrigerator, a tiny kitchenette with a stove and sink, a miniscule bathroom, and a narrow cot with a fitted sheet and an OD green blanket folded at the foot.

"Not bad, Major. Not bad. Pretty smart to have a safe room built in your house. And the secret switch to allow you to bypass the keypad when you're running for your life was ingenious. Of course, it didn't help you this time, did it?"

Breaking his silence, Barclay spoke up, his voice shaky, "How did you know there was a panic bypass button?"

"I didn't, Major. Not at first anyway. But I figured it out."

"You keep referring to me as a major. I was a colonel when I retired, not a major."

"You were Major Barclay when you and I knew each other."

"What did you say your name was?"

Slater said nothing for so long that Barclay began fidgeting in his chair. "Stop moving around, Major. You make me think you might want to be a hero and do something stupid."

Barclay frowned. "I truly don't have any idea what you're trying to accomplish here. But I do know that you've assaulted a federal official, and for that, you can get many years in a federal penitentiary."

Slater shrugged. "Been there. Done that. Won't do it again."

"What do you mean?"

"Are you telling me you really don't know who I am?"

Confusion crossed Barclay's face. "No idea. I assume you must have been in the military since you referred to yourself as a sergeant. I spent twenty-five years in the Army, and I encountered literally thousands of soldiers in that time. Why you think I would remember you is beyond me."

Slater's eyes narrowed, and the knuckles on the hand holding the gun grew white as he gripped it hard. "You son of a bitch! You lied and got me sent to prison, and you don't even remember me?!" he raged, his voice cracking.

Barclay leaned back in his chair, trying to create as much distance as possible between himself and Slater. As he scrutinized Slater's face, recognition suddenly flared. "You're Slater. Sergeant Von Slater. You were the sniper who killed the wrong man."

"I sure as hell did, thanks to your bad information! Instead of taking responsibility for your own damn screw up, you lied to the military investigators and then got some of your asshole buddies to cover for you and lie on the stand, too," he said, his breath coming fast.

Barclay responded, "Now, Sergeant, that's *your* story, whereas *my* story is quite different. Mine is that I testified truthfully at the court-martial. Just because the verdict went against you doesn't make my version false and yours true."

Barclay's cell phone rang at the same moment Slater shouted, "Wanta bet, asshole?!" as the big forty-five roared in his hand.

Outside the house, the SWAT team arrived and assumed control of the perimeter. Operators covered all sides and approaches to the house. Clay briefed everyone on their assignments before climbing into the department's special ops van and positioning himself at the radio and telephone console. The equipment would not only record both ends of any conversation but also allow others in the van to hear everything being said.

With a wave of his hand for quiet, he dialed Barclay's cell number and waited while it rang and rang. Just as he began to think the call would go to voice mail, Slater answered. "What do you want?"

"Is this Von Slater?"

"Yes. Is this Commander Randall?"

Hiding his surprise at how quickly Slater identified his voice, Clay said, "It is. I'd like to talk to you about what's going on. Would that be possible?"

"Anything's possible, Commander. Why don't you tell *me* what's going on. I'm sort of incommunicado with the outside world right now, seeing as how I'm locked up in a reinforced room inside the home of the world's biggest asshole."

"Mr. Slater, is Senator Thomas Barclay in that room with you?"

"Hold on," he said. "Let me check. Commander Clay Randall wants to know if a Senator Thomas Barclay is in here with me. Is he?"

Clay listened intently for a response, hearing nothing.

"No, I'm sorry, Commander. No one responds to that name in here."

"Mr. Slater, Is Senator Barclay okay?"

"That depends on how you define okay."

"Please don't do anything that will make the situation worse."

"First, I'm not sure how things could be worse than they are right now. And second, I don't want to talk about that lying piece of shit. Instead, let's talk about you, Commander. I'm guessing since you're on the other end of the line that you haven't been arrested for the murder of your mayor."

"That's a good guess," Clay responded. "Can I assume you're the one who killed her and tried to frame me for her death?"

"Commander, there will be time to discuss all that later."

"May I speak to Senator Barclay?"

"No, that's not possible."

"I know he's in there with you. He called 9-1-1 and said he was there."

"Let's just say he's indisposed."

"Is the senator injured, Mr. Slater?"

"How about we dispense with all this formality? You call me Von, and I'll call you Clay."

"Okay, Von. So, back to the question. Is Senator Barclay injured?"

"You could say that."

"Does he need immediate medical attention?"

"I don't know. Let me ask him."

As Slater put the phone down, Clay faintly heard him say, "Hey, asshole, your buddy Clay Randall wants to know if you need medical attention."

Although keeping the phone pressed tightly against his ear, Clay heard nothing.

"Sorry, Clay. He's not talking."

Worried that Barclay was seriously injured, if not already dead, Clay said, "Von, what can I do to convince you to release Senator Barclay."

"Oh, don't worry. He'll get out of here."

"When?"

"When I decide, I'll let you know," Slater said, hanging up.

Barclay's scream abruptly cut off as the forty-five caliber bullet dug a groove in the side of his head, ripping off the top of his left ear. Hardly slowing, the round punched through the door to the bathroom and embedded itself in the wall. Barclay fell over sideways in the chair, knocked unconscious by the force of the impact as blood began to drip from the wound down the side of his face and onto his shirt. Slater watched the man he hated, almost wishing he had put the bullet between his eyes instead of deliberately grazing him.

The insistent ringing of the phone finally got his attention, and he answered. After the brief conversation with Clay, Slater went to the sink and grabbed a roll of paper towels. He wet a handful and wiped the blood off Barclay's face. He examined the wounds to his head and ear and was satisfied the man wouldn't bleed to death.

Checking drawers, he found a first aid kit and wrapped a full roll of gauze around Barclay's head, adding several wraps of paper tape to secure it. Seeing the blood had barely seeped through, Slater moved back to his chair. He pulled out a pack of cigarettes and lit up as he watched the man begin to stir.

Slater felt phlegm gathering in the back of his throat. Feeling a coughing spasm coming on, he hit himself several times in the chest with his open hand until it began to loosen. He coughed up a mouthful and spit it onto the floor. This time, there was even more bright red blood mixed in with the mucus.

Slater took several shallow breaths, afraid a deep one would start another coughing jag, a situation he didn't need now that Barclay was coming awake. He watched as the man blinked several times and sat up slowly. He groaned, putting his hand to the side of his head. Feeling the bandage, he gasped, "You shot me!"

"Very observant on your part, Major. Don't worry. You're not going to die. At least not right away."

Barclay's eyes widened at Slater's words, but he said nothing.

"Now, listen up, Major. We have things to talk about."

Barclay swayed in the chair as he tried to sit up straight. Keeping a hand to the side of his head, he mumbled, "What things?"

"Let's see. Do you know why I'm here with you in this room?"

Barclay squinted at Slater. "I guess you want revenge for what you think I did to you."

"It's not what I think you did, Major. It's what I *know* you did. And you know it, too."

"I'm not going to argue with you. As you said, you've got the gun."

"That's right. So let's talk, you and me. And just so you know, I'm not here only because you screwed me over way back then in Iraq."

"Why, then?"

"Does the name Denise Adams mean anything to you?"

Barclay's eyes shifted away before coming back to Slater. "Of course, it does. She's the mayor here. Or she was until somebody killed her."

"Know anything about that, Major?"

"About what?"

"About who killed her and why."

"I assume from what's happening here that you must have killed her. As to why, I have absolutely no idea."

"Are you sure, Major?"

Leaning forward, Barclay exclaimed, "Quit calling me Major! I'm a United States Senator!"

"Hey, chill out. Okay, *Senator*," Slater said with a grin. "Back to the question on the table. Are you certain you don't know why Ms. Adams was killed?"

"I already told you. No."

"Are you absolutely sure, Senator?"

"Is that what this is really all about? You think I had something to do with Denise's death?"

Slater shrugged but said nothing.

"What are you, a close friend or something? Somehow you figure that by attacking me you can avenge Denise's death?"

When Slater remained quiet, Barclay continued. "Well, here's the deal. Denise Adams worked for my campaign several years ago. She did a great job, and to repay the favor, I campaigned for her when she ran for mayor. That's the sum total of my connection with her. It was a strictly professional relationship."

"Interesting. That's not what Lou Dunlop said when he hired me to kill her."

"I don't care what . . . wait a minute. What are you talking about?"

"You mean about Dunlop hiring me to kill Denise Adams?"

"Are you saying that my chief of staff hired you to kill Denise?"

"That's exactly what I'm saying. For fifty thousand dollars, of which he paid half and stiffed me on the rest."

"I don't know anything about that, I swear. If Dunlop hired you, he did that completely on his own. I had nothing to do with it, and that's the truth."

"So you expect me to believe that Dunlop hired me to kill the mayor totally without your knowledge."

"That's right, and I don't give a damn whether you believe me or not."

"What about the newspaper article? I saw you reading it when I got here. Care to explain the claims in there that you and Ms. Adams were having an affair? An affair that started before your wife died of cancer?"

"Don't you talk about my wife, you bastard!"

Slater leaned forward, the gun held inches from Barclay's face. In a deadly cold voice, he said, "I'll talk about your wife and your girlfriend and anyone else I choose to."

Barclay leaned back without speaking, his eyes locked on the gun.

Slater smiled. "You didn't answer my question. What about the newspaper article? Is all that stuff about you and the mayor just a bunch of lies like you claim everything else is?"

Barclay crossed his arms and turned away. "I refuse to discuss this any further. If you've got evidence that my chief of staff engaged in illegal activities, take it to the police and let them deal with him."

"Oh, they're dealing with Dunlop as we speak."

"Since you seem to have inside information, how exactly are they doing that?"

"You know, the usual crime scene stuff. Taking pictures, measurements, the sort of things cops do when they're conducting a murder investigation."

63

While Slater continued his interrogation of Barclay, Chief Wilson climbed into the special ops van. Clay brought the chief up to date on Barclay's situation as well as Dunlop's murder.

"So you think this Slater killed Lou Dunlop?" Mike asked.

"No doubt in my mind," Clay said. "He said he wasn't ready to talk about it yet, but I'm convinced he took out Dunlop and intends to kill Barclay before he's done."

"What's your plan?" Mike asked.

"Since they're locked inside Barclay's safe room, I'm sending the team into the house. They'll take up positions covering the door to the room while I keep trying to talk Slater into giving up."

"Okay, make it happen."

Within minutes, the SWAT team had secured the lower level of the house and taken up positions covering the master suite on the second floor. Clay moved into a small office directly across the hallway while the chief stayed in the ops van. The phone line was kept open so Mike could follow along with the conversation.

When everyone was ready, Clay dialed Barclay's phone.

"Hello, Clay," Slater answered.

"Von, Can I speak to Senator Barclay?"

"You're a very persistent man. Barclay can wait. First, I want to talk to you about the Mexican restaurant and the young woman's story about someone scratching my SUV. Do you know what I'm talking about?"

Clay hesitated before answering. "I do."

"Does she work for you?"

"Yes, she's one of my detectives."

"What about the big guy who pretended to be her husband. He one of yours, too?"

"No. He's a sergeant with the Nye County Sheriff's Office."

"Was it your idea to create the distraction so someone could take the stuff that had my DNA on them?"

"No, actually, that was my detective."

"Well, it was inspired, I have to tell you. She sounds like a smart cop. And I assume my DNA was found at the mayor's house."

"It was. Since we're talking about it, did you kill Mayor Denise Adams?"

"Yes."

"Okay, I appreciate your honesty. Now, if you don't mind, can we go back to why we're here?"

"Sure, let's talk about the current situation. What do you want to know?"

"Is Senator Barclay okay?"

"He's fine, although he seems somewhat shaken by the death of his chief of staff."

"Did you also kill Lou Dunlop?"

"I did. The world is a better place with that sorry son of a bitch gone."

"Why do you say that?"

"Because Lou Dunlop was evil personified. He was a pervert, plain and simple. Did you know he was into child porn?"

"Yes, we did. We were in the process of filing charges on him, but now—"

"Let me guess. I saved the taxpayers the trouble and expense of a trial. You should thank me."

Overlooking the comment, Clay pressed on. "Can I talk to Senator Barclay?"

Slater was silent for so long that Clay thought he had hung up. "Von, are you still there?"

"I'm here, Clay. I was just thinking about your request. How would you like to come inside and have a face to face conversation with the senator?"

This time, it was Clay's turn to hesitate as he mulled over Slater's suggestion. It was contrary to every principle of tactical operations and hostage negotiations. He figured Mike Wilson was right then racing from the special ops van into the house to get in his face and refuse to allow such a potentially dangerous move.

In spite of his training, there was something about the idea that made sense to Clay. He had a feeling about Slater that was difficult to articulate. Somehow, he didn't think the killer meant to do him harm.

As those thoughts ran through his mind, the chief came charging down the hall, stopping abruptly when he saw Clay standing in the office. Winded from his run, he was only able to gesture wildly at Clay, sliding a finger back and forth across his throat.

With a nod, Clay said, "Von, that's an interesting invitation. I need to think about it and call you back."

"That's fine. The senator and I aren't going anywhere," Slater said, clicking off.

Still breathing hard, Mike wheezed, "What are you thinking?! You never voluntarily put yourself into a hostage situation!"

Clay held up both hands in a calming gesture. "Hang on, Mike. You need to sit down before you fall down."

Dropping into a chair, Wilson continued breathing hard. "I swear, this job is going to be the death of me."

"Well, if you got a little more exercise . . ."

The chief's head came up rapidly, his eyes narrowed, "Don't go there!"

"Okay, okay," Clay said. "Just listen for a minute before you go off. I've got a feeling about this. Slater isn't some wild-eyed crazy who's trying to figure a way to get out of that room and escape. He's admitted killing Denise and Dunlop. He knows he's either facing the death penalty or life in prison, and he doesn't care."

"All the more reason why I'm not letting you go in there. You said it. He doesn't care, so why would he worry about taking out a cop along with a United States senator?"

"Listen, Mike. There's more to this than we're seeing. I didn't tell you exactly what Slater said when he went into the safe room. He referred to himself as Sergeant Slater and Barclay as Major Barclay. I have a gut feeling that none of what's going on right now is about Denise or Dunlop. Instead, I think it has something to do with his military career. In my first conversation with Slater, he referred to Barclay as a lying piece of shit. I'm guessing Barclay might have been involved in some way in Slater being court-martialed and getting sent to Fort Leavenworth."

"All that's very interesting," the chief replied, "but that still doesn't make me feel good about letting you go in there."

"Tell you what. I'll call him back and try to find out why he wants me to come into the safe room, but I won't commit either way. How's that?"

With the chief's reluctant agreement, Clay called back, putting the phone on speaker so Mike could hear Slater. "Von, I have a couple of questions."

"I thought you might. Shoot."

"Why can't I just talk to the senator on the phone?"

"Because you really need to look the man in the eye as you, as *we* have the conversation."

"Why?"

"So you can tell when he's lying. I could use the old joke about knowing he's lying because his lips are moving, but I'm serious here, Clay. Barclay is a man who wouldn't tell the truth unless he thought it would benefit him directly. Since I will have a gun pointed at him as we speak, he's more likely to be truthful."

"About the gun, Von. I have a problem with that."

"I'm sure you do, just as I would have a problem with letting you inside if *you're* armed. In order to make this happen, you must, and I stress *must*, be unarmed. Not even a pair of fingernail clippers."

"If I were to agree to that, what would stop you from shooting me as soon as I stepped through the door?"

"Two things. One, you have my word. I know that probably doesn't mean anything to you, but people who know me have absolute faith that, when I make a commitment, I *always* follow through. And two, I have no beef with you. In fact, you and I have a common grievance against Senator Barclay."

"I can't imagine what that would be," Clay said, puzzled.

"Mine is because my former Army major lied and caused me to be sent to prison. Yours is because he was responsible for trying to frame you for Mayor Adams' murder. Now, he might try to tell you that he had nothing to do with it. That it was all Dunlop's fault. I'll concede it's at least possible that Dunlop may not have told Barclay every step he took, but the man knew the end result that his boss expected. Therefore, Barclay's responsible. Just like in the military. When the troops screw up, the person in charge almost always gets the ax. Of course, that wasn't the case with Major Barclay. He's led a charmed life. At least until now. So, what do you say? Do you accept my terms?"

"Another question. If I agree to come inside unarmed, what happens after our conversation with Barclay?"

"I'll surrender my weapon to you and go quietly to jail. And I'll plead guilty to all the charges."

"I'll call you back," Clay said, hanging up.

"What do you think, Mike?"

Wilson shook his head. "I don't know. The guy sounds reasonable, but this is a huge risk you would be undertaking. If I let you go in there and something bad happens, I'll never forgive myself."

"I understand, but I think this has a real chance of working. If we don't agree, I'm afraid he'll end up killing Barclay. As much as I detest the man for everything he's done, he doesn't deserve to die. If we can bring this situation to a peaceful conclusion, I think we have to try."

The chief sat for several minutes without speaking, then said, "I'm agreeing to this in spite of having very serious doubts. God help me if I'm wrong."

Clay called Slater back. "Von, I'm coming in. What do I need to do?"

"Be sure you're unarmed. For my comfort level, I'll need you to strip as soon as you step inside. My weapon will be pointed at you until I'm satisfied you aren't coming in with guns blazing, so to speak. When that's done, you and I can have our talk with Senator Barclay."

"Okay," Clay agreed. "Will you be opening the door, or can you give me the code for the keypad?"

"No, I prefer to stay back until I'm comfortable with our arrangement. There's a button on the top left corner of the doorframe. Push it, and the door lock will release."

"Okay, I have to brief my boss, and then I'll be coming in. I'll bang on the door before I push the button."

Clay removed his pistol and left it on the table. He dumped the contents of his pockets beside the weapon before turning to face Mike.

"Clay, are you absolutely sure about this?"

He shrugged. "No, if you want to know the truth. But I think I have to do it if we're going to have a chance of ending this peacefully."

In all their years of working together, Mike Wilson had never exhibited deep emotion. Without warning, he grabbed Clay and squeezed him in a bear hug. "Don't get yourself hurt, or I swear I'll demote you to parking enforcement."

Clay grinned as Mike let go. "Damn, Chief. I didn't know you cared," he said as he turned and went into the master suite.

He directed the SWAT team members to deploy themselves out of sight of the door to avoid spooking Slater. When they were in position, Clay banged on the door three times, reached to the top of the doorframe, and pressed the button. The door opened with a soft click, and he stepped inside the safe room.

As Clay came in, his eyes immediately went to the gun pointing unwaveringly at him. Slater had positioned himself against the far wall so he could easily watch both men.

"Close the door, Clay," Slater directed. "And keep your hands where I can see them at all times," he added.

Clay did as instructed and turned around, his eyes falling on Barclay. The blood from the head wound had partially soaked through the bandage, but the man otherwise seemed alert as he glared at Clay.

"Before we get to our discussion, I need you to strip to your underwear," Slater said.

Without responding, Clay took off his shirt and pants and dropped them on a low table near the door. Slater watched him closely, then said, "Hold your arms away from your body and turn around."

Clay did as instructed, making a slow, complete turn. "Good?" he asked.

"Almost. Step away from your clothing."

Clay moved to the other side of the room as Slater cautiously went to the table and searched the pockets of his pants and shirt. Satisfied, Slater went back to his original position.

"You can get dressed now, Clay. And thank you for not trying anything."

With a brief nod, Clay silently retrieved his clothes and quickly dressed. "What now?" he asked.

"Have a seat on the bunk over there," Slater said. "That way, Senator Barclay can see us both as we have our discussion."

Clay went to the bunk and sat down, his hands resting on his knees. Slater moved back to his chair, his eyes shifting between Clay and Barclay. He rested the pistol on his leg, his hand curled around the butt.

"Okay, let's start. First, Senator . . . oh, hell, I'm done with calling you that. You'll always be Major Barclay to me. Get used to it," he said with a mocking smile.

Barclay remained quiet as he gently touched the bandage covering his head.

"Alright, I think Clay would like to know why you went on this campaign of attack and destroy against him. Care to explain?"

Barclay's eyes shifted to Clay before coming back to Slater. He said nothing.

Slater let the silence stretch out over a minute before raising the gun toward Barclay. "You've apparently misunderstood the ground rules, Major. When either Clay or I ask you a question, you answer. If at any point you fail to respond, I'll be forced to notch your other ear, which won't bode well for photo ops on the campaign trail."

Barclay's put his hand to his uninjured ear as if to protect it. He said, "I haven't done anything to Randall."

Clay spoke up at that. "Senator, while you personally may not have pulled all the crap I've endured, you ordered it done."

"You?! Endured?!" he barked. "You don't have any idea what the word means. Try having your daughter killed and your granddaughter permanently disabled. You've taken my whole family away from me. And for what? Just because you couldn't handle the thought of a poor homeless guy in a wheelchair daring to show disrespect to you."

Clay looked at Slater in disbelief at Barclay's outburst. Turning to Barclay, he snapped, "You call it disrespect, Senator? I call it attempted murder! When a guy with a butcher knife is trying his best to stick it in your chest, that goes way beyond disrespect!"

"Alright, this is good," Slater said. "And your rebuttal, Major?"

"I'm not playing this game," Barclay growled.

"Trust me, Major," Slater retorted. "You *will* play this game, or you *will* die right in that chair. What's your decision?"

Barclay looked fearfully at Slater and then at the gun pointing at his head. "I'll answer the damn questions."

"Good. That's what I wanted to hear. Now, do you have a rebuttal you'd like to share with Commander Randall?"

Barclay shook his head.

"Okay, then I'm giving that round to the commander. Go ahead, Clay. Ask your next question."

"Did Dunlop ever tell you he hired Von Slater to kill the mayor?"

"I've said it, and I'll say again. I didn't know what Lou was going to do."

"But he told you about it afterwards. Right?"

Reluctantly, Barclay replied, "You have to understand. Lou's job was to take care of things so I could concentrate on my job. There have been hundreds of things he's handled without checking with me. I trusted him to do the right thing. In most cases, he did exactly what I wanted. In this situation, I just–" Barclay stopped.

"Just what?" Clay jumped in. "Just wanted to ruin my life, right? So your boy Dunlop picked it up and ran with it."

Barclay shrugged but didn't respond.

"While we're talking about Dunlop," Slater said, "he specifically requested that I plant an item at the mayor's house that would point a finger directly at Clay. All so he would be blamed for her death. I'm sorry now that I agreed to do it because I've come to the realization that Clay didn't deserve it. I don't say that lightly seeing as how I have no particular love for police considering my occupation. My question to you, Major, is, did you know either before or after the mayor's death that implicating the commander here was part of what I was paid to do?"

"I don't recall Lou saying anything about that, no," Barclay answered.

"Well, that's certainly convenient. Tell you what. Seeing as how it's been more than ten minutes, I'm going to have a smoke. That should give you enough time to search your memory and give me a definitive answer to my question," Slater said.

"Want one?" he asked them as he lit up.

Barclay scowled, "No." Clay just shook his head.

"No problem. I'm going to sit here and enjoy one last cigarette and then finish this."

"What do you mean?" Barclay asked, suddenly wary.

Slater didn't answer as he continued to draw deeply on the cigarette, his eyes never leaving Barclay's face. He took another lungful of smoke and coughed. And coughed. And coughed again, deeper each time. Suddenly, he was hacking so hard he had trouble drawing a breath. The gun began to waver in his hand. A violent spasm caused him to lean forward, and the weapon and cigarette fell from his hands as he pounded on his chest trying to draw a breath of air into his lungs.

Before Clay could react, Barclay leaped from his chair and snatched the gun off the floor. He stood over Slater as the man continued to emit deep, rasping coughs. With a triumphant sneer, Barclay pointed the gun at Slater's head, his finger curling around the trigger.

"Barclay, don't do it!" Clay shouted.

The senator's eyes locked on Slater, watching the man's face turning red as he tried and failed to catch his breath. Within seconds, Slater's face had turned a dusky blue.

Clay jumped up and quickly went to Slater, slamming his fist into the man's back between the shoulder blades. Twice more he did it, until Slater sucked in a breath of life-giving air.

Turning to Barclay, Clay put out his hand, commanding, "Senator, give me that weapon. Now!"

Barclay shook his head, glaring at Clay. "No. I don't trust you any more than I do this filth," he exclaimed, his eyes going back to Slater as he moved away.

Slater remained slumped forward as he fought to get his breathing under control. Ropy strings of bright and dark blood dripped from his mouth. He slowly raised his head enough to see Barclay through eyes that were still watering. His face was no longer blue; it was now a pasty white.

Wiping his mouth with the back of his hand, he croaked, "Can you get me a glass of water?"

Barclay glanced toward the counter where several plastic glasses were stacked beside the refrigerator. "No, I don't think so," he said with a big smile.

As Clay went toward the counter, Barclay swiftly pointed the pistol at him. "Don't move, Randall."

Clay stopped and turned around. "Don't do this, Barclay. You're a victim of Slater's crime. But if you don't hand that weapon to me right now, you're committing a crime of aggravated battery against a police officer. Do you really want to face a jury on that charge?"

Momentarily distracted by Clay's demand to turn over the gun, Barclay didn't immediately see Slater get to his feet and take a step toward him. However, before he could reach Barclay, Slater coughed again. Barclay whirled around and shoved Slater hard in the chest, sending him sprawling on the floor.

Barclay stepped back so he could keep Clay and Slater in front of him. He watched with a smile as Slater went through another round of deep, chest-rattling coughs as he lay on his side. When it finally eased, Slater very slowly sat up, his head down.

"Get up," Barclay ordered.

Slater gave no sign he heard the command.

"I said, get up!" Barclay repeated loudly.

"Can't you see he's out of it, Barclay?" Clay said. "Let me help him!"

Barclay didn't respond right away, as his eyes went back and forth between the two. He said, "Okay, Randall. Get him up and put him back in the chair. But don't try anything."

Clay lifted Slater to his feet and half-carried him to the chair. Easing him down, he held onto Slater's arms until the man was able to sit up without falling.

"He's fine, Randall. Get back over there," Barclay said, waving the gun in the direction of the bunk.

"The man is no longer a threat, and he needs medical attention. Let me get the officers in here so they can take him into custody. And once again, I'm ordering you to give me that weapon," Clay said, holding out his hand.

"Yeah, give him the gun, Major," Slater croaked.

"I don't think so," Barclay sneered. "In fact, considering how circumstances have changed, I'm debating whether or not I should kill you right now. You know, to save the taxpayers the trouble and expense of a trial, as you said a while ago."

"Think that will help your campaign for president?" Slater asked.

Clay could almost feel the waves of hate coming off Barclay. Both men appeared to have forgotten he was there as they glared with animosity at each other.

"Of course, it will," Barclay said. "I'll be a hero. United States senator singlehandedly defeats the hired assassin who killed the mayor of his hometown and his chief of staff."

"Not that it matters now, but you never answered the question about whether Dunlop told you he hired me to kill Mayor Adams," Slater pointed out.

Barclay shrugged his broad shoulders and took a deep breath before answering. "You're right. It doesn't matter. But since you asked, I didn't know about it beforehand. However, I–" he stopped, cutting his eyes over at Clay. He smirked, "I knew nothing about it and would never have condoned such a heinous act because that would be wrong."

"Spoken like a career politician," Slater said, his voice growing weaker. He examined the hands that had caused so many deaths since that fateful night in Iraq. He didn't regret for a second killing Dunlop as well as most of the others since he started down his dark path. Denise Adams bothered him, though. The more he thought about it, the more he realized she had done nothing to deserve death. Not by his hand, anyway. Life was full of choices and consequences. He had made his choice, and he was ready for the consequences he knew were coming. By one means or another.

Gazing up at Barclay, he said, "Since you're going to kill me anyway, why don't you at least admit you set me up in Iraq."

Barclay scrutinized the gun in his hand, a curious look on his face. "You can't let the past go, can you? So you did a few years in the USDB–"

"A few years?! It was fourteen damn years, you–"

"Shut your mouth, asshole, or I'll shut it for you! Right now!" Barclay yelled, his finger tightening on the trigger.

Barclay glared at him for several seconds, and then, with heavy contempt in his voice, said, "Sure, I set you up in Iraq. So what? Not that it matters what I say in here. I'll deny it outside this room, and it'll be the word of a respected United States senator against a murderer and a lying cop. Who do you think people are going to believe? Besides, you have nobody to blame but yourself, Slater. You got out of prison while you were still a relatively young man. You had the whole rest of your life in front of you. Instead, what did you do? You decided to stick with what you know best. Shooting people down like dogs. I have to say I'm not impressed with what you've made of your opportunities."

"My opportunities?" Slater wheezed, his voice cracking. "Go to hell! Pull the trigger!"

Barclay suddenly grinned as he waved the gun back and forth. "You know, now that I think about it, I don't believe I will. Remember your big talk about me only having the perception of power? Well, now who has the real power? I think we know the answer. And I think we both know who had it all along. So, here's what's going to happen. Instead of killing you, I'm going to turn you over to this man here," he said, acknowledging Clay for the first time in several minutes.

"Then, I'm going to take great pleasure at the thought of you sitting in a jail cell after your conviction awaiting your execution down the road. My only hope is that I'll still be the president when your last appeal is denied. When that time comes, be sure to tell your lawyer not to bother with an appeal to me for clemency. I'm thinking it won't receive favorable consideration."

Barclay then turned toward Clay, demanding in a loud voice, "Randall, get this *asshole* out of my house."

Instantly, Slater lashed out with his foot, connecting with Barclay's knee and driving it sideways with a loud crack.

Barclay bellowed in pain, staggering, grabbing the back of his chair as he fought to keep from falling.

Clay stepped toward Barclay. "Give me the gun!" he yelled.

"NO!" Barclay screamed, pointing the pistol at Clay. "Get back or I'll kill you!"

Clay stopped as Barclay swung the gun back toward Slater. Hobbling on one leg, using the chair to support his weight, Barclay inched closer to Slater, positioning himself so the man couldn't kick him again.

He jammed the pistol against the side of Slater's head, his hand shaking in frenzied rage. "DIE, YOU SORRY MOTHER–", his screaming curse suddenly cut short.

The bullet tore through flesh, shattering bone in the process as it accomplished its objective. The second round went wild, ricocheting off the steel door and flying straight back in the direction it had come. It, too, found a target.

65

Mike Wilson and the SWAT operators all heard the noise of gunfire inside the safe room. The chief ran forward and banged his fist repeatedly on the door, yelling Clay's name.

Suddenly, the door opened a crack. SWAT officers immediately trained their weapons at the small opening.

"Everyone stand down! It's under control!" Clay yelled from inside.

Mike called back, "Clay, are you okay?"

"Yes, I'm opening the door!"

Clay swung the door open wide and told the closest officer to call rescue units for two gunshot victims.

Slater was semi-conscious, muttering something Clay couldn't understand as he bent over him. He could see where the bullet had struck Slater's belt buckle before entering his lower abdomen. There was already a small pool of blood on the floor, while a slight amount trickled from the hole. Clay wasn't sure if that was good or bad. He could be bleeding out inside for all he knew.

The first rescue team came running in moments later and immediately started working on Slater.

The second rescue unit arrived shortly after and began administering treatment to Barclay, who was moaning in pain as he gripped his knee with his uninjured arm. His other arm hung useless by his side.

Barclay raised his head and saw Mike Wilson standing at the door. Pointing at Clay, he howled, "He shot me! I want this man arrested! I want him charged for trying to kill me!"

Mike turned to Clay. "You shot the senator?"

"You bet I did. Shot him in the arm."

"Why?"

"Because he was a half-second away from killing Slater."

"I was justified!" Barclay roared. "He was holding me hostage. He destroyed my knee! I had every right to kill the son of a bitch!"

"Actually, Barclay got his hands on Slater's gun and threatened to kill both of us," Clay said.

As an EMT pulled an oxygen mask over Barclay's nose and mouth, Mike said, "Sounds to me like Commander Randall saved you from being charged with a homicide, senator. You should thank him."

Clay and Mike could hear Barclay continuing to shout threats even as the EMTs carried him down the stairs and out the front door.

"I'm confused," Mike said. "How did Slater get shot?"

Clay winced. "Barclay had the gun pressed against Slater's head and was squeezing the trigger when I shot him in the upper arm. He jerked just enough from the hit that the round missed entirely. Unfortunately, it hit the steel door and ricocheted straight back and hit Slater as he stood up. Fortunately, the round caught his belt buckle first, and that slowed it down a little bit. Otherwise, he'd probably be dead."

Mike watched the EMTs working to stabilize Slater a moment before asking, "Where the hell did you get a gun? Slater told you he was going to make you strip."

Clay smiled as he pulled a tiny revolver from his pocket. "My backup. It shoots twenty-two caliber long rifle hollow points, and they pack a punch," he said.

"He didn't make you take your clothes off?"

"Oh, he did, but I was counting on him not wanting to see my junk. And I was right. He told me to keep my underwear on. Before I went in, I stashed it in the only place it wouldn't show. I have to admit though, wearing briefs, it was fairly uncomfortable until I pulled it out."

"Considering where you had it stashed, how did you manage to reach it without Barclay seeing you? Or Slater?"

"Their hatred toward each other was so intense at that instant that I think they both forgot I was here. I'm glad because I'm sure they would have wondered what I was doing if they had seen me ramming my hand down the front of my pants."

Mike stared at the pistol before saying, "You probably should wash your hands first chance you get."

Hearing a groan, they turned to see the EMTs lifting Slater onto a stretcher. The injured man had an IV in his arm and an oxygen mask covering his mouth and nose. His eyes were closed.

"We're ready to take this guy," the EMT said.

"Get going, and don't let him die on you," Clay responded.

"We'll do our best, Commander," he said as they began rolling the stretcher out of the safe room. Suddenly, Slater put a hand on the door facing to stop the stretcher. When the EMTs paused, Slater waved at Clay.

"You need immediate medical attention, Slater."

Slater shook his head, reaching up and pulling down the oxygen mask. The EMT at his head grabbed the mask and tried to force it back on his face, but Slater kept moving his head side to side to prevent it.

"Have to . . . tell you something," he whispered, his eyes boring into Clay.

Clay gave the EMT an inquisitive look, receiving a shrug in return. "I can't promise he'll make it if we wait," the EMT responded.

Slater reached out and squeezed Clay's arm with surprising strength. "One minute. Alone," he rasped, pointing at the EMTs.

"One minute and not a second more," he answered, waving the men away.

"Okay, what do you want, Von? Just be aware that I haven't advised you of your constitutional rights, so anything you say will–"

"I don't care . . . about rights," he said haltingly, his breathing more labored. "Listen to me . . . have something . . . for you."

"What's that?" Clay asked.

"Shirt pocket," he said, pausing to catch his breath. "Cell phone. Don't let anything . . . happen to it. Check recordings. Very . . . informative."

Clay pressed the outside of Slater's shirt pocket, feeling the outline of a cell phone. He pulled it out.

His voice starting to fade, Slater continued, "If I make it . . . , I owe you . . . full confession. I'm . . . man of my word." Dropping his hand from Clay's arm, he passed out.

Two months later

By mid-October in Northeast Florida, the summer heat has begun to ease. Typical temperatures at the beach top out in the low- to mid-eighties, and bright sunshine dominates most days. That is, unless a hurricane is threatening.

On this Saturday morning, it was one of those perfect days as Clay rode his bicycle on a group ride to St. Augustine and back. The cyclists were forty miles into the ride and on the return trip when Clay's cell phone rang. He made it a point never to answer his phone while riding after witnessing a spectacular crash when a cyclist lost control while trying to retrieve his cell phone.

He hit the button to kill the ringer, figuring if someone needed to talk to him, they would leave a message. Sure enough, a minute later, he heard the ding of a voicemail message. He kept pedaling, thinking he was only a half hour or so from finishing the ride. Surely, on a Saturday morning, nothing critical was happening.

Less than five minutes later, he heard the ping of a text message. Shaking his head, he signaled to the riders behind him that he was breaking out of the pace line. Waving them past, he slowed to a stop in the bike lane.

He read the text message and groaned. The terse comment was from Chief Mike Wilson. "Call me NOW!"

Okay, he thought. This wasn't good. He had a feeling his relaxing weekend was done before it really got started. He checked the number and saw it was from the chief's straight line in his office. Reluctantly, he hit the call back button.

"Clay, where the hell are you?" Mike asked.

"Right now, I'd say I'm a couple of miles the other side of Mickler's Landing."

"Are you on that friggin' bike?"

"Of course I am. It's Saturday morning. I'm on my bike every Saturday except during tropical storms and hurricanes."

"I need you to get in here as soon as possible. There have been developments that we need to discuss."

"Such as?"

"I'll tell you when you get here, which will be how long?"

Clay checked the time before answering. "It's ten-thirty now. It'll take me about thirty minutes or so to get home. Then I have to shower and—"

"Forget the shower. Come straight here."

"O-o-kay. In that case, I'll be at HQ in forty minutes."

Forty-five minutes later, Clay rolled into the parking lot of police headquarters. Wondering if Mike Wilson would have something sarcastic to say about being five minutes late, he grinned to himself as he pushed his bike through the door and headed into Administration. He leaned the bike against the wall as he strolled into the chief's office, stopping when he saw Joey and Summer in chairs across from the chief.

"I'm here, so what's going on?" he asked as he stood by Joey's chair.

"Whew," Joey exclaimed, waving his hands in the air. "Could you move away? You're a little ripe!"

"That happens when you ride a bike for fifty miles in Florida," Clay said. He moved to the other side of the room and leaned against the wall, crossing his arms. "Is this better?"

"Much," Joey laughed.

"Alright, enough chitchat," the chief said. "Let's talk about why I called you three in on a Saturday."

Clay said, "Does this have anything to do with Von Slater?"

"It does. I got a call from the hospital a little while ago," the chief said. "Slater died early this morning."

Clay wasn't sure how he felt. The man was a hired killer with a long and bloody career under his belt. He had killed Denise Adams within an hour of Clay leaving her house and then tried to frame him for her murder. He had killed Lou Dunlop, someone for whom Clay had great difficulty finding any sympathy.

He had also confessed to Clay that he was the one who killed the real Jeremiah Smith, the undercover FBI agent, and had used Smith's name as an alias while he continued his lethal career. In Clay's mind, there was neither understanding nor forgiveness for such actions.

The interviews with Slater had taken place over a two-week period almost a month after the incident at Thomas Barclay's home. Because of Summer's outstanding work on the case, she was included in the interviews. That turned out to be a good idea since Slater seemed to make a connection with her. He addressed her most often while answering questions, regardless of who asked. Only in a subsequent interview did he tell them that Summer reminded him of his deceased daughter.

They had interviewed Slater in the hospital where he was slowly recovering from the gunshot wound. The cancer that started in his lungs had metastasized, spreading to his liver, one kidney, and his colon. He knew beyond any doubt that he was a dead man. He was okay with that.

They had obtained a search warrant for the Lexus and recovered the Barrett sniper rifle and the expended cartridge. Ballistics linked the shell casing to the rifle, although damage to the projectile had prevented an additional match. It didn't matter since Slater gave a detailed and convincing confession about how he had set up and subsequently killed Dunlop.

Slater began the first interview by saying the only hit he ever regretted was Denise Adams. He had come to believe she was a total innocent and didn't deserve such a dishonorable end. That set the tone for the rest of the interviews, which included details of the sixteen people he had murdered in his career as a hired killer.

He admitted upon questioning that his third wife had not killed herself. He had caught her cheating on him and shot her, setting up the death to look like a suicide.

During the final interview, Slater asked Clay if he could send the cash he had left to his first ex-wife. He said he liked her the best of his three wives and thought she deserved some compensation for the hell she had gone through with the death of their daughter.

Clay had initially planned to file a request to seize the money for the police department's use since Slater had earned it in his criminal occupation. However, after reading the suicide note written by Slater's daughter, and learning of the horror she had endured at the hands of her stepfather, horror that led directly to her suicide, Clay began to have second thoughts. He told Slater he would pass along the man's request to the state attorney's office and abide by their decision.

Joey asked Slater about Dunlop's connection to the man named MacKay. He told them Mackay was a powerful political fixer in Washington, so he guessed Dunlop knew him through the dark underbelly of political wheeling and dealing. Slater said although MacKay had reached out to him for job several times over the years, he had never met him, but he gave them the man's phone number. Clay passed the information to the SAC of the Jacksonville FBI office, who committed to follow up on it right away.

The information gleaned from Slater's cell phone provided a treasure trove of evidence against Lou Dunlop. Slater had recorded every telephone conversation with Dunlop. He also had recorded the conversation in Dunlop's car in the parking lot at the Jacksonville Zoo as well as the final confrontation in Barclay's safe room. All three of them were amazed by each new revelation that came out of the recordings.

"Clay, where did you go?" the chief said, snapping his fingers.

He blinked. "Oh, sorry. I was just thinking back about everything that happened and how Slater recorded everything. The guy was unbelievable."

Mike said, "Besides wanting to let all three of you know about Slater dying, I wanted to tell you about a call I got from a friend of mine at the Department of Justice in Washington. This is not for publication yet, so what I'm about to tell you can't leave this room until it becomes official. All of you got that?"

All three nodded in unison.

"Okay. The word is that Senator Barclay will announce this afternoon that he is resigning from Congress, effective immediately. In addition, he no longer intends to run for president. His official reason will be the ongoing struggle dealing with the death of his daughter," Mike said, glancing at Clay, "and the continuing medical issues involving his granddaughter."

"Bullshit," Joey said behind his hand, covering the curse with a fake cough.

Mike smiled at Joey. "It is exactly that, but he may not walk away completely unscathed from all this. At the very least, the things he said that Slater recorded are going to be extremely embarrassing, if not criminal."

"Good!" Clay said, vehemently.

"My buddy at DOJ said there's a hush-hush investigation underway by the military. They're reviewing the statement Barclay made admitting he set Slater up on the killing in Iraq. It's been over twenty years, so my buddy didn't think the Army would bring charges against him for that. It's also possible but doubtful that the Army would go back and take away his military pension and rank after this long. Regardless, when you take all the underhanded stuff he's done and said, his chances of being re-elected to Congress, much less president, are nil. The man's political career is over, and he knows it. Which is why he's resigning from Congress."

Joey said, "He deserves that and more."

As Mike turned to retrieve something from the credenza, Joey said, "By the way, Chief, I haven't had the opportunity to express my concerns to you about Commander Randall copying me."

Mike turned back. "Copying you? What are you talking about?"

Joey cut his eyes at Clay, seeing confusion on his face. "I didn't know until the big shootout in Barclay's safe room that he's been carrying a little twenty-two exactly like mine. Don't you think he should have checked with me to, you know, get my approval first? After all, I'm the original Little Heat."

"Oh, give me a break," Clay said before Mike could respond.

The chief looked at Joey so long he started to squirm in his chair. "I think, Sergeant, considering his rank, that Commander Randall can carry whatever backup pistol he wants for as long as he wants."

"Thanks, Chief," Clay said. "And Joey, you named your peashooter, 'Little Heat'. Considering my higher rank, I'm going to call mine, 'Big Heat'."

Everyone laughed but Joey as he sat there unable to think of a suitable retort.

Mike said, "Okay, if you're both done with the clowning around, I have a couple more things to share. I've watched you two," he said, pointing at Joey and Summer, "as you worked these cases almost around the clock. You busted your butts to dig up the evidence against Slater, and the investigation out there in Nevada was outstanding. Especially your ruse to get his DNA, Summer."

"Thanks, Chief," she said, smiling.

"Yeah, like I've always said, I taught her everything she knows, Chief," Joey boasted.

"I know that because you've told me and everyone else who would listen at least a thousand times."

"Just sayin'," Joey mumbled.

"Anyway, I've made a couple of personnel decisions that I will share with the three of you shortly. But first, I need to let you know that I fired Jack Hargraves yesterday afternoon. It turns out he was the author of that anonymous letter about Clay he claimed to have found on his car. Our IT guy was cleaning Hargraves' office computer from a virus and found the letter in a Word file dated two days before he said it mysteriously showed up.

"I called him in and questioned him on both the letter and your challenge coin, Clay. He denied it all until I showed him the evidence from his computer. Then he broke down and started crying. He confessed to everything, including stealing the coin. He said Dunlop didn't tell him why, just that he wanted him to take something that people would immediately recognize as belonging to you. He assumed Dunlop was going to use it to harass you in some way like with the pizza and topsoil deliveries."

Seeing Clay's surprise, he continued, "Yeah, he also admitted he was the one who ordered all that stuff to be sent to your house. He also told me, and I tend to believe him, that he would never have given the coin to Dunlop if he had known what the man intended to do with it. He said when he heard it was found at the crime scene, he panicked. He wanted to come tell me then, but he was too scared. Afraid he would be implicated in the mayor's murder. The state attorney is going to review everything and make a decision about criminal charges on him. Regardless, he won't ever have a job in law enforcement again.

"And one more thing, since the cases were solved, there was no need to pay for a rush job to match the DNA on the coin to anyone. I got a call from the Tampa lab supervisor late yesterday afternoon. In fact, right after Hargraves left my office. Hargraves told me he used a latex glove when he stole the coin and dropped it in a Ziploc bag before passing it to Dunlop. That was apparently the truth. The lab supervisor told me Dunlop's DNA was the only one on there, on both sides of it. He must have taken it out of the bag for some reason. But why? We'll never know."

The chief suddenly stood up. "And now, back to the personnel decisions I mentioned. I find that I am one commander short. Sergeant Crutchfield, for your outstanding work on this case and many others, I am hereby appointing you to the rank of commander in charge of the patrol division, effective Monday. Here's your new badge, Commander. You deserve it," he said, handing Joey the badge and shaking his hand.

Joey sat stunned, unable to say a word.

"Wow! Joey 'Little Heat' Crutchfield is struck speechless for the first time in his life," Clay laughed. "Congratulations!"

Joey said, "Thanks, Chief. I'll do my best."

"I know you will. And my second personnel decision involves you, Summer."

"Yes, sir?" she said, sitting forward in her chair.

"I am now one sergeant short with the promotion of your sergeant to commander. You're ranked number one on the current eligibility list, so, effective Monday, I'm promoting you to sergeant. Congratulations, and here is your new badge," he said, shaking her hand. "You'll stay in the detective division and assume the duties Sergeant, make that Commander, Crutchfield performed."

With a huge grin, Summer said, "Thank you, sir!"

Mike said, "And with that, I believe we all deserve to go home and have a quiet rest of the weekend."

"Chief, one comment," Joey said.

"Yes, Commander?"

"Now that Commander Randall and I are the same rank, I believe I'll change my nickname to 'Big Heat One', and he can be 'Big Heat Two'. It seems only fair."

Before Clay could go off on his friend, the chief's phone rang. He picked up and listened for almost two minutes without responding. "Okay, I've got just the people to respond right here in my office. I'll send them that way in a minute," he said, hanging up.

He rubbed his face with both hands, then said, "It seems the surfers and fishermen at the pier have gotten into it again. Some surfers got too close to the pier, so one of the fishermen got pissed off and cast in their direction. Then one of the surfers retaliated by cutting the guy's line. That led to several other fishermen casting heavy sinkers at the surfers. One of the surfers was hit in the head and knocked unconscious and fell off his board. I guess his buddies pulled him to shore and then stormed the pier where they got into a huge fight with the fishermen. They had to call for help from Neptune Beach and Atlantic Beach PDs to get it under control. Several idiots on both sides are injured and are being transported to the ER.

"S-o-o, forget what I said about a quiet weekend. Commander Crutchfield? Your promotion is effective immediately since this involves patrol officers. And Sergeant Hayes? Your promotion is also effective immediately. I'm sure Commander Randall will want you heading up the investigation into any possible felony offenses. And I have no doubt he will be accompanying the two of you to the pier."

Chief Wilson stood and gestured toward the door. "After you."

Clay said, "I'll leave my bike here and ride with you, Commander Crutchfield."

"No, no, no," Joey said. "I'm not letting you ride in my car the way you smell."

As the two of them headed for the exit, continuing to argue good-naturedly, Summer looked at Mike Wilson with a massive eye roll.

Clay glanced back as they went out the door.

Joey said, "She rolled her eyes again, didn't she?"

With a quick wink at his new sergeant, Clay said, "Who, Summer? Nah. No way."

THE END

A COMMENT FROM THE AUTHOR

Perception of Power is the third installment in the Detective Clay Randall Series, preceded by *Body Toll* and *The Six O'Clock Rule.* The novels are best described as police procedurals as well as thrillers. Many readers have asked me whether they should read the books in a particular order. My response is . . . it depends.

If you like to start a series at Book One and move forward as the characters grow and develop (and sometimes die), then start with *Body Toll.* If you like to pick a novel at random and find you like it well enough to try another, then go for it. As an avid reader myself, I've found that both methods work for me.

I decided it would be interesting to ask Detective Commander Clay Randall, the main character in my novels, what he thought about it.

The following conversation took place when I asked his opinion:

"You gotta be kidding me! I'm up to my ears in homicides and robberies, and you're asking me what order my stories should be read? *Good thing he can't read my mind since I'm really on a fifty-mile bike ride with my buddies. Besides, why is he bugging me on the weekend? I'm off duty.*"

"Uh, Clay. You know I can read your thoughts, don't you?"

Silence for ten seconds, then, "Aw, crap. I forgot. Okay, anyway, why do you care what order the stories should be read?"

"Well, actually, many of the readers have asked that question."

"Oh, okay, as long as it's them asking. I guess I'd say to read them in any order they want since I'm in all three. One caution though. Some of the stuff I've faced in my career has been tough to deal with, so I wouldn't want readers to get the idea that my stories are lighthearted comedies. Don't get me wrong. There are humorous incidents and a few crazy characters, but there's also plenty of action and danger and, in some cases, tragedy. And now, if you don't have anything else, I've got a ton of work to do. Oops, forgot about that mind-reading thing again. I need to get back to my ride. Later."

And there you have it . . . straight from the guy in charge.

Connect
with Bruce

www.BruceThomason.com

 Bruce@BruceThomason.com

CPSIA information can be obtained
at www.ICGtesting.com
Printed in the USA
LVOW13s1512141216

517260LV00012B/986/P